Mrs. Mohr Goes Missing

Mrs. Mohr Goes Missing

Maryla Szymiczkowa

TRANSLATED FROM THE POLISH BY
Antonia Lloyd-Jones

Mariner Books
Houghton Mifflin Harcourt
Boston   New York   2020

First U.S. edition

Copyright © 2015 by Jacek Dehnel, Piotr Tarczyński
English translation copyright © 2020 by Antonia Lloyd-Jones

This translation is published by arrangement with
Społeczny Instytut Wydawniczy Znak Sp. z o.o., Kraków, Poland.

First English-language edition published in Great Britain and Australia by
Point Blank, an imprint of Oneworld Publications, 2019.

Originally published in Polish by Znak as
Tajemnica domu Helclów, 2015.

hmhbooks.com

Library of Congress Cataloging-in-Publication Data
Names: Szymiczkowa, Maryla, author. | Lloyd-Jones, Antonia, translator.
Title: Mrs. Mohr goes missing / Maryla Szymiczkowa ; translated from the
Polish by Antonia Lloyd-Jones.
Other titles: Tajemnica domu Helclów. English
Description: First U.S. edition. |
Boston : Mariner Books/Houghton Mifflin Harcourt, 2020. |
Series: A Zofia Turbotyńska mystery; 1 | Originally published in Polish by
Znak as Tajemnica domu Helclów, 2015. | Translated from the Polish.
Identifiers: LCCN 2019025605 (print) | LCCN 2019025606 (ebook) |
ISBN 9780358161462 (trade paperback) | ISBN 9780358274247 (hardcover)
| ISBN 9780358150954 (ebook) | ISBN 9780358311232 | ISBN 9780358307082
Subjects: GSAFD: Mystery fiction.
Classification: LCC PG7219.Z93 T3513 2019 (print) | LCC PG7219.Z93 (ebook) |
DDC 891.8/538 — dc23
LC record available at https://lccn.loc.gov/2019025605
LC ebook record available at https://lccn.loc.gov/2019025606

Book design by Greta D. Sibley

Printed in the United States of America
DOC 10 9 8 7 6 5 4 3 2 1

In memory of

Krystyna Latawcowa née Dutkiewicz

CONTENTS

*Ignacy on the technical superiority of the fork, and has a
terrifying dream.*

*the Alhambra, learns that not every widower's wife is
actually dead, and finally that the police do not let the
grass grow under their feet.*

AUTHOR'S PREFACE

B y the end of the eighteenth century, Poland had been partitioned by three empires: Russia, Prussia, and Austria. And throughout the nineteenth century it did not exist as an independent country. Cracow, Poland's former capital, had special status: in 1815, following the Napoleonic wars and the Congress of Vienna, the city and its vicinity became a semiautonomous, small-scale republic under the control of all three empires. As a result, the capital of the Austrian partition of Poland — the region known as Galicia (unrelated to the Spanish region of the same name) — was the historically less significant but larger city of Lemberg (now Lviv in Ukraine). The tiny republic's freedom was increasingly suppressed, which led to resistance, mainly from the gentry and the nobility.

Toward the middle of the nineteenth century, Europe was experiencing intensifying unrest, culminating in a wave of insurgencies in 1848 known as the Spring of Nations, when various nationalities, especially the Hungarians and Poles, tried to regain their independence within the empires. In 1846, with an uprising about to erupt in Cracow, the Austrian authorities incited the peasants to massacre the nobility. In spite of this action, which came to be known as the Galician Slaughter, the uprising occurred and was bloodily suppressed. Afterward the republic was abolished and Cracow was incorporated into the Austrian partition, where it continued to take second place to Lemberg, which was growing larger and richer.

Still, the Spring of Nations led to a change of power in Vienna. In December 1848, the eighteen-year-old Franz Joseph Habsburg became emperor. He would rule for almost sixty-eight years, longer than Queen Victoria; just as she did, he brought a distinctive character to the entire epoch. In 1867, in an attempt to save his vast domain — more than twice the size of the British Isles — from disintegrating, he transformed it into Austria-Hungary, combining the empire of Austria and the kingdom of Hungary, each with its own parliament and government and equal standing in this newly consolidated empire, but united still by a single monarch.

In 1893, when this story is set, Cracow was home to a diverse mixture of ethnicities, languages, and religions from all over the empire. Apart from Poles and Austrians, there were Czechs, Slovaks, Italians, Hungarians, and Ukrainians (known as Ruthenians in those days), and above all, Jews. The Jews accounted for more than a quarter of the city's population, but most of them were not assimilated and led their own separate lives. Even those who were assimilated into society were treated as second-class citizens.

Despite its wealth of cultures and its great historical past, Cracow was a provincial city. Made into a bastion surrounded by forts, it could not expand and had only about seventy thousand citizens. Galicia was backward, the poorest region not just in Austria-Hungary, but in all Europe at the time. Yet greater freedom prevailed there than in the German and especially the Russian partitions of former Poland, where frequent uprisings continued to erupt against the oppressive partitioning powers. The Poles were represented within the parliament, and even the government of the Austro-Hungarian empire; they were freely allowed to study in the Polish language at schools and at the Jagiellonian University — which dated back to medieval times, when Copernicus studied there — and to found cultural institutions. Cracow became a major center for culture and learning, a vital place not just for Galicia but for all the Polish lands, home to many leading authors, scholars, and artists.

Not surprisingly, many Poles regarded themselves as loyal subjects of His Imperial Majesty, and saw the dual monarchy of Austria-Hungary—that curious country familiar to us from the novels of Joseph Roth and Robert Musil—as their motherland; though in political terms it was fairly liberal within the context of contemporary Europe, in terms of society and culture, it was painfully conservative, full of hypocrisy and social inequalities, a place where the desire for change was gradually increasing.

PROLOGUE

❦

In which not much can be seen, and not much can be heard.

At this hour the corridor is entirely empty, but the pale blue glow of the moon shining through the branches of the trees outside is making strange patterns on the door and walls that merge now and then to form figures — a nun in a wimple and flowing tunic, an old lady bent double, or a brawny watchman. But there's nothing there, nothing at all.

How much easier it would be if the room were in a side wing, around a corner — but this door can be seen from the glazed area at the end of the corridor, brightly lit by a lamp; this is where the ladies' and gentlemen's halves of the building meet, and Cerberus, in the guise of a Sister of Charity, is usually on guard in the duty room beside the locked door; but now, thank God, Cerberus is not there.

Someone returns, doing their best to move silently. This person slips into the room and goes up to the corpse in the rumpled bedclothes; it has clearly been through its death throes, and yet the face looks oddly serene, as if dying brought on a state of bliss.

The hardest thing is grabbing hold of it. A naked heel protruding from the blanket raps against the floor. Shh, not a sound! No, there's no one coming, nobody heard a thing. All that's left is to make the bed. And *heeeave!* Who'd have thought her body weighed so much? More than when alive. How heavy could she have been? Eight stone? A hundredweight? No, less than that. She was a scrawny creature, nothing but skin and bone, with the head of a sparrow and the hands of a squirrel. The life has only just flowed out of her, but it's like lifting a cathedral bell. Was that a gasp? No, nothing of the kind. It's just the feeling that at any moment the corpse is going to come back to life and wreak its revenge. Just a few more yards, four, three, two to go. This corridor doesn't usually look so wide, but now crossing it seems like a struggle. Fortunately there's no door here, no lock, and the way up is clear. At any rate, this is where the stairs begin. How lucky that they're new and don't squeak.

CHAPTER I

✦

In which we meet the household at an apartment on St. John's Street, learn how Vienna is taking its revenge on Cracow, what one can do with seven stallions, and how to cure many a case of cholera; we also hear about the great value of certain books, the equally great rapacity of the ladies from a certain society, and the tragic accident that befell the Hungarian envoy all because of a bottle of slivovitz.

It was Saturday, 14 October 1893. All morning a large cloud, dark gray with streaks of sapphire blue, had been hanging above number 30 St. John's Street in Cracow — known as "Peacock House" because of the fine sculpted bird above the main entrance — threatening rain.

"Come along, Franciszka," said Zofia Turbotyńska gloomily, fearing the worst — by which she meant having to pay twenty cents for the ride home in a cab. "The shopping won't do itself."

And then, ignoring the cook's aphoristic answer ("On Saint Jerome's, either it rains or it don't" — though in fact this particular sacred figure had been commemorated a fortnight ago), she went into the hallway, did up two rows of small black buttons on her boots, pulled on her cherry-red kid leather gloves, donned a new hat bought at Marya Prauss's fashion emporium, and examined herself in the mirror.

Zofia, née Glodt, wife of Professor Ignacy Turbotyński of the medical faculty at Cracow's Jagiellonian University, was approaching her fortieth summer, but she noted with approval that she was really quite comely. Perhaps over the past year she had gained a minimal amount of weight, but she carried herself erect and still had an alluring figure. A healthy complexion with no pimples and very few wrinkles — just one was more distinct, on her forehead, between the brows, perhaps too often knitted. An oval face, the features rather stern, but softened by nicely defined eyebrows and keen eyes with dark lashes . . . a slightly hooked nose . . . and lips — well, the lips could have been fuller, but she consoled herself that her thin lips gave her the look of a refined Englishwoman.

She reached for an umbrella from the porcelain stand, which was bristling with her husband's walking sticks. Briefly her fingers fluttered over the handles — a silver parrot's head with topaz eyes, a rolled-up elephant's trunk, an ivory knob (donated a couple of years ago by his grateful students), and a small, glossy skull (a souvenir of his last year at medical school) — and finally extracted a Chinese dragon chasing a pearl: a present, as Zofia liked to mention, from her sister, who lived in Vienna. Just one more backward glance into the mirror — playful enough for her to find herself pleasing, and stern enough for Franciszka not to dare counter it with a smirk — and they were ready for the march to Szczepański Square.

They went the usual way: down St. John's Street, then St. Thomas's, with an occasional reluctant glance at that cloud, which was gathering, swelling, and seething over the Piasek district.

"It's sure to be pouring in the outskirts by now," said Franciszka, seemingly into space, though with patent reproof. But she knew that in the life of Zofia Turbotyńska there were sanctities greater than the elevation of the host, including a proper Sunday luncheon, and thus an equally proper Saturday shopping expedition.

By now they had reached the end of St. Thomas's Street, and so Franciszka, who was walking slightly behind with a basket over her arm, knew what would happen next: as soon as they came level with the Alchemist's house, the bow on Zofia's hat suddenly twitched and turned to the right, followed by the rest of the hat and her head. The time had come for a groan, for this was where "that crime" came into view, "that hideous shack, worthy of a station halt in a garrison town" — in other words the enormous bulk of the covered emergency staircase, tacked onto the City Theater a couple of years ago after the fire at the Ring-theater in Vienna.

"I realize that almost four hundred people burned to death there," Zofia would say, "but is that a reason for Vienna to take revenge on Cracow with this monstrosity? Fortunately we'll have our new theater in a matter of days!"

And so there was the ritual groan, and then the bow moved back into place. Now they had to move on to serious matters.

Szczepański Square opened wide, edged with squat little houses; here and there crooked booths sprang from the dirty cobblestones; they were roofed in shingle and crammed with tables large and small, barrels of pickled cabbage and gherkins, piles of wood, bunches of brushes and wicker baskets creaking from an excess of pears, apples, potatoes, and cauliflowers carted here by peasants from the villages outside Cracow — and so it was, all the way to the other side of the square, which was closed off by the longest booth of all, divided into yet more stalls, with the saleswomen and their customers buzzing about in front of them, as well as a handful of grubby urchins scenting the opportunity to swipe an apple or seize a dropped coin from the ground, despite being repeatedly shooed away. But maids and cooks were in the majority — Zofia had her own opinion on the topic of ladies of the house whose servants went shopping unsupervised: "they leave with a handful of crowns and return with a single parsnip, and a rotten one at that"; of course, she occasionally sent the girl to the market, the pharmacy, or the haberdasher's for a trifle or two, but she had to take personal command of the Saturday shopping.

As she walked among the booths, her brain was working away like an arithmometer: entire days and weeks were organized in her mind, accounting for breakfasts, luncheons, teas, and suppers and the requisite amount of flour, butter, milk, cream, lard, sugar, and honey; pounds of fruit; and measures of wine, capons, goose breasts, schnitzels, and aspic. Between a basket of apples and a table piled with cheeses wrapped in horseradish leaves, she could mentally convert seidels and vedros, lots and stones, bushels and achtels of the foodstuffs that she would administer for the next few days, weeks, or months. She only lost her way in the new coins. Last year Vienna had replaced the silver guldens with golden crowns, so now there were two currencies in circulation: both the good old kreuzers and the new hallers, which were worth almost half as much as their predecessors and commonly known as "cents," leading to constant misunderstandings at the market, as every housewife carped about the high prices: "Twenty cents for a kilogram of kohlrabi? That's banditry!" And the tradeswomen would mollify them by saying: "There's no need to get in a stew, madam. It's in new cents, not old!"

Be that as it may, after reaching the meats that she had seen to in advance—the schnitzels for today's luncheon had already been prepared, and the lad from the butcher's on the Small Marketplace was due to deliver the poularde for tomorrow's by four o'clock—Zofia's thoughts had moved on to cakes, when suddenly her mental arithmetic was interrupted by a tuneful cry: "Cousin Zofia! Cousin Zo-fiaaa!"

Beyond the figures of two old biddies from the countryside, wrapped in shawls, selling mushrooms they'd picked at dawn, she discerned a tall, austere figure taking tiny steps in her direction—Józefa Dutkiewicz. In fact, they were only distantly related through an aunt whom they had last seen some thirty years ago—and who had long since resided in a graveyard—but they were more closely associated by a long-standing, ardent mutual dislike, or to be precise, they had been sticking pins in each other for years, fighting a duel in which each blow was masked by exaggerated courtesy. The final outcome was not yet apparent.

Mrs. Dutkiewicz, née Korwin-Kunachowicz—and, thanks to her husband, as she often stressed, the bearer of the Trzaska coat of arms—was without doubt from a better family than Mrs. Turbotyńska (whose own was quite ordinary), and one of her cousins was counselor to the governor of Galicia. Yet Zofia came out on top, thanks to her husband's status—the wife of a Jagiellonian University professor beat the widow of a Mutual Assurance Society official by several lengths. Moreover, old Dutkiewicz had passed away less than a year ago, and Józefa's modest widow's pension was not enough for her to keep a cook and a maid at once; with a heavy heart she had been obliged to dismiss Franciszka. "It is easier to teach a maid to cook than vice versa," she had explained in her tuneful tone, "and after Jan's death I found it tiring to have quite so many souls hovering about the house."

Zofia would not have been herself if she had failed to take advantage of the situation, especially as she had constant trouble with servants and was always on the lookout for someone new, having either just sacked the maid or the cook or being on the point of doing so. At once she scouted the matter — as a tireless gatherer of intelligence, she always had an eye on most of what was happening within the reach of Planty Park, which surrounded the city center — and effectively ensnared both her cousin and her cook; a week after the first conversation, the girl had transported her small wooden trunk from Mrs. Dutkiewicz's house on Floriańska Street to Zofia's on St. John's. And this was one of the best transactions that Zofia had performed in her life to date: Franciszka Gawęda, who had come to Mrs. Dutkiewicz a decade ago straight from Kęty, her native town, as a raw fourteen-year-old, was adroit, honest, and bright; had been trained for all work; and in addition had gained such mastery of the traditional Galician cuisine, with a special focus on desserts, that in comparison with her virtues, the primary driving force of the intrigue paled: Zofia's joy at impoverishing her rival by taking away her long-term servant.

Perhaps if Franciszka had come to the Turbotyńskis' house from the domestic services procurement agency, Zofia would have found an excuse to dismiss her within a month, in her usual way; but as it involved a triumph in the war against Mrs. Dutkiewicz, she had merely clenched her teeth a few times — and six months on, she could not imagine life without this slim, reticent girl, with her large eyes and big red hands.

"Zofia, what a joy it is to see you!" Mrs. Dutkiewicz — who had sidestepped two porters with jute sacks to reach the middle of the square, her maid in tow, laden with shopping — insincerely exclaimed.

"Józefa, how marvelous," replied Turbotyńska just as insincerely.

Not proficient at interpreting these society ladies' battles, every encounter of this kind made Franciszka feel awkward, so at the sight of her former mistress, she cringed. In fact, Mrs. Dutkiewicz was loudly expressing her satisfaction that "faithful Franciszka" had found "such a worthy employer," but the stern glance she cast at her former cook left no room for illusion. In Cracow "forgiveness" was a purely theological term, with no practical application in everyday life.

Franciszka bowed politely, mumbled a courteous inquiry into Mrs. Dutkiewicz's health, and stepped to one side, leaving the field to the mighty adversaries. At a modest distance she inspected some old posters: *SIDOLI'S GRAND CIRCUS — today, Saturday, 16 September! A grand, spectacular, splendid show . . . Miss Mary Annie Gordon, presenting Attila the Russian black stallion running free . . .* Franciszka's heart instantly beat faster at the thought of it.

And just a few feet away, a genuine spectacle had begun to unfold. Those two splendid mother hens were sparring, with their servants behind them like medieval pages, bearing baskets full of vegetables instead of helmets.

Still in mourning, as she would be for the rest of her days, with her white hair pinned up, Mrs. Dutkiewicz was squeezed into a smart but unstylish dress from two seasons ago, but she held herself erect and with great class. More than a decade her junior, Mrs. Turbotyńska was dressed far more colorfully — some might have said garishly — but gave no ground to her rival; Zofia had never been a beauty, but in the thirty-eighth year of her life she still passed as a "handsome woman." And the rare streaks of gray in her chestnut hair merely enhanced her looks — in this, she trusted all the ladies who complimented her on them.

The two women stood almost motionless; words, phrases, and sentences were uttered, but nothing of the least importance — nothing but local gossip and courtesies. What mattered was what passed between the words: the gestures, grimaces, and dodges. It was clear who was losing the round: Zofia was distracted, casting hesitant glances now at the cloud, now at the row of cabs outside the theater; if it began to pour before they could reach home, she'd have to pay the same price for the short ride as for a quarter of an hour parading about town — as much as twenty cents. Daylight robbery. Although the cloud was still billowing, turning a darker shade of blue and now taking up a larger piece of sky, for the time being it was holding back the rain.

Finally they managed to bring the conversation to a conclusion that left neither lady feeling offended, and went their separate ways, dragging their tails behind them — namely, the two burdened servants.

Having bid Mrs. Dutkiewicz farewell, Zofia swiftly worked her way past a few more stalls, pointing with a cherry-red kid leather finger at an especially fine cauliflower or, on the contrary, a bruised pear, while Franciszka bustled about, putting paper cones into the ever-fuller basket. And so they came to the edge of the square, where her mistress said, over her shoulder: "Let us make a small detour past the pharmacy," and they entered Szczepańska Street.

"Please, madam, could I have Monday morning off?"

In other circumstances, Zofia might have stopped and thrown up her hands, but there was no time for that now; she merely cast the cook a withering glance and, without slowing her pace, launched into a tirade:

"Franciszka, Franciszka, off to Sidoli's circus again? How old are you? Fifteen or almost twice as much? Are you going to waste money watching those capers on horseback again? Or that rascal who titillates the hoi polloi by jumping from a balloon by parachute while additionally mounted on a bicycle?"

Franciszka was silent for a moment, returning in her mind to the incredible evening she'd spent there, when, from her place in the cheapest seats, she hadn't once torn her gaze from the uniforms dripping with gold and the splendid rows of horses. The flashes as the trick rider stood up in his stirrups, the whoops of danger and delight! If she only could, she'd go to the circus twice a day, especially as the program — or so the posters plastered all over the city proclaimed — was *rich and ever changing.* But that wasn't what this was about.

"No, if you please, madam, I'd like to go and see my grandma at Helcel House."

Like a true member of the Cracow bourgeoisie, Zofia Turbotyńska was not a fan of the day off; spare time could be devoted to something useful, such as cleaning the silver or washing a few windows. But so be it. Half a day once a week had to be relinquished, as guaranteed not only by contract but also custom — that is, the rules of the Dutkiewicz house, which Franciszka had brought with her from Floriańska Street to St. John's. And it was the lesser of two evils for her to be paying a visit to old Mrs. Gawęda rather than traipsing about at circuses or fairs. Zofia herself had long since been an orphan, and had no elderly relatives whom she might look after or visit at Helcel House retirement home; nor could she count on anyone visiting her in forty years' time at a similar refuge, but on principle she approved of involvement in family life.

"Of course, Franciszka," she said, nodding her head, hat, bow, and all; and then, without slowing down, she made the decision to go on an outing herself.

In her daily struggle to become the perfect Cracovian lady, whom no one would dare to remind of her provincial origins, Zofia Turbotyńska conducted all sorts of campaigns,

including social ones. Until recently it had been her dream
to become chairwoman of the ladies' section for the XIX National Exhibition in Lemberg, but unfortunately, at the general assembly held at the Savings Bank, there hadn't been
any ballot; Mr. Marchwicki, exhibition manager and deputy mayor of Lemberg, had mounted the rostrum and announced in a sugary tone that the wife of Mr. Polanowski,
initiator of the exhibition, had been chosen as chairwoman,
and a circle of grand ladies had been selected as her subordinates: Princess Sapieha, Countess Badeni, and Mrs. Las-
kowska, wife of the governor's representative in Cracow. To
this group he had also added his own wife. Those rapacious
females had snapped up everything: Badeni was in charge
of the orphanages, the cottage hospitals, and the charitable
works; Polanowska had taken on peasant education, teach-
ing home economics, childrearing, and servant-training; and
Mrs. Marchwicka had annexed handicrafts, courses in wom-
en's work, and bazaars, and on top of that the entire wom-
en's charity committee too. What an insatiable creature! The
Messalina of charitable works, the Jezebel of the cooperative
movement!

So Zofia had resolved to follow a different path, closer to
home, and to make her contribution in the care of Cracow's
sick and needy. She didn't have vast capital at her disposal
— and even if she had, she wouldn't have handed it out too
liberally — but she was resourceful, ambitious, and knew
how to get people to do things for her of their own accord.
Her chosen field of activity was the Charitable Society, and

her chosen aim was to become a committee member on the board of the ladies' section. Of course, the president's and vice president's chairs were occupied by the Countesses Potocka, and the other vice president was Mrs. Gwiazdomorska, wife of the deputy chairman of the general council, and beyond that, if not a princess, then a countess was chasing off a baroness. But there were some ladies without their own coats of arms among the committee members — and Zofia was holding on to this aim, though fully aware that she was not the only one with her sights fixed on it; other ladies of the same social standing, extremely fervent in their efforts to care for the elderly, had been racing off to Helcel House lately, as well. One had to go there, to show oneself, and to form acquaintances with the nuns who ran the home.

"Let us go together, Franciszka," she said, as she walked through the door of the Golden Tiger Pharmacy.

❧

"Two bottles of wine against cholera," she said to the shop assistant.

The newspapers were reporting new cases every day, and the *Cracow Times* had even started running a regular column headed CHOLERA. So far, the names of faraway cities and towns had featured there, but ever since the ominous name *Rymanów* had been mentioned, a town just twenty-five miles away, Zofia had felt as if cholera were standing at the gates, and that it was time to protect herself from it. Unfortunately, her husband had his own tiresome medical opinion on how to treat this illness, which was that wine may well taste good, and might even fortify the organism as a whole, but wouldn't keep cholera at bay; he droned on tediously about the comma bacillus and hygiene, insisting that the only cure was to build proper waterworks. But Zofia knew her facts: washing one's hands was not half as effective as wine *recommended by the medical authorities.*

"Bilberry, made by Schwarz of Vienna or by Gutunić?"

"And Gutunić is where?"

"Also Vienna. It's Dalmatian," said the shortsighted assistant, raising the bottle to eye level and slowly reading off the label, "'containing tannin. Against maladies of the stomach and intestine.'"

"Perhaps the bilberry from Schwarz," she replied graciously. *Gutunić,* she thought to herself, *what sort of a name is that? Definitely not Viennese.*

Franciszka stood silent; she too had her opinion on the matter of cholera, but was ashamed to reveal it, since being reproached on several occasions by her past as well as her present employers for repeating old wives' tales. She had her own medical oracle that she heeded in every case: *The Angel's Aid for Defense and Protection in Dire Need.* If asked which book was the most important in the world, as a good Christian, she would unhesitatingly have answered "the Bible." But were one to plumb the deepest recesses of her heart, there one would find *The Angel's Aid.* For though the Bible was full of wise and instructive stories, Judith's problem-solving methods or Tobias's medical practices were not applicable in daily life, where a person encountered troubles of every possible kind.

And here *The Angel's Aid* was a most useful source of information on techniques for taming domestic animals; infallible methods for dealing with freckles, vomiting, flies, cramps, and fear of water; the best infusion for causing one to remember everything one reads or hears; how to be rid of warts, how to make a barren marriage fertile, and how to cope with prolonged rain and thunder.

Though the book did not express itself with particular precision on the question of cholera, Franciszka persisted in her research, and sometimes fell asleep while leafing through its greasy pages. So far, on learning that cholera was accompanied by diarrhea, she had concentrated on methods for treating white diarrhea and bloody diarrhea. If afflicted with the former, one must take a piece of red clay the size of a hen's egg, dry it in the oven, grind it in a mortar, and then dissolve and boil it in a quart of river water, which must be scooped in the direction of the current. To remedy the latter, one drinks two spoonfuls of powdered blueberries dissolved in warm wine, followed by fatty beef broth, then takes care to keep warm and rub the umbilicus once an hour with nutmeg oil. She had the nutmeg oil, the blueberries, too, and beef could always be bought. She was prepared. Sometimes, as she nodded off, she'd imagine the glorious scene in which the professor and his wife would be fading fast, he raving about the waterworks, she letting a glass of bilberry wine slip from her hand; but by applying the recipes from the mocked and despised *Angel's Aid*, Franciszka would save their lives by feeding them blueberries dissolved in warm wine and rubbing their navels once an hour with nutmeg oil, in the process earning herself not only their undying gratitude, but also respect for her little book.

"And something for tonsillitis. Yes, and some mustache pomade as well."

"Mustache pomade? For Dr. Turbotyński? Unfortunately we're out of stock, but you can try Wiszniewski's on Floriańska Street . . ."

"For *Professor* Turbotyński. My husband is now *a full professor of medicine at the Jagiellonian University*," she said, pronouncing each syllable even more slowly and precisely than usual. "These two months past."

"My most sincere apologies, madam."

"A trifle," she said, laughing insincerely, "a mere trifle. How much do I owe you?"

In fact Ignacy's professorship was certainly not a trifle, but the long-desired crowning of a consistent climb up the rungs of Cracow society. For Zofia Turbotyńska, née Glodt, was not a native of Cracow. She was born and raised in the provincial city of Przemyśl, not counting the year she had spent at the Order of the Blessed Sacrament convent school in Lemberg, which was not a happy memory. Having received a thorough domestic education thanks to the invalu-

able Miss Buchbinder, she had married Ignacy Turbotyński
— of noble descent, he came from a respectable though
not affluent family resident in Cracow for generations —
and ever since, she had done everything in her power to be
sure that no one would think of her as an outsider. In fact,
with time, she too had virtually forgotten her own origins.
She had adopted all the habits of the Cracow bourgeoisie,
and stuck to them so strictly that her husband sometimes
couldn't restrain a compassionate smile: she shopped at the
Cloth Hall market, bought all her colonial foods at Antoni
Hawełka's store, went to High Mass at St. Mary's Basilica,
and the only newspaper she read was the *Cracow Times*.
She could be tested on the family connections of all the
greater houses to several generations back, and as for gossip, within the scope of Planty Park there was no one to
rival her.

They left the pharmacy, and had just reached the front
door of Peacock House when the first raindrop fell on the
bow atop Zofia's hat; they were saved. And so were the
twenty cents they hadn't spent on a cab.

"Good morning, Ignacy," said Zofia, facing the mirror
to take off her gloves and lay them in a Japanese black lac-
quer box.

A moment of silence followed; in the gap in the door she
saw her husband, or rather a small part of him: the shiny
bald patch on the top of his head, poking out above the
open newspaper, and his fingers holding its edges. On the
table lay a pair of scissors and a couple of cuttings.

"King Humbert fell off his horse," said Professor Turbotyński at last, "but luckily he wasn't injured."

"How splendid," replied Zofia with genuine joy, as if the news involved a good friend; she was always interested in hearing about the crowned heads, even the Italians.

"He was much luckier than the Hungarian envoy, Mr. Bokros, who fell out of a window while trying to catch a bottle of slivovitz," added her husband without looking up.

"Well, as I always say, the immoderate consumption of alcoholic drinks is bound to end in tears," said Zofia categorically.

CHAPTER II

❦

In which we learn that some people save tens of cents on cabs, while others throw millions of crowns away, and that even countesses like to gawk; we also learn how to climb Olympus, and what most often goes missing at charitable institutions.

Zofia Turbotyńska rarely asked herself questions of a theological nature; she considered herself about as religious as her peers — she said a Hail Mary and an Our Father at bedtime, went to High Mass on Sundays, and, depending on the time of the liturgical year, performed various extra rituals, but God did not often occupy her thoughts. Only occasionally, as this morning, did it briefly cross her mind that some higher authority was watching over her: Providence, or the Divine Eye, peeping out of a triangle edged with a halo of golden rays, as above the high altar at the Sisters of the Presentation; it was God in His infinite goodness who had sent her this splendid weather, knowing that she and Franciszka were heading off to Helcel House, and would have to walk to Planty Park, cross it, leaving the city center, and then tramp the length of Długa Street into areas that no self-respecting woman should really frequent.

They walked in silence; on St. John's Street, Pijarska Street, or in the park, there might have been someone to bow to, but they didn't encounter a single familiar face, despite the glorious sunshine, particularly bright for the time of year. On Długa Street, Zofia stopped looking out, because she knew she wouldn't run into anyone of her acquaintance here, but only bakers, bricklayers, and market traders. They were just passing Krzywa Street when, from the far side of Słowiański Square, the odor of the slaughterhouse drifted toward them: the smell of blood flowing into the gutter and sides of meat baking in the surprisingly sultry air. Zofia winced, and turned away. She thought of her spiritual exercises: she was going to show her best Christian side, as a lady who gave charitable support to the poor, and felt she should attune herself accordingly. Perhaps she should do a good deed? She considered giving Franciszka a whole crown—why not let her help her old grandmother, why not let her buy her something nice? But this of course was whimsy, concocted by her overgenerous soul; the virtue of charity is a fine one, but not when it blatantly contradicts the virtue of thrift. Oh, no. Since the good Lord had so benevolently afforded her fine weather, since He had illuminated all Cracow with those rays of sunlight shining from the golden triangle, why shouldn't she give away the twenty cents He had saved her? Forty, for the journey in both directions? *Though let's not be carried away — we cannot tell what the weather will be like an hour from now,* she deceived herself, for there wasn't a wisp of cloud in the clear blue sky (like all intelligent people she was a master of self-deceit). Moreover, she didn't know how late they would stay at Helcel House, but luncheon still had to be served on time, which might necessitate rushing home at high speed, whatever the expense. *And so let us stop at twenty cents,* she thought. But even this demanded justification. Franciszka's name day was exactly five months away, but deep down Zofia could already think of those twenty cents as a contribution toward her annual name-day gift.

"Franciszka?"

"Yes, madam?"

"Here," she said, stopping to open her shell purse, which shimmered in the beautiful sunlight, and pick out a twenty-cent coin. "Buy a treat for your grandmother on the square. Old people adore anything that's sweet."

Franciszka curtsied, said thank you, and rushed among the stalls, while Zofia stood in the shade of a tree half stripped of its leaves and yielded to pleasant musing on the secrets of her generous heart, capable in a flash of parting with money purely to benefit an old person whom she didn't know. Smiling cheerfully, she watched as the girl bought some biscuits or caramels and, clutching her paper cone like a trophy, piously crossed herself beneath a statue of the Blessed Virgin Mary.

From the square stretched a breathtaking view of the Ludwik and Anna Helcel House for the Poor, the seat of Cracow's newest and biggest charitable foundation. All the talk was in praise of it as an example of outstanding Christian charity, so Zofia too had been duly chiming in with the pious oohs and aahs at this great bounty. Though at times it occurred to her that to spend more than two million crowns on the poor quite so freely, one would have to have been truly spoiled by a life of infinite wealth from the day one was born . . . Was it really necessary to build a full-scale palace for paupers fetched out of hovels, mildewed basements, or garrets where the wind howled? The combined fortunes of the Treutlers and the Helcels, including a bank, six large residential houses, four of which were on the Market Square, four stalls in the Cloth Hall, unlimited fortunes — all this had gone to perdition. The Sisters of Charity could just as well have cared for the old and the sick in a far less impressive building. The fields alone, bought from several Kleparz district families, and then Pryliński's design, the construction work, the materials, some of which had come all the way from Lemberg and Vienna, and finally all the fittings — the total cost had been more than six hundred thousand, as much as the city's entire annual budget.

Though one had to admit, it was quite a sight to behold.

Just three stories high, but imposing, with a tall cupola on top, the building looked as splendid as on that day in July three years earlier when His Eminence had consecrated the chapel. Zofia liked thinking back to that day when, still a humble doctor's wife, she had found herself among the great and the good of this world (for her, Cracow was the entire world, though perhaps there was room in her heart for Vienna too). She felt as if she had climbed Mount Olympus — and indeed, as the congregation could only stand in the chapel doorway until the bishop and priests had performed the ceremony, the guests were led up a steep, narrow staircase to the organ gallery. And up there, close to the ceiling, close to the capitals of the Corinthian columns, everyone was bathed in the golden glow emanating from the brand-new altars. In truth, Zofia had stood among the lower ranks — some girls from a refuge run by the nuns, and the craftsmen who had built this edifice — but there before her were some real gods and goddesses: city councilors, court advisers, distinguished countesses from the ladies' section of the Charitable Society, the great painters Juliusz Kossak and Jan Matejko, and above all His Excellency Count Tarnowski, president of the academy, a bearded, thunder-wielding Zeus — Cronos even, who, as the man in charge of the *Cracow Times*, set the course for all that was dear to Zofia Turbotyńska's heart. Below, in the chapel, she could see Cardinal Dunajewski, Apollo-like in a golden robe, shining with heavenly light to the strains of the cathedral choir. "His Eminence looked magnificent with the miter on his silver hair," she had enthused afterward to Mrs. Dutkiewicz and anyone willing to listen.

She owed her admission to this ceremony to Sister Alojza, a nurse at the refuge, whom she had come to know while organizing a charity tombola for the benefit of the girls' home run by the nuns. Alojza, who had spent her whole life within the order (first as an orphan, later as one of the Sisters of Charity of Saint Vincent de Paul), had acquired a virtue that Zofia found invaluable — the quality of being almost entirely devoid of free will; having fallen into Zofia's clutches, Alojza obeyed her every command. In fact, the role of helmswoman of Sister Alojza's life should officially have been performed by Mother Juhel, the entire order's mother superior, but the young nun had a natural ability to sense strength of spirit; Mother Juhel was indeed called "stern" by those who liked her, and "that French battle-axe" by those who did not, but she paled in comparison with the professor's wife.

Once she had gone through the gateway and crossed the threshold — passing beneath the facade adorned with a Latin inscription, two coats of arms, and an image of the Virgin Mary of Częstochowa, designed like a shop window display to glorify the piety and charity of the two merchant clans that had endowed the home — Zofia at once parted ways with Franciszka, who set off for the rooms for needy residents to offer her granny the sweetmeats and the latest gossip from town. Meanwhile Zofia slowly ascended a flight of steps between two rows of Doric columns lining the vestibule and then turned left, toward the office, where she expected to find Sister Alojza. But the door was locked. So she headed toward a white door the height of the passage with finely latticed glass panels, and went through it in search of her acquaintance. She passed at least three Sisters of Charity going in different directions, one of whom was leading a decrepit old woman along by the arm; in the tall passageways they all looked small and puny, though Zofia knew that some of the nuns were stronger than many a man. Suddenly she heard energetic footsteps behind her; she turned around and came face-to-face with the mother superior of Helcel House, Mother Jadwiga Zaleska — small and plump, with a face that, though friendly, was roughly hewn, and made even rounder by the shadow of her broad, snow-white wimple.

"Jesus Christ be praised, Mother."

"Forever and ever, amen," replied the nun, clearly in a hurry, but to be polite, she stopped. "To what do we owe the visit of such a welcome guest?"

"I have come to see Sister Alojza about prizes for a raffle to benefit scrofulous children."

"Delightful, delightful. God will assist, for the cause is noble."

"There has been so much charitable work in our city of late — some endow splendid facilities, such as the Helcels or Prince Lubomirski, while others, such as I, the common rank and file . . ."

"Oh yes, Lubomirski . . ." said the nun indignantly. "His

new refuge may be a fine edifice, but why does it have that cupola?" At this point she lowered her voice. "When the mother superior of our order, Mother Juhel, wrote to Mrs. Helcel from France, at once she mentioned Les Invalides. And so we have our own beautiful chapel, topped with a truly Parisian or Florentine cupola . . . and here, as if to spite us, only a mile and a half away they're building another one."

"Reverend Mother, surely there's no cause for contention. First, it's all staying in the family, for the Sisters of Charity are there too, and secondly" — here Zofia lowered her voice — "the prince left far less funding than the Helcels, as one can see from the building itself. Here the chapel is almost freestanding, like a separate church, tall and slender, but there the cupola has simply been fixed onto the roof. No proportion and no charm."

"Aha," said Mother Zaleska, smiling radiantly. "The main thing is that it's all for the glory of God and to help indigent boys, our children, who shall know the boundless love of the Everlasting and the value of hard work. No matter," she said, frowning, clearly having remembered some unpleasant duty. "I must go. Sister Alojza should be upstairs." And she headed off energetically, setting the wide sleeves of her habit in a flutter.

Only now, as she glanced down the wide passageway, did Zofia realize that something was amiss. Of course the nuns were devoted to their patients, but one couldn't say that they were rushed off their feet; they generally walked without haste, gently leaning forward to proffer a glass of water or bandage a hand, always at a slow, contemplative pace. Yet the ones she had passed earlier had been moving much too rapidly, nervously, including the dry, bony nun escorting an old woman who was struggling to keep up with her. Something out of the ordinary must have occurred at Helcel House — could it be a visit of inspection by one of the ladies from the Charitable Society? In less than a month His Eminence was due to open the Lubomirski Refuge; perhaps he was planning to visit the mother superior at Helcel House to confirm some of the details? This Zofia Turbotyńska must know as soon as possible. Fortunately, just at that moment, down the steps came — or rather bounced like a ball from step to step, no, jumping two steps at a time — Sister Alojza.

"Jesus Christ be praised."

"Forever and ever, amen, Mrs. Turbotyńska, forever and ever, amen!" gasped the nun.

Yes, she was in a fluster, too; she stopped, but it was as if different parts of her body wanted to keep going in opposite directions. Only her eyes were fixed on Zofia, without moving, but full of tension. Quite apart from that, Alojza had suffered all her life from exophthalmos, so it always looked as if she were gazing at the world with a mixture of fascination and incomprehension, if not — considering that, as well as bulging eyes, she had rather prominent incisors too — alarm.

"I am here to see you. This time with a request."

"A request? Oh . . ." Alojza looked around tensely, as if in search of something that might help her with this conversation. "But in the office . . . right now it's not possible to go to the office . . . perhaps another time? No . . ." She realized it wasn't appropriate for her to fob off the professor's wife in this manner. "Perhaps we could go through to the garden?"

"I don't wish to trouble you," replied Zofia, which meant of course that she had no intention of discussing serious matters just anywhere, under the nearest maple or ash tree, but properly, in the office.

"Not in the least . . . we can even exchange a few words right here . . . if you don't mind." Well, nobody ever said that disseminating charity in Cracow was simple, easy, or enjoyable.

"I am helping to organize a raffle for the benefit of scrofulous children," Zofia began, patently averse to being received in the corridor like a common tradesman. "I recall that the sisters have some splendidly equipped workshops here. Perhaps it would be possible to ask the residents for gifts of the heart to be raffled for this purpose — Christmas cribs, maybe, or some pretty little baskets, or needlework . . ." She paused to watch one of the gardeners run in through the main entrance, knock the mud from Saturday's rain off his boots, and purposefully race upstairs.

"No, that's quite enough," said Zofia, changing tack so sharply that Sister Alojza all but jumped. "That's quite enough," she said in a tone that brooked no opposition.

"Will you please tell me what's going on here? Why all this running about? Is the bishop coming? The canonical visitor? Or is a very important person coming to reside here?"

"Perhaps we had better go outside," whispered the nun cautiously. "It's quieter there."

They turned into a corridor, then passed through a side door, down some steps, and along the side of the chapel, all the way to the garden that was laid out between the wings of the building. Oh dear, those saplings, the little lawns, the benches, flower beds, and paths — to Zofia all this was yet another vulgar display of the combined fortunes of the Helcels and the Treutlers, who even had to show off their profligacy in the garden, though one could perfectly well have put a vegetable plot here and built some profitable residential houses on the site of the present kitchen garden. They sat down on a bench, Zofia straight backed with her chin raised and her hand resting on her umbrella, stabbed into the freshly raked path, and Alojza with rounded shoulders, huddled forward. Even from here one could tell that something was brewing in the house; curtains twitched and figures flashed past furtively.

"Well, then?"

"It's nothing much," said Sister Alojza, trying to make light of the matter, but it's hard to make light of things when you're goggle-eyed, so her efforts to play down the situation seemed desperate, and to some extent they were. "It's just that we've lost one of our lady residents. It happens quite often."

"Quite often?" said Zofia, raising an eyebrow, plainly vexed that the nun was doing her best to conceal something from her. "So do you simply take in someone else in her place? And if she happens to be found, make her into schnitzels to cover up the truth?"

Sister Alojza gave her a look in which incredulity and fear that this might in fact be a genuine suspicion were mixed in equal measure.

"Not in the least! We look for them. They usually turn up fairly quickly. And it's always the same ones — those whose minds are somewhat muddled by old age. One of them, who'd been brought up in the countryside, used to go and sit in the stable, covered in straw. Another would ferret about in the pantry, eat her fill, and then fall asleep with a slice of bread in her hand. The younger ones, the male convalescents" — she glanced skyward — "occasionally slip out at night on godless errands, always the best sign that they've fully recovered. But this time . . ."

"This time she hasn't been found?"

"Indeed, she has not. So Mother Zaleska has summoned the cooks and the gardeners to help, and the sisters who aren't attending anyone at the moment, and even the servants from the upper floor . . . Oh, I didn't say — the lady who has gone missing . . . not only is she quite all right in the head" — at this point her glance was full of respect — "but she's from the upper floor!"

As well as its reserve fund, Helcel House had a fixed income, too; it was designed to be a permanent foundation that would guarantee support for the sick and poor, acting as a charitable perpetuum mobile. The neediest residents, known as *almsmen* and *almswomen*, who were sent to the institution by the municipality, did not pay for their own keep, but lived in shared dormitories without special amenities; those who were still capable earned some income by making things in the workshops. Whereas the rest, taken in whenever a place became vacant, were divided into three classes, according to which they paid for their accommodation, with an additional contribution to cover board and lodging for the charity cases. The wealthiest kept their own servants here and occupied two-room apartments, as a rule furnished with items brought from their former, grander lives. Through their half-open doors one might spot a Louis XVI armchair, its covers rather shabby by now, a Biedermeier chest of drawers from a country manor or bourgeois drawing room, an ebony crucifix, a bouquet of artificial flowers under a glass dome, photographs, papal blessings in gilded frames, or portraits of long-deceased husbands and parents.

"Someone important?"

"Mrs. Mohr, the image of respectability, a very quiet, pious woman, the widow of a high court judge. Yesterday evening I wished her good night, but this morning there was no sight or sound of her. Every room in the entire house has been thoroughly searched . . . but she has disappeared without a trace!" Alojza broke off, clasped her hands together so tightly that her fingers went white, and then spoke again, this time with a slight hesitation. "As for the raffle, Mrs. Turbotyńska, I can't make any promises, because it all depends on Mother Zaleska, but I will put a word in her ear, and I'll pray for a favorable response. I wouldn't wish to trouble you . . ."

"It's no trouble," replied Zofia, raising her left eyebrow. "I shall pay you another visit once this not very peaceful rest home is in a more peaceful state, and Mrs. Mohr is back between her bedsheets. God be praised, Sister Alojza."

She stood up, and the nun sprang to her feet too, assuring Zofia that she'd gladly escort her back to the vestibule. So they walked through the garden, one tall and slender, the other squat and round, like female versions of Don Quixote and Sancho Panza. Finally they parted ways.

"And what are you doing here, Franciszka?" Zofia said to her cook, finding her politely waiting by one of the columns. "You have the morning off, haven't you?"

"Yes, but . . . I didn't want to leave without saying goodbye."

"No, no, this is your free time. There's not a minute to lose . . . 'Let us love each other like brothers but count like Jews,'" said Zofia, who often quoted such typical sayings of the times as a safeguard, ever since grasping in her girlhood the subtle hints that Granny Glodt was not descended from quite as Catholic a family as it might appear — an inkling that, if proven true, might raise an eyebrow among some members of Cracow society. "I shall manage to complete the luncheon preparations on my own. In any case, just about everything is ready. I trust you found your grandmother in good health?"

"Yes, madam."

"Excellent. Don't waste time on foolishness."

"Yes, madam. Goodbye, madam."

Once again, an anxious-looking nun ran past them. Evidently Mrs. Mohr was not yet back in her bed.

"Goodbye," replied Zofia, and descended the steps at her most dignified, regal pace, something she had mastered at deportment classes for young ladies in her hometown. Once in the blood, always in the blood.

❧

On the return journey she paid even less attention to her surroundings than before; now and then she merely took hold of the small watch edged with blue enamel that was pinned to her chest and glanced at its face, as if seeking there the solutions to life's major problems — but invariably the watch showed nothing but the time.

Just as everything was astir in Helcel House today, so for quite a while something had been astir in the heart of Zofia Turbotyńska, trying to find an outlet. She had no children, and despite visiting doctors in Lemberg and Vienna, despite conquering her embarrassment and resorting to consultations with Ignacy's colleagues, there was clearly nothing to be done. An affair? Impossible. Some women assured themselves offspring by that means, but it was out of the question. She loved as everyone else did: she'd been in love, and so had married; as a married woman, she continued to love her husband, but without overdoing it. She expressed her devotion by serving the meals on time, running the house to perfection, and supporting him in his career.

Though only ten years older than his spouse, Ignacy Turbotyński looked much more mature. Perhaps it was down to the bushy but graying sideburns that he grew as a mark of loyalty to the ruling house, or perhaps this was how his attitude to the modern day revealed itself; of the times, the only ones to interest him were the past, and the *Cracow Times* newspaper, to which he subscribed.

On completing his studies in Cracow and Göttingen, Ignacy had taken up a post in the anatomy department. For many years he had worked as second and then first junior lecturer, then he had become a senior lecturer, and finally a full professor at the Jagiellonian University, in his own view achieving all that he possibly could. Or rather, all that he would never have achieved if not for his wife. It was Zofia —though if asked about her husband's specialty, she would drop her gaze in confusion and pretend to be incapable of telling a tibia from a fibula—who for years on end had been skillfully developing various acquaintances and connections, scheming away, whispering a word in one ear or another, gradually paving the way for Ignacy to gain further promotion. For he was regarded as solid and reliable, but not much more. "No need to close the window," people would meanly say. "The turbot is not an eagle, it won't take off."

Turbotyński had no major works to his credit, and wasn't terribly interested in the novelties so eagerly introduced by his younger and more ambitious colleagues, with the enterprising Professor Kostanecki, well versed in the world of German science, at the forefront. Ignacy specialized in preparing anatomical samples, which he had learned under the watchful eye of Professor Ludwik Teichmann, whose first-rate specimens — as Turbotyński was keen to stress — had "won awards at world exhibitions." Though Turbotyński's own specimens had not achieved fame throughout Europe, thanks to his conscientious efforts the Theatrum Anatomicum's museum collection had been enriched by many new exhibits, including — of this the professor was particularly proud — the splendidly prepared arterial system of *Eretmochelys imbricata*, the hawksbill sea turtle.

Professor Teichmann, who lived nearby on Floriańska Street ("His daughter married a *baron*," Zofia would reverently say, a fact that in her opinion entirely removed the mild stain of the scientist's profession of the Calvinist faith), was Ignacy's mentor. Next year he would be retiring from his post as head of the faculty, but it was already known that Kostanecki would replace him, and not Turbotyński, who — unlike his wife — showed no managerial ambitions and was not in the least bit interested in competing for any post at all. He would come home, wreathed in the odor of the formaldehyde and glazier's putty he used to prepare his exhibits, settle in his armchair, light a cigar, and read the newspaper from cover to cover, sharing with his wife the more interesting — in his view — items of news from the world at large.

Zofia was aware that for the time being she could not achieve any greater honors for Ignacy; perhaps in a decade or two there'd be something to do with seniority, general eminence, and advancing years: a medal, an honorary degree, or a collection of congratulatory writings from his colleagues. But for now, she had done all that was in her power for her husband, so the time had come to do something for herself. She hadn't succeeded with the Lemberg National Exhibition, and it was hard to rise up the ranks of the Charitable Society without a title or a husband among the top city or provincial authorities. At the same time, in everyday life, managing the servants and exchanging gossip, she felt as if trapped in a tightly laced corset. Sometimes, as she reclined on the sofa, she would lay her book on her lap, marking the page with an index finger, and ponder the fact that in another era she might have done better in life; she could see herself as Cleopatra, as Zenobia, the English queen Elizabeth, perhaps, or Joan of Arc—in any case as an imperious woman, leading her troops onto the field, attired now in splendid armor, as if straight from a painting by Matejko, now in a sumptuous gown from a canvas by Jacques-Louis David or an ancient tunic from the work of Delacroix . . . Meanwhile, she had to be content with giving orders to Franciszka, planning the meals for the coming week, and making sure the poularde was removed from the oven in time.

CHAPTER III

A long but pithy chapter, in which we learn about Cracovian conservation practices, and that — mark my words — Matejko will live for some time to come, that one can keep procuring new staff for years on end, what one must do to lie down beside Mrs. Helcel, and finally, what the watchman found.

"Ignacy," said Zofia cautiously, "I cannot imagine that, as a university professor and a *distinguished* person, you have not been invited to the gala opening of the new theater . . ."

Typically, Zofia already knew of course that a special committee, convened by the city council, would soon be focusing its attention on a matter that was stirring lively interest in most Cracovian households: the distribution of spare tickets for the celebrations due to take place less than a week from now. Although the new building was large and impressive, everyone was aware that it couldn't accommodate all of Cracow's bourgeoisie simultaneously.

"Zofia," gasped Ignacy, setting a shred of bay leaf on the edge of his plate with his fork, "surely you don't mean to tell me you wish to attend that feast of fools?" Ignacy, who was not terribly interested in cultural matters on the whole, had an extremely critical attitude to the new theater; he was of the opinion that the prodigious sums of money the city council had spent on building and furnishing this temple of Melpomene should have been granted to the goddess for whom he cared far more, namely Hygieia. "As you know, I'm most concerned about culture," he said, ignoring his wife's meaningfully raised eyebrow. "And I think highly of the national arts" — the eyebrow went up a notch — "but the gentlemen at the council must have been suffering a mental aberration, *confusio mentis,* when they decided that a *theater* is more important than the waterworks that Cracow has lacked ever since the Swedes destroyed the reservoirs and pipes over two hundred years ago. Cholera! Typhus! Dysentery! Not to mention alcoholism — the water in the wells looks nasty and tastes disgusting, so when in need of a drink, with nothing to quench their thirst, the common folk are all the more willing to reach for a beer mug or a shot glass, bringing moral disaster on themselves."

Having said this, he reached for a wineglass himself, drank a little Riesling, and carefully set it down again on the ring it had impressed on the tablecloth earlier. Zofia was silent; she had known from the start that bringing up this topic would prompt her husband to deliver a tirade, and so she was waiting out the storm, focusing on her zander and on planning her next move.

"Never mind that the central conservation committee in Vienna called for the preservation of the ancient Holy Spirit Hospital on that site, never mind that none other than Count Tarnowski appealed for the salvation of that relic of the past! Oh, no, those miserable reformers railed so furiously against its 'hideous stone walls' that this barbarity was committed—approval was given to demolish the hospital, with the single caveat of a promise to the imperial committee to keep the little Holy Spirit Church intact . . ."

Zofia gazed at him as he poured out the familiar facts and opinions that he cited every single time in exactly the same order, and with her entire bearing did her best to express her undivided interest.

". . . until suddenly last year, when the theater was already up, and the church was not blocking the view of it at all, they approved its demolition too. Barely had Matejko made an offer to the city council to restore the church at his own expense, when the very next day word got out that the roof had collapsed, and the church would have to be destroyed because it posed a threat to life, certain death for children, et cetera . . . It's most peculiar that the vault caved in as if on command, as if at the sound of the trumpets of Jericho. And the danger was so severe that they couldn't take the church apart for several months after." As he spoke,

Ignacy's face went redder and redder, making his sideburns look like bursts of electricity surrounding a purple ball. "Vandals! Matejko was right to return his honorary citizen's diploma to the mayor and declare that he'd never be buried in the National Pantheon at St. Michael's. Quite right!"

"That's nothing but hot air. He has only just had his fiftieth birthday; he'll live as long again. He'll have plenty of opportunities to be reconciled with the councilors, then he'll rest in peace at St. Michael's, and no mistake," said Zofia, unable to restrain herself. In fact, she loathed the troublesome liberals just as much as her husband did, but in her heart of hearts the thought of the beautiful new theater pleased her, even if it had been built on the site of a medieval barn. "I'm sure Matejko will be present at the opening. And Count Tarnowski, too. Regardless of your views about the theater, the city's elite are bound to attend the gala opening. And tomorrow, as a university professor, you will walk across from St. Anne's to the Collegium Novum with the other professors for the inauguration of the academic year. In a gown!" She all but quivered at the thought of this memorable moment. "So say what you like, but I cannot imagine that we can fail to appear at the opening of the theater."

"My dear Zofia —"

"Ah, there's dessert as well," said Zofia. She crumpled her napkin, tossed it onto the tablecloth, and went into the kitchen. Time off is a sacred thing. Yet the fact that she could not eat her meal in peace, but had to keep going to and fro, from dining room to kitchen and back again, was bound to give her stomach ulcers in the end; for now it just put her in a rage. She came back carrying a tray, on which stood two cups filled with lemon flummery, her hands shaking so badly that the cups shook too, causing their edges to chime against each other. Franciszka may well have done the cooking, mixing, and grating, but it was the lady of the house who had to interrupt her meal, go into the kitchen, and come back with the tray. And then clear away the unappetizing remains, plates smeared with sauce and little balls of allspice, the dirty knives and forks . . .

"Ignacy," she began — rightly regarding the matter of the tickets as settled, so now Ignacy would bend over backward if necessary to obtain them — "Franciszka cannot cope on her own anymore. It's beyond her strength. She cannot do the cooking and also clean the entire house."

"I see no obstacle, Zofia," he replied, grabbing a teaspoon and a cup of flummery with surprising agility. "You'll need to pay another visit to one of the domestic services procurement agencies — let them take care of it. Mrs. Vogler's, perhaps? On Szpitalna Street, or Mrs. . . . . what's her name?"

"Mrs. Wolska? No, no, whatever you may say, Mrs. Mikulska is Mrs. Mikulska; she has been in the business for over twenty years. Hers was the first agency in all Cracow to be licensed by the governor and I've always been to her . . ."

"And you have always dismissed the girl after a month or two . . ."

"Ignacy!" said Zofia, burning with righteous indignation, as ever when confronted with the truth.

"And the one who's been with us the longest is Franciszka, who came from your cousin, not from Mrs. Mikulska. Why don't you ask Józefa if she has anyone else up her sleeve?" he said, struggling to suppress a smile.

"Sometimes you are quite impossible."

They sat awhile longer in silence, each engrossed in their own thoughts. She was plotting how to get back at him for those cutting remarks, and he was pondering how to leave the table in a civil manner, without exposing himself to anger, meaningful looks, and snorts. If Franciszka was at home, he merely had to ask her to clear the plates or serve tea in his study, but on days like this he was entirely at Zofia's mercy. In theory he could pretend to have dozed off at the table, but he was two years short of fifty, and that sort of ruse seemed inappropriate, for it would make him into an old codger — at once he'd have to swap his frock coat for a traditional *czamara* overcoat and his sideburns for a handlebar mustache, and nod off before the fire, occasionally waking up to utter a few words of upper-class waffle and then go back to sleep again. He wasn't ready for that yet. So he sat up straight, shifting crumbs about the tablecloth with a fingertip.

"I think I'll go and read," said Zofia at last. "If you're still in here when Franciszka returns, please make sure she clears the table. And tell her not to disturb me."

He assented, and then listened to her receding footsteps: still loud in the dining room, quieter and quieter in the passage, until he heard the key grate in the bedroom door. He knew her movements by heart: now she'd go up to the shelf with her favorite books, hesitate a moment, take out a German edition of Edgar Allan Poe, and reread "The Murders in the Rue Morgue" or "The Gold-Bug" once again. Or possibly one of the books by Gaboriau that she'd bought in Paris on their honeymoon or acquired later, as a young wife. Something about crime and punishment, but not by Dostoevsky. He could see her finger gliding across the spines of the books and . . . yes, he could hear the groaning of the springs as she sat in the old armchair she'd brought here from her hometown. And then nothing but silence, pure silence.

❧

The next day, Zofia's main concern was the ceremonial inauguration of the academic year at the university, where, with immense satisfaction, she saw Ignacy in his gown — incidentally, it occurred to her that she must make sure he didn't wear that costume like an ordinary frock coat, but rather with the distinction due to it. Yet on Wednesday she decided to visit Sister Alojza again to bring her raffle plan to a happy conclusion.

Mother Zaleska was not a wasteful person, and regarded the objects produced in the workshops as a form of tribute that the almsmen and almswomen owed to the palace — for what else was Helcel House, if not a palace? — and so her response to any attempt to grab if only a few of the wooden spoons they made was generally unfavorable; but Mrs. Turbotyńska had her way of dealing with this, too. First of all, she was on good terms with one of Mother Zaleska's ancient and extremely bossy aunts. Secondly, she provided the nun with her favorite dessert — figs, of which she had grown fond while living in Smyrna for many years; she always thanked Zofia for them wholeheartedly, although she did occasionally mention that even the best figs from the colonial shops in Galicia were no match for the ones she'd had in the past. Thirdly, Zofia had once done her a small but essential favor of the kind one can never forget — if only because the person who did the favor is more than happy to remind one of it.

She passed the door into the office and glanced curiously down the passage. Nothing seemed out of order: all the excitement of two days ago had died down now, the agitated voices were silent, and once again the only people in sight were convalescents slinking along with dark rings around their eyes and old ladies dragging their feet — some had probably been born in the previous century. In between, the nuns flitted past majestically in their white wimples, at their natural tempo *moderato* once again. Zofia retraced her steps and stopped at the office door.

"Jesus Christ be praised," she said with a slight bow as she crossed the threshold. "I am pleased to see that this time you are in your place and we won't have to go into the garden — the weather has just deteriorated." She rested her umbrella against an armchair and, though gazing at Sister Alojza with a degree of benevolence, was not yet going to let her speak. "And we have a whole host of matters to discuss! I assume the poor lost sheep has returned to the flock by now?"

"Forever and ever, amen, Mrs. Turbotyńska," stammered the nun. "We've been praying to the Lord Jesus night and day for her return."

"Oh?" said Zofia, tilting her head a touch to the left like a guinea fowl, then cleared her throat and began in a less jovial tone: "Not that I would wish to educate you in matters of faith, but perhaps it would be more appropriate to try Saint Anthony of Padua? Though after so many days perhaps Saint Jude would be the better choice . . ."

Alojza didn't know what to say; from the day she was born she had never understood jokes, or irony, or allusions, so she did as she saw fit in such instances: she raised her eyes to the ceiling and gazed upward for a while, as if tracking a fly or a spider crawling around the lamp.

"Are the doors into the institution locked at night?" came a question out of the blue. Alojza was lost. She was still wondering whether to pray to Saint Anthony for help to find the lost old lady, as for a mislaid rosary or a comb dropped and kicked beneath a chest of drawers, or whether Saint Jude would indeed be the better choice by now, but here was another turn in the path.

"The doors?" she replied. "Yes, the doors are locked.

And there's a watchman. Nobody went out. There's no sign of her."

"And who has occasion to walk about the corridors at night?" For the time being, Zofia had dropped all thought of prizes for the raffle, of paste-and-cardboard Christmas cribs, embroidered napkins, hand-carved walking-stick handles — in short, all the junk that she would then have to force on Cracow's gentlefolk for the benefit of scrofulous children. "Particularly on the top floor? The sisters? Servants? The residents themselves?"

"Occasionally . . ." said Alojza, blushing, "if one of them chooses not to employ the chamber pot but prefers . . . to make her way . . . to the water closet . . . though as a rule they prefer to stay in their rooms. But some are very bad — if the chamber pot stays in the room, even if it's covered with a thick cloth and hidden in the bedside closet . . . they wake the maid and tell her" — talking about human physiology was such an ordeal for the poor nun that she was almost gasping for breath in the search for reasonably bearable euphemisms — "to deal with . . . the unpleasantness."

"And has someone spoken to them?"

"To whom?"

"To the sisters and the servants."

"But what for?" Alojza's eyes grew even larger and more bulbous. "It's not about talking; it's about finding the unfortunate Mrs. Mohr — goodness knows where she's hidden herself. She may be unconscious, she may not be alive, may the Lord protect her . . ."

"Is Mother Zaleska here at the moment?"

"No, she has gone to see the bishop, to—"

"Splendid. In that case, let's get down to work!"

❧

The blood of the Glodts was starting to rise in Zofia's veins, pharmacist's blood that thrilled at the thought of forms to be filled, columns to be added up, and accounts to be balanced. What excitement for a heart so fond of novels about the detection and punishment of crime!

As Mother Zaleska could be back at any moment, Zofia had to find a place where she could officiate for an hour or two.

"Mrs. Mohr's room?" she asked in a tone that wasn't really interrogative.

"But it's her room, her things are in there. It's her property . . ."

"By now," said Zofia, casting Sister Alojza an indulgent look, "after three whole days it is probably her estate."

Sister Alojza put a hand to the bunch of keys hanging from her belt, chose one, and turned it in the lock. Inside, the room was neat and tidy to a fault—every single item was carefully positioned to a point of obsession: symmetry reigned throughout. Every trinket on the little shelf was matched by another, every cushion on the armchair had a twin; some of the books were arranged like a pipe organ, the tallest in the middle, with smaller ones in descending

order on either side. While Alojza briefly went to check
if Mother Zaleska was on her way, Zofia settled comfortably at the writing desk, involuntarily peeping into several
drawers as she did so: the same order ruled there too.

"I asked Sister Teresa, who cleaned in here on Sunday
morning," said Alojza, back from the first floor. "The bed
had been made; only the blanket was missing. She didn't
find any objects out of place. She just removed a vase of
wilted flowers and some dirty dishes. Nothing special
caught her eye."

"Splendid, splendid," muttered Zofia, making a note in
the little book where she usually wrote down recipes, the
first lines of poems, and the more elaborate pieces of gossip; seconds later she had a new thought, to do with her
other mission, the charitable one. "It would be quite appropriate for me to go and see the ladies on this floor . . . And
as for the employees, ideally I would summon them all here
at once, but we cannot paralyze the entire functioning of
the house." Alojza fully agreed with these words. "So perhaps you would bring each of them to me in turn?"

Physically Alojza was put to the test for the next hour
or two as she ran to and fro between the first floor and
the third floor, up and down hundreds, if not thousands,
of steps. By turns she watched for Mother Zaleska, sup-
plied Mrs. Turbotyńska with various pieces of information,
brought the watchman to see her, then the gardeners and
the cook—people with whom Zofia would rather not talk
in person, but such were the rules of the game she had de-

cided to take on, the rules of reinventing herself as a detective from a novel. Of far greater interest to her than the plebs were the residents of the top-floor apartments—the female residents, that is, for after lights-out the door separating the ladies' wing from the gentlemen's was locked, meaning that for now she could limit her focus to this community, consisting of a few ancient noblewomen, rich widows, and old maids, the last heiresses to bourgeois fortunes. And the servants who kept them company.

Each of these women, as Zofia was perfectly well aware, represented a separate world, which was either joined to other worlds by an intricate web of connections, or which had most definitely cut itself off from them. Here were long-standing animosities that had first budded at society balls and in the large somber drawing rooms of Cracow's residential houses, under Renaissance beams and Baroque ceilings; here too were some heartfelt ties that dated back to the days when these wrinkled old women delighted their parents as little girls in muslin frocks—though no doubt deep in their souls they were already mean and spiteful then; and finally, here were the strangest yet most enduring relationships, in other words animosities blended into one with alliances: hate-filled friendships. On this she was counting the most, for nobody gossips as ardently as a friend filled with hatred. And perhaps some significant detail from the life of Mrs. Mohr, "the image of respectability," might emerge along the way.

Equipped with her little notebook, Zofia went from

room to room and, regardless of whether she found the resident to be a willing or unwilling interlocutor, questioned each of them in turn. Without forgetting in the process that she had her own mission to complete at Helcel House: the raffle.

❧

"*Entrez*," Zofia heard at last from inside, after knocking at the door for several minutes; a key grated in the lock and a small stout maid with a face as smooth and yellow as a billiard ball admitted her into the hall of Countess Żeleńska's apartment.

The lady was already in view from the doorway; she must have spent the past few moments getting ready to give an audience. She was sitting in a tall, rather worn-out armchair, as if trying to look like the pope benevolently receiving a delegation of Cracow bourgeoisie. The final corrections were still being made as she adjusted the velvet ribbon on her neck, arranged her lace mantilla, and nestled down in her armchair like a mother hen.

"*Entrez*," she wheezed again. Zofia entered the drawing room, bowing low.

Countess Matylda Żeleńska de Zielonka, in terms of status the most distinguished resident at Helcel House, occupied the most spacious three-room apartment on the third floor. Thanks to its dark green wallpaper and heavy, snuff-colored curtains, the drawing room in which she received her guests was rather gloomy. The windows of the room—like those of the entire ladies' wing—faced west, so the curtains were designed to stifle noise from the outbuildings, the stables, and the laundry, but something about the way the thick fabric was arranged reminded one of the drapery of a catafalque. Countess Żeleńska had furnished a family mausoleum for herself while still alive: here and there on the walls hung a wrinkled male ancestor or a lovely young female ancestor. (On closer inspection it proved to be the hostess in the spring of her life, in the days of the Spring of Nations.) The room smelled of dust, powder, and withered roses.

After introducing herself, Zofia began cautiously with the standard courteous inquiries about health, but was soon convinced that this was prompting a negative rather than a positive response, so she came to the point.

"Your ladyship, I would like to talk to you about a charity raffle that I am helping to organize for the benefit of scrofulous children."

"Ah, yes, yes, those poor children with the English disease," said the countess, for whom the names of all illnesses suffered by lesser mortals sounded alike, or were perhaps one and the same ailment: poverty. Zofia was well aware that correcting the countess would defeat the purpose, so she continued in an unruffled tone:

"If your ladyship were to be so kind," she said, modestly dropping her gaze to the dusty rug, "and would agree to take the raffle under her patronage . . ."

Philanthropy was the favorite pastime of almost all the local aristocratic ladies, who despite their advanced age vied with each other to organize charity balls, and before Easter, wrapped in thick wool stoles, they solicited donations in Cracow's ever-chilly churches. The *Cracow Times* eagerly informed its readers which lady would be holding a collection in which church and at what times. In this city no self-respecting charitable enterprise could exist without its own countess — these were the rules, and Zofia *nolens volens* (but more *volens* than not) had to abide by them. Matylda Żeleńska could become *her countess,* whose patronage would make Zofia's enterprise into an *event,* meaning that next year in the column headed EASTER WEEK COLLECTIONS, alongside the familiar names of the most distinguished aristocratic ladies, the name *Zofia Turbotyńska* would appear.

Seeing vacillation on the countess's face, Zofia decided to play her trump card.

"If your ladyship's state of health will not allow for it, then naturally I understand. Perhaps Countess Tarnowska would be agreeable ..." It was an open secret in Cracow that these two ladies had a genuine mutual loathing, ever since a much-publicized inheritance case several years ago. The countess took the bait.

"Not allow for it?" she said, almost rising from her chair. "My dear madam, there is nothing more noble than philanthropy! We should take my cousin, the late lamented Mrs. Helcel, as our model for the selfless and righteous provision of aid to our needy neighbors in the name of Christian charity." The fees that the countess paid were certainly enough to keep several, if not at least a dozen, paupers, but it was no secret that a place had been found for her at Helcel House on account of a clause in the donor's will, giving priority admission to the founders' own relatives. "It shall be my pleasure to help, my dear madam."

In her excitement at hearing these welcome words, Zofia felt the blood rush to her head, and suddenly her corset was too tight. The countess must have noticed.

"Are you feeling all right? Do take a seat," she said, pointing with the feeblest gesture to another armchair. "It is sure to be this terrible business with Mrs. Mohr. We are all greatly unsettled by it," said the countess, shaking her head. "What on earth can have become of the unfortunate woman?"

Zofia, who had fully recovered by now, instantly seized the opportunity to discover some new facts.

"Was Mrs. Mohr in the habit of going outside the bounds of the institution?"

"How could she, my dear madam?" said the countess, frowning. "Mrs. Mohr was in poor health — she hardly ever emerged from her room. Her knees," she added in an embarrassed whisper.

"Did she receive guests?"

"Rarely. She was a widow, she had no children . . . Well, she did have, but the poor little things had died, of cholera it seems. Her sister sometimes visited her, but they weren't on the best terms. I don't like to gossip . . . but every time she was here, they ended up quarreling. It was most unpleasant. She came to see her last Sunday, in fact . . . She must have stayed late, because I could still hear them arguing after dinner, about food again. Old people don't have the appetite they once had," she said, sighing. "Most of the visits are on Sundays. It should really be a day of rest, but there's such a commotion from the lower floors . . ." Her face took on the expression of a martyr from a canvas by Delacroix.

Children & chol., wid., Sun. p.m. arg. w. sister, Zofia jotted down in her notebook under the heading *Co. Żel.* The blood of the Glodts was happily bubbling away. As long as Mother Zaleska did not come back too soon. There was always the hope that before her audience with the bishop she would have to spend an hour or so waiting in an anteroom.

"Many thanks indeed, your ladyship, for those valuable observations. And of course, for your promise to support the raffle," she said, smiling so sweetly that her head seemed made of sugar. "I shall speak with Mother Zaleska as soon as possible. I would like to obtain some of the residents' artifacts to be donated as prizes." She noticed a wisp of sympathy in the countess's eye; so she too was aware that the conversation would not be easy. "And then I shall take the liberty of coming to see you again."

"We should not spare any efforts for the poor," concluded the old lady sententiously. "And whom shall you interview now?"

"Visit. I shall visit the ladies who reside in the neighboring rooms."

"Aha, Banffy. And Mrs. Wężyk. Well, each of us has a cross to bear," she said, smiling with one side of her mouth.

"Banffy? Like the Hungarian politician?"

"Apparently a relative, but a very distant one. Whatever the case may be, I wish you luck, my dear Mrs. . . . ?"

"Turbotyńska."

". . . Turbotyńska."

❦

Alojza had just clambered to the third floor, bringing two gardeners, who were now standing hesitantly in the corridor; one was crumpling his cap, the other was chewing his fingernails, and both were shifting from foot to foot. But Zofia waved a hand to say it wasn't yet time for such secondary matters — she was just about to knock on the door of Baroness Banffy when a very small, shriveled old lady emerged from the next room.

"Mrs. Wężyk," whispered Alojza, who, a little out of breath, had managed to run up to Zofia now. Then she began explaining to the old lady that "the unfortunate Mrs. Mohr" still hadn't been found, and "this dear lady will ask a few questions."

"More? More what?"

"Judge Mohr's widow, who lives in number four," said Zofia, joining in.

"It's the first I've heard of her."

"She went missing the day before yesterday."

"I haven't found her," said Mrs. Wężyk rather angrily, "but then I haven't been looking for her either."

"Nobody expects you to. It's just that she's gone—"

"Gone, quite so! Goes to and fro, stamps her feet, so I can't sleep at night!"

Mrs. Wężyk, bent double at first, now straightened up, full of fury out of nowhere, and rapped her thin walking cane against the floor.

"I do not wish it! And Aniela should not keep urging me, or I shall dismiss her!" she shouted into Zofia's face, or rather into her bodice, for she reached roughly the height of it, and then agitatedly headed down the corridor.

"Yes, I thought that would be pointless," said Alojza, sighing. "Mrs. Wężyk is not—"

"Not in her right mind, I can see that."

"Not very patient when it comes to conversation, I was going to say. She thinks she's still living at home, and we are her householders and servants."

"Is Aniela her maid?"

"Aniela has been dead for years. At first Mrs. Wężyk used to visit her grave at Rakowicki Cemetery, but since last year . . ."

"I see. Did Mrs. Mohr have similar problems with her memory?"

"Not in the least! Her memory was legendary—she only had to have seen a person once in her life to recognize them fifty years later. She could recite whole books by heart. Oh, no, hers was an unusual mind!"

"Really?" said Zofia, making another note. "What else? Ah yes, the baroness, and then I'll deal with the next person you've brought here."

Baroness Banffy occupied two rooms next door to Countess Żeleńska. The door was opened by her maid, who looked a little older than Zofia; a well-built figure with graying hair gathered in a large bun. Zofia uttered the same formula as for the previous visit.

"Her ladyship is not receiving anyone," snapped the woman icily, glaring at Zofia like Cerberus.

"That will do, Polcia," came the baroness's voice from inside. "Ask her to come in."

Zofia had been sure this conversation would be in German — the language of her forebears on the paternal side — but as it turned out, the baroness spoke Polish very well. As they talked, Zofia realized that she must in fact be a Pole who, after several decades in Austria and Hungary at her husband's side, had acquired a slight, indeterminate accent. She must once have been a handsome woman, thought Zofia, but the years had not been kind to her. She appeared robust, despite being seventy, at a guess, but tiredness showed in her face, and not even a thick layer of powder could hide the dark shadows under her eyes. Zofia rejoiced at the thought that regular use of Rix's Pompadour Milk was sure to spare her complexion a similar fate.

"A charity raffle . . . I am sorry to say that I cannot

help you," declared Baroness Banffy. "I no longer have the strength to contribute to such events. A few years ago, perhaps . . . at my late lamented husband's estates in Transylvania I myself organized charitable fetes . . . ach, how fine they were—excellent Tokays, superb company, Gypsy bands, cymbals, a dancing bear . . . But today, in this venerable sanctuary, I myself am in need of *solicitous* care." She cast a glance at her Cerberus-like maid. "I am sorry," she said again in an almost apologetic tone.

Having already won the countess round, Zofia was not dismayed by the baroness's refusal, so she opened her notebook and smoothly moved on to questions about Mrs. Mohr.

"I don't know her."

"You and she are neighbors."

"Yes, so I have heard."

"Do you not lead a social life within the house, your ladyship?"

"My dear Mrs. Turbotyńska"—Zofia was very pleased that her interlocutor had remembered her name at once—"if I wished to lead a social life, I would not have come to live in this dying place. My only desire is peace and quiet in my homeland."

"Her ladyship's only desire is peace and quiet," repeated the maid, as if translating from another language.

"And did you see anything troubling on Saturday evening, during the night, or on Sunday morning? Any unfamiliar people? Or suspicious faces?"

"Almost everyone here has a suspicious face," replied Polcia, who was plainly in the habit of assisting her mistress in conversation. "Even those from so-called society . . ."

"Polcia . . ."

"I'm just saying what everyone can see anyway," she said, pursing her lips.

It was clear that she stuck by her mistress as a faithful housekeeper who, judging by their intimacy, must have been there at the late lamented Baron Banffy's estates in Transylvania, where, instead of notaries and councilors' wives, bears danced at the charity fetes, and instead of a string orchestra, nothing but cymbals played . . . *Honest to God*, thought Zofia, *if a Transylvanian brigand were to spring from behind the wardrobe, this big-boned woman would send him to kingdom come, if only with the bunch of keys that jingled at her apron.*

"No, I noticed nothing out of place," said the baroness after a pause for thought. "Everything is so ordinary and repetitive here that any deviation from the norm sticks in the memory — the fact that one of the almswomen has died, that marzipan muffins were served for dessert, or the laundry was a day late, even changing the bedsheets becomes an event. No wonder the house thrives on the slightest gossip . . ."

Zofia pricked up her ears. "And have you heard any gossip about Mrs. Mohr?" she asked.

"What sort of gossip do you imagine there can be about an ailing widow who, apart from a Sunday outing to Mass, never pokes her nose outside the door of her room? Too late for a wedding, and too soon for a funeral," said the baroness.

"That fortune hunter may have had a go at her," said the maid, laughing knowingly.

"Polcia!"

"What fortune hunter?" asked Zofia.

"I'm not saying a thing," said Polcia, scowling.

"And quite right too," the baroness concluded for her, in a tone implying that the conversation was at an end. It only remained for Zofia to thank her for her time, bow politely, and withdraw under the vindictive gaze of the snooty maid.

❧

The time had come to question the house's various employees and servants. Most of them answered timidly, stuttering and drawling one word after another rather than formulating whole sentences. They sat on a small chair that the watchman carried into the missing woman's room and set down opposite Zofia's armchair; the small chair came from the little room beside the door separating the ladies' wing from the gentlemen's, where one of the nuns was on duty all night. The nun who had spent the whole of Sunday night there had already made her statement to Mother Zaleska. She hadn't seen Mrs. Mohr leaving her room, nor had she heard any suspicious noises. She had said it was so quiet you could hear a pin drop. Everyone else had said much the same — nobody knew a thing; nobody had noticed anything out of the ordinary.

Meanwhile, Zofia questioned them thoroughly. Earlier she had thought all this searching for the missing Mrs. Mohr — toward whom she felt quite indifferent — would bore her within an hour, but now she had lost track of time. At first she had persuaded herself she was only doing this in order to impress Mother Zaleska and secure the prizes, and, along the way, a countess who would lend her name and title to the raffle. But now she was far less concerned about that, and increasingly intrigued by the mystery, or at least the illusion of a mystery, because deep down she was expecting to discover that Mrs. Mohr had gone on a trip, or simply wandered out of her apartment at night and died of an aneurism in some remote corner of this enormous building. But it was fascinating to find how much people revealed when pressed for an answer — and especially how much they revealed unconsciously, while trying to hide something or other. By now she knew who disliked whom, who had not been at Sunday Mass, and who griped about the food. The game of interviewing all these people, taking notes, and recording their statements was more fun than any of her favorite pastimes. She had the same feeling as on that afternoon when, already engaged to be married, she had accompanied her father on a visit to the mayor of Przemyśl and had been shown a large doll's house belonging to his daughter. Oh, if only she could have knelt before this beautiful, fragile construction and picked up the tiny dolls . . . she could have played with them like a little girl! At the time she had restrained herself, but now she had decided to yield to the temptation and play the game of solving the mystery — and it was making her feel splendid. Even if these particular conversations were monotonous and uninteresting, and her notebook wasn't gaining any crucial facts.

"Next," she said now and then. "Next . . ."

"Mrs. Turbotyńska, Mrs. Turbotyńska," panted Alojza, interrupting her somewhere in between the cook and the gardeners; she was out of breath again from running up the stairs. "Mother Zaleska is back."

"Let us rejoice at her safe return from the bishop's palace," replied Zofia, and then in a hushed tone she added: "And for the good of her health let us not allow her to come up here." Then, speaking louder again, she turned to the gardeners. "Were either of you gentlemen here on the day Mrs. Mohr went missing?"

Most of the employees had observed the Sabbath, so only the core staff had remained: the nuns, two cooks who had made the dinner, two of the almswomen who had helped them to distribute the meals, and Morawski the watchman, who had left his post several times during the night to inspect the orchard and garden before returning to his lodge. He hadn't noticed anything unusual. No, no dogs barking or suspicious shadows either. Had anyone been up to the top floor after visiting time? Apart, Zofia remembered, from the missing woman's sister, who had stayed late and started an argument after dinner was served. A doctor, perhaps? No, none had been called. Any of the nuns? The ones who delivered the evening doses of medicine. Who else? A little earlier the women distributing meals, mostly the residents' maids. Yes, the maids might have had something interesting to say too, but it was plain to see that there was no love lost between them, and one would stab another in the back if she betrayed her or her mistress's secrets, so they'd probably prefer to hold their tongues. What about men? No, there hadn't been any visits from the gentlemen's wing either. The gardeners never came up here, apart from that special day when they'd searched the whole house for Mrs. Mohr.

Zofia came out of the room for a while.

"So here we have the residents' apartments," she said, drawing the corridor in her notebook with the various rooms leading off it. "She's definitely not in any of those. Considering her bad legs, she's unlikely to have gone down the stairs . . ."

"Oh, no, ma'am, Mrs. Mohr couldn't 'ave dragged 'erself to the end of the corridor, let alone the stairs," stammered the countess's maid tearfully, who moments earlier had been quite shamelessly eavesdropping at the door. "She could 'ardly drag her little feet along, she were so feeble . . ."

"At the end of the corridor," said Zofia, marking it on her map, "are the bathrooms. They've checked in there, I'm told. Who searched the bathrooms?"

"Sister Teresa and Sister Józefa," Alojza was quick to answer, doing her best to be as helpful as possible. "They didn't find anything."

"Are there any locked doors in there, broom cupboards or laundry rooms?"

"The laundry rooms are in the next building, and there aren't any cupboards."

"I see. Here is the exit onto the stairwell. Here are the rooms. Here are the bathrooms." Zofia turned around and pointed to a wide passage. "And what's over here?"

"The stairs up to the attic."

"Who checked in there?"

"The watchman."

"Excuse me, my good man," said Zofia to one of the cluster of staff who hadn't gone back to their jobs but were still trailing about on the top floor, exchanging whispers. "Please bring the watchman back here to see me."

Moments later, he appeared. Asked if he had searched the attic thoroughly, he shrugged and said, "But how could Mrs. Mohr have clambered up those stairs? She could hardly walk to the bathroom, and not without one of the sisters to support her."

"Did you do a thorough search?"

"I went in and looked around—there's nothing but sheets hanging up to dry."

"And the whole roof is open plan, with no enclosed areas, no storage spaces, cupboards, or closets?"

"There are no closets, just a small box room, low and dark, where our residents' trunks are stored on arrival."

Momentarily Zofia imagined all those trunks, coffers, and traveling chests with labels from Nice, Venice, and London, once smart and new, but which, in a year or two, five at most, would be packed with a deceased aunt's or grandfather's belongings and moved to the loft of an apartment building or the attic of a suburban manor house, forever out of fashion, doomed to the secondary role of junk.

"She could have lain down in a trunk. Slammed it shut. Fainted and fallen inside," said Zofia, sensing how freely she was floating on the churned-up waves of her own imagination. "Go and check again," she finally commanded, "and this time do it properly!"

Alojza came running from the direction of the stairs again, just about on her last legs after racing all the way downstairs and back.

"Mother Zaleska," she gasped, somewhere in between a shout and a whisper. "Mother Zaleska!"

"Splendid," said Zofia with great composure, having just about completed her interviews. "We shall have the opportunity to discuss the prizes for the raffle. Countess Żeleńska has promised to provide her patronage."

As she said this, she glanced through the open door at the chair brought earlier by the watchman — someone was sure to remove it shortly; the cooks and maids would return to their jobs and she to her everyday life at Peacock House.

From here she could see that a white wimple had appeared on the stairs above floor level. Mother Zaleska had just come into sight when a loud cry came from the attic, surprisingly high-pitched for a man built like a wardrobe, followed by the patter of feet.

"A doctor!" shouted the watchman. "Fetch a doctor! And a priest! Help!" He came running down the wooden staircase in such a rush that he almost fell — in fact he did, but was caught by a gardener standing nearby. "Fetch a doctor!"

At this point almost everyone began vying to push their way to the attic staircase; the women appeared to be squealing, weeping, and shouting, but plainly, in the interval between one sob and the next, they were eyeing each other closely; it took the joint action of Zofia and Mother Zaleska — women who in two quite different companies were known for their gruff, military tone and the ruthless obedience that they inspired in others — to bring the cluster of curious onlookers under control. One of the young gardeners was sent to fetch the house's head doctor, but by the time he came back, alone, someone had remembered that Dr. Wiszniewski was not at work today but had gone to his cousin's funeral in Tarnów.

"Dr. Zakroczymski!" exclaimed Alojza suddenly. "He came to see his sister today. Perhaps he's still here." And, hitching up her habit, she bolted down the stairs.

⊰❦⊱

A short while later, Dr. Zakroczymski did indeed appear, walking with his usual awkward gait. Zofia regarded him with a mixture of sympathy and dislike. He had his reputation, indeed he did, but, be that as it may, even a doctor with such a badly tarnished reputation would be capable of confirming a death.

Finally, the four of them went upstairs: the watchman, the doctor, Mother Zaleska, and Zofia Turbotyńska. The attic smelled of dry timber, dust, fresh laundry, and mice. On the left-hand side they could see the door leading into the box room. No wonder the first time he had looked the watchman had failed to spot Mrs. Mohr; she may have been "the image of respectability," but not of imposing stature. Indeed, she hadn't fallen into a trunk or been buried by a pile of dry sheets. But for some reason she had made her way up to the attic. Perhaps she'd been walking in her sleep, or perhaps she'd had a temporary brainstorm. Then she only had to wake up, take fright at not knowing where she was — and a heart attack was inevitable. She had indeed slipped into the small box room with a sloping roof where the trunks and suitcases were kept, and in such an unfortunate way that her body couldn't be seen from the middle of the attic. She was lying in a corner, still wrapped in the blanket taken from her bed, and shielded by the half-open door.

First the doctor checked her pulse, and then he and the watchman grasped the corners of the blanket and carried her little body closer to the stairs, to a spot that was better lit. There was nothing shocking about the corpse — no dark stains, bruises, or blood; the face was peaceful and the cheeks still ruddy. The doctor's fingers clumsily undid some buttons.

"Not counting a small bruise that she must have sustained while falling and landing against that trunk, I can't see any injuries," he said. "She fell into a faint, which could have happened for various reasons, and then died of exposure. Yes," he said, straightening up, "naturally I will draft the relevant report and leave it for Dr. Wiszniewski's inspection. For now, I suggest moving the body to the mortuary."

Apart from the doctor, nobody said a word. From below, at the bottom of the stairs, came a clucking chorus of voices telling each other tall stories. Though death was not an unusual event at Helcel House, every time it occurred it stirred strong emotions among the residents.

CHAPTER IV

❧

In which we discover that students are rogues, on the day of the grand opening of its new theater Cracow is corked like a bottle, a cousin can be the age of a grandmother, the foyer is swarming with flora and fauna, a princess sleeping on a glass mountain is woken by a boy in a peasant coat, and one corpse is too few.

The days ahead belonged to the theater, so Zofia Turbotyńska devoted her spare time to alterations to her dress—which she had bought far enough in advance, as usual, at Marya Prauss's emporium—and to devising a detailed plan for that evening: with whom she must speak, what topics to bring up, and what to say about the work on display. Yet she still found a moment to make her way to the employment agency on Gołębia Street, where she presented Mrs. Mikulska with a list of requirements for a future maid, greatly reduced — so as not to scare off potential employees — but still the longest on the company's books. *And what if Ignacy's older brothers were suddenly to die, what if he were to inherit the estate and had to go back to managing his patrimony?* she thought as she filled in the boxes on the form with her shapely handwriting. *Then what would I be looking for?*

Land stewards, Bailiffs, Foresters, Estate administrators — she read, running an eye down the poster hanging in a display case — *Distillers, Craftsmen, Farmhands for field work and harvesting* . . . definitely not *Fröbel nurses, Polish girls, German girls,* or *French girls,* because the rattle-and-diapers chapter of her life was forever closed, but what would it be like to run all those acres of farmland and manage such a large retinue? Maybe then she wouldn't feel the aching void that had filled her slightly hard but vivacious heart of late?

She wanted something more in life — but if someone, Ignacy for instance, were to ask her, "Zofia, my dear Zofia, but what more do you want?" she wouldn't have been able to answer; all she knew was that in the past few months the only time she had felt truly alive were those few short hours when she had helped to find the missing old lady's body, while toying with the thought that here in Helcel House a dangerous, whisker-twirling murderer was on the prowl, and she was the investigating magistrate who'd track him down and hand him over to Imperial-Royal justice.

But the conclusion had been quite banal: a small heap of emaciated limbs wrapped in a blanket and a nightshirt. She could not forget the sight of the unfortunate woman's body, dragged from behind a chest and laid on the bare floorboards among the sheets stretched on washing lines. It hadn't looked like the other bodies she had seen before: on their deathbeds, surrounded by white lace, or on catafalques in various churches. The face had not seemed as waxy and transparent — on the contrary, it was rosy pink and flushed; it looked as if Mrs. Mohr had fallen asleep and was dozing, dreaming of her youth or her long-dead husband. Mother Zaleska, who had clambered up the steep staircase in Zofia's wake, had noticed the same thing. "It looks as if she has just closed her eyes and is praying to the Virgin Mary, doesn't it?" she had asked in a saccharine tone. For her it was a happy moment; it meant bidding farewell to her fears that a rumor would spread about Cracow to the tune of "old ladies go missing without a trace at Helcel House!," but here was just another death in this sanctuary, where a high mortality rate among the residents was bound to be an inherent feature. But for Zofia it was a sad moment; it meant abandoning her new vocation and returning to the tedium of her daily life. The idea of tracking down an assassin had taken such possession of her mind that one afternoon she nodded off while reading, and dreamed she was presenting the police with a criminal caught with her own fair hands.

And now she was back in her usual life again, in Peacock House on St. John's Street, the same old place where she had lived for the past few years, in a city twice the size of shabby Przemyśl, yet not terribly large either, in the musty mire that was Cracow, the city she loved and hated all at once. If only she could do something great, create a work of art, be celebrated like the writer Maria Konopnicka, or a Polish Sappho ... but it was out of the question; when she had finally dared to send her poems to the *Illustrated Weekly* she had read in reply: *To Mrs. Z. T. No, the* Weekly *cannot publish "poetic works" of this kind; they lack rhyme, rhythm, and . . . meaning. Why not send them to a journal that is better disposed toward you than the* Weekly, *though it won't gain any credit?* What other options did she have? She scoured the housewives' calendars, looking for occupations worthy of a good wife, such as sewing little cloth bags for lavender to hang in the wardrobes and place in the linen chests. Outside it was gray, and she was at her sewing table, flashing away with her needle. October already, but in the chaos caused for lack of a maid there had been no time yet to put away the summer clothes while also preparing the fur collars and Ignacy's beaver-fur coat for the winter . . .

"The professor's student is here," said Franciszka, interrupting her musings.

"Please ask him to come in," said Zofia, putting her material, needle, and thread on the sewing table; let it lie there as proof that she was the model wife, seeing to the welfare of the household — she was Hera, not a hetaera.

In the drawing room doorway stood a youth of about twenty, slim, well built, with an oval face, as if carved out of wood, and dark hair combed to one side. He greeted Zofia with a slight bow of his sculpted head, and even introduced himself, but all she caught was the first name, Tadeusz; the rest was drowned by the wheels of a carriage that rattled over the cobblestones outside. But rather than ask him to repeat his surname, she focused on his appearance. Twenty years ago, Zofia Glodt would have considered him handsome, but today Zofia Turbotyńska's first thought was *a rogue*. She had a poor opinion of students in general, and Ignacy's students in particular; she had heard too much about the disgusting pranks they played. No, not from her husband, but she had her sources ... there are things a spouse will never tell his wife, but that a female acquaintance is only too happy to reveal to her over a cup of tea and a slice of Pischinger cake. Thus over tea and cake she had heard about the ham rolls the students ate while dissecting corpses, and about their larks tasting human urine; it was over tea and cake that she had finally learned that one day Ignacy had entered the dissecting room unexpectedly, only to see that, for a joke, the students had placed a cigarette in a female body's *nature;* of course he hadn't uttered a word about it at home, but apparently, extremely agitated, his voice quivering, he had started his lecture by saying: "Gentlemen, make light of what you will, but always show respect for the reproductive organs!" Who knows? Perhaps this was the rascal responsible for that odious deed, especially as a dubious smirk was flickering on his lips.

"Good day, sir," she muttered curtly, rising from her chair; a reel of white thread that must have been in her lap slid down the folds of her dress, rapped twice against the floor, and rolled to the feet of the student, who instantly bent down, picked it up, and handed it to her.

"Thank you," she said.

"I have taken the liberty of disturbing you, madam, because the professor instructed me to deliver this invitation to the gala opening of the theater into your hands in person." He passed her a rectangular envelope; she took out a cream-colored card, checked that the name had been written without mistakes and with the correct title, and, most importantly, that the invitation was for two. "He said the servant might forget."

"I refuse to hear critical remarks about Franciszka," Zofia suddenly interrupted him, having noticed which seats they had been assigned: in the upper circle, and at the back as well, on extra chairs. For some strange reason it all came together in her mind — suddenly she felt sure this must be the boy who had desecrated the corpse and scoffed ham rolls in the dissecting room. "And I particularly refuse to hear them from my husband's errand boy."

The student was at a loss for words; plainly he couldn't understand why the sudden attack. He stood on the spot, staring at this matron, so ill disposed toward him, whom he had already privately nicknamed "the Hysterical Harpy."

"I am most terribly sorry," he said at last, as if with great respect, but still with that smirk on his lips. "I was merely citing the professor's words."

"Quite needlessly. I thank you for your trouble. Goodbye," replied Zofia, then sat in the armchair, reached for the sewing table, and started stitching again. The boy was too bewildered to respond; then, after a pause, he bowed and left.

On and on she sewed, her needle occasionally reflecting the light from beyond the window: the tinny glow of a filthy autumn day. Why did she have to do that? He had brought the invitation, he had been polite, it was the first time she had ever seen him, and she didn't even know his name, except that he was Mateusz or Tadeusz; yet she had exploited her obvious advantage merely in order to ... well, quite — to what end? To make herself feel better? That she did not. Suddenly she realized that she had sewn up the fourth side of the bag, so it couldn't be turned inside out or filled with lavender; she sighed and started searching the sewing table for a small pair of scissors to unpick the last seam.

❧

From the Turbotyńskis' house to the new theater building it was actually only a ten-minute walk along the city walls, but Zofia insisted that it would be *more fitting* to drive up in a carriage. Thus for the past twenty minutes they had been at a standstill on the corner of the Small Marketplace and Szpitalna Street, advancing at a snail's pace. The queue of one-horse droshkies, two-horse fiacres, and large landaus with coats of arms waiting their turn to drop off their impatient passengers in the theater forecourt stretched all the way to the porch of St. Mary's Basilica.

"This is absurd," gasped Zofia dramatically, who, though far more resourceful in life than her husband, sometimes liked to assume the role of a feeble little woman. "Do something, Ignacy. You are a university professor, after all."

"I've been saying for some time that our city's narrow streets are not fit for quite so many vehicles," said Ignacy, clearing his throat. "But nowadays everyone wants to go everywhere by carriage. I don't think the crown will fall from our heads if we get out and walk, my dear."

Zofia bristled; agreeing to her husband's suggestion meant admitting that he was right, if not directly conceding that taking a droshky had not been the best idea, but so be it — unfortunately there was no alternative. Luckily, she consoled herself as she alighted from the carriage, they were not the only ones to suffer this humiliation — a procession of people in evening dress was moving up Szpitalna Street.

As "by reason of limited space" the ladies had not been able to attend the gala opening held several hours earlier, now they were all the more eagerly heading for the inaugural performance, where they intended to draw twice the attention to themselves. The invitations instructed that ball

dresses were de rigueur, and for several days Cracow's leading fashion houses on St. Anne's Street had been in an unusual stir as the final fittings and alterations were made,
ensembles were created and accessories added that would
turn the other ladies green with envy. Now those same sophisticated ladies, who days before had been smiling at
their reflections in the shop mirror as they stroked their
taffeta gowns, were on their way to the theater, raising their
skirts high enough to avoid contact with the omnipresent
mud, but not so high as to breach propriety by revealing
their calves. With both hands, but gently, to avoid crushing the material, Zofia Turbotyńska held up her elegant Na-
ples-yellow dress and walked toward the Municipal Theater
with a look of infinite suffering on her face. Suffering, let us
add, of the elevating kind, endured for the sake of art.

Brightness shining from the theater building came into
view halfway down the street, glittering on the taut silk of
opera hats, fur collars, and stoles, and causing brooches
and diamonds to sparkle from afar. Zofia found the elec-
tric light almost dazzling, like something from Mr. Verne's
novels brought to the very heart of Cracow. The French association was all the more apt in that the theater resembled
the Parisian Opéra, which—also newly open to the public at the time—the Turbotyńskis had seen while on their
honeymoon. Preoccupied by hopping across puddles and
avoiding splashes of mud from under the shoes of other
Cracovians, Zofia did not pay much attention to the facade; knowing there would be time for that in the future,

she merely noted with satisfaction that the mascarons and attics were similar to the ones on the Cloth Hall. Beneath an inscription reading CRACOW FOR THE NATION'S ARTS she tidied her husband's tailcoat and her own dress, and together they entered the temple of art.

The performance was due to start at half past six, but plainly the commotion caused by the queue of carriages was going to delay proceedings. The theater foyer was gradually filling up, and every language of the empire could be heard. There was no lack of visitors from Prague, Vienna, and Trieste, even from Warsaw, but most of the audience were people who *meant something* in Cracow, as Zofia liked to say. On the landing of the large marble staircase, beneath a bronze bust of Count Kruzer, the generous donor, Count Tarnowski himself was conferring with Prince Sanguszko, marshal of the National Assembly, and with the deputy mayor of Lemberg, who had come at the head of a delegation from the capital. Everyone was waiting for the governor of Galicia, Count Badeni, to arrive, so the entry of Professor and Mrs. Turbotyńska did not stir anyone's interest; not a single head turned to look at them and there were no theatrical whispers in which the ear might detect the words *new, professor,* or *university.* Unabashed, Zofia began to scrutinize the assembled crowd in search of suitable company.

Under one of two giants (the unquestionably female one, as she noticed, somewhat surprised by the boldness of the decor) supporting the passage she spotted Ignacy's colleague, Dr. Zaremba the laryngologist, and his wife. She wasn't fond of them — he was profoundly deaf, and she was profoundly stupid — but she couldn't find anyone better, and standing alone in the corner would mean social disgrace; vigorously dragging Ignacy after her, she breezed through the crowd toward the Zarembas like a yellow galleon in full sail. The conversation took shape in a predictable manner: amid the prevailing din, Zaremba heard even less than usual, and as ever Mrs. Zaremba talked nineteen to the dozen: "My cousin, Mrs. Pomianowska, has lovely hair. Mine is nice, but hers is *looovely!*"

But Zofia's thoughts had gone back to Mrs. Mohr. What was a woman who could hardly drag her feet along doing in the attic in the middle of the night? How on earth had she managed to clamber up the stairs? Indeed, sleepwalkers had sometimes been known to do things in their sleep that they were not normally in the habit of doing, but they did not gain supernatural strength — a handicap is a handicap. And why was she lying in the box room? Nobody had mentioned her ever escaping from her apartment before, either by night or by day; they said she had an excellent memory, she had never been known to walk in her sleep, nor did she share another old lady's passion for hiding in various corners. If she had fainted in the middle of the attic, the nuns hanging out the washing would have found her in the morning, and perhaps she would still be alive and well . . . though on Sunday they wouldn't have been working, so they wouldn't have found her until Monday. But then again . . .

When all the important guests, including the governor, had finally arrived, people stopped exchanging niceties and started to take their seats — an activity involving far less politesse. The counts and countesses, princes and princesses, city councilors and other guests of honor moved up the broad steps to the boxes on the first and second floors, while everyone else began to crowd a narrow staircase leading to the third floor. Zofia was still upset about the seats assigned to them.

When she had received the envelope containing a cream-colored card (a white invitation was for the gala opening at noon, and a green one for the banquet), she had been overjoyed. But when she saw the details . . . On the way to the theater she had continued to fulminate about the seats, "unworthy of a Jagiellonian University professor," and now she was having to push her way through the crowd, like at the Kleparz market.

"Professor Turbotyński! Professor!" she suddenly heard behind her. She turned around and there was the very same errand boy with the rather derisive smirk (surprisingly well dressed for a common student, it occurred to her), evidently trying to attract her husband's attention.

Well, I never, she thought, *fancy addressing your mentor in that tone! What are the young people coming to?* But before she could come up with a fitting reproach, she heard Ignacy say: "Mr. Żeleński, how pleased I am to see you. Zofia, you've met my new assistant, Tadeusz Żeleński, haven't you?" Zofia felt the blood rush to her head. "He's the son of our great composer who runs the conservatoire, and I have no doubt at all that he represents the future of Polish anatomy. I tell you, this young man will go a long way!"

"Yes, we have already had the pleasure," she stammered.

"Oh, yes, indeed we have," said the young man, smiling more radiantly than ever.

"It is to the patronage of Tadeusz's cousin, Countess Żeleńska, that we owe our presence here," Ignacy went on, and Zofia felt herself flush again.

"Talk of the devil," said Żeleński, as the countess came into view, looking like an old vixen wearing too much powder. The young man ran up and offered an arm to his cousin, who could just as well have been his grandmother, and towed her up to the Turbotyńskis.

"You're looking queasy again, Mrs. Turbotyńska," remarked the countess, once the greetings and introductions were over. "October is a dangerous season for the health. Not to mention the cholera, which they say is nearing Przemyśl—"

The young man interrupted her digressions on diseases.

"The main thing is the theater's standing, though they all said it would collapse before it was completed. Apparently, some joker even went up to the architect on the site and asked, 'Excuse me, but is it true the building's at risk of caving in?', to which he replied, 'The only thing at risk of caving in is your face.'"

"Tadeusz," the countess scolded him, "what a thing to say in front of the ladies, especially the wife of your mentor and the man himself!"

"I most humbly beg your pardon," said the student, addressing the Turbotyńskis, blushing slightly, though maybe just for show, and clicked his heels. "Perhaps you'd like to join us in our box, madam? It's sure to be stuffy higher up, and we've had a seat come free, because our cousin Gorayska won't be in attendance. Tonsillitis. Just one seat, unfortunately," he explained apologetically, looking at the professor.

Zofia, still embarrassed—the smirk that never left the lips of the young Żeleński perplexed her even more—glanced hesitantly at her husband. Could Żeleński be planning his revenge? Invite her to the box, and once there, reveal to the countess how badly she had treated him? In her mind's eye she was already imagining the total failure of her charity raffle and social ostracism, sniggering at banquets, hideous tittle-tattle.

"Don't worry about me," Ignacy assured her, mistakenly interpreting his wife's look as an expression of concern for him. "The upper circle will suit me splendidly."

He thanked the countess for the tickets and for taking care of his spouse, bowed, and trudged upstairs, while in the company of the Żeleński cousins, Zofia hesitantly headed for the box they had hired—number three, on the left-hand side of the auditorium. The view from there was undoubtedly better than from the upper circle; she could admire the decorations surrounding the stage, appreciate the elaborate carvings on the balconies supported by caryatids, the deep-pink curtains, the paintings on the ceiling, and the vast chandelier hanging from its center. But above all she directed her gaze toward the audience, trying to pick out persons who might notice her, sitting *in a box.* And with *a countess,* too. *Oh, what a pity my cousin Dutkiewicz isn't here to see this!* she thought with regret. As the young Żeleński was still being extremely nice and polite, she calmed down, took several deep breaths, and reached for her fan. She felt as if, after years of exile, she had been allowed to return to Olympus, where once in the past she had briefly appeared on the occasion of that other grand opening. She set about scrutinizing the deities.

Opposite, in a box on the stalls level, almost on the proscenium, sat the young Count Potocki and his wife, with the count's mother beside them — the eccentric old dowager countess, sister-in-law, as Zofia remembered well, of the great bard, Zygmunt Krasiński. Shielding half her face was an enormous, unmissable hat, adorned with clusters of grapes.

"Look at that," said the young Żeleński, addressing his cousin, "the Hanging Gardens of Babylon."

The old lady raised her opera glasses and giggled, whereas Zofia did not know how to react. Was such mockery of venerable matrons considered appropriate among the aristocracy? She glanced to the right, toward the imperial box, where the representatives of His Majesty were sitting: the governor and the marshal, in the company of the vice chancellor of the university, the great artist Matejko (*He* has *come! I was right!* she thought with satisfaction), and other prominent persons. Count Tarnowski and his wife had just taken their seats. Thin and pale, with a squint, she settled in her chair, folded her hands in her lap, and squinted even more, gazing at her surroundings with a look of utter boredom on her face.

"Doesn't she look like a female kangaroo?" said Żeleński. "*Das verrückte Känguru* in person!"

"Tadeusz!" exclaimed the countess with feigned indignation and giggled again, overjoyed by the spiteful remark aimed at her unloved rival.

"But, my dear cousin, we all call her that," said Żeleński, laughing.

Zofia was utterly dismayed. Was this a sophisticated form of revenge? Was Żeleński trying to lure her into mockery of the wife of the president of the academy, to use it against her afterward?

"Please don't be shocked by Tadeusz's direct manner," the countess said to her. "It's all one big hornet's nest. To survive here, you must either have armor, or a sting."

"Cracow?"

"Helcel House, Cracow, Galicia," she said, smiling. "The whole world, in fact."

For a while, in mutual understanding, they scanned the boxes and the stalls through their opera glasses; the countess was looking for cousins, while Zofia was still in search of deities, and the young Tadeusz was probably spying out the prettier young ladies. He also waved casually to his father, originator and permanent director of the conservatoire, who, sitting in the imperial box among the top brass, could not wave back to him at all.

The performance had already been delayed for a good fifteen minutes, but there were still guests pouring through the main entrance, people who had chosen to stick firmly on the side of dignity and drive up to the forecourt in a carriage, so they were waiting for the entire traffic jam to be unblocked. Every couple of minutes they came in, agitated, often purple in the face; from the balcony their peeved expressions were plain to see, and their pouting lips forming the words: "It's a downright scandal!" or "It couldn't have been foreseen!"

"Oh, there's Mr. Fikalski," said the countess, laughing. "Have you had the pleasure of his acquaintance, Mrs. Turbotyńska?"

"Fikalski ... Fikalski ..." said Zofia, searching her memory, but she couldn't connect a face with the name, nor a function or title.

"He's a convalescent, staying at Helcel House — he suffers from gout. A well-known figure."

"Is he famous?" asked Zofia.

"Infamous, more like. Known for being a dowry hunter. He got into the house thanks to patronage, never mind whose" — at this point a faint scowl crossed her face — "and he's lying in wait for the next rich widow. Some ladies" — here there was a note of envy in her tone — "simply cannot rid themselves of his inopportune advances."

"Over there?" asked Zofia, pointing with the tip of her fan.

"No, two seats to the left. Who else do we have here . . . ?"

"Who's that next to Mrs. Nemeczek, the notary's wife?"

"Where?" said the countess, all but leaning out of her chair.

"Over there, on the level above, in the magenta dress. I can't see her properly because her hat is in the way . . ."

"Oh, they'll shove anything on their heads," said Tadeusz, "grapes, parrots, veils . . . I wouldn't want to be sitting behind that lady. I'd swear one could see nothing but the wings from behind her."

And so, commenting on the décolletages, the jewelry sets, the sideburns, wrinkles, and hunchbacks, the ladies surveyed the entire auditorium, with the young Żeleński putting in his three pennyworth now and then. They had splendid fun — not once did it occur to Zofia how horribly dull it must be for Ignacy, who was not in the least interested in this vast display of the Cracow bourgeoisie, gentry, and aristocracy — and they were actually sorry when the performance finally began.

First a Chopin polonaise rang out, orchestrated by the military bandmaster Jan Nepomucen Hock, who took great pleasure in building up the brass and percussion sections, which made it sound as if they were playing a cross between

the Radetzky March and a musical portrait of the execution
of the emperor Maximilian; apparently, all these years on,
His Majesty's face still stiffened at the very mention of Mex-
ico. Barely had the final crash of the drums and cymbals resounded than the entire company of actors came onstage,
who hadn't been seen since the old theater had closed,
and who were greeted by their fans with raucous cheers
and applause. The honor of performing the *Prologue*, specially written for the occasion by the acclaimed poet Adam
Asnyk, fell to the actor Józef Kotarbiński, newly imported
from Warsaw:

"*Plaudite cives!*" he began in a booming voice. "Wel-
coming the muses hospitably, our new theater opens wide
its doors to laughing Thalia and sad Melpomene, who come
with their grateful choirs; miraculously they change this
stage unfurled into a scene encompassing the world . . ."

Zofia Turbotyńska would not have been herself if on
hearing these rhymes she had failed to think of the humiliation she had experienced at the hands of that hack working
for the *Illustrated Weekly*. Further on, the phrase "Rejoice,
O nation, rejoice!" was repeated several times, so it stuck
in her mind; then came something about King Lear, where
crown rhymed with *clown,* and *forswear* with *despair,* then
something about the whip of satire, and about the motherland; and to finish off some nonsense about a boy in a
peasant coat who will finally awaken the sleeping princess
on the glass mountain, meaning Poland, perhaps — but
Kotarbiński's interpretative efforts were in vain, for Zofia

was busy devising torments for the spiteful little editor. Next came an overture by Moniuszko, a scene from Fredro's comedy *Revenge*, a short piece from Słowacki's tragedy *Balladyna*, and at last a very welcome interval.

"Such an engaging program, don't you think?" said Ignacy, interested as usual in the least interesting thing of all, in other words the show, rather than the audience. "How charmingly they've arranged it all . . . both drama and comedy . . . we have Moniuszko from the Congress Kingdom, Mickiewicz and Słowacki from Lithuania, but also the émigrés, like Chopin, from abroad. Then there's Asnyk from here in Cracow and Fredro from Lemberg, and we still have Liszt's Hungarian *Salve Polonia* to come," he said, leafing through the program printed by the *Cracow Times*'s presses.

The countess and her cousin would happily have made use of the interval to greet their relatives and acquaintances, but as they had taken the professor's wife into their box, it was up to them to look after her; especially as the countess understood without being told that Tadeusz was relying on making a good impression on the Turbotyńskis.

Meanwhile, vanity fair continued around them, as the ladies scrutinized each other and the gentlemen twirled their mustaches or flaunted their sideburns; diamonds and rubies were compared, costumes were checked to see which of the merchants had failed to spend money on a new outfit for his wife. The dowry hunter flashed past in the crowd, immediately followed by the lady in the magenta dress, but both instantly vanished. Then, a little later, the magenta dress emerged again, and now, in the bright light, with her veil drawn aside, they saw none other than Baroness Banffy, who nodded slightly, probably greeting Countess Żeleńska rather than Zofia Turbotyńska, and sailed onward.

"What a frightful color," muttered Żeleński. "It makes her look like *une fille du régiment.*"

"Tadeusz, that's too much!"

"But, cousin, I don't mean anything indecent, just the association with the color of the uniforms."

"I take it the baroness is not very popular at Helcel House," said Zofia, watching her movement across the room, which, because of the crowd, was like a knight's move on the chessboard.

"Not specially. Nor is her maid, whom my own maid particularly dislikes. I can't quite say why, but as I'm sure you know, servants thrive on intrigue and want to be important at any price. They must have argued over the fact that one of them works for a countess, the other for a baroness . . . that's a recipe for trouble. They say" — here she lowered her voice — "that maid of hers has a large legacy coming her way and often boasts about it."

"Perhaps the dowry hunter should be courting her, Mr. Fi . . ."

"Fikalski," said the countess, laughing. "Yes, that's quite conceivable . . ."

Just then Count Tarnowski and his wife walked through the middle of the foyer, generously dispensing bows, like monarchs. Meanwhile, Matejko stood in the corner, myopically squinting at the spectators and the decor by turns. Soon they heard the second gong, and everyone shuffled back to their seats to listen to Liszt and the second act of Mickiewicz's drama, *The Bar Confederates.* It was Polish enough to put the Royal Castle to shame.

❧

The final applause rang out at half past nine, then the crowd began to pour from the boxes and balconies, come down the staircase, throng in the cloakrooms, and finally spill out of the building. Zofia waited downstairs for her husband to descend from the upper circle, but as the audience vacating the better seats was kept apart from those leaving the worse ones, first Ignacy had to come down to the first floor and then find his wife, whom the Żeleńskis were still politely keeping company; almost simultaneously the magenta Baroness Banffy reached their small group.

"I am returning by carriage," she said at once. "Countess, perhaps you would like to accompany me?"

"No, thank you. My cousin and I are going on to the reception," said the countess.

Indeed, Zofia had noticed that as well as the cream-colored cards, the countess had green ones, too. She hadn't even dared to dream of such luck, but she felt a pang of heartache all the same.

"We, however, have dismissed our carriage," said Zofia

to Banffy, "so if you have two spare places, your ladyship . . . we live nearby, on St. John's Street."

"Oh?" Baroness Banffy was plainly not thrilled by this turn of events, nor was she going to hide the fact, but with a courteous nod she said, "With the greatest of pleasure."

Battling their way through the whirl of the cloakroom, making their bows, and saying their thank-yous and good-byes took another quarter of an hour. While the baroness hailed her coachman, Zofia, with Ignacy dutifully glued to her shoulder, was standing in the forecourt, squinting into the darkness in an attempt to see what sort of vehicle would be taking them home. She was expecting a coach with a he-raldic crest, mantling, and a crown with seven tines, but what drove up was the most ordinary, one-horse, covered droshky. But never mind — what mattered was that she had spent the evening in a countess's box and was being driven home by a real baroness. What a grand life they had! By now the crowd had largely ebbed away, mainly because many people, chastened by the bitter experience of their outward journey, had decided to go home on foot, but there were still plenty of carriages in Szpitalna Street and St. Mark's Street; they flashed past the windows of the droshky, walk-ing along the pavement, almost all straight from the the-ater: top hats above beards and scarves, and gowns of every color, now wrapped in capes and shawls.

"What a splendid evening," said Zofia reverently, "and what a day for Cracow! I may not have taken in every word of Mr. Asnyk's sublime poem, but I shall certainly reread it in the privacy of my own home. I trust you enjoyed Mr. Kotarbiński's recitation, your ladyship?"

"I gained greater pleasure from the extracts by Mickiewicz. They plucked at the heartstrings."

"Cracow may not be Vienna, or Budapest," Zofia went on, "but have they a building as grand as ours in Lemberg? Their Skarbek Theater is an ugly block—I wonder if they have tacked a hideous wooden staircase onto it as they have to our old theater . . ."

She rambled on, but nobody was listening. Ignacy was tired, and as Baroness Banffy did not feel specially bound to play the role of hostess in the carriage, she made no effort to hold up her end of the conversation. In any case, by now they had turned into St. John's Street. Then came thanks, bows, assurances of undying gratitude, and other such ceremony. But, as the scriptures say, to everything there is a season, and a time to every purpose under heaven, including opening the heavy, ancient door of Peacock House, climbing the stairs, taking off one's gloves, and removing one's hatpin. The great day for Cracow—and for Zofia Turbotyńska née Glodt, professor's wife and noblewomen's factotum—was at an end.

Meanwhile, the cab in which the baroness had driven the Turbotyńskis home whirred down the cobbles of St. John's Street and down Pijarska Street, then Sławkowska. Shortly afterward, the cabman asked if madam would like to turn into Pędzichów Street or carry on along Długa, but the baroness merely waved a hand indecisively. As she drove up to

Helcel House, usually in total darkness at this time of night, she saw lights burning at the front, figures flitting past the curtains, and in some of the windows the terrified faces of old ladies and convalescents who must have gone to bed long ago, but were up and about; wrapped in blankets, they were trying to find order in all this chaos. Not even the thick stone walls could stifle the raised voices coming from inside. Along the path came the doctor with his bag; he passed the baroness, raised his collar, and left through the gateway into Helcel Street. In the vestibule two nuns were consoling a third, who had plainly had a fit of hysteria minutes earlier, and now, dabbing her eyes with a handkerchief, was staring wildly at the opposite wall. It looked as if no one were in control of the situation — people were rushing past each other on the stairs as if on a busy street; as soon as the baroness set foot on the first step, Mrs. Wężyk excitedly grabbed her with a clawlike, arthritic hand and cried: "Have you heard, Aniela? Murder! It's murder!"

But Zofia Turbotyńska would only hear the news the next day.

CHAPTER V

✢

In which the professor's wife glowers through a half-open door, reveals her past experience as a detective (the celebrated case of the silver sugar bowl), lectures Ignacy on the technical superiority of the fork, and has a terrifying dream.

"It was here, Mrs. Turbotyńska, this is where she was found," whispered Alojza. Red from crying, her face looked even more wretched than usual. "Jesus Christ have mercy on us, what a tragedy," she babbled.

Through the open door into one of the four-person rooms where the almswomen lived, they could see chaos: an overturned nightstand, scattered objects, and shoe prints. *Heavy police boots for the most part, which are sure to have wiped out all the evidence,* thought Zofia scornfully.

"It is not a tragedy, dear Sister Alojza," she said sharply, trying to conceal her excitement. "It's a crime."

Before eight that morning, when Franciszka — still in her mobcap but with a dressing gown thrown over her nightshirt — had knocked at the door of the master and mistress's bedroom and said in a whisper that a boy had come running with a message from Sister Alojza, Zofia had not hesitated for an instant. She'd had him sent to Szczepański Square to fetch a cab on the double ("Look lively, boy, and you might get a tip!"), and had set about dressing — in a hurry, but quietly enough not to wake the still-sleeping Ignacy. She had pinned her hat to her bun in the droshky. But beneath the hat and bun, her thoughts were in a whirl — who had perished? And why? Could her vague suspicions — or rather hopes — have come true? Could it be that Mrs. Mohr's death was no accident, and the murderer had struck again? Murder is a dreadful thing, of course, but instead of horror, the emotion rising in her was quite different; once again she felt like the investigating magistrate at work. Unfortunately, when she reached the site of the crime, it turned out that the role of investigating magistrate had already been cast.

All the residents had been moved out of the ladies' dormitory on the second floor, where the corpse had been found after last night's supper, and a young policeman had been posted on the door. If not for the surprisingly tough stance adopted by Alojza, who had taken advantage of the respect typically shown by countryfolk from the villages in the Cracow area toward any sort of habit, cassock, or surplice, they would never have gained a peep inside—but as it was, the young policeman simply looked in all directions and then set the door open for half a minute. He informed Zofia that the inquiry into the killing, the victim of which was one Julia Krzywda, was being conducted by the Cracow police in the person of investigating magistrate Dr. Rajmund Klossowitz. But if Mrs. Turbotyńska had any relevant information to offer, Dr. Klossowitz would be sure to spare her a few minutes, as soon as he finished interviewing the witnesses. She felt just as the actors from the old Cracow City Theater must have felt when they learned that at the opening ceremony Mr. Asnyk's prologue would be performed by an actor from Warsaw.

Naturally, she did not expect the investigating magistrate to hear what she had to say, then instantly clap his hands and open an inquiry into a double murder, but she certainly didn't expect what actually did occur. When she was invited into the office, she noticed that Dr. Klossowitz was sitting at Mother Zaleska's desk, while the nun herself, pale as the wall, sat listening in on his interviews.

"I'm told you have some information concerning the crime that has been committed here," Klossowitz began at once, without even showing Zofia to a chair. So she helped herself to one and said, "*Crimes*, in the plural, if you please!"

At these words Mother Zaleska went even whiter, while Klossowitz narrowed his eyes and stroked his mustache.

"What do you mean by that?" he asked, pronouncing each word separately, with distinct emphasis. *I wonder where he gets that mannerism from?* thought Zofia. *Isn't Polish his first language? Or maybe he speaks with exaggerated clarity to make himself understood by Jews, Highlanders, Ruthenians—in short, all the inhabitants of Galicia who speak Polish badly, and whom within this mixed ethnic and linguistic environment he has to interview from time to time? Or perhaps it's simply the result of a lack of intelligence, or a desire to sound clever and earnest.* But for now she laid this thought aside as nonessential, and came to the point.

"As I am sure you are fully aware, less than a week ago in this very institution the body of Mrs. Mohr, the judge's widow, was found, may her soul rest in peace."

"And in your view that demise," said Dr. Klossowitz, one word at a time again, while gazing idly out of the window, "is connected with the murder committed yesterday, if I understand correctly?"

"That's it exactly!" declared Zofia with a note of triumph, convinced she had made the right impression on the detective.

"Do you have any proof of that?"

"Not yet," she admitted hesitantly. "But there is evidence. Not least the fact that the bed was still made, whereas someone sleepwalking—"

"Madam, allow me—"

"I am certain that a postmortem examination—"

"Madam, allow me to ask a question," Klossowitz interrupted her, and stood up. "How many inquiries have you conducted before now?"

"I'm sorry?"

"I would like to know," he said, standing in front of her and rocking to and fro, shifting his weight from the heel to the toe and from the toe to the heel of his perfectly polished boots, "if you have ever succeeded in bringing a criminal to justice?"

"I once caught a housemaid who was stealing the sugar," said Zofia proudly. "I trapped a fly in the sugar bowl, which demands a degree of dexterity, and the next time I looked inside it . . ."

"So the housemaid had murdered someone, had she?"

"You must be joking," said Zofia indignantly, and as the situation was growing uncomfortable, decided to appeal to the highest authority. "You don't understand. My husband is a scholar. A professor of medicine! At the university!" she immediately added, to avoid being taken for the wife of a schoolmaster.

"No, my dear madam, it is you who must be joking. I am conducting this inquiry, which only concerns the brutal murder of Mrs. Krzywda. Please leave it to the experts to decide on postmortems and the like. My dear madam, do forgive me, but your husband's profession is of no consequence here. And the qualifications required for investigative work are beyond the scope of ladies, who aren't in need of higher education anyway."

❧

Well, nobody had said it would be easy, she consoled herself after leaving the office. In fact, Zofia Turbotyńska did not question the view that some things in this life fall to the lot of the male sex, and others to that of the female; such was the status quo, and it was quite unnecessary, possibly even harmful, to confuse matters. For instance, in the debate ongoing for several years about whether to accept women at the Jagiellonian University, on the model of French or American academic institutions, Zofia was guided by her husband—an expert on the topic, after all—who firmly took a conservative stance: as the ladies had never had any need to study before, why on earth would they suddenly have one now? But as we all know, theory is not always in harmony with practice. Today, for instance, theory demanded that at this time on a Sunday morning she should be getting ready to attend High Mass at St. Mary's Basilica, not flying about Helcel House like a spinning top, as was happening in practice.

For while investigating magistrate Klossowitz, assisted by two policemen and two nuns assigned to him by Mother Zaleska, was busy interviewing the residents and employees of the house in turn, Zofia decided to conduct her own . . . no, it wasn't an inquiry—for fear of ridicule, she refused to let herself think of it as such, nor would she have described it that way to others; she preferred to think of it as research, browsing, seeking the truth, or even innocent female reconnaissance. Most of the people who interested her were waiting in line to be interviewed by Klossowitz, so she started with Alojza. She sat her on the first chair to hand in Mrs. Mohr's room, which she had already chosen as her headquarters earlier that week, and began to question her. From Alojza's account, between sporadic bouts of sobbing, she learned that the body had been found after dinner at about 8:30 p.m., when Mrs. Andrusik had entered the dormitory that she shared with three other residents.

"She went to fetch a prayer book so she could attend vespers, like all the residents whose health allows it. Mrs. Krzywda was lying in bed, under a quilt, and it looked as if she were asleep, poor thing. But when she didn't respond to Mrs. Andrusik's questions, Mrs. Andrusik put on the lamp to see if she was all right . . ." At this point, the nun interrupted her account with a mournful *"Kyrie eleison"* before starting up again. "And she noticed that the wretched woman wasn't asleep at all . . ." Alojza burst into tears.

"It's no time for weeping, Sister," said Zofia, handing her a handkerchief, one of the four dozen she had received in her trousseau and which, as a thrifty person, she tried not to use too often.

"Of course," said Alojza, calming down a bit. "It's a time for prayer. Mother Zaleska has already arranged a Mass for the soul of the poor murdered woman."

Murdered women was Zofia's immediate thought, but all she said aloud was: "You and the other sisters are more than capable of praying without me — that's not why you summoned me here, is it?"

"But I don't know why I summoned you," said Alojza, opening her eyes even wider. "Or why I sent the boy with that message . . . I was expecting you to pay a visit today, as it's Sunday, and . . . I don't really know . . . I think it's that I didn't want you to come without warning that . . . the over-turned nightstand . . . So I thought . . ."

"Splendid, Sister Alojza, quite splendid." Zofia inter-rupted her, turning a deaf ear to her rambling speech. "But in this particular instance, please allow *me* to do the thinking."

Sister Alojza meekly fixed her unfortunate gaze, like that of a benign basilisk, on the floor.

Presumably, thought Zofia, *the two old ladies were united by the same fate, and perished at the hand of the same person. Could someone from the outside have killed them? The watchman assured Alojza that he saw nothing and nobody. Of course, there's always a way* . . . She imag-ined a brawny, athletic man creeping across the roof of Hel-cel House in the dark, wielding a rope, lowering it, and then slipping through the open window of the dormitory, before seizing upon the innocuous old woman and mercilessly taking her life. His body tenses, his raven-black mustache shines in the lamplight as his victim gasps for breath . . . *But,* she thought almost bitterly, *it is nothing like the mur-ders in the rue Morgue in Mr. Poe's story. The windows, in the dormitory as well as in here, are locked from the inside, so the murderer must have entered the room the usual way, from the stairwell. Anyway, it may be October, and it may be true that darkness falls earlier than in the summer, but there are people in the streets, all the trees around Helcel House are young and small, and the view is splendid — the murderer wouldn't have risked being seen, but would have waited for a later hour. Moreover, if the same person killed both women, he had to creep in here at night on two occasions, a week apart, commit each crime, and make his getaway. Whereas one of the householders . . . If one includes the residents, the nuns, the cooks, and so on, the householders form a large crowd, we have quite a choice. But if one were to insist on a single culprit, then how would one explain the difference in the methods of killing? Mrs. Mohr was so sickly that she never actually moved from her room, and no one would have been surprised to find her lying dead in her bed, with no evidence of murder at all. I've already examined the bedclothes — there are no slits or tears, and not a drop of blood. In which case, why drag the body out of the room and conceal it? If the murderer killed her in a fit of passion, he might have panicked and simply wanted to get rid of the corpse, and a rarely used corner of the attic seemed a splendid hiding place, and wasn't far to go either. But then what? Corpses start to stink.*

At this point in her ruminations the waxy face of Granny Glodt appeared, whom many years ago she'd had to kiss on the cheek, right beside the bluish tip of her nose, amid a stifling odor of putrefaction and lilies, placed in bunches around the open coffin. *That would give the murderer . . . two days? Three? Five? A week at most. Perhaps he intended to move the body to another site later on? Or maybe he took off at once?*

"Has anyone left the house since the day of Mrs. Mohr's death?" she asked.

"Has anyone left?" repeated Alojza; taken by surprise while wondering whether she should pray harder for the salvation of the victim or the killer, she was totally confused. "I'd have to check in the office . . . but the investigating magistrate is in there. Let's think . . . one of the gardeners went away. And came back. But no, that was earlier on . . . There's Mr. Majer, but he simply died of pneumonia, a day after Mrs. Mohr, and he's already been buried. No, nobody."

Zofia fell silent again, while Alojza, her eyes bulging more than usual, waited for more questions. *If he didn't take off,* thought Zofia, *then either he hadn't planned the murder and panicked, with no idea what to do with the body, or else he'd had wider aims and wanted to kill Mrs. Krzywda too. But what is the sense in killing Mrs. Mohr so furtively, and Mrs. Krzywda in a way that made the crime instantly apparent? Never mind that for now. I wonder if . . .*

"Has Mrs. Mohr been buried too?" she asked at last.

"No, not yet, we're waiting for her sister to arrive. Her body is lying among blocks of ice in our mortuary, at the end of the garden. The funeral will be late."

"But has the body already been washed? Who washed it?"

"Sister Aniceta."

"Let's go and see her."

Of the entire staff of sixteen nuns who worked at Helcel House, Zofia only recognized a few — Mother Zaleska of course, and Mother Juhel, the French mother superior, then there was Alojza, and maybe two or three others. But which one was Aniceta? As soon as she laid eyes on her, she told herself she would never have remembered that face, not even if Sister Aniceta were introduced to her several times, because it was devoid of any characteristics at all. Neither young nor old, neither pretty nor ugly, neither chubby as a Baroque cherub nor skinny as a medieval hermit, it was one of those faces without color or expression that one sees in the back rows at the theater, in a far corner of the office, or in the cluster surrounding a market stall. The very picture of nobody — who had, however, been born, and was destined to remain in this impersonal shape to the very end.

They found her in the laundry, a separate building next to the pigsty, where, in a white apron, her head covered not with a wimple but a modern mobcap, she was ironing the residents' nightshirts, taking an occasional sip of water into her mouth from a glass, and liberally spraying it out again with a loud *pfffff* sound.

"Jesus Christ be praised . . ."

"Forever and ever, amen," she said, nodding. *Pfffff!*

"We're here in connection with Mrs. Mohr. Was it you who washed her body, Sister Aniceta?"

Without interrupting her ironing, she shrugged, and then muttered: "Why shouldn't I have washed her body? I wash them all, so why should I refuse to wash Mrs. Mohr? She died, so I washed her." She put down the iron, picked up the nightshirt, shook it, turned it the other way up, and resumed her ironing. "Nobody else here does it, if you please, madam. Either they don't know how, or they don't want to. But I learned to wash the dead when I was a little girl." Zofia imagined this face as the face of a child; smaller, but just as inscrutable as now, flat as a chopping board. "So yes, I certainly did wash Mrs. Mohr."

"You didn't notice any unusual marks on her, did you?"

"Unusual," she said, casting a suspicious glance, "meaning satanic? Moles sprouting hair?" *Pfffff.* "No, none at all."

"No, not moles. Marks. Bruises, as if someone had been wrestling with her, stab marks, puncture wounds from a dagger . . ."

"Holy Mary, Mother of God!" The words "puncture wounds from a dagger" had such an electrifying effect on Sister Aniceta that she put down the iron and raised her arms toward the ceiling. "What an idea! No wounds, no bruises. She lay in perfect peace, pink as a rosebud, as if she had only just left this world and flown straight into the arms of the Lord Jesus, so serene she was."

"But did you examine the body carefully?" pressed Zofia, feeling in this hot, damp air as if she were in the tropics, in a land from a print in a travel book or the *Illustrated Weekly*, Celebes perhaps, or Brazil — in any case, a place where one streams with perspiration and where the correct attire for

Cracow in October is decidedly unsuitable. "Are you certain nothing escaped your notice, Sister? A scratch under the hair, a small bump . . ."

Sister Aniceta was plainly piqued.

Pfffff. She snorted, and then said nothing for a while as she carefully pressed on the iron. *Pfffff.* "No, nothing escaped my notice, and nothing ever shall. I shall find every pinprick. When I wash a body, I do it thoroughly, for that is our final earthly ablution. When I wash a body, I do it as carefully as I would wish to be washed when my time has come." *Pfffff.*

"We are all full of praise for Sister Aniceta," said Alojza, hurrying to provide assurance in an attempt to mitigate the brewing conflict. "She is extremely fastidious in her work."

"But I believe you, Sister, without a doubt!" said Zofia, suddenly laughing, in the tone of a worldly-wise lady, confident of settling the matter this way. But not a single muscle twitched on Sister Aniceta's wooden face.

❧

Zofia thought hard about the two victims' bodies, tracing little squares on Mrs. Mohr's floorboards with the tip of her umbrella as she did so, while one story below the examination of Mrs. Krzywda's corpse was taking place. It had first been examined earlier on by Dr. Wiszniewski, chief physician at Helcel House, who had pronounced her dead. But now the experts were carrying out a proper postmortem—

the police doctor Paleczny and Dr. Wachholz from the forensic medicine faculty at the university.

Mrs. Andrusik, a tailor's widow from Gołębia Street, who had just given evidence to the investigating magistrate, must have been very surprised when Sister Alojza quietly told her that someone else wanted to have a word with her too. Her amazement was even greater when that someone turned out to be a lady in a tilted hat, sitting for reasons unknown in a room on the third floor.

"You're from the late Mrs. Krzywda's family?" she mumbled, neither asking a question nor stating a fact. "My condolences, madam."

"No, my dear," explained Alojza, shuddering at the thought that anyone could suspect Zofia, to her the epitome of refinement, of being closely related to an almswoman. "This kind lady is Mrs. Turbotyńska, the professor's wife, and she'd like to ask you a few questions about Mrs. Krzywda."

"What do I know, Sister? I've already told it all to the magistrate. I came in, found her, and screamed . . . well, I admit I took the Lord's name in vain, but I had a dreadful fright when I pulled back the quilt and there she was, with that tongue of hers lolling and those terrible goggle eyes staring at me . . ." She stopped short, casting a cautious glance at Alojza's ocular defect.

They couldn't extract much from Mrs. Andrusik apart from the known facts: at what time she had entered the dormitory, the appearance of the corpse, typical for strangulation . . . Nothing had grabbed her attention, but then she'd been too shocked to focus on anything apart from the body. By now her primary source of offense was that she'd been transferred to another dormitory. All right, murder is murder, but why should she have farther to go to the bathroom? Nor was she able to tell them much about Mrs. Krzywda. They hadn't talked to each other often, only about house-related matters. When asked about Mrs. Mohr, she muttered that she'd never heard of such a person.

Without even taking out her notebook, Zofia cast a glance at Alojza to tell her to remove the surly Mrs. Andrusik from the room. When Alojza came back, she found Zofia in exactly the same pose, her hat tilted at just the same angle.

"Well, then. Why don't *you* tell me about Mrs. Krzywda?"

"Mrs. Krzywda . . . was alone, with no family, and no one came to visit her. About sixty years old? I can look up her age in the office if it's important. A cheerful disposition, though a little reclusive. She came to the house on the recommendation of an important lady; that I remember, but I can't remember why that was necessary — maybe there was a brief lack of places."

"What was the lady's name?"

"Oh, that I don't recall," replied Alojza, "but her letter will be in the office. Every letter that arrives is kept in the archive. I'll go and look as soon as the investigating magistrate is on his way."

"All in good time. And so: she was alone in the world, not young, and a pauper, seeing she didn't pay for her keep but was an almswoman. She spoke Polish."

"Yes, I never heard her speak any other language. But if she had another, maybe she had no one to talk to in it."

"And where was she from?"

"From Cracow or hereabouts, but where exactly I don't know. Somewhere in this vicinity, anyway. That should be in the documents too."

"Please explain to me, Sister," said Zofia, suddenly remembering the raffle prizes. "Do all the almsmen and almswomen contribute to the house in some way, lighting the stoves, or doing jobs in the orchard and the workshops?"

"Not all of them, just the ones whose health allows for it."

"Of course, of course. What work did Mrs. Krzywda do?"

"Hmm, if only I could remember . . ." said Alojza, growing anxious, which made her look the image of Mrs. Zaremba's unhappy pug dog. "But Sister Felicja will know. I think she used to help with the ironing . . . no, it wasn't the ironing. Something like that, to begin with. And then she asked to be transferred to the kitchen because, apparently, she used to be a cook, and from then on she helped with the cooking."

To Zofia, murdering a cook at a time when it was so hard to find properly qualified servants, when nothing but clumsy dolts applied for the job, unable to tell the difference between a spear of asparagus and a piece of string, was not just a crime but an act of outrageous profligacy. She loosened the strings of her velvet reticule, took out her jotter, and wrote: *Krzywda prof. cook, check what before.*

"Please look up what she did when she first arrived, Sister. And whether she then worked in the kitchen every day, or on specific days." Alojza nodded, but Zofia wasn't sure if everything was getting through to that nodding head. "And if only on specific days, then was she there on the day of the murder, on the day before, on the day of Mrs. Mohr's death, and on the day before that. Very good, what else? Where was Mrs. Krzywda from, what place in particular? What did she do apart from being a cook? Where did she cook, for what family? Who was her husband? Was she a widow, or had she run away from him?"

Alojza no longer resembled a pug dog in a wimple; now she was like a pug dog in a wimple on top of whom a landslide has fallen. Every question was a mystery.

"I shall look into everything I can. I'll ask the sisters in the office and the ladies from Mrs. Krzywda's dormitory," she gasped, "every single thing."

"Very well, very well now, Sister. I have no doubt you shall do it with all due care. And" — here she raised a finger — "discretion."

"Discretion, yes, of course," said Alojza.

Zofia dropped her hand to take hold of the watch that was pinned to her chest. *Here I am, chattering away with Sister Alojza nineteen to the dozen,* she reproached herself. *Here I am playing detective games, snooping among dead bodies, while there are genuinely important things to be done at home!* At eleven the first applicants were to appear from Mrs. Mikulska's agency.

"That will be all," she said, getting up from Mrs. Mohr's favorite armchair, which in a matter of days was sure to go to her heirs. "I shall look forward to a full report on the case," she said, repeating a sentence straight from a novel; she couldn't remember which, but it made her feel like a bona fide imperial-and-royal high-ranking official, merely awaiting a soft "*Jawohl!*" from Sister Alojza, but it didn't come, so she said it to herself instead. As she pressed the door handle, she turned briefly and said: "Please inquire of whomever possible whether Mrs. Mohr and Mrs. Krzywda were connected in any way — did they know each other, did they like or dislike each other, were they from the same district, did they ever come into contact in any way, could Mrs. Krzywda have worked for Mrs. Mohr, or did they ever talk to each other . . . I am interested in the smallest, even the most apparently insignificant piece of information. God be with you."

"And also with you," yapped the sad pug dog left behind in the room.

❧

Many a time did the Cracow trumpeter climb to the top of St. Mary's Basilica tower to play the hourly signal before the Turbotyńskis sat down to supper that evening, carried to the dining room table by Franciszka in stages: slices of faux salmon made of roast veal, and roast partridges served with pureed peas.

Following her morning visit to Helcel House, Zofia had made her way back to St. John's Street; Ignacy hadn't asked why she wasn't at home when he awoke, but just in case, she had remarked that charitable work demands many sacrifices, such as forcing oneself to get up at first light. Then she had discussed the business of the day ahead with Franciszka, and by ten to eleven she was sitting in the drawing room, waiting for the girls from Mrs. Mikulska's agency to arrive. Zofia had finished making lavender bags by now, but she decided to make it look as if she had some urgent needlework to do. They should know at once that the lady of the house hadn't a minute to spare, and did not waste time on romantic novels or superfluous gossip: abandon all hope of idleness, ye who enter the service of Mrs. Turbotyńska! Then there was luncheon with Ignacy, who that day had announced that he'd be eating with his wife instead of guzzling a late breakfast with his colleagues, meaning one of the famous sandwiches served at Hawełka's restaurant, washed down with lashings of pilsner. Later, Zofia had paid an afternoon visit to Mrs. Zaremba, the doctor's wife, dull as ditchwater, but from whom she planned to wheedle a certain favor that she needed in order to obtain another favor from someone else; taken a short nap; leafed through an article on the psychic experiences of the medium Eusapia Palladino in a back number of the *Illustrated Weekly;* and finally sat down to supper.

Ignacy rather greedily helped himself to the thin slices of veal coated in fragrant mayonnaise blended with anchovies and capers. At moments like these he resembled a sleek tomcat that had finally got its paws on the fish.

"Whatever, I decided not to make the task easy for them. They sat in the hall, and Franciszka brought them in by turns, while I sat by the window; on entering the room, they could immediately see the ottoman, from which the cushion appeared to have slipped. It was quite plain to see where it should be. No doubt about it. Two of the girls picked it up in passing and put it back in place. Entirely automatically. That's the only proper way to test them . . . Ignacy, eat your partridge, not just that veal, you must have something hot to eat before bed, it's not healthy to fill your stomach with all that cold food . . ."

"My dear Zofia," he said with a sigh, "I defer to you entirely on matters of cuisine and the servants, but please don't lecture me about anatomy, healthy eating, and the workings of the stomach. The stomach is a resilient organ, almost as springy as the uterus . . . if one were to remove a uterus, place it on the cobbles, and drive a cart full of stones over it, no harm would come to it — it would instantly return to its original shape." He briskly went into mid-lecture, but realizing that he had overstepped the mark, he suddenly broke off his account of deliberately crushing bodily organs under cart wheels.

"So the remaining two still hold some promise. I have arranged with Mrs. Mikulska for them to come by turns for a week. We shall see how they cope with various tasks, whether they are capable of cleaning the silver without marking the surface as they polish, whether they get on with dusting the lamps and the plaster moldings of their own accord . . . and then there's their personal hygiene, exemplary so far, but they may have washed extremely carefully today—in a week it will be easier to tell. I also need to ascertain what they have been taught in previous houses, whether they know what a fork is for, apart from eating . . . Ignacy?"

"Hmm . . . what's that? A fork?" said the professor, looking up from his plate.

"You were not listening to me, Ignacy, were you?"

"But, my dear Zofia, how can you say that? Of course I was listening."

"Is that so? Then what was I talking about?" she said, raising her voice (and her eyebrow); she was very quick-tempered.

"About tableware?" began Ignacy hesitantly. "I don't think there's anything to stop us from ordering a new set—after all, you were given these when we married, and that's a good many years ago . . ."

"No, Ignacy," uttered Zofia crisply. "I was talking about combing the fringes with a fork."

"The fringes?"

"You see, you were *not* listening," she said, her reproach tinged with triumph. "About combing the fringes of the rugs and about how disastrously the hoydens sent by Mrs. Mikulska set about it. And that's not all. The first one did not wipe the mud off her shoes upon entering the house, but soiled the entire hall—would you credit it? Of course, that was the one who failed to pick up the cushion. I contrived the first possible excuse to say thank you and good-bye at once . . ."

"But why a fork?" wondered the faux-salmon fan.

"Ignacy, for a university professor you sometimes show extraordinary ignorance. A fork is the best tool for the job."

❧

The Turbotyńskis' apartment was by no means immense, nor was it dripping with luxury, but it did have its own grandeur; for grandeur was what Zofia Glodt had cherished most of all in her youth. On proposing to her, Ignacy had made sure the future couple's nest corresponded — as far as possible — to all his *dear Zofia*'s dreams, and the bedroom was perhaps the most faithfully realized dream of all. As Saint Teresa of Ávila would say, more tears are shed over the prayers that are answered than those that are not.

His dear Zofia, whose favorite reading matter included the novels of Walter Scott and the epic works of the Polish romantic poets, had wanted a Gothic bedroom: dark, with antique furniture; crossing its threshold took the couple into a magical grotto, somewhere between Merlin's and Morgan le Fay's, or an enchanted princess's castle. Ignacy had had it all made to order in Brünn, at Holoubek's famous studio.

Two large wardrobes with tracery, as if cut out of the windows at St. Mary's, resting on lion's feet. Two nightstands decorated with heraldic lions. A large looking glass with a pair of entwined snakes on the frame, biting each other, as above the entrance to Lizards House on the Market Square. A chest of drawers with a washbasin, and on each drawer a fallen knight with a pennant — lying so awkwardly that Zofia had her suspicions: the knights had once been standing, and were probably intended for the doors of a dresser that hadn't been collected from the workshop, so the carpenter had refashioned them a bit, changed the landscape into a green sward and reused them. And at the forefront of this collection of somber, heavy, dark furniture, beneath a chandelier featuring Melusine and some antlers, were two equally dark, equally heavy, and equally somber beds, which had always looked like deathbeds. On the wall above them hung a large crucifix. And wallpaper with a Gothic pattern.

Occasionally Zofia thought this was why she and Ignacy had no children: in this bed, a double one, with its high backboard crowned with pinnacles, looking like the tomb of King Kazimierz in the Wawel Cathedral, no life could possibly have been conceived; sometimes she dreamed that she was dying, and that Ignacy had brought a craftsman to the house and was saying, "Please make my wife's bed into a coffin — it's a shame for a piece of furniture like that to go to waste."

Ignacy had gone to sleep long ago, and with a nightcap pulled over his head, was now quietly snoring. It occurred to her that his gray sideburns looked like soft moss growing on the pillow. Melusine on the chandelier was gently turning on her chains — reminding Zofia that in the daylight she had seen dust on her; as soon as she decided which of the maids to hire, she would have to set her to cleaning the lamps throughout the house — and the antlers were casting long shadows across the ceiling.

If not strangulation, or stabbing, she wondered, *then what could have been the cause of Mrs. Mohr's death? It was unnatural, of course, a natural one wouldn't interest us. Could she have been poisoned? That would imply that the murders were not committed in a fit of passion, but were carefully planned. And if so, what poison was used?* Zofia remembered dreadful scenes in various historical novels involving choking, vomiting, and spitting blood; toxins raced through the body like fire. But why in Mrs. Mohr's case the blissful facial expression and those rosy cheeks, despite several days having passed since she died? And if the murderer had such a fail-safe method to hand, why had he brutally strangled the second victim, instead of giving her a lethal dose of the same substance?

She fell into a shallow, fitful sleep. She dreamed that the young Żeleński was prowling about Helcel House, murdering more women, wearing that roguish smirk beneath his stiff, curly, waxed mustache, and then sticking in their *nature* not cigarettes, but rolled-up sheets of paper with the poems she had sent to the *Illustrated Weekly*. Or maybe they were now-redundant invitations to the opening of the Municipal Theater: green, white, and cream colored? Or Ignacy's professor's diploma cut into pieces? She too was present in the dream, running along the rooftop of Helcel House, urgently trying to discover what Żeleński was making into little scrolls, but the roof was cluttered with large versions of the donors' coats of arms, and it was impossible to move across them.

She woke up clammy with perspiration, her pulse racing. But at least the day did not begin with the news of another murder.

CHAPTER VI

❧

In which Zofia Turbotyńska shows no interest in the digestive tract of the salamander, lurks in a gateway, and brings up topics at table that a woman of propriety should not discuss while eating catfish.

Zofia was sitting at her dressing table, applying Dr. Rix's Pompadour Milk Substitute for Powder to her face, though in fact she was occupied with something else: by slightly tilting the left of the dressing table's two mobile side mirrors, she could closely observe Antosia, one of the applicants for the post of housemaid, as she made the bed: whether she carried out the tiniest duties in the correct order, how much time she devoted to smoothing the creases and plumping up the pillows, and whether she took the opportunity to dust the little bell and the ribbon attached to it. *She will do,* thought Zofia, *though she is very far from ideal.*

To Zofia's own surprise, over the past few days even an issue as important as the choice of a housemaid had taken second place in her thoughts to the inquiry. Yesterday evening the *Cracow Times* had informed its readers that the investigating magistrate, Dr. Klossowitz, after a high-speed inquiry, had unmasked the degenerate responsible for the hideous murder of Mrs. Krzywda, an indigent almswoman at Helcel House. Everyone relevant had been questioned. Karol Morawski, the watchman, had sworn that in the time frame in which the crime had been committed he had not left his booth by the entrance to the grounds of the institution. Meanwhile, several witnesses had seen him creeping upstairs after dark, plainly doing his best to conceal his presence, trying to flit past stealthily, stooping low to make himself look smaller . . . He still denied it, but the witnesses had no reason to lie; what's more, they all gave the same evidence separately and independently. It was an open-and-shut case — he had come upstairs with murderous intent, had committed the crime, and fled the scene. "The watchman did it," the whole city was saying. Only Zofia was unimpressed, because nothing in this scenario added up. Why on earth would the watchman have first poisoned Mrs. Mohr with such finesse and without leaving a trace? And when he found the body in the attic, why had it made such an electrifying impression on him? If, of course, the same person had killed the poor old lady and then strangled

Mrs. Krzywda—and deep down Zofia was convinced that was the case. *It's not him,* she said to herself. *It's not him.*

She consulted all her crime novels, but—except for frightening an old woman with fatal consequences—nowhere did she come upon a method for killing a human being without leaving any visible traces on the body. Except for poison, of course. As a good housewife, naturally she was aware of the dire consequences of eating tainted meat, fish that was past its best, or lethal mushrooms, but poison generally featured in the books as an unnamed liquid in a small bottle, poured into wine by an evil marquise. She didn't know which substances had to be injected, which poured in the mouth, or, as in *Hamlet,* the ear, and which merely had to be sniffed. So she decided to visit Ignacy at the university.

She entered his study unannounced, as if she were at home, pretending that she happened to have been passing along the next street and had decided to drop in on him. But instead of looking at her husband, her eyes were fixed on his bookshelves; she was trying to find her way around the various scientific almanacs that occupied shelf after shelf, but he kept being a nuisance, gabbling away about the difficulties of dissecting the digestive tract of a salamander.

"Good day to you, madam," she suddenly heard behind her. She turned around, and there in the doorway stood the young Żeleński, who came lugging some large bottles of liquid for specimens, fetched from a remote corner of the academy and clearly needed by Ignacy.

"Aha," she said, "good day, Mr. Żeleński. Once again, thank you for delivering the tickets, it was an extremely kind gesture."

"A trifle, a mere trifle."

"And that wonderful seat in your box. What an unforgettable evening." At these words Żeleński smirked in the usual way. "In fact, I have something to ask you about, to do with your aunt and our charitable activities . . ."

"My cousin."

"Oh, yes, of course, your cousin! But it is rather a personal matter," she said, raising her voice, and casting reproachful glances at Ignacy. "So perhaps . . ."

"Don't worry about me, my dear Zofia," said Ignacy, with a note of guilt audible in his tone. "I'm just off to Hawełka's for breakfast. You and Tadeusz can talk freely." And at once he started stuffing papers into his briefcase at high speed, as if his wife were standing over him with a blazing sword.

"Well, I never, what a perfect coincidence," she muttered with satisfaction. He knew his place.

As soon as the door had closed behind Ignacy, the student Żeleński, in silent anticipation until now, asked how he could be of help to Mrs. Turbotyńska. Zofia blinked as she gathered her thoughts.

"I would not wish to overburden you with my affairs," she began cautiously, "but . . . are you closely related to Countess Żeleńska? What degree of kinship do you have?"

"Oh, it's distant," he said, waving a hand. "Very distant, even. But we are close, because she was close to my father when he lost one of his parents. He was not quite nine at the time."

"Your grandmother died in childbirth, I presume?" asked Zofia, putting on a sympathetic face. "Maybe that is the source of Professor Żeleński's artistic soul, his wistful nature and penchant for music . . ."

"Oh, no, on the contrary. It wasn't my grandmother, but my grandfather who died. The penchant for music is from him: he was said to be the best pianist in all Galicia, and he even did some composing. He was killed during the peasant uprising, in February 1846, in the park at our family manor in Grodkowice. He died defending my grandmother, his wife. She had been wounded" — at this point he began to stammer — "he saved her, but he couldn't save himself. The peasants also cut down our cousin Stański, who had come to visit on his honeymoon, and two servants. One of the peasants went up to my grandfather with an axe and hacked off his jaw because, as he said, 'He liked to gnash his teeth' . . ." As he said this, he automatically drew a hand across his cheek. "Now there's a cross on that spot with the inscription 'Lord, forgive them, they know not what they do,' which I used to play under as a child. We even have an exercise book containing my grandfather's variations on themes from an opera — *Fra Diavolo*, I think — stained with blood, because when the peasants carried off his corpse to claim payment for it from the Austrian government, his head was lying on those notes. It's ancient history now. At the time my cousin was very kind to my father, hence the affection, though genealogically we are connected by some very remote forebear."

Zofia was thrilled with this tale — she'd had no idea how to jump from Countess Żeleńska to the topic of grisly murder, but it had all fallen into place like the perfect game of patience. She came close to rubbing her hands together with joy, as she usually did when an extremely tricky game of Napoleon's Tomb unexpectedly came out right, or when, after the first of the three attempts allowed, an entire game of Paganini worked out perfectly.

"That is a horrific story, but I don't need to tell you that. You, sir, as a doctor, are sure to have seen all manner of atrocities at close hand . . ."

"As a *future* doctor," he said, laughing, "it is all ahead of me. For now I have seen more horror in the prints in medical handbooks than in hospital wards or the dissection room."

"Wounds? Tumors? Blood?"

"Skin diseases. Filth, neglect. But we were going to talk about my cousin . . ."

"Oh," said Zofia, waving a hand dismissively, so that motes of dust began to swirl, "it's a trifle, it can wait. What about poisons? Are you interested in poisons, by any chance?"

Żeleński looked at her hesitantly and mumbled that yes, up to a point.

"And what can poison us?"

"Oh, there's no lack of poisons around us. There are

some treacherous plants growing in our climate alone, such as deadly nightshade, also known as belladonna. What else . . . ?" He dug in his memory, trying to remember the lecture. "There's monkshood containing aconite, hemlock, digitalis, henbane . . . And mushrooms, of course. The death cap, Satan's bolete, the agarics . . ."

"Yeees," said Zofia, nodding, "indeed? Please go on."

"And then there's curare, and datura, yellow oleander, and other exotic poisons, not to mention venomous snakes. There really is plenty to poison oneself with, Mrs. Turbotyńska. Or to poison someone else with," he added meaningfully, knitting his brow as if to suggest that he did not support the idea of dispatching Professor Turbotyński to the next world.

"Well, yes, but I was thinking of something closer to home . . . what about rat poison?"

"That's usually arsenic or strychnine. There's also cyanide . . ."

"But what are the symptoms of such poisoning?"

Żeleński spread his hands.

"I'm not a toxicologist; my knowledge is very limited. Everything I know I learned at Dr. Iwaniec's lectures."

"Dr. Iwaniec? The redheaded fellow?" she said, perking up. "With the half-blind wife who's ashamed to wear spectacles?"

"Indeed," he replied guardedly, "Dr. Iwaniec does have reddish hair. Though I have not had the pleasure of his wife's acquaintance."

"You haven't missed a thing," she declared, making a note in her book. "In any case, the next time you met, I'm sure she'd fail to recognize you. To her we are all nothing but blurred splashes of color, like variegated mist . . . Well," she said, rising to her feet, "I hope I haven't taken up too much of your valuable academic time."

"And the matter you wanted to ask about . . . ?"

"Oh, it's trivial. A mere nothing. I shall ask her about it in person. *Au revoir, Monsieur Żeleński.*" She added in her most refined tone of all, "*Au revoir!*"

And hurried off, summoned by matters of great importance.

❧

"What a splendid coincidence!" Mrs. Iwaniec was surprised to hear, while staring down as usual, because of her poor eyesight, at Gołębia Street's treacherous, uneven paving. In fact, for this very reason every encounter was a surprise to her; from only three feet away she saw very little. But spectacles would have "aged" her, and she regarded the wearing of pince-nez by women as newfangled nonsense suited to crazy emancipationists; on rare occasions she resorted to the use of a lorgnette, which seemed to her more dignified and feminine. "Good morning!"

A tall, smartly dressed figure sprang up before her out of the blue, like the genie from Aladdin's lamp. It could have been anyone, from a fireman to a bishop. Someone with flashes of gold here and there, at any rate.

"Good morning, good morning," she said, stopping and squinting. Her left hand began to fumble at her ample bosom in search of the thin chain. Finally she found it with her fingertips, grabbed it, and pulled, thus extracting the lorgnette from her pocket; then at the push of a button she unfolded it and held it up to her eyes. "Ah, Mrs. Turbotyńska, how very nice!"

"How long is it since we saw each other last? Not since the Resurrection Mass, I think? Or was it the Holy Sepulcher? No, it was the Resurrection, but here we are in chilly October already!"

"But it's a very fine October," Mrs. Iwaniec timidly protested, having only just left her warm apartment; Zofia was of the opposite opinion on the question of autumn temperatures because her hands were numb with cold. She had spent the past hour and a half lying in wait, hidden two doorways along, keeping an eye on Dr. and Mrs. Iwaniec's house; fortunately the watchman happened to be away, but if anyone had asked her what business she had come on, she planned to answer with a question: "Is this where Councilor Hoesick lives? He advertised that he'd like to sell a piano, hardly used, mahogany, with candleholders." In any case, it had been hellishly windy in the gateway.

"Aha, one day it's glorious, the next day there's rain . . . and they say it's March that comes in with a roar and goes out with a whimper," she said, laughing gaily, revealing her predator's teeth. "Whatever the case, the time has gone by in a flash. We must see each other more often!"

"Decidedly," replied Mrs. Iwaniec noncommittally, unaware that she had just sealed the fate of an evening in the near future. At once Zofia unfurled the vision of a delightful supper party, to which she had invited persons from the best social sphere, among whom Dr. and Mrs. Iwaniec were indispensable. After a quarter of an hour of sweet talk, subterfuge, thank-yous, most-kind-of-yous, and "matchless company," the invitation had been accepted. And the frozen Zofia could finally race home, where at once she called from the doorway: "Franciszka, make me a cup of hot tea this instant! And top up the stove!"

Organizing a supper party, not even a particularly lavish one, almost from one day to the next was quite a challenge. The provisions — wine, lemonade, meats, fish, and aspic — could all be obtained, bought, and prepared with the help of Franciszka and the new girl, Antosia, who in the process would have the chance to pass the final test for the post of housemaid. The real problem was the guests; assembling a group at such short notice was not so easy. In her invitation to Dr. and Mrs. Iwaniec, Zofia had somewhat embroidered reality. She had spoken of "a small but select company" that would gather for supper on Thursday. It was indeed small —

apart from Żeleński, who agreed to accept the invitation by way of thanks for the tickets, for the time being it consisted of no one but Dr. and Mrs. Iwaniec. Zofia was counting on inviting the Teichmanns, maybe even with the daughter who had married a baron, but unfortunately Antosia came back with the news that the professor was in poor health, and his wife was busy caring for her husband. The Olszewskis too sent their apologies, and so did the Wicherkowskis, the Żelskis, and the Pomians, excusing themselves either with illness, earlier commitments, or church obligations. On a tide of desperation, sighing heavily, she sent the girl to Szewska Street, to the Zarembas. Thanks to their physical and spiritual debilities they were not the most popular guests in Cracow society, so one could invite them at the drop of a hat. Zofia meanwhile clenched her teeth, and with a heavy heart headed off to Floriańska Street, as if to Canossa, to invite her cousin, Mrs. Dutkiewicz. And although the point of it all was not social success, but the opportunity to interrogate Dr. Iwaniec, deep down she could not help regretting that the "small but select" company was turning into a small but random one.

While the guests were slowly gathering, Zofia ran to and fro between the kitchen and the drawing room to see to Franciszka, and to keep a close eye on Antosia, though once again she had to admit that so far the girl was acquitting herself quite well. Dr. Iwaniec, in a rather faded green frock coat, was the last to arrive. His stout wife had squeezed herself into a pale pink dress; on her face she wore the same disoriented look as usual. In fact, she only went where her husband led her, tripping along the way, first over the lion's foot at the base of a chair leg, then over a potted palm. The remaining guests — the Zarembas, Mrs. Dutkiewicz, and Żeleński — were already in the drawing room, where Ignacy was trying to amuse them with conversation, though it was hard to find a topic they would all find entertaining. Luckily Mrs. Zaremba had an endless supply of prattle at her disposal. With the entry of Dr. and Mrs. Iwaniec came a string of introductions. Meanwhile, Zofia discreetly signaled to Antosia, pointing at the door into the dining room; Antosia took a few hesitant steps and stopped, unsure what she was meant to do, then opened the door and closed it behind her from the other side. As quietly as possible. Zofia rolled her eyes to the ceiling, opened out both leaves of the door herself, and invited the guests to take their seats at the festively laid table, while she ran to see if the first course was ready to be served. She didn't give Franciszka any orders or instructions, but simply nodded like a general at the front. Operation Supper Party had commenced.

When she came back and took her place at the table, Ignacy and Dr. Iwaniec were discussing politics: they were talking about the late French president, Marshal MacMahon, and how in his day he had crushed the Paris Commune (Ignacy was for him, Iwaniec strongly against); about the latest electoral reform proposed by the prime minister, Graf von Taaffe (Iwaniec was for it, Ignacy not necessarily); and also about the audience that His Excellency the governor had given on Monday here in Cracow, at the Spiski Palace (here they were in agreement that it was a highly significant event, testifying to the city's superior status). Zaremba couldn't hear much, so he concentrated on the soup and the drinks, nodding perhaps in agreement, or perhaps because of too much of the latter. His better half had trapped Żeleński and was telling him in agonizingly tedious detail about a charity collection in which she had recently taken part for the benefit of a church in distant Paraguay. Mrs. Dutkiewicz and Mrs. Iwaniec, sticking to the topic of life eternal, though undoubtedly a more secular version, were exchanging comments on the medium Eusapia Palladino, who, as rumor had it, was soon to arrive in Warsaw.

"Could you gentlemen not bring Miss Palladino here to us in Cracow?" asked Mrs. Iwaniec loudly.

"That charlatan? Good God, Leokadia," replied her husband. "Medicine is a *science,* and a serious scientist does not waste his time on nonsense."

"Is that so?" said Mrs. Iwaniec, bristling. "She is traveling to Warsaw at the invitation of a group of the local doctors. For whom the company of that extraordinary woman is evidently no dishonor. What's more, I read in the press that medical authorities throughout Europe have testified to the authenticity of her experiments, including Dr. Lombroso!" Mrs. Iwaniec was undoubtedly well prepared.

"Lombroso? Bishop Lombroso of Fiesole?" Mrs. Zaremba interjected.

"No, my dear lady, an Italian doctor who claims to have

described the typical physical features of criminals and fel-
ons," explained Żeleński, overjoyed that at last the subject
had changed.

"Claims to have?" said Iwaniec, raising his voice ir-
ritably; driven into a tight corner by his wife, he had decided to get out of it by launching a cruel attack on the
weakest section of the enemy's defenses, an action worthy of Marshal MacMahon himself. "Young man, surely
you don't presume to question the findings of a first-rate
scholar? Correct me if I am wrong, but I don't think your
academic achievement to date gives you the right. Moreover, one does not have to look far to perceive the accuracy
of his theories. The watchman at Helcel House, who only
days ago cruelly took the life of an innocent woman, is a
typical example of Lombroso's 'criminaloid': an overprom-
inent jaw, large ears, a low brow, and a hunched posture. It
all fits. Every last detail."

"Do excuse me, Doctor, but it so happens that on my
visits to Helcel House, where I act in a charitable role, I
have seen this man at close quarters, and I must say that
he made an entirely positive impression on me," said Zofia,
"nor did I notice the jaw of a troglodyte."

The Italian doctor's theory, which naturally she had
heard of before now, seemed to her doubtful; if physical appearance were inevitably linked with a penchant for crime,
Sister Alojza should long since have slit the throats of in-
fants in their cradles. But she decided to keep this thought
to herself. Instead, having finally spotted an opportunity to

steer the discussion on to the right track, she asked: "What about a poisoner? Does a poisoner have typical physical features, too? Why, Lucrezia Borgia sent whole hordes of victims to the next world without ceasing to be a beauty, did she not?"

"Indeed, Mrs. Turbotyńska, poison is the weapon of women, but the female sex is different from the male, as we are perfectly aware," declared Iwaniec and laughed heartily, glancing at Antosia, who had nearly gathered up the empty mushroom soup plates.

"The Borgias poisoned their victims with arsenic, didn't they?"

"They did indeed. Arsenic oxide looks like sugar or flour, and unlike strychnine, which is extremely bitter, it has no smell or flavor, so no wonder it was the favorite poison for all those years, not just for rats. *La poudre de succession* —inheritance powder, as the French would say."

"What are its effects?"

"Stomach pain, vomiting, and other complaints best not mentioned at the dinner table . . ." said the doctor hesitantly.

"But on the contrary, please go on. This is fascinating."

On the other side of the table, one of the women audibly suppressed a groan.

"Complications . . . of the intestine, damage to the heart," Iwaniec explained patiently. "The victim usually dies within fifteen hours or so, though sometimes it takes longer. The actual death is very violent — in cases where large amounts have been ingested, of course. But if it is dispensed slowly, in small doses, the poisoning can go on for months, years even. And it doesn't always happen consciously — arsenic is sometimes to be found in wallpaper or domestic paints. Paris green, for instance," he said, pointing at the dark green walls of the Turbotyńskis' dining room, at which Mrs. Dutkiewicz, already pale, went as white as chalk.

"Arsenic is sometimes prescribed for skin diseases, and it's an ingredient in the popular English patent medicine Fowler's solution," added Żeleński, wanting to show off his knowledge.

"So it is, young man, so it is. But I would not wish . . ."

Just then Antosia began to serve the catfish, but, unabashed, Zofia mercilessly carried on.

"Do all poisons have an equally brutal effect, making it instantly plain to see that the victim was poisoned, rather than dying of any other cause?"

"Well, most of them, yes. Strychnine, for example, prompts very strong spasms, making the unfortunate victim stiffen, as if suffering from tetanus" — at this point Iwaniec convincingly assumed a dramatic scowl — "the face twisted into a sardonic smile. But if morphine, for example, is administered in excessive doses it merely stupefies, causes heaviness of the limbs, somnolence, and finally a gentle death in one's sleep. The pupils shrink to the size of pinheads, and from the arms of Hypnos one falls straight into the embrace of Thanatos."

"Zofia, my dear, let that be an end to this topic, eh? Cousin Józefa appears to be feeling weak," said Ignacy.

"She's not the only one," added Mrs. Zaremba, and glanced at her husband, counting on his support, but he was busy with his catfish and only scraps of the conversation were getting through to him.

"What if the dead person looks healthy?" Zofia pressed.

"Healthy?" said Iwaniec, frowning. "No dead person ever looks healthy. The cessation of life is a symptom of a decided lack of health. A definitive one, I would say."

"What if their cheeks are pleasantly pink?" asked Zofia, then, seeing that Mrs. Dutkiewicz was ostentatiously fanning herself with her napkin, added: "Antosia, open the drawing room window a little, would you, please? But not far enough to cause a draft." Mrs. Zaremba began clucking about the fatal consequences of sitting in a draft.

"Oh, that sort of redness is not a sign of health; it's a morbid blush. Lethal!" said the doctor, raising a finger. "Cyanide. It causes a headache, breathlessness, numbness, and heart palpitations.

"No wonder it can easily be confused with a heart attack. But it brings certain death, and gives off a characteristic odor of bitter almonds . . . Stronger doses cause bruising, but if they're moderate, especially in the case of shop-bought cyanide, contaminated with other salts, the skin remains pink for quite a time. From the chemical point of view of course, it's to do with . . ."

"Damazy, please," said Mrs. Iwaniec, who though she could not see the reaction of the other guests could sense it all too strongly.

"It is I who must apologize," said Zofia repentantly; now that she had achieved her aim, she instantly transformed herself into the perfect lady of the house, "but medicine is truly *fas-ci-nat-ing*. I feel blessed by God for giving me a doctor as a husband. A man who saves the lives of others."

"My dear Zofia," grunted Ignacy, "I don't save any lives."

"But you could!"

"I feel blessed, too!" chimed in Mrs. Iwaniec, at which Mrs. Zaremba exclaimed: "The fortune of a wife is indeed a blessing . . ."

Suddenly they all fell silent, remembering that Mrs. Dutkiewicz was a widow.

"My late lamented husband," she said reverently, "was a man of great goodness. His task may have been more modest, but as an officer of the Mutual Assurance Society he too saved lives. Take, for example, the families of those who died prematurely, whom he helped to obtain financial compensation amid great tragedy."

"A truly Christian soul," said Zofia, seeking to minimize the nasty taste.

"I have heard that he is still remembered with great devotion by his colleagues," added Ignacy.

"But his greatest gift was the children he so generously bestowed on me," Mrs. Dutkiewicz went on. "*Six* of them," she said, casting a triumphant look at the ladies present. "Indeed, children — what a comfort for an elderly widow. My Maria and her Bruno have just produced a daughter."

"They have given her the name Zofia, haven't they?" said Zofia with feigned delight, piqued by the topic of motherhood.

"Indeed," said Mrs. Dutkiewicz, "but I am sure she will not be my only grandchild."

And so somehow they waded through to the end of supper. Antosia served the dessert, Żeleński told them how as an adolescent he had spent the holidays at the family mansion in Grodkowice, where he was tremendously bored, because there was nothing in the library but old copies of *Czech's Calendar*, Cracow's annual who's who ("An extremely useful publication!" Ignacy had interrupted him), books about farming, and a couple of Fredro's comedies, where someone had added crosses to mark which scenes should not be read to young ladies. Then the gentlemen had gone into the library, where Ignacy and Zaremba reminisced about their student days, while in the ladies' circle Mrs. Zaremba made a long speech about the properties of certain face powders and rose water.

When the door closed behind the final guests, Zofia told herself with satisfaction that the supper had been a great success. Though of course she realized that she was alone in this opinion. For a long time to come Mrs. Zaremba would talk of the "bizarre habits prevalent in *that* house," and Mrs. Dutkiewicz would cast suspicious glances at any dark green wallpaper.

CHAPTER VII

❧

In which Zofia runs up expenses because of her fatal addiction to detective work, gets to the bottom of a dessert, and from there to two queens and one king.

The day before, as Franciszka was preparing the catfish specially for Dr. Iwaniec, Zofia had announced: "It's time for you to visit your grandmother again. Time passes more quickly for the old, it trickles through their hands, and she hasn't seen you for simply ages . . ."

"Only two weeks," said Franciszka, looking up from the fish and rubbing her hands on her apron. "No, not quite ten days, I was there on the sixteenth, on Saint Maxim's day, and today it's the twenty-fifth, Saint Crispin's, the patron saint of cobblers . . ."

"You mustn't count out your forebear's time like a pharmacist," Zofia said, criticizing her. "We shall go there together." And seeing the girl's dissatisfied look, with a heavy heart she added: "Don't fret, you shan't lose your day off. But not a word to the professor. I shall see to it. You shall have your full day's pay."

That point was obvious to her: Ignacy could have no suspicions that instead of occupying herself with matters appropriate to her sex and social standing, not to mention the rules of an honest marriage, his wife was wandering about public buildings in search of an evil strangler. And sometimes she would have to pay a price for his ignorance, if only a full day's wages to Franciszka, though it was not actually her due, seeing she would be merrily spending the afternoon in the bosom of her family, at her grandma's side.

❧

After ascending the front steps into Helcel House and then several more in the vestibule, Zofia had come to a stop and was leaning against a marble column to catch her breath — though autumnal, the day was strangely oppressive. Just then a dark-haired youth went past her, briskly walking, or even running, out of the building. His thick head of hair, parted evenly on either side, was slightly combed back and heavily pomaded; his clothing was elegant to a fault, and with it his face may have been handsome, but was too tanned to go with such a starched collar. He didn't so much as glance at Zofia, but he stuck in her memory for looking as if his head had been transferred from another chess piece — as if the top of a pawn had been put on a bishop. He came downstairs at a rapid, springy pace and vanished from sight, first behind the ornate front door and then the gate of the institution.

Neither Mother Zaleska nor Sister Alojza was in the office, just a young nun who ventured to say, "Sister Alojza is to be found on the third floor."

"Knowing her kind and charitable heart, I can say with full responsibility," hissed Zofia, "that at no price would she wish to drag me up and down those awkward stairs, but would certainly advise me to wait here for someone to fetch her down."

The girl cast her a reluctant look but left the room immediately, with her habit shuffling along the floor. Zofia looked around the interior. It was here, at the heart of the institution, the thought flashed through her mind — for her thoughts always raced at the speed of a quadriga — that the presence of the Helcels was most palpable in the heavy, bourgeois pieces of furniture that they had left to the foundation, destined to furnish the office. The large carved desk, which had once stored the income and expense books for their stalls in the Cloth Hall, correspondence with banking houses, contracts, and wills. Or the cupboards in which the Helcel library had been replaced by fat registers, in some of which Sister Felicja — the nun with the neatest handwriting—recorded the accounts for the higher-class residents, and in others the proceeds from the sale of the items sewn, woven, sculpted, and glued together by the almsmen and almswomen in the house's workshops. But above all, the Helcels were present in the two large portraits in heavy carved frames: he had been painted in a nobleman's robe, with a ceremonial saber, a silk sash, and a pearl collar stud at his throat, like a genuine old-style Polish aristocrat; she in flattering full light where the wrinkles disappear, in mourning dress, so that the hands emerging from her wide sleeves all but shone against the black background.

"Don't you think this is an exaggeration, Sister," said Zofia to Alojza as she entered the room, "these national costumes, like an insurgent's attire? Anyone would think Mrs. Helcel was a heroine of the independence movement who raced about the woods with a hunting rifle, shooting off the Cossacks' caps . . ."

Sister Alojza was utterly confused, because she was still pondering the knotty question of a feud between two of the female residents, so she merely spread her hands doubtfully.

"I am not a fan of this sort of public show of political sentiment. Expressions of our national art or culture are a good thing, by all means," Zofia went on. "The same goes for Czech, Hungarian, or any of the other cultures that flourish under Viennese rule. But to have oneself portrayed in Polish national mourning more than thirty years after the January Uprising, well, really! And that chapel of theirs at Rakowicki Cemetery. Did you know, Sister, that any of their cousins and distant relatives may be buried there but on condition that they spoke Polish? Absurd!" She smoothed a wrinkle in her dress with the back of her hand. "Is that smart young man who just left a visitor, or a patron of the institution?" Zofia suddenly asked. "He's not an employee, is he? A relative of one of the sisters, perhaps?"

Again, Alojza couldn't keep up. She was only just starting to wonder whether the venerable founder of the house really had run about the woods with a rifle in her youth, but meanwhile Mrs. Turbotyńska's thoughts had moved on to something else entirely; Alojza girded her loins and, stammering a bit, replied: "Young? Smart? Hmm, I don't know. He must have been visiting someone, but I can't say whom. We don't have many visitors — most of our residents are entirely alone in the world, but there are some who still have visitors. And the people who come here from outside include some real originals! We used to have a gentleman who could eat hard-boiled eggs whole, shell and all, and he'd entertain the lady residents with this trick, until one night . . ."

"Very good, very good, Sister. Let us return to our affairs!"

Alojza fixed her gaze on the professor's wife, as if not understanding what "our affairs" meant at this moment.

"But why? It was Mr. Morawski who strangled . . . Mrs. Krzywda's murder has been explained . . . Mrs. Turbotyńska, it is not our role to question the magistrate's judgment. 'Render to Caesar the things that are Caesar's, and to God the things that are God's . . .'"

"Oh dear, Sister, Sister! That's all very well, but doesn't

the Gospel teach us that even Caesar's judges sometimes made mistakes? And so have you looked into the facts I asked about?"

Though undoubtedly extravagant, the theological argument proved effective, at least for a while.

"I shall," said Alojza resignedly, as if accepting that there was no turning back, and that the moment when she had informed Zofia Turbotyńska about the murder had sealed her fate as this inquisitive woman's accomplice. "All I have learned so far is that before she went to the kitchen, Mrs. Krzywda didn't help with the ironing—she worked in the orchard, because it was the apple- and plum-picking season. Our head cook, Mrs. Sedlaczek, was going to consult her notes to see which days she worked in the kitchen, but I thought it didn't matter anymore . . ."

"Thank you, Sister," said Zofia, jotting down a few words (*orchard, then kitch.*), then leafed back a few pages to see what else she had wanted to ask about. "Ah, yes, one of the nuns was on duty in the corridor the night Mrs. Mohr went missing. May I speak to her later on?"

"Sister Bibianna," said Alojza, making an effort to remember. "Yes, it was Sister Bibianna, formerly Barbara Zakroczymska."

"Aha, the doctor's sister! So that's why he . . . I see. But that can wait. First, let's go to the kitchen."

"I'm sorry, Mrs. Turbotyńska, but I have a lot of work to do. Now that . . . er . . . two places have come free and we can take in some new residents, Mother Zaleska has told me to go through the letters from the people waiting to come and live here, and the letters are long."

"But of course, Sister, I shall manage on my own. Please just show me the way."

❦

Located on the first floor at the far end of the right wing, the kitchen was not an old-fashioned, soot-blackened chamber with a row of copper pots hanging above the hearth, but a thoroughly modern laboratory designed by specialists, a genuine factory for food. The system for fetching firewood, the proximity of the food stores in the cellar and also the two superbly functioning hand-cranked lifts, which carried meal trays to the higher floors, meant that the cook at Helcel House felt like the manager of a large enterprise, and treated her underlings, almsmen and almswomen, cordially but quite gruffly. Serving up several hundred dinners was an operation that demanded rationing the sentiments and courtesies in favor of effective action.

"Make haste! Chop ze carrots!" shrieked Mrs. Sedlaczek at a group of old people who were sluggishly peeling vegetables. "How can I help?" she asked Zofia, showing in the process a distinct lack of enthusiasm for the fact that a strange woman was causing an obstruction in her kitchen. Suddenly she squawked more or less at Zofia, and more or less at someone behind her: "Mrs. Nawalka, hurry up wiz zose beans! Speed, not sleep!" Zofia turned and saw that these words were addressed to a shriveled old crone sitting on a little stool, who lurched and began shelling the beans a little more briskly.

"Madam, we are working here, dinner will be served soon," declared the cook in a reproachful tone when she discovered what this fancily dressed grande dame had come to ask, distracting her from ordering her minions about. By now, thanks to her strange accent, Zofia had realized she was a Czech. "I know nozing about zat poor woman who was strangled by ze watchman . . . Don't sleep!" she screamed at Mrs. Nawałka again.

"Sister Alojza said that you keep a record of who helps in the kitchen on which days . . ."

"Zat I do, I do, because ze sisters order me to, but it just takes up time."

"Do you happen to remember whether Mrs. Krzywda worked here last Sunday? It was Saint Teresa of Ávila's day," she said, prompting her.

"Zat I need not check; she always helped on Wednesdays and Zundays! Zough she knew next to nozing about cooking. All she knew, she learned here . . . And even zat day, I remember perfectly, she argued wiz one lady. Zere was a *hádka* . . . a quarrel. But I don't remember wiz whom. Anyway, I don't like to gossip," she said, having second thoughts. "Is zat all?" She cast a glance at the old people hunched over the carrots.

"If you could also tell me what the residents of the third floor had for supper that day."

"How inquisitive you are, madam!" grunted the cook, and with an offended look on her face reached for a large book bound in thick canvas. "Wait a moment . . . Terrine of hare and roasted capons. And lettuce," she said through clenched teeth, "because it's *healthy*," she added, sounding as if lettuce were her greatest enemy on the nutrition front.

"And for dessert?"

"Almond mousse, as every Zunday. Zis time wiz chestnuts."

"Aha!"

The cook had no idea what this nosy woman in the hat with a feather was so pleased about, but she too was pleased that the conversation was finally at an end and she could get back to work, to her bean soup and boiled beef with saffron milk caps. "I won't disturb you any longer," said Zofia on her way out. "Just one more question: Did you tell the investigating magistrate about Mrs. Krzywda's cooking?"

"Of course not, madam. Anyway, nobody asked me about it — why should zey?"

❧

There was one thing that Zofia Turbotyńska thoroughly loathed . . . No, that's not right. There were a number of things that Zofia Turbotyńska thoroughly loathed, but right now, as she was leaving the kitchen and its oppressive smells of boiling vegetables and frying oil, she felt that what she hated most of all were these foul, stifling aromas, reminiscent of shameful body odors. She walked down the corridor, twisting her face to left and right, but the stench of cooking clinging to her dress, hair, and hat continued to assail her nostrils.

To make matters worse, a few yards ahead she spotted a familiar figure: Mrs. Grabowska from the ladies' section of the Charitable Society, who visited Helcel House decidedly too often and was also sure to be on the prowl for raffle prizes from the workshops. Zofia stopped, hid behind a spreading palm tree in a brass pot, and then waited a while until her rival had vanished into one of the rooms.

Sister Bibianna, Sister Bibianna . . . Why would she . . . she kept on thinking. Of course, she was familiar with the name Zakroczymski—in her mind it was infamous. Not because of the sister, who had not entered the convent in the wake of a scandalous escapade—no one had asked for her hand and then abandoned her, nothing of the kind. But the conduct of her brother, the doctor, more than sufficed. Siblings, but how very different they were. Suddenly she had a brain wave that made her stop in her tracks.

"It all makes sense!" she said out loud, prompting two old ladies sitting by the window to turn their guinea fowl heads in her direction.

"Does the doctor visit his sister often?" she asked, putting her head around the office door.

"Who? Sister Bibianna?" said Alojza, reacting unusually quickly. "Of course, they're siblings. I can't see anything odd about that . . ."

"Aha!" exclaimed Zofia a second time, more to herself than to the nun. "Why yes, of course! Now it all makes sense!"

"What should I find out about her?" asked Alojza.

"Oh, nothing. I can manage by myself," said Zofia, smiling. "If you could just point me in her direction, and then leave us on our own. I'd like to have a little chat with her."

The nuns did not live in a separate part of the building; their bedrooms were located all over the house, in between the larger rooms assigned to residents, so that even in the middle of the night, the sisters were not at a distance, but close to their charges.

"Thank you for agreeing to spare me a few minutes, Sister Bibianna," said Zofia politely as she entered one of these little rooms.

The decor was austere: a cross on a whitewashed wall, and three narrow beds separated by screens, with a very thin belt of personal space around them. The only evidence of privacy were some locked suitcases stored underneath the metal bed frames and mattresses.

"It's very cozy in here," said Zofia, lying through her teeth.

"I'm glad you like it," the nun said, lying through her own teeth in return, "and I am always happy to help those who perform acts of charity."

"I'm here on a different matter today," replied Zofia in a fairly casual tone. "Not to ask about raffle prizes yet, but about the night when Mrs. Mohr's life came to an end."

"You mean Mrs. Krzywda? May she rest in peace . . ."

"No, Mrs. Mohr. The lady whom we found in the attic, behind the door into the box room."

"Oh, yes! That night I was on duty in the cubicle next to the door between the ladies' and gentlemen's wings. I gave all the details to Mother Zaleska. Nobody came through the door, because I have charge of the only key. I noticed nothing out of the ordinary."

"Can you swear to that?"

The nun took mild offense at the expectation of having to support her words with an oath as well, but then she replied: "Yes, I can. Though I don't see why . . ."

"And you didn't sleep a wink all night?"

"No. I can swear to that as well."

Zofia stopped by the window and ran a fingertip down the edge of the curtain.

"I am in no doubt," she replied at last, "that your conscience is clean. At least as far as the oaths are concerned," she added with a sigh of disapproval. "But not in relation to all the events of that night."

Sister Bibianna suddenly went crimson, as if her face were an empty vessel into which someone had funneled creamy beet soup from above.

"How dare you say such a thing?" she exclaimed. "My conscience is between me, the Lord God and my confessor, and nobody who turns up at Helcel House out of the blue and starts throwing their weight around is going to dictate to me on what matters . . ."

"But I know you haven't told any lies. You've simply been economical with the truth. It's true that you never slept a wink all night. And that you noticed nothing unusual. Because it's hard to sleep on the march . . . though they say it does happen, especially to the infantry. For a short time in the middle of the night you left your post."

"What calumny! Please leave my cell this instant!"

"You went to deliver a valuable package for your brother, and it's a long way to the doctor's room and back. Especially if you don't want to be noticed. And that is exactly why you didn't see or hear anything that night."

In fact, not everything was crystal clear to Zofia, but she had decided to go for broke, knowing, or rather believing, that no one could possibly drag a corpse down a wide corridor and then up the stairs to the attic without attracting the attention of the person on watch. But the solution that had occurred to her was pure speculation; after all, Sister Bibianna could simply have fallen asleep. Yet now she had instantly gone pale, as if the beet soup had suddenly drained from her face, leaving nothing but a pale mask. She began to sway a little, then sat down on the edge of the bed — not her own one, a fact that Zofia noticed at once with some satisfaction. It meant her blow had struck home.

"The fact that your brother, Dr. Zakroczymski, is a morphine addict is no secret in Cracow, especially for someone like me," she said slowly, "whose husband is a doctor, not to mention a professor at the university medical faculty. Allow me to say that the premature ending of Dr. Zakroczymski's career was a great disappointment for Cracow's entire medical community . . ." Here she broke off; it wasn't the first time she had caught herself repeating set pieces that were really Ignacy's preserve. Meanwhile Sister Bibianna was no venerable antique, but a pretty young woman of little over thirty, though she had ugly furrows running from her nose to the corners of her drooping mouth. And now, her mouth drooping even more, she sat on the bed, convulsed by spasms of weeping.

"Now, now," said Zofia to calm her down, not so much out of genuine sympathy but a dislike of emotional outbursts, "it'll be all right."

"Aaall right . . . hooow . . . can it be . . . aaall right?" sobbed Bibianna, now red again, this time from weeping. "I was seen . . . it has aaall . . . come out . . . Mother of Goood . . . heeelp me!"

"Indeed," said Zofia, sitting beside her and speaking softly, as if to a child, "you were seen. Never mind by whom. It is up to me to make sure Dr. Wiszniewski doesn't find out about this. But I do have conditions which you are going to meet. Wash your face now," she said, with a nod toward the washbasin, "and cool off."

Sister Bibianna walked across the room mechanically, like a puppet, and raised the lid of the washstand, causing the mirror fixed inside it to cast sunbeams on the wall. She poured water from a jug into the china bowl, washed her face, and then dried it with a fresh towel she took from a drawer. Briefly she stood gazing into the mirror, then returned to her place. Zofia was standing by the window, looking outside and trying her best to recall nice Dr. Zakroczymski who had once even flirted with her in passing at a carnival ball; she had been only about thirty at the time. She remembered his fine, pink complexion, the glint in his eye, and his pitch-black mustache — he was like Ares cast in the role of Asclepios. She had occasionally seen him since then, looking weaker and weaker, until the day came when his frock coat was too big, drooping on his shrunken shoulders, and his eyes were burning with a very different glow. All the doctors had known for ages what was wrong — he wasn't the only one to have problems with morphine — though a conspiracy of silence still prevailed in the city, where people simply made roundabout comments to the effect that "a mysterious illness is eating away at him."

"These are my conditions: first of all, swear to me that this was the last —"

"I swear."

" — the very last time. The person who saw you can check whether the morphine supply in the doctor's room has dwindled again. And Dr. Zakroczymski's entreaties cannot change a thing. He —"

"He was such a . . . such a . . . good boy! And so . . . handsome . . ."

"That is quite irrelevant to us," Zofia lectured her. "And so: regardless of your brother's entreaties, you will no longer allow yourself to break the seventh commandment. Secondly: should the need arise, you will confess that you weren't in your place. I will think up a plausible explanation. Thirdly: you will report to me on anything that seems unusual, odd, or suspicious." *For I don't know,* thought Zofia, *how much longer Alojza will have patience for me, seeing that she has already started to grumble.* "Fourthly and finally: if I ever need to ask you a favor, I shall not have to remind you more than once. Is that clear?"

Sister Bibianna, formerly Barbara Zakroczymska, sat on the bed like a teenage girl, huddling awkwardly, with her arms extended and her hands folded, as if to pray, in the dip in her habit between her knees. She nodded.

"Do you swear?"

"I swear."

"Splendid!" said Zofia suddenly, with a smile. "Goodbye, until we meet again in better circumstances. And please give your brother my best wishes for a rapid return to health!"

❧

"How was your day, dear heart?" asked Ignacy after supper from his end of the table; lounging in an armchair, he was reading the newspaper, noisily rustling the pages, which always drove his wife into a silent fury.

"Franciszka and I were at Helcel House—she went to see her grandmother," said Zofia, occupied with a game of Napoleon's Tomb solitaire, which as usual was failing to come out right. "It is most Christian of her."

"Helcel House, eh?" said Ignacy, brightening. "A dangerous

place. The scene of a murder. And no wonder — as the old adage goes, 'Długa Street leads straight to the scaffold.'"

"Ignacy, the scaffold was demolished a hundred years ago."

He let this pass without comment; she herself was perfectly aware that in the venerable city of Cracow "a hundred years ago" was tantamount to "yesterday morning."

"But listen to this — even the most seemingly harmless places and objects can be lethally dangerous . . . listen to this . . . now, where was it? Aha! There's a report from Brazil that Admiral Mello declared Mr. Lovena to be president, and a man called Pei . . . Peixoto . . . these foreign names are diabolical . . . 'made an attempt on Mello's life with the use of an album filled with dynamite that he sent him as a gift.'"

"No thank you very much is what we say to gifts like that," she replied, wanting to please him.

"Well said! And what if the album ended up in the wrong person's hands? What a faux pas that would be. There's nothing but murder and mayhem wherever you look. Even in our own backyard. They'd only just locked up that vicious watchman when Dr. Jordan's bicycle was stolen. Listen to this: 'From a lockup in Dr. Jordan's park an unknown culprit stole an almost brand-new bicycle, marked *Spezial*, the property of Dr. Jordan. When the theft was noticed, an attempt was made to catch the bold thief, but he fled into the city on the bicycle, riding it perfectly. The police are in search of the culprit, and have issued a warning against acquiring a stolen bicycle . . .'" He rustled the pages again. "What awful times these are, when even such a benefactor of mankind, such a loyal proponent of all that is wholesome and Polish as Dr. Jordan, the Habsburgs' personal stork, who has delivered so many members of the ruling house into the world, loses his bicycle at the hands of a common thief!"

"The hands and feet," said Zofia, who, several years ago, seeking help with her childless state, had had dealings with Dr. Jordan as a gynecologist. And although he too was from Przemyśl, her memories of him were not fond; truth be told, she was pleased to hear about the theft. Though naturally she would never have admitted it at any price.

While Ignacy went on rustling his newspaper, she picked up the cards, shuffled them, and laid them out again.

Let's take stock, she thought to herself as she played the game. *The two murders are closely connected. Cyanide, and as such, no wonder it was in an almond pudding to hide the smell . . . and now the cards that go crosswise . . . A simple woman would have used rat poison, which isn't exactly in short supply in that huge building, but instead she chose a more sophisticated substance. But even if we were to suspect a simple almswoman of such refined use of poisons . . . Ah, the ace of diamonds . . . hmm, the two doesn't really fit here . . . even if we were to suspect her, then of course there's no possible connection with the murder of which she herself was the victim. The idea that she poisoned Mrs. Mohr, and then someone happened to break into her room and strangle her . . . no, that's impossible. Mrs. Krzywda, a simple woman, was given a commission. Maybe the person who hired her knew that she was particularly eager for money? After all, for such a poor wretch some extra cash in her old age would be a priceless thing . . . Queen of spades, queen of diamonds, king of hearts . . . She got a job in the kitchen, and poisoned Mrs. Mohr. The contractor waited for that moment, then he lugged the body to the attic and hid it. But what for? Wouldn't it have been easier to leave it in the bed? Was he trying to hide something from someone? Or maybe it was the body he wanted?* She broke off her deliberations and went on laying out the cards for a while. *Preposterous. Either way, he wanted to make sure the death was discreet. And the second murder was sudden, brutal. Risky, too, because he could have been caught at any moment . . .*

Antosia came in, curtsied, cleared the teacups from the table, and left the room. Despite being new to the house, she was already aware that when the mistress was playing patience and the master was reading, it was better not to disturb them.

Which means he must have been in danger. In one way or another. Blackmail? Mrs. Krzywda could have been blackmailing him, demanding money that he'd promised her but didn't have. Or extra money beyond what they had agreed in advance. Bah, she could even have had pangs of conscience and let him know she was going to give herself up to the police. I must find out with whom she communicated in the last few days, whether she had a close friend or relative in the house, a confidante ... Maybe she was given severe penance in the confessional box; maybe she was lying prostrate; maybe she suddenly had more money and was buying herself sweetmeats or trinkets which could have given the game away ... One way or another, Mrs. Mohr is the key to the murders. Who could have been so eager to rid the planet of this particular old woman, when she was halfway to the next world anyway, and why?

Through a strip of window between the heavy, dark red velvet curtains, Zofia could see the darkness pouring down St. John's Street. She lost another game of Napoleon's Tomb, but no matter: of the two games of patience that she was playing, it was the less important.

CHAPTER VIII

❦

In which a peacock feather parades about Cracow on a Saturday, the watchman yields to the voice of Sarah Bernhardt, Zofia inspects the spot where imaginary treasure was buried, makes a dubious deal, and finally discovers a thing or two in a love nest.

On Saturday, just before noon, a green hat with a wide brim and a peacock feather secured by a gold-plated brooch cautiously emerged from the gateway of a house on St. John's Street. First the hat hesitated, as if wondering if it was going to rain — inevitably changing the streets of Cracow into muddy channels with streams of dirty water racing down them — and finally set off ahead. It passed the stone peacock adorning the facade of the house, then crossed the little bridge between the Piarist Monastery and the Czartoryski Palace, continually under repair. At St. Florian's Gate it turned right, and narrowly dodged a fast-moving carriage. The peacock feather quivered angrily, then headed in a straight line toward the towers of St. Mary's Basilica. It passed the house where, as all of Cracow knew, for years on end Mrs. Matejko had been having terrible rows with her famous artist husband, and a little farther on the house where Mrs. Dutkiewicz had not had any rows with her husband for the past two years, since he had been laid to rest in Rakowicki Cemetery. Past the junction with St. Thomas's Street, at house number ten, the hat abruptly stopped and tilted.

How can I have failed to remember that earlier? thought Zofia, amazed at her own forgetfulness, as she gazed at a statue of Saint Joseph gracing a facade. A few years back, also in the autumn, an appalling tragedy had occurred in this narrow two-story house, ending the life of Mrs. Bałucka, mother of a famous comedy writer. Once the owner of a small café on St. Mary's Square, she had died at the hands of a woman whom she had helped financially with great generosity. One day, when this woman, the wife of a bookbinder who liked a drop of the hard stuff, called to ask for further charity, she was let into the house as usual. But Mrs. Bałucka's Christian gesture was met with the recompense of Judas — a gag, some ropes, and a lethal blow to the head with the base of an iron, and then the corpse was hidden under a bed. The felon stole valuables and fled to a nearby town. The whole city talked of nothing else, including Zofia. She had even been moved to write a poem about the irony of a bad soul causing a good soul to give up the ghost with an iron. She thought it was quite accomplished, and for a while she planned to send it to a journal, but her recent experiences with the press had made her lose heart and the poem was still lying in her desk drawer beside her other literary attempts, correspondence with Ignacy from the days of their engagement, some ringlets of her mother's hair, and the rest of yesteryear's treasures, which had lost value with the passage of time but couldn't possibly be thrown away.

The classic crime committed for easy gain — though was it actually so easy? When the bookbinder's wife was arrested she was drunk; apparently she'd been drinking ever since the murder — she couldn't cope with her own conscience. Anyway, the Krzywda case was completely different. The almswoman had nothing, for she couldn't possibly have had anything; the corpse had not been hidden, as if the killer didn't care about keeping up appearances or needing time to escape. The alleged culprit, the watchman, hadn't even run from the scene of the crime. *No,* she thought, *it certainly can't have been an ordinary crime. None of it fits together.*

The hat moved on, turning left at St. Mary's, passing the slaughterhouse on the Small Marketplace, and entering Mikołajska Street. It stopped at the last building before Planty Park. Ducking under a low entrance, yet still catching the feather on the lintel, the green hat and all the rest of Zofia Turbotyńska's elegant attire crossed the threshold of one of the nastiest places in Cracow, which the wives of university professors usually did their best to keep at a distance: the local police station and jail.

✦

"Mr. Morawski, I know that you are innocent," said Zofia in a tone so soft that she'd had to practice it in advance at home, locked in her boudoir. "I don't just believe it; I *know* it for a fact."

If the watchman had been less browbeaten by the events of the past few days, including the inquiry, his arrest, and the reports of his accusation in the Cracow press, he would surely have noticed that the sweetness of the elegant lady's tone bore no relation to the look on her face; she was eyeing him up and down as if planning to draft a detailed map of his oval face and its hard features afterward. She made sure she'd remember it well: the jaw was standard, the forehead high, made markedly higher by a receding hairline, and the ears weren't large at all — though she couldn't be sure of this particular detail because they didn't shave the prisoners here, so at least half his ear was hidden beneath his randomly cropped mane. She imagined him sitting still as a pair of flashing scissors danced around his head in the hands of one of the almsmen, given the role of barber at Helcel House because he had some notion of cutting hair, though his eye was not the same as in the past, nor were his arthritic fingers quite so dexterous.

Morawski said nothing. It looked as if he had swallowed

the hook, but he still didn't know this woman's intentions, or the reason why the guard had summoned him from his cell and escorted him to the low, dark hall that served as a visiting room.

"I want you to tell me why you were walking about the house at night. That will help me to get you out of here."

"I have nothing to say."

"A charge of murder is a serious matter. You can lose your life for that."

Something passed across the thick skin of his face, a sort of nervous twitch, or maybe just impatience. But he was as closed to her as a door with no handle.

"That remains to be seen," he replied quietly.

"A man in his prime who kills an old woman? For no reason?" said Zofia, flicking crumbs off the wooden table-top. "I don't think the court will be lenient."

There was a moment of awkward silence. It's hard to hold a fluent conversation about the imminent execution of one of the interlocutors.

She had come here full of hope, but this unresponsive man was starting to annoy her. Not that obtaining a visit had been all that difficult: this was Cracow. The whole place was run by officials, each of whom had a wife, a mother, or a daughter, who in turn had a friend, a cousin, an aunt — in short, each of them had a thin thread of connection to another. So, step by step, from one person to the next, it was always possible to find friends in the right places. And the wife of the man in charge of the jail had been at school with a lady whom Zofia had once helped — knowing that she had a wide range of useful contacts — with an extremely shameful matter. One conversation had been enough for a message to be sent by private means saying that the wife of a university professor and doctor — and thus, by implication, a person with a wide range of useful contacts — a benefactress of Helcel House, had felt a sudden urge to bring Christian succor to a man burdened with the heaviest charges, whose soul was in direct danger of eternal damnation. There weren't many doors in Cracow, including prison doors, that Zofia Turbotyńska could not open. Or at least set slightly ajar.

Stubborn as a mule! she thought angrily. The watchman gazed in silence, now at his unexpected visitor, now at the flakes of paint peeling off the wall. Of course, if he started to talk he'd help her with her investigation, so to some extent she was here in her own interests — but since admitting the truth could save him from the noose, he was the one with more to gain.

"It is regrettable," she said, dropping the gentle tone entirely, "that the use of torture has been abandoned. If put to the rack, you'd have admitted to the investigators why you were walking down the corridor at night."

"Even if they put me to the rack I wouldn't say."

Silence fell again. A friendly chat about torture is not among the simplest either.

Of course, in purely theoretical terms, she thought to herself, *he could have been a tool in the hands of the mysterious king of hearts who murdered Mrs. Mohr. If the first hireling went off the rails and demanded extra money for the poisoning or threatened to expose the culprit, then maybe a second person was contracted, the watchman, for instance. The jack of spades, let us say. But that's a vicious circle. As the killer took the risk of rapid exposure, and as he switched from subtle poisoning to brutal strangulation, he must have had a knife at his throat. And persuading a house employee to commit murder would take some time — you can't simply walk up to a sheepdog and ask it point-blank: "Maybe for a nice round sum you'd be willing to change into a wolf and do in this troublesome ewe over here?" Definitely not. The watchman has to be innocent. But seeing he's ready to risk his life, his reason must be very important.*

"Think, my good man, how much your mother will suffer when —"

"My mammy died in the days of the old emperor," he said, giving her a pitiful look. "And my pappy in this one's day."

"Well, your brothers or sisters —"

"I'm all alone in this world," he wheezed. "I were the firstborn and my mammy died giving birth to the second. So there won't be much lamenting over me."

But just then Zofia's eagle eye espied a split second of hesitation in the watchman's long, chiseled face. No, not hesitation, but maybe regret? She latched on to it like a harpy.

"The man has yet to be born," she declared sententiously, "for whom no one shall weep. I am already aware of at least one Christian soul who . . ."

He shifted on his chair, as if suddenly feeling uncomfortable.

"Who?"

". . . who will have reason to lament — who is already lamenting."

"It's all gossip. It's not worth listening to idle chatter."

"At Helcel House the walls have ears. And eyes," she said, pulling the thread, though nobody had said a word to her about a Christian soul bewailing the watchman's imprisonment, "and tongues, too. Is it worth being quite so stubborn when the facts are already known?"

"What facts are known?" he suddenly shouted. "What facts are known? Nothing is known, it's just that people make up nasty gossip, because they're . . . petty. They're petty and they see everything that's petty, nasty, and vile. Just because I'm a watchman does it mean I haven't got a heart?" He went red in the face as he spat out each sentence with greater fury. "Does it mean I'm incapable of love? That I'm just dragged along . . . like a dog?"

And suddenly this large, burly man burst into sobs that sounded like an acute attack of hiccups. Ignoring the cost and her disgust, Zofia took a handkerchief with the monogram *ZG* from her pocket, and with an inviting gesture placed it on the table. But the watchman quickly regained his self-control, sniffed a few times, and fixed his gaze on the floor. She put away the handkerchief.

"Why the obstinacy?"

He said nothing, but his gaze shifted from the tips of

his shabby boots across the floor tiles, up the spittoon, then onto the wall, and almost got as far as Zofia's face.

"I am a watchman," he said at last, "so they despise me, as if I were no better than a beggar. But my pappy was a watchman, and my grandpa before him, and my great-grandpa before him, and the line goes back further. We've worked for some of the best, for counts, for princes, for bishops. When they hired me for Helcel House it was because everything there is the best, the dearest, of the best quality, so even the watchman is first-rate, from a long line of watchmen. And we watchmen have our principles. If I were to say why I was walking about at night, I'd not just bring shame on myself, but also on the Christian soul who will weep for me. Worse, if the court were to give credit to various old gossips, they might jail me for six months for adultery, too, because her old man, that son of a dog, that bastard of the first order, if you'll pardon the expression, is still breathing his last in prostitution on Długa Street . . ."

"In destitution . . ."

"Yes, like I said, in . . . er, in poverty, in a dark basement. But he can't last much longer. Amen."

"Do you not think that when your life is at stake, you might drop those watchmen's principles for once?"

"Our principles are sacred."

She sighed, as it occurred to her that the things people hold sacred cover the oddest spheres and are to do with the strangest things: for one person a sum of money put aside for a rainy day is sacred, for another it's their mother's memory, and for a third it's an unwritten professional code.

"Let us suppose," she began, "that as a watchman you admit to nothing. You go to the scaffold. And then the murderer calmly kills another old woman."

"God forbid!"

"Was it not your duty as watchman to protect Mrs. Krzywda from being murdered?"

He folded his arms, let his head droop, and hawked noisily.

"Yes, it was."

"Indeed it was. And is it so very important to keep a little secret if it might mean sacrificing another victim's life?"

"How can you know he'll be back again? Maybe he only planned to do it the one time."

"Two times — first he killed Mrs. Mohr."

"What the devil? But she was —"

"Poisoned," said Zofia in a sepulchral tone; in her youth she had dreamed of a career as a great actress and often flattered herself with a mental comparison to Sarah Bernhardt.

After this single word, the grimness of which echoed off the low ceiling of the visiting room, the rest of the encounter was a mere formality. The guard — who thanks to the instructions of the prison chief's wife was at Zofia's beck and call — brought some paper, Zofia skillfully asked some supplementary questions, then drafted the statement at lightning speed, and the watchman added his angular signature. As a farewell gesture she was going to reach into her bag and fetch out a picture of Saint Leonard, patron saint of prisoners, which she had brought specially to give to him; but it occurred to her that she'd do better to offer him a pair of lovers from Shakespeare or Goethe than a gloomy hermit.

"The Christian soul," she whispered instead, "will be beside herself with joy that you have come to your senses."

He glanced at her with some embarrassment — and definitely with more gratitude than if she had given him the tonsured Saint Leonard, carrying manacles and chains smartly coated in silver paint.

Once she was out of the prison gate, she briefly stopped to gather her thoughts, and smiled again, remembering how confidently investigating magistrate Klossowitz had boasted in the newspapers of exposing the murderer, and Dr. Iwaniec had classified the watchman as Lombroso's typical criminal. This would put their noses out of joint — what a pleasant thought! But meanwhile the green hat had to hurry back to St. John's Street, thence to the little shelf above the coat hooks, for the luncheon would not supervise itself.

❧

As every Sunday, Zofia and Ignacy went to High Mass at St. Mary's, recently decorated by the great painter Matejko and his pupils to look like a medieval casket: gold stars were strewn across a sapphire-blue background, and angels, whose faces were lent by the prettiest daughters of the Cracow bourgeoisie, and also — thanks to special patronage — a rather less pretty daughter, but that's best skated over. As they were leaving, several requisite greetings and good-byes were said, and like a morphine addict consumed by her habit, Zofia was on the point of abandoning Ignacy to head for Helcel House, when the company began talking about the imaginary treasure hidden under a bench on Virgin Mary Square, as described in the *Cracow Times.*

A man called Rybarczyk, who sold groceries on Szpitalna Street — according to Mrs. Zaremba a very decent fellow, though somewhat sluggish — had dreamed three nights in a row that someone had buried treasure underneath the bench. The first time he took no notice, the second time he went to inspect the bench and spent several hours examining it, and finally the third time he dreamed that if he didn't act immediately a woman would beat him to it. By now he felt as if the treasure, forced on him by his dreams, actually belonged to him. So he gathered up the appropriate tools and in the middle of the night set out with Wincenty Gargul, an apprentice carpenter, to dig up the ducats and precious stones from under the city bench.

Indeed, the cobbles had plainly been disturbed. Mrs. Zaremba gazed at them as if at priceless antiques that had witnessed great historical events, when all they had actually seen was the routine arrest of two men by a police patrol, which marched them off to the clink on Kanonicza Street to flush the nonsense out of their heads by morning. Clearly having a flair for research, Mr. Zaremba nudged a cobblestone with the tip of his boot.

"What if there really is some treasure down there?" his wife asked naively.

At that point, excusing herself with "acts of charity close to my heart," Zofia finally set off for her desired destination, reflecting on the boundlessness of human folly.

✦

She entered Helcel House, but before pressing the handle of the office door, through the whitewashed glass of another inner door, she saw Sister Bibianna standing on the threshold of the chapel. She appeared to be signaling, so Zofia went a few paces closer. Bibianna had just pushed a bath chair to this point; in it, huddled under a blanket, sat a wrinkled old resident, evidently wishing to say his prayers in a more venerable place than his own bed.

On seeing Zofia, Bibianna was plainly confused.

"I have something for you, madam, but not here," she whispered.

"By the coffins."

"What coffins?"

"The residents' coffins. Left-hand entrance to the cellar. In . . . half an hour," she said, glancing at the wall clock.

✦

"Mother Zaleska, I know you have plenty on your mind," said Zofia after taking a seat in the office, "but Christmas will be here in no time, and a raffle without prizes is like a bread ring made of nothing but the hole . . ."

To say that Mother Zaleska had grown wan in the past few days would be putting it mildly. There she sat at her desk looking crestfallen, her wimple plainly not the freshest; her round, ruddy face was drawn and drooping, and her eyes, reddened either by sleepless nights or weeping, had lost their glow. She didn't respond, but nor did she have to, and Zofia knew the reason. Ground down by a double scandal — not just the murder of Mrs. Krzywda but also the guilt of the trusted watchman — Mother Zaleska was afraid that Helcel House would lose its good name, and the residents of the upper floors would gradually start to withdraw, along with their capital, which was one of the pillars of this enterprise. In this situation, persuading her to provide prizes for the raffle would be harder than ever. Even if Alojza tried to win her over in her clumsy way, Mother Zaleska now saw the wooden canes, woven baskets, and Christmas cribs made by the poorer residents as the last source of income for the institution, compromised as it was by murder.

"I'm sorry to say it is out of the question. The items produced in the workshop by the almsmen and almswomen are their recompense for shelter, board, and lodging. We cannot be prodigal with these gifts of the heart," said Mother Zaleska almost automatically, without looking at her visitor.

"I was under the impression that we had already reached a decision. Countess Żeleńska herself has agreed to—"

"The countess may lend her name in support of the raffle, and we are ready to back it with our prayers, like any worthy aim, but as for the prizes . . . that is quite another matter."

So neither the many strings of figs, nor winning over the nun's bossy aunt, which really had taken a lot of trouble, nor the polite requests were of any use. In the far corner of the room Alojza was clearly embarrassed, and didn't know where to look; she went on shifting papers from pile to pile, in the hope that this entire unpleasant scene, in which one of the pilots of her soul was battling with the other, would finally come to an end. But Zofia would not give up.

"It is no secret to anyone in Cracow that the institution has suffered a blow, and you are suffering with it," she said. "Yet it so happens that I am in possession of information that will clear the watchman of blame. It will not bring Mrs. Krzywda back to life, or Mrs. Mohr . . ."

"Ah, we're not expecting the resurrection of the dead! Not from you, in any case," added Mother Zaleska scornfully. "But rather from some men of great piety, mystics, people of great faith. But clearing the watchman's name—"

"But clearing the watchman's name will take some trouble, so I hope you will entrust the joy it brings you to God, and also thank him by providing suitable gifts for the raffle."

Such unambiguous plain speaking, such obvious blatant barter took Mother Zaleska by surprise. The atmosphere in the office was thick enough to cut with a carving knife. Or at least a schoolboy's penknife. Alojza held her breath — at such length that she'd have gone blue if Mother Zaleska had not finally yielded.

"Such God-sent miracles are always worthy of gifts," she hissed through her teeth, then stood up, bowed with an energetic, military nod, and headed for the door.

"I shall hold you to your word, Mother!" said Zofia, smiling, then turned to her trusty Sister Alojza. "And I shall continue to trouble you for your help with my charity collection, for no one makes such a fine effort on behalf of the scrofulous children!"

"God be praised," came Mother Zaleska's voice from the corridor, her valediction sounding not unlike a threat.

At surprising speed for someone squeezed into a dress with a sizeable bustle, Zofia turned on her chair and questioned the nun: "What news of our dear departed friends? Do we yet know what Mrs. Mohr and her sister talked about? When will I finally be able to speak to her? Do we know anything about Mrs. Krzywda's family? Was there any connection between them? You were to check these things."

Alojza shook her head.

"No, absolutely nothing. It's as if she sprang from nowhere, out of thin air," she said, throwing up her hands. "No one knows anything about her. Not what village she was from, nor who her husband was . . . no living relatives have come to light, not a soul. Perhaps she was an orphan? The only thing is this letter of recommendation." She stood up with a soft grunt.

She walked over to a large, four-part bookcase made of dark wood, took out a file, and from it a small rectangle of smart letterhead — as Zofia mentally noted — with a family crest embossed in the corner.

"Mrs. Krzywda was accepted at Helcel House thanks to the intercession of Countess Wielhorska. From Krzeptów. Here is the letter in which she writes that 'she is a woman of great piety and many virtues . . . a widow . . . falter . . . no, fallen. Fallen into financial difficulties.' Nothing but generalities. I showed the letter to the magistrate, but I don't think he was interested. There's nothing in the letter to say when and for whom she worked as a cook. Maybe for this countess? I don't know."

Zofia held out a hand, examined the letter on both sides, then quickly jotted down a few words in her notebook (*C. Wielhorska, widow, financial*) and before she had finished writing, asked: "And Mrs. Mohr? It's too bad there's no information on Mrs. Krzywda . . . though if you do happen to hear anything, I want to be the first to know. But what about Mrs. Mohr?"

"There's not much more than you already know, Mrs. Turbotyńska. The widow of a judge, a wealthy woman, with bad legs. Her only family was a younger sister . . ."

"And where is she? Where has the sister got to?"

"Apparently she's on her way back. She was taking the waters, in Karlsbad, I think."

"How long does the journey from Karlsbad take?" said Zofia impatiently, who had been wanting to talk to this key

witness for ages. "One just boards the train, Prague, Pardu-
bitz, Ostrau, and the Cracow city limits are in sight!"

"But if one has paid for the Kurhaus in advance ..." said
Alojza, relishing the word *Kurhaus*, which was softly wreathed
in a mist of forbidden pleasures: luxury and comfort.

"Did she leave a long time ago?"

"I'm afraid she left on the day Mrs. Mohr went missing.
By the time we found the body, by the time the sister could
be located in Karlsbad, which took a lot of trouble, as she'd
changed hotel because of the bedbugs, in short —"

"Of course, of course," interrupted Zofia, "on that fateful
day — well I never. She evidently took the evening train, if
they had time to quarrel after dinner. As soon as —"

"As soon as she arrives I shall let you know."

"And at the house? Did anyone quarrel with her, or
argue?" Zofia was sure that the mystery of Mrs. Mohr was
at the bottom of it all; but how was she to get to the bottom of it? Where was she to pinpoint it? With whom was it
connected? It crossed her mind that Mrs. Mohr's age was a
complicating factor: she had lived so long that she could have
made enemies right back in the days of the old emperor, in
times that were truly immemorial. How much easier it would
be to conduct her inquiry in a kindergarten than an old people's home ... "Perhaps someone was vying with her?"

Alojza knitted her brows. She was plainly trying to
bring herself to say something, endeavoring to express her
opinion. And finally she did it: "But why would anyone vie
with Mrs. Mohr? She had no sort of life any longer, she was

quietly fading away . . . Nooo . . . And the idea that someone disliked her . . . various people didn't like her."

"Anything else?" asked Zofia, without looking up from her
notes.

"There is one thing. Mrs. Mohr hardly ever left her
room, did she? But she wanted to talk to a certain lady, so
she asked the almswoman who came to clean her room to
ask that lady to visit her the next day. But when the next
day came, she'd vanished from the room . . . and . . . and we
know the rest. We know it all. We know it all, it's known to
all . . ." she said, getting in a tangle.

"What is that lady's name?" said Zofia, who was due in
the cellar now.

"Mrs. Walaszek."

The left-hand door into the basement was set slightly ajar.
Zofia went down the steps, and at the bottom she looked
in both directions; here were the house's spacious store-
rooms, where fruit and vegetables were kept, blocks of ice
in the ice store, and coal in the boiler room; in summer the
almsmen and almswomen pickled gherkins here, and in autumn they shredded cabbage and stacked the shelves with
preserves made in the kitchen. Sister Bibianna was standing there waiting, leaning against a door painted gray.

"What are these coffins doing here?" whispered Zofia.

"What do you expect? They're just standing here. The almsmen and almswomen buy their own coffins in advance, whatever kind they wish," said Bibianna, pulling on the doorknob to reveal a small space lit by nothing but a tiny window. A wide variety of coffins was neatly arranged against the wall: dark ones, light ones, some varnished black or white — in other words, for old maids — decorated with all sorts of crucifixes, handles, and cherubs.

"How can one tell which is whose?"

"They're signed. Look at this . . ." said Bibianna, moving a lid aside to expose a piece of paper with a name on it.

"What a memento mori," said Zofia. "These people really do think about death!"

"Amen."

"But we're not here to talk about coffins. It seems you have something for me."

"Yes, though . . . I feel uncomfortable in the role of a telltale . . ."

"This is not telling tales," interrupted Zofia, "it simply means having your ears and eyes open."

The nun closed the door of the coffin store and brushed her hands against her habit.

"Well then, Mr. Fikalski used to say dreadful things about Mrs. Mohr. Sometimes the way he looked at her at dinner made my flesh creep beneath my habit."

At the thought of Sister Bibianna's creeping flesh, Zofia herself felt the chill of the cellar beneath her bodice.

"At any rate, she wasn't in debt to him," the nun continued. "She sometimes gave him the stare of a basilisk too. And lately one of those ladies from upstairs . . . Mrs. Wężyk, yes, Mrs. Wężyk saw Fikalski quarreling with Mrs. Mohr! Publicly! But in such monosyllables that nobody knew what it was about."

"Mrs. Wężyk sees various things," muttered Zofia dubiously.

"Maybe so," said Bibianna, shrugging, "but others saw it as well, including two of my fellow sisters. They're the ones who told me that Fikalski . . ." — here she leaned toward Zofia — "that wretched Fikalski is from the place where Mrs. Mohr had a house. From Bochnia. Maybe they were arguing about that house, I don't know."

Upstairs, or perhaps in another part of the cellars, a bucket clanged. They waited a while in silence.

"Anything else?"

"Apparently, after Mrs. Mohr's disappearance Mrs. Krzywda spent a couple of days ardently praying in the chapel. Although I did not actually see her there. And that's all for now."

"God be praised."

❦

Fikalski, Fikalski, Zofia was sure she had heard that name somewhere before. It was true that Countess Żeleńska had mentioned Fikalski at the theater a week ago, but there was something else . . . What a bore! She was no spring chicken anymore, but perhaps Dr. Gwiazdomorski should prescribe her some herbs for these problems with her memory . . .

She thought of dropping in on the countess to ask her a few questions. And she'd take the opportunity to find out who could introduce her to him — when the house was being searched from top to bottom for the missing old lady she didn't have to explain why she was questioning everyone. But now it would be odd for her to conduct a private inquiry — the first death was officially an accident, and though the second was murder, the culprit had been identified and arrested. Anyone could tell her to mind her own business. So if she was going to discover anything, she'd have to make it sound like an ordinary friendly conversation.

Unfortunately, the countess had gone out and her maid couldn't — or wouldn't — say when she'd be back. So Zofia knocked at the other door on the same floor. For a moment she thought Baroness Banffy had opened it in person, but it was just her maid, Polcia, as hefty as her mistress.

"I'm afraid her ladyship won't have time for you," she muttered through pursed lips.

"I realize she has more than enough to occupy her," said Zofia, refusing to give way. "But this is no trifling matter." Polcia, however, gave no reply, but merely pushed the door shut.

Oh well, all that remained was to hope for a stroke of luck — maybe she'd track down Fikalski or Mrs. Walaszek, manage to converse with them, and draw them out. It was too early for dinner, and yet the corridors were deserted; she glanced out of the window and realized what was up. After a doubtful morning, the weather was rather fine now, quite warm for the end of October. Although it was a Sunday, there were gardeners buzzing about by the wall coated in a bloodred vine that separated the grounds of Helcel House from the railway embankment, but in the courtyard, among beds of variegated chrysanthemums, asters, and dahlias, social life was in full bloom, too. Zofia ran down the steps beside the chapel and scanned the garden, trying to spot Fikalski. She had no great hope of recognizing him—he had only flashed past her briefly at the theater, at a distance too, and she had no idea what Mrs. Walaszek looked like.

It seemed all the residents whose state of health would allow for it were outside in the garden. Some were strolling under the young lime trees growing along the avenue that divided the area with flowers from the vegetable garden; others were sitting on benches, basking in what were sure to be the last rays of sunshine this year. Several old men were sitting beneath a slightly lopsided statue of Saint Joseph. *No wonder,* thought Zofia—she knew from Sister Alojza that the stretch of wall behind the statue had once been a point for smuggling alcohol from the marketplace into the men's wing; perhaps the practice still continued. One had merely to approach the wall, shouting, "He whose trust is in the Lord . . ." and minutes later one would hear: ". . . hereby claims his just reward"; over the bricks one hand passed some money, the other a bottle, and without setting eyes on one another, the parties to the transaction would be off to see to their own business. But that was not what interested her. She spotted a familiar figure — Sister Aniceta, who did the ironing, walking along a path with a laundry basket. When Zofia asked if she happened to know where she might find Mrs. Walaszek and Mr. Fikalski, a well-practiced scowl of moral disdain bloomed on her face.

"Of course, I know perfectly well where those *persons* are to be found," she snapped. "Over there. *Together.*" And she waved in the direction of a latticed pergola standing in the depths of the garden under a spreading plane tree that must have been here in pre-Helcel days. Zofia said thank you; hardly had she set off that way before a man emerged from the pergola. He was not very tall, stout, but fashionably dressed. His age was only apparent from the way he walked, leaning at each step on a stick, which was not a light cane but a solid staff strong enough to bear the weight of his broad shoulders. Despite hobbling, he was walking fast — in fact, he made it look as if he were trying to get away from the pergola as fast as possible, but Zofia effectively blocked his path with the entire width of her dress.

"Mr. Fikalski?" she asked, though she already knew the answer.

Under a large, beaky nose a small mustache twitched, and at lightning speed a hand adjusted a monocle and smoothed some graying sideburns. Zofia noticed that his bald patch was covered by a comb-over, subtle indeed but far from adequate.

"That's right, Alfons Fikalski . . . How may I help you, my fine lady?"

"Indeed, yours is a famous name . . ."

"Oh yes," said Fikalski, pleased, "quite so! In my time I've done some directing, organized sleigh rides, picnics, wedding parties, and dances; I've run lotteries and cotillions at balls — once upon a time I was quite a figure! No evening in Cracow can possibly succeed without Fikalski — that's what they used to say! Sadly such gallopades are in the past for me now; I'm afraid I won't be able to help you. The gout, don't you know. Though I still have all my masculine powers, ahaha!" he guffawed. "But I can recommend the right person."

"That is not what I wish to discuss with you — I'm hoping to ask about the late Mrs. Mohr."

Fikalski's face stiffened and the mustache quivered. Dyed, as Zofia noticed to her amusement.

"I don't recall."

"Apparently there was an altercation between you and the unfortunate lady . . ."

His tone changed too.

"Madam, I would advise you not to take notice of old gossipmongers," he hissed, "alive or dead. I did not know the lady. Excuse me, please, I'm in a great hurry . . ."

"In that case I don't wish to take up more of your time. You're sure to be hurrying to Mass, as it's Sunday today," said Zofia, smiling wryly and nodding toward the chapel. She waited for Fikalski to clamber up the steps and disappear inside the house, and then headed for the pergola.

Inside it sat a woman who had to be Mrs. Walaszek. Dark complexioned, with rounded shapes, she was a good many years older than Zofia, but her hair was still raven black. *Hmm, not the subtlest form of beauty, perhaps, but it might appeal to some,* thought Zofia, feeling a stab of jealousy. *Though women of her age should not be involved in this sort of thing.* Her hands were folded in her lap, and on a small table before her lay a volume of poetry, covered by one of her gloves — considering the dreamy look she had in her eye, Zofia thought it possible that there may have been a kiss planted on a hand in here. In broad daylight.

"Good morning, madam. I'm not disturbing you, am I?" said Zofia in the sweetest tone imaginable.

"No, please be my guest."

It sounded like "gayest." *What's that strange accent?* wondered Zofia. They exchanged a few polite comments on the weather, until finally Zofia couldn't hold back.

"Forgive my boldness," she said, "but you come from abroad, don't you?"

"Yes, from abroad. My home ceety's Udine."

Zoodinay? Zofia was quite incapable of locating that place on the map. *Could it be in Bohemia?* she thought. *Or in Bukovina, far away across the river Prut? She's sure to be a converted Jew.*

"Lidia Campiani, by marriage Meesees Walaszek," the lady introduced herself.

An Italian! exclaimed Zofia mentally.

"Zofia Turbotyńska. My husband is Professor Turbo-tyński."

"*Professore!*" exclaimed Mrs. Walaszek aloud in a tone betraying respect. "My 'usband worked on ze trains. He fought beside Garibaldi against Austria, for *risorgimento,* and fell so much in love weeth Italia that he brought a wife 'ome—to Austria, eento capteevity again. *Ironia, davvero?* But he is no longer alive. Are you veesiting someone 'ere?"

A member of the Carbonari! thought Zofia in horror, but politely replied: "In a manner of speaking. I was acquainted with Mrs. Mohr. I take a lively interest in her fortunes. That is, I used to . . ."

"Oh, poor Mrs. Mohr. *Povera,*" said the Italian, shaking her head.

"Sister Alojza told me that you were friends."

"*Davvero?* I would not 'ave been saying so." Her Polish was surprisingly good, but here and there it still caused her problems, so she spoke slowly and clearly, not in the least how Zofia imagined an Italian would speak. "We talked a few times, she was een Eetaly several times; she liked to tell about Naples, though I was never there. What a peety, a nice lady. She wanted to talk to me on that day when she died. *Poverissima.*"

"You don't happen to know what she wanted to talk to you about?"

"It was strange. She said . . . *come si dice . . .* it was a matter of life and death. No, life or death. A leetle *dramatico,* no?"

"*Dramatico* indeed," repeated Zofia somewhat mechanically. "Thank you very much for our conversation, it's so nice to know that Mrs. Mohr had friends here."

She stood up, and adopting the friendliest of smiles, she said as if in passing: "A fine-looking fellow came out of here a while ago."

"Oh yes, he's very nice," said Mrs. Walaszek, beaming. "*Signore* Fikalski. He's a weedow, I am a weedow — *molto simpatico.*" And her farewell smile revealed her pretty white teeth.

"Oh yes, *simpatico,*" replied Zofia, forcing another smile. "Good afternoon, dear lady."

An antiquated Juliet waiting for her balding Romeo, she thought. As she walked away from the pergola she couldn't restrain another smile — a broad, sincere smile of the sort that only schadenfreude can prompt.

CHAPTER IX

✤

In which Zofia Turbotyńska is forced to resort to some morally dubious acts, realizes that a sizeable chapter has been torn from the book of her life, sets two belligerent bucks against each other, comes upon a suspiciously shabby cross between an Alpine chalet and the Alhambra, learns that not every widower's wife is actually dead, and finally that the police do not let the grass grow under their feet.

"The doctor says please come in," said the nurse grudgingly, "but he only has fifteen minutes."

"That will entirely suffice," replied Zofia confidently, tapping the tip of her umbrella against the floor for greater effect.

Last night over a game of patience in her boudoir before bedtime she had planned the entire morning in detail;

her actions needed to be swift and coherent, like surgical incisions: first, she had to bring Dr. Zakroczymski entirely under her control, and then the investigating magistrate Klossowitz, while at the same time pacifying Mother Zaleska, were she to take a stand. And she needed to do all this in the fewest moves possible. So she had started in advance, by sending Sister Alojza an urgent request to get Klossowitz to come to Helcel House on the excuse — a valid one, in any case — that she had some crucial information for him, relevant to the case. Then, on the pretext of escorting Ignacy to work, she accompanied him to Kopernik Street, and on the way back she called at Dr. Zakroczymski's consulting room in St. Lazarus's Hospital.

"Ah, it's Mrs. Turbotyńska in person. My sister remembered you to me. I feel flattered," said the doctor with a note of derision. "To what do I owe this undoubted honor?"

Zakroczymski looked awful. His frock coat hung even more sadly from his skinny frame, and his eyes were duller than ever.

"I am pleased you did not say 'undoubted pleasure.' That will spare us any disenchantment," replied Zofia in a neutral tone as she sat down uninvited. "I have come to see you about the late Mrs. Mohr, a resident of Helcel House, a place you know extremely well. It was you who confirmed her demise and drew up the death certificate."

"Indeed I did."

"May I take a look at it? You are sure to have a copy."

"It is highly unusual," said the doctor slowly, drawing

out each syllable, "for a person . . . who is the wife of a doctor of medicine . . . a professor of medicine . . . to be unaware of medical confidentiality . . ."

"The person is aware of it," said Zofia, interrupting him. "The person also knows that there may come a point when your erroneous, I repeat, erroneous diagnosis is challenged by the higher courts. But then you will not be able to do anything about it, and it will rebound on you with multiplied force. I am concerned about time, and you should be concerned about correcting your mistake in advance."

Zakroczymski didn't reply, but after a short pause he slowly opened a desk drawer, took out a document, and, still silent, passed it across the desk to Zofia.

POSTMORTEM EXAMINATION of Antonina Mohr, née Januszkiewicz, age 81, dated 17.X.1893.

External examination
1) The corpse of a woman, 4´10″ long, build and nourishment good.
2) Posthumous stains, bright red, extensive, rigor mortis throughout the body.
3) On the body are the following lesions:
a) on the left hand, abrasion of the epidermis, the size of a 10-haller coin;
b) on the sixth right intercostal space at the nipple line, a bruise slightly smaller than a 1-gulden coin.

No other external injuries.

Conclusions

1) The bright-red coloring of the posthumous stains indicates, especially in accordance with the current inquiry, that the deceased most probably died as a result of hypothermia.
2) The bruising on the sixth right intercostal space and the epidermal abrasion on the left hand were the result of light injuries unrelated to the subject's death.

Signed:
Dr. Juliusz Zakroczymski

"As you can see," he recited monotonously but not very coherently, "Mrs. Mohr's death was purely the result of natural causes. Dr. Wiszniewski has told us about her medical condition, all entirely natural at her age anyway. She must have risen during the night and wandered up to the attic in a lethargic state, where she fell over, hence the abrasion and the bruise, and died as a result of hypothermia. A tragic incident, but not unheard of. I really don't know what more could have been done."

"You could have performed an internal autopsy. The poor woman's body is still lying in the mortuary at Helcel House."

"Is that so?" spluttered Zakroczymski, which must have been quite an effort for him. "Are you an expert on medicine as well now? I'm telling you, there are no signs to suggest that performing an autopsy is necessary."

"I admit that I find it surprising, but it turns out that I do know better than you. Did it not cross your mind that reddening of the body is an indication of the effect of poison?"

"Nonsense."

"Are you sure?"

Without a word, Zakroczymski just stared at Zofia with an absent gaze.

"What about potassium cyanide?" she pressed.

"In theory it's possible, but . . ." admitted the doctor, tugging at his graying mustache, "but it's hardly likely—"

"It is highly likely. I would say almost entirely certain. Typical intense pink stains, giving the body a suspiciously healthy, glowing appearance. In relation to which—"

"You're not going to force me," he said, his hackles rising.

"Cards on the table, Doctor. We are both perfectly well aware of your reason for being at Helcel House that day. Your addiction, though undeniably morally repugnant, is a matter between you and your Creator. However, I cannot accept it as a reason for neglecting your duties as a doctor. It could be said that in this particular instance your fate depends not just on the Almighty, but also on me."

"What exactly are you going to do?" he asked calmly, straining to raise his heavy eyelids. "Inform your husband?

Inform the medical faculty? They know already, besides which I don't really care what they think."

It was true — the medical set turned a blind eye to Zak-roczymski's addiction; in memory of the brilliant start of his career, he was still allowed to work at the hospital, where he treated the simplest cases, under the watchful eye of his superiors. *In spite of all,* thought Zofia, *holding a conversation with a morphine addict is not among the easiest of tasks. He doesn't realize what a complex and serious situation he is in.*

"I shall be obliged to inform the relevant authorities about Sister Bibianna's nocturnal expeditions," she declared equally calmly. Life finally appeared in Zakroczymski's lusterless eyes.

His narrow pupils seemed to run Zofia through like daggers. "Your own fortune may be of little concern to you, but I doubt you are equally indifferent to your sister's fate."

"But you made her a promise . . . How . . . how I despise you!" he stammered.

"No matter, I am not concerned about your respect," she coolly replied, "but I do want a *professional*" — she emphasized this — "to perform a competent autopsy. I expect you to amend your report by twelve o'clock today and send it to whom it may concern. Or deliver it in person, for there can be no delay, in view of the need to identify the killer and also to save your reputation. Magistrate Klossowitz will be paying a working visit to Helcel House today. At noon?" she said, rising to her feet, and then added: "I think my fifteen minutes are up — thank you for sparing me your time."

And she left, her skirts shuffling across the disinfected floorboards of the consulting room.

❧

Indeed, as the trumpeter on the tower of St. Mary's began to play the second part of the hourly signal, Dr. Zakroczymski, his face tense and rigid, knocked at the door of Mother Zaleska's office; meanwhile, instead of the squat figure of the mother superior, sitting behind the wide desk was the increasingly impatient investigating magistrate, Klossowitz. Zofia, Mother Zaleska, and Sister Alojza were there too, standing beneath the portraits of the founders.

The previous half hour — for Klossowitz had been brought in by Alojza at half past eleven — had been spent on an exchange of nasty remarks between the magistrate and the professor's wife, who endeavored to expound her reasoning, and to persuade him that the watchman could not have committed the murder. But he had requited each bit of her elaborate statement with a coarse comment about the garrulous nature of women. Not much more of that and eventually she'd have revealed, too soon, that this was not actually about Mrs. Krzywda's death but Mrs. Mohr's, but she didn't want Klossowitz to dismiss "these fairy tales" out of hand and leave, so for the time being she focused on this death, regarded by everyone as murder from the start. However, the atmosphere was extremely intense. By the time Zakroczymski finally crossed the threshold, it felt as if, had he rashly entered the room with a lighted cigarette, the toxic fumes in there would have exploded, reducing the entire costly edifice to a heap of rubble.

After the standard exchange of bows, Zakroczymski cast an eye at Zofia, then at Klossowitz, then at Zofia again, before finally starting to speak, rather haltingly.

"A doctor's work . . . is like the work of an inventor who toils into the small hours, trying to fathom the mysteries of the universe . . . sometimes he doesn't add a line to his notes for weeks on end, until suddenly in the middle of the night he cries, 'Eureka!'"

Klossowitz looked at him with suspicion, but for the time being didn't stop him.

"And it's similar for a doctor. He thinks he has made the correct diagnosis, but something keeps bothering him, something won't give him peace . . . and all of a sudden he comes to an entirely new conclusion. That's what has happened here. At first, guided by the age of the deceased and the lack of evidence—"

"Just a moment," interrupted Klossowitz. "You didn't examine Mrs. Krzywda's body—there was more than enough evidence!"

Thrown off orbit, Zakroczymski had to gather his thoughts, and stood blinking nervously.

"No," he began, "I'm not talking about that demise at all. This is to do with the death of Antonina Mohr, née Januszkiewicz, aged eighty-one. Mistaken for death as a result of hypothermia, when in fact . . ."

Only now did Klossowitz realize that he had been set up. He rose to his feet, almost overturning the chair, and then, picking up a document file from the desk, he roared: "This is un-for-giv-a-ble. The police force has work to do! Real work! Here I am, frittering away my time in office hours, listening to tales about old ladies who died in attics while there are thefts, adultery, assaults, and brawling going on in Cracow! What a total lack of respect for the police force!" He wagged a threatening finger at them all and added, "Total and utter lack of respect!"

Zakroczymski, however, who had already endured one unpleasant conversation today, lost his temper and puffed himself up; now they stood facing each other like the angry rival males of some aggressive species; the females who chanced to be in the office did not protest — in the natural world they'd probably have kept to the edge of the clearing, chewing the grass, but for lack of anything to eat, they stopped at silent observation of the conflict.

"I'm trying to explain medical complexities to you, and you're telling me it's a waste of time? When a citizen reports to a policeman, and when he's a medical doctor who may have made an erroneous diagnosis and in time has come to have doubts, and who might be able to help expose the murderer who's lurking here, then at least in the name of common human decency —"

"That's enough of your decency! I'm trying to conduct an inquiry! An inquiry!"

"And this is part of that inquiry!"

"Absolutely not. It is irrelevant. The inquiry concerns a murder, and that is just a case of someone collapsing and dying."

"Actually, of being poisoned and dying."

"Poisoned?" Klossowitz simmered down a little and poked a finger into his overtight collar. "Poisoned with what?"

"Cyanide. There's plenty to indicate that we're not dealing with death by natural causes, not least the stains on the body."

The steam went out of Klossowitz and slowly, with small, almost imperceptible movements, he went back to his recently abandoned chair, then sat down at the desk again.

"We have an additional circumstance, too," said one of the female deer in full courtship colors from her corner of the clearing, "namely the dessert."

Both men looked at her with a patent lack of comprehension.

"The last thing Mrs. Mohr ate was a dessert. And curiously, it was an almond mousse. It's a well-known fact that in contact with water, potassium cyanide gives off . . ."

"As a result of hydrolysis it exudes hydrogen cyanide, which does in fact smell like bitter almonds," said Zakroczymski, coming to her rescue.

"Quite so. Which made it all the easier for the murderer to kill the victim."

Throughout the conversation no one had paid any special attention to the mother superior, who was now the picture of misery. At first she'd been standing, but had soon sat down, and the longer the exchange of comments had continued, the more she had slumped in her armchair. By now she was half supine, her head drooping, her elbows on the armrests and her fingers knotted together, making her look like Stańczyk the jester in Matejko's famous painting, in a wimple instead of a tricorn cap and bells. If not just one, but two murders had been committed at Helcel House in barely a week, the reputation of this sanctuary lay in ruins, and the entire fortune of the Helcels and the Treutlers had gone to waste.

"Will it be possible to find evidence of poison in the contents of the stomach so many days after the death?" asked Klossowitz finally.

"The potential exists. I've made that suggestion in my amended report," said the doctor, taking a sheet of paper from his briefcase. "Fortunately, exhumation won't be necessary, because the body is still within the grounds of Helcel House, properly refrigerated."

"In that case," said the magistrate, sighing heavily and casting a reluctant glance at Zofia, "the body will have to be sent to the forensic medicine unit . . ." At this point Mother Zaleska groaned. "Or as a last resort, if conditions allow for it, a doctor will have to be summoned to perform an autopsy here."

"They do allow for it, they do," said Alojza, speaking for the first time since she had greeted Klossowitz in the office doorway.

"Excellent. It is ... twenty past twelve. May I use the telephone?"

Zakroczymski stared inquiringly at Zofia; feeling his gaze on her, she turned to face him and by slowly blinking she indicated to him that the matter had been duly settled.

✤

"It could be that we Cracovians are asking for trouble by opening that theater—just listen to this, my dear." Ignacy rustled the newspaper as he folded it in two to make it easier to bring the questionably illegible column closer to his nose. "There's been a theatrical scandal in Budapest involving a Polish singer, Madame Nussbaum. *'On entering the rehearsal room at the opera with her husband, she ran into Count Vasquez-Marron, who was escorting his own wife, also an opera singer . . .'*"

"What times we live in," muttered Zofia, "a count married to a singer! Maybe she's a circus rider, too?"

"*'. . . also an opera singer . . .'*"

"On the other hand," she interrupted him again, "what sort of a name for a count is that? It's quite absurd."

"*'. . . to the rehearsal. On seeing the count, Mr. Nussbaum ran up to him, crying: "You scoundrel! At the last performance you booed my wife!" At which the count slapped Nussbaum twice on the cheek. The incident took place before witnesses . . .'* I really can't see a thing by this lamp . . .

anyway, the manager canceled the lady's subsequent performances. *'Furthermore a duel took place . . .'"*

"Excuse me, madam," said Franciszka, coming in from the kitchen to take away the tea tray. She leaned toward Zofia and asked in a whisper: "Am I to tidy the tomb by myself this year?"

"'. . . a duel took place between Nussbaum and Count Vasquez. The result of the duel is not known.'"

Zofia was dumbstruck; for a while she couldn't utter a word, though not because of Ignacy's rather boring anecdote. How could she have forgotten that All Saints' Day was approaching, and with it the traditional visit to the family tomb? Indeed, October was almost over. How could that be?

The events of the past few weeks had eaten a hole in her calendar — she couldn't think where the time had gone; all she could remember was the gala opening of the theater, and then, in extremely fine detail, her visits to Helcel House. But all the other days, mornings, and evenings had gone by without leaving a trace in her mind. Something must have been going on, someone must have chosen the dishes for their meals, supervised the cleaning of the silver and the insertion of lavender between the sheets; someone must have hired the carter to bring coal for the winter, but all these things had happened beyond the consciousness of Zofia Turbotyńska.

"Have the other girl go."

"The other girl, madam?"

"What's her name . . . Anielka? Anielka. The new girl."

As she gripped the tray full of teacups, side plates, and a bunch of knives and forks like a bundle of silver brushwood, Franciszka cast her an uncomprehending look.

"But you dismissed her, madam."

"I did? What a suggestion! Why would I have dismissed her?"

"She broke four cups from your wedding-present dinner service. Through negligence, although I told her to take special care."

Ignacy cleared his throat discreetly from his armchair, then started cutting the article about the Nussbaums out of the newspaper, to stick in his album of curiosities. And so the murder at Helcel House really had preoccupied her as much as dissecting a salamander's or tortoise's intestines usually preoccupied Ignacy; his students liked to say that when he was dissecting you could nail him to the floor and he'd never notice.

"Of course, of course," she said with restraint, "then have the next one come."

"But you haven't sent to the agency for a next one, madam."

"Why don't you go along tomorrow and ask, Franciszka? And when she comes, show her this and that and send her to the cemetery right away. Or you and I can go, I'm not sure yet."

Franciszka nodded.

"That's all for now. We shan't be needing you again today," said Zofia.

"Thank you, madam, and good night."

"Good night."

"Good night, Franciszka," said Ignacy from his corner, and then addressed his wife again. "Extraordinary news, my dear, just listen to this. Dr. Jordan is still looking for his stolen bicycle, and is offering a reward of one hundred crowns. *'A brand-new bicycle, with pneumatic tires, white handlebars, and marked with the word* Spezial. *The spokes were decorated with off-yellow crepe paper and tied with string, which was no obstacle to riding it'* . . ."

"Ignacy," asked Zofia, sounding exasperated, "are you thinking of looking for Dr. Jordan's bicycle? Are you eager to win the hundred-crown reward?"

Disconcerted by the sharpness of her tone, Ignacy folded the newspaper on his knees.

"I think," he said slowly, a little offended, "pinning down the culprit would be an extremely public-spirited act."

❧

If one were to look down on Cracow from above, from a point higher than the towers of St. Mary's Basilica and the Wawel Cathedral, and if one could see through stone, as well as the roofs and walls of railway carriages, one would know that at precisely 10:34 a.m., just as Zofia stepped on board the train, Dr. Teodor Chościak placed a report on the desk of investigating magistrate Klossowitz, headed: *Autopsy performed on the body of Antonina Mohr née Januszkiewicz, age 81, dated 30.X.1893,* and concluding with the key statement: *The forensic medical opinion contradicts earlier findings that the cause of death was hypothermia. Following additional chemical analysis of the contents of the stomach and intestine, in which considerable amounts of potassium cyanide were found, there can be no doubt that the cause of death was poisoning by means of the said potassium cyanide.*

But no one has such all-pervading eyesight, so the co-incidental timing of these two events would never come to light.

The people of Cracow were used to a stuffy atmosphere; in fact, they were brought up, matured, and died in one, but the stuffiness prevailing in the second-class carriage on the Galician Railway of Archduke Carl Ludwig was intolerable, even for a woman like Zofia, who regularly frequented the stuffiest of drawing rooms, last aired in the days of Emperor Joseph II. Here was the combined odor of sweaty wool, of male and female bodies, of mothballs that permeated the winter furs lately brought out of the wardrobe, of meals consumed in the station buffet, provisions crammed into traveling bags, and the coal smoke that shrouded the entire train.

Small but neat, the station at Bochnia was like many others: a pair of two-story buildings joined by a ground-floor waiting room. But on the same side as the tracks there was a platform roof running the entire length of the waiting room, supported by about ten wooden arches, some wider, some narrower, with a latticed balustrade below, spinning-top-shaped pinnacles above and, over the exit to the tracks, an ornate gable with a sign saying BOCHNIA. All this fine openwork in lacy patterns made the place look like a cross between an Alpine *pension* and a Moorish palace.

Beyond the station things only got worse — no more Alps, no more Alhambra, nothing but the usual shabby Galicia. Zofia passed a couple of Jews in midargument, and several ragged porters, for whom the handful of passengers from Cracow guaranteed no income, boarded a very tatty cab and told the driver to take her to the marketplace. Almost all the houses were the picture of poverty and despair — many of them were not much more than country cottages: small, hardly off the ground, with little wooden porches and roofs sagging with age, covered in rotten shingle or poor-quality tin. Here and there, the tops of mine shafts with metal wheels protruded — after all, this was a mining town, though it was really just mud and decay. Worse than that, there were gaping holes in the plaster, revealing bricks or more often reeds stuck together with clay, and wooden beams underneath them. In the small gardens the remains of late apples still hung on the trees. Here and there was a rotten balustrade or a single loose shutter hanging off a hinge; above the low shop doors hung small signs, crookedly painted by bad itinerant artists.

Fortunately for Zofia it was a Tuesday, not a Thursday, the regular market day in Bochnia — two days later the local poor would be reinforced by the visiting poor: aged beggars, Jewish ragpickers, peasants from the neighboring villages as long as they had the strength to get here, selling what they had to sell, and drinking away the money in the tavern. The marketplace was a large dirt floor with a central column supporting the lopsided statue of a saint — no, on closer inspection through her lorgnette it turned out to be a lopsided statue of King Kazimierz the Great. Around it were what must have been Bochnia's most prominent buildings: a church with a hideous wooden bell tower; a veritable dog kennel of the kind found in only the poorest villages; a local administrative building topped with a broken roof, resembling a synagogue; and some houses, a few of which even had upper floors. One of them must have belonged to Mrs. Mohr, or rather to her heirs — a fine inheritance, undoubtedly. Zofia inspected the facades and shop signs: Zimmerspitz's paper, school supplies, and haberdashery shop; Feniger's restaurant and his honeys from Janowice, Dalmatian and Hungarian wines from his own vineyards in Sárospatak; and there was Urbański's: a wide sign, painted by a very unskilled hand. She went into each in turn; Feniger's was too crowded for her to ask any questions, and Zimmerspitz's was empty apart from an old salesman with a nasty, sallow face, like a shriveled lemon — she could tell at first glance he was the type that doesn't talk but only listens and takes mental notes. What Zofia needed was a different sort of person entirely. She headed for Urbański's shop.

It was a colonial store like any other, but not as lavish as the ones in Cracow: it had dark fittings, jars of toffee, small kegs full of dates and raisins, and loaves of sugar neatly aligned on the shelves. She looked around her as she waited for the brawny matron behind the counter to serve her—this was sure to be Mrs. Urbańska, keeping a firm hand on the shop and also on Mr. Urbański, if he were still alive, of course, and hadn't politely died and left the firm to his widow for her sole management.

"Are you just passing through, madam, or staying awhile?" she asked at last.

"I? Oh, I have come to buy salt from its point of origin. I like products of the best quality, and plenty can happen to it between Bochnia and Cracow. Something added here, something removed there . . ."

Urbańska agreed sympathetically.

"And how do you like Bochnia?" Without letting Zofia answer, she smiled broadly and began to brag: "Our Bochnia's beautiful, isn't it? Ever since the railway arrived, and it's coming on for thirty years now, there's so much prosperity! We've erected a fine statue of King Kazimierz, Matejko himself drew the—"

"Matejko? Well, I never . . ." said Zofia, shaking her head, and thinking to herself that even the great master's hand could occasionally slip.

"We've such big schools, all brand-new, only just launched, one for the boys, the other, St. Kinga's, for the girls, designed in Vienna. And just three days ago we had the grand opening of the new county council . . . an architect from Cracow . . . Canon Father Wąsikiewicz blessed it, Canon Father Lipiński said Mass, the entire council was there, all the officials, everyone, simply everyone, the whole of Bochnia came! A feast for sixty, the chairman raised a toast to His Majesty, to the Bishop of Tarnów . . ." Mrs. Urbańska was almost out of breath, but Zofia patiently let her gabble on, while plucking at the finger of a glove. "We've got a singing society, too, it's called the Lute; they sing so beautifully; my husband is a member. It's so nice . . . and there's the Falcons sports club—they've just opened a section for cyclists. Yes, please don't be surprised, all sorts of novelties are arriving here"—she was all but blushing with joy—"even bicycles! You're sure to think that out here in the provinces we live in ignorance, but we do visit Cracow, yes we do, I even go to the theater . . ."

"I was at the gala opening," said Zofia, unable to control herself. "I didn't really want to go, I can't bear the crowd at first nights, but my dear friend Countess Żeleńska insisted that I do her the honor of joining her in her box. Mr. Asnyk's prologue was a great work of poetry."

There was no answer to that—a countess and a gala opening trumped every other card, even the new county council.

"It's a lovely town" was all Mrs. Urbańska could finally gasp, as if she had run out of air.

"The countess and I are organizing a raffle for the benefit of scrofulous children. She recently went to reside at Helcel House . . . in the very best rooms, of course. And I think one of your fellow townswomen has been living there, too, Mrs. Mohr . . ."

"Mrs. Mohr, widow of Judge Mohr, yes, I know her, I do."

"Or rather you did. The poor lady has passed away."

"Passed away? Ha," said the shopkeeper philosophically, "she was old, and so she died."

"She had a house here, didn't she?"

"Yes, she did. Over there" — she nodded in a vague direction — "left her by her husband. He was a Bochnian through and through, an important man, he was a judge in Bilsk and then in Cracow. But it's a few years since he passed away . . . his parents are buried on Oracka Street, here, but as for him, you know . . . the squire, he's in Rakowicki Cemetery, with his wife's family," she added, scowling at this betrayal of his lesser homeland.

"Is Mrs. Fikalska buried in Cracow too, or did her husband have her buried here?"

"Not at all, her husband died before she did, in my parents-in-law's day, a good thirty years ago . . ."

"How can he have died when he's alive? Alfons Fikalski," Zofia retorted.

"Yes, I've heard that Mr. Fikalski Junior is in fine form," hissed Mrs. Urbańska, "like a pig in clover. But you can't say the same of his wife."

"Well, quite, that's who I was asking about. Is it long since she died?"

Mrs. Urbańska clutched her sides, laughing. "How can she have died when she's alive?" she roared. "Who's there in the house on Solna Street, then? Though truly I don't know what sort of a life it is: all alone, shut in her room, tied to the bed — sometimes she yells so loud it carries the length of the street. All because of him. Haven't you heard?" A glimmer of excitement flared in Mrs. Urbańska's eye. "No? He was a womanizer, ugh! And a wastrel. She was from a good family, they had a shop, the corner house. She brought him that as a dowry because she was an only child, but Fikalski . . . was such a ladies' man. He'd organize a ball, lead the figures of the cotillion or the mazurka, he'd play cards, he would. A year and a half it took him. Eighteen months!" She banged her fist on the counter; she had quite a fist to bang, and the counter was pretty solid too. "And he'd squandered the entire dowry. Goods, shop, house, and all. And he was left with debts, too. Her parents had thought they'd live out their days in peace under their own roof, but they had to go and live in a corner of some relatives' place in Opatów. And the girl went mad. Mrs. Fikalska went off her head — she lost her wits completely. She just lies in bed, shouting. If you go over there, to Solna Street, and stand outside her cousins' house, sometimes you'll hear her."

"And what exactly does she shout?"

"Nothing, just made-up stuff, gibberish. Sometimes she sings — well, they say she's singing, but to my mind she's roaring like an animal. But what will become of her now, if Mrs. Mohr is dead?"

"What does it have to do with Mrs. Mohr?"

"They say," said the shopkeeper, leaning over the counter confidentially, "it's not the parish priest who provides care for her at all, but Mrs. Mohr who paid for it. She knew Mrs. Fikalska's parents; they were friends — Judge Mohr lived right next door to them, and when she found out that they'd both passed on in Opatów, she resolved to care for their wretched daughter. They say she wants for nothing, and yet the whole business has aged her—she looks like an old woman, with matted white hair . . ."

"While Mr. Fikalski is flourishing."

"Flourishing?" Mrs. Urbańska banged her fist on the counter again, making the glass lids of the jars of toffees and marshmallows jingle. "There's no justice in this world."

"Maybe not," muttered Zofia partly to her, and partly to herself, "but maybe someone tried to see justice done and paid for it with their life . . . Well, here we are passing the time chatting, but I've come on an errand. The very best, authentic Bochnia salt—I presume I can buy it here?"

"Yes, madam, the very best salt of all." This time Mrs. Urbańska struck her own chest, which was just as solid as the counter, so she did herself no harm.

❧

The return train rattled along at an even pace; the fug was no less awful than in the morning, but Zofia was oblivious—she sat pressed in between a bearded man in a thick frock coat and a thin student, or maybe shop assistant, of Jewish appearance, and looked through the notes in her little book. Mrs. Mohr had had an excellent memory for faces, so there could be no question of her failing to recognize Fikalski—especially if she had provided so generously to support his mad wife. Had she wanted to warn Lidia Walaszek née Campiani about him? Could Fikalski, who had got it into his empty head to become a bigamist and squander a second dowry, have been capable of committing murder—both murders? Supposing he'd schemed to do away with the old lady who was trying to foil his plans —had he teamed up with Mrs. Krzywda and offered her money to spike the almond dessert with cyanide? But later on, it turned out he had no money, because he'd long since frittered away everything he, his wife, and his parents-in-law possessed—all he had left were the clothes on his back and the hope of a dowry, the wealth of the Campianis of Udine . . . Maybe he'd actually been planning to marry and leave for sunny Italy where the lemons ripen, without paying the fee for the murder? Either way, Mrs. Krzywda had revolted. Or perhaps her conscience had started to bother her? *A nice round sum seems to quell most people's pangs of guilt*, thought Zofia, *whereas a sum that's expected but never paid is going to increase them immensely . . . So the disappointed almswoman blackmails Fikalski, things are getting hot for him, it's an urgent, dangerous situation. He loses his sangfroid and strangles the poisoner . . . no, he doesn't strangle her. He was at the theater—I saw him there myself.*

Though the train was gently rocking her to sleep, she tried to retain her clarity of mind. *The watchman? Could he be the real . . . no, not murderer, but the tool in the murderer's hand? In the end,* she thought, *the fact that he defended the honor of his beloved does not exclude him from also being the murderer. A large sum of money from Fikalski would allow him to marry the woman with whom he has been united by Cupid's arrow, fired rather rashly down the corridors of Hel-cel House. And so: Fikalski commissions Krzywda to poison Mohr, then blackmail ensues, and another commission, carried out with less finesse than the first . . .*

"Excuse me! Excuse me!" cried the bearded man in the frock coat. "Excuse me!" And with a fat leg tightly wrapped in trouser material, he tried to squeeze through to the exit.

"Is this Cracow already?" asked Zofia in a drowsy voice. "Cracow station?"

The thin student, or shop assistant, silently nodded.

❧

Hardly had she crossed the threshold, hardly had she called out: "Ignacy, I went all the way to Bochnia to buy you first-class salt!" — which was not in fact greeted with an outburst or even a rumble of satisfaction — hardly had she removed three hatpins — one with a brass cicada, one with a little crescent moon made of garnets, and one with a turquoise stone — than Franciszka was at her side.

"Madam," she whispered, vigorously wiping her hands on her apron, "this afternoon a messenger came with a letter from Sister Alojza. An urgent one. The master asked what it was, but I merely replied that it was to do with the servants, and he didn't ask further questions."

"Quite right," Zofia said, taking hold of one of the pins

and hastening to open the envelope with it in lieu of a paper knife. She ran her eyes down the lines of Sister Alojza's neat, clerical handwriting.

Helcel House for the Indigent, Cracow, 31.X.1893

Esteemed Mrs. Turbotyńska,

With a heavy heart, placing my suffering in the care of Jesus Christ, Savior of the world, I must admit that you are right: Mrs. Mohr was indeed murdered. This morning, as soon as Dr. Chościak confirmed that she was poisoned, investigating magistrate Klossowitz launched an inquiry and before noon sent some policemen to us.

You were correct, though the result of the inquiry prompts no joy. Not only is the watchman in prison, it was the cook who did the poisoning. It turns out that Mrs. Sedlaczek served a lengthy jail sentence for poisoning her husband, and she was sent down by none other than the late lamented Judge Mohr, Mrs. Mohr's husband. The poor woman fell victim to hideous revenge for the fact that a fair trial placed a husband-killer behind bars. What times we live in!

God bless you for all your kind help,

Alojza, Sister of the Infant Jesus

Zofia folded the sheet of paper and put it back in the envelope, and the envelope into her pocket.

She examined herself in the mirror. Bochnia had tired

her a little, but the turnabout in the investigation had pumped fresh blood into her veins — her color had returned, and her eyes were glittering again like gemstones.

"Ignacy," she announced in a dramatic tone as she entered the drawing room, "we need to install a telephone. I cannot imagine organizing the raffle for scrofulous children without it. I'll be doing nothing but running to Helcel House and back again . . . See to it, please, Ignacy!"

CHAPTER X

❧

In which Zofia does not agree with the Cracow Times *but adheres to ancient customs, and Cracow suffers an irretrievable loss. A day of triumph changes into a day of surprises, accusations are put off for now, and Rakowicki Cemetery is visited by Odysseus, who has something to say on the subject of every grave.*

Of late, Zofia Turbotyńska had found few things as annoying (except for clumsy maids, Mrs. Zaremba's blather, and of course, the inept Cracow police, incapable of perceiving the obvious) as the announcements that kept appearing in the *Cracow Times,* such as: *Instead of buying lamps and wreaths for the family grave, Mrs. So-and-So has sent twenty-five crowns to the Brother Albert Refuge to buy fuel for the poor,* or: *Instead of a wreath on the grave, Dr. and Mrs. Such-and-Such have donated ten crowns for hungry children.*

It was all the fault of the wretched letter that had reached the editors of the newspaper less than a week earlier. *Instead of wreaths, memorial lamps, and fripperies that only bring the living the satisfaction of amour-propre and seem reminiscent of pagan ritual, how much more positive it is to donate a sum of money to charity in the name of the dead whom we are mourning,* wrote the anonymous author. The editors of the *Cracow Times,* who had long since disapproved of this allegedly pagan custom imported from the West, with an obstinacy worthy of better things, concurred with this absurd idea and were zealously stirring up their readers.

"As you know, Ignacy," explained Zofia, "I have nothing against philanthropy — on the contrary, I devote a great deal of my time and energy to it. Especially in recent weeks. Today I am going to Helcel . . ."

"Off to Helcel House again," said Ignacy, casting her a suspicious glance. "I can't think why you spend so much time there. Particularly when it has been a dangerous place of late. There are so many other foundations in town. You could devote yourself to poor children . . ."

"But that's exactly what I am doing. Scrofulous children," she retorted, but not as confidently as she would have wished, for it was some time since she had given any thought to the raffle, "and I am trying to obtain prizes from the mother superior. For children indeed. Countess Żeleńska is providing her patronage, and she is a resident there . . . as you are aware, it involves a lot of trouble . . . courtesy . . . and visits."

"Quite so, quite so," he said, nodding, but still looking mistrustful.

"So of course charity matters, but how can one let All Saints' and All Souls' go by without decorating the family grave? Can you imagine such a thing? Thousands of people coming to the cemetery only to see the Turbotyńskis' neglected tomb standing out from its neighbors like a sort of romantic ruin? That would be a scandal!"

"I think you may be exaggerating a little, Zofia," replied her husband. "Besides, I suspect people may have more important things to do at the public cemetery than examine the grave of my dear departed parents."

Zofia turned a deaf ear to this remark.

"What about all the announcements? Nothing but cant and hypocrisy! Believe me, there's nothing worse than hypocrisy!"

"Mm," he mumbled.

"In any case, as long as *I* have something to say about it," she continued, "your father and mother's grave will look as a grave at such a fine site deserves. In a prominent row, far away from the suicides."

The Glodt family had been laid to rest in the main cemetery in Przemyśl, of course; the oldest stone from the ancestral tomb had been transferred there from the old cemetery after it was closed down, but it was hard to feel proud of the plain plinth and its long-outmoded inscriptions. Whereas the old Turbotyńskis were buried in the Cracow public cemetery, near the chapel, in a small but elegant tomb, erected according to the fashion of the time in neo-Gothic style and discreetly adorned with the family coat of arms.

"But of course, my dear, you do have something to say about it. When it comes to decorating the tomb, I am counting on you as usual," said Ignacy, then went back to reading the newspaper, in which, thought Zofia, further buffoons were sure to be informing all and sundry of their great generosity, as meted out in solid Austrian currency.

❧

Tomorrow was All Souls' Day, and the weather was unfavorable, yet on the way into the cemetery, one had to push through a serried throng of people in heavy overcoats, furs, and capes. Zofia couldn't bear crowds, but she had no alternative — the grave must be tidied and decorated today — All Saints' Day, November the first — to look smart first thing on All Souls' Day, November the second, and stir the envy of other families. It mattered even more to her than the inquiry — she had answered Sister Alojza's letter with a succinct note, thanking her for the information and promising ardent prayers for Helcel House. *If Fikalski were going to run away he'd have done it long ago. Half a day won't save anyone, not even the watchman,* she reasoned, *and the grave won't tidy itself. One should know one's priorities.*

On the eve of the holiday, she was too busy to bring the

new maid along, so it was Franciszka who had come to the cemetery with her and was now clearing the way for them with a wreath and a birch broom for sweeping the grave. Now and then Zofia saw familiar faces — Mrs. Fabiańska, Mrs. Hrehorowicz, the Sokulska sisters — while noting with satisfaction that not all the ladies in this city had let themselves be taken in by the *Cracow Times,* and after the All Saints' Day Mass were hurrying to Rakowicki Cemetery to dress their family graves, as any decent Cracow matriarch should. Outside the chapel — another grand edifice sponsored by the Helcels — she ran into one of them, her cousin Józefa, whom she hadn't seen since the memorable dinner. Whatever one might say, when it came to cemetery traditions one could certainly rely on her.

"Ghastly weather, isn't it?" said Mrs. Dutkiewicz to open the conversation.

In customary Cracow style they exchanged a few remarks about the climate, recalled how fine it had been on All Saints' last year, how sunny, how unusually warm, how low the barometer had fallen then, how the wind hadn't blown out the memorial candles or knocked over the flowers, which in this year's conditions would probably be reduced to bald stalks in a couple of days.

Apart from the weather, the favorite topic of conversation at the cemetery was health, especially the health of more or less important people. Thus with the acquaintances encountered one discussed Count Tarnowski's chill and Cardinal Dunajewski's bronchitis, but also Councilor

Horowitz's nasty ailments. So not surprisingly, the great artist Matejko's ulcers were eagerly and lengthily debated.

"But my dear Zofia, have you heard? Matejko is very ill," said Mrs. Dutkiewicz earnestly, adjusting her hat.

"It's sure to pass, Józefa," declared Zofia in the tone of an expert.

"I wouldn't be so sure of that, cousin. Last night Professor Paszkowski and three of his colleagues were summoned to his house. I saw them from the window."

Zofia felt a stab of envy—just as her cousin intended. Ignacy was not a medical celebrity; in fact, he had ceased to practice years ago, but to fetch someone like Paszkowski all the way from St. Anne's Street when Turbotyński lived just around the corner . . .

"In *medical circles*," she said firmly, "they say that Matejko's last trip to Karlsbad to take the waters has put him back on his feet splendidly. Rest assured, many a masterpiece has yet to appear from his reliable hand."

"If you say so, my dear," conceded Mrs. Dutkiewicz surprisingly meekly.

"Ignacy and I will be sure to come and light a candle for Jan tomorrow," said Zofia in a conciliatory tone. "Perhaps we'll meet."

"Much appreciated, my dear. It's sure to be the last time at the old site. My sons and I have bought a new plot and are making plans for a mausoleum, so we'll have Jan moved into it."

"Really? In which part of the cemetery?"

"In the newest part, near the Warsaw road."

"Ah, of course. *There*," said Zofia, her smile as radiant as it was insincere. "Farewell, Józefa!"

Then, as if to thin air, she said: "And I can see our grave from here!" She turned to the cook, who had been shifting from foot to foot for quite a time, perhaps out of impatience, perhaps because of the cold. "Come along, Franciszka, we've work to do."

❧

Once she had carefully tidied the grave, brushed it clean of leaves, and weeded out every blade of grass and every timid clump of moss, Franciszka left the field to her mistress, who opened a large traveling bag and started fetching out a complete set of accessories: candles with tinfoil collars wide enough to stop the dripping wax from staining the stone; small lamps of various shapes; wreaths, garlands, and crosses, some made of fir, others of russet-and-gold everlasting flowers. Gradually she used them to decorate every free space on the pretty neo-Gothic monument, which entirely vanished beneath them. She lit the candles, inspected the result of her work with satisfaction, and then slowly extinguished all the flames — no one was going to notice them today, and she didn't want to pay for the candles twice. Now they were merely waiting for the woman employed to keep an eye on the decorations, who cost far less today than to-morrow, when almost everyone would leave their own maid or hired warden to keep watch.

"Get a move on, Franciszka," she boomed as soon as she saw the woman approaching. "We still have plenty to do today!"

And in less than fifteen minutes, after squeezing through the crowd again—in which she noticed that the widows in mourning did most of the pushing and shoving, evidently regarding themselves as more important than anyone else on this particular day—they reached the gate.

"There's Mrs. Dutkiewicz again," whispered Franciszka, pointing ahead.

Zofia squinted.

"What do you mean?" She snorted. "That is someone else entirely. Józefa has gone almost completely gray."

Franciszka shrugged. "How should I know? In hats all the ladies look alike."

This time Zofia shrugged, and then looked around for a cab. Soon after, shuddering as the cold leather seat sent a chill through every layer of her clothing, she was sitting beside Franciszka in a rather uncomfortable vehicle. They set off.

She gazed gloomily through the small window, remembering her first visit to Helcel House at the beginning of October, on that sunny day she'd have been happy to describe in a poem, rhyming "sunlight" with "bright" and "autumn crocus" with "focus." Meanwhile the long, dismal central European autumn had set in, a time of foul weather, wading through mud, and lethal drafts, which every self-respecting Cracow lady dreaded even more than cholera, for cholera did little harm, but a cold draft was as grim a reaper as the Black Death in the Dark Ages. The trees lining the road were almost entirely stripped of their leaves by now, revealing black clumps — balls of mistletoe, with rooks and ravens lurking among them.

"There," said Zofia, handing Franciszka twenty cents, "on you go. Here's the money for a cab fare of up to fifteen minutes."

Then she clambered out of the cab in front of Helcel House and told the driver: "My servant will pay — you will drop her outside the house or once fifteen minutes have elapsed, and that's the limit. But with watch in hand, not at your discretion!"

The driver nodded and halfheartedly raised his cap. Zofia walked off, spreading a hand to keep hold of her hat as gusts of decidedly autumnal wind attempted to tear it from her head.

Inspired by her sense of recent triumph when, in a single morning, she had subdued both Dr. Zakroczymski and Klossowitz, now she intended to press on like a storm, like King John Sobieski's hussars at the Battle of Vienna, like an unvanquished heroine treading her enemies' corpses underfoot as she closed her gloved hands on the neck of the guilty party. Fikalski, that repulsive philanderer, dowry hunter, virtual bigamist, and out-and-out murderer, would squirm at her feet this very day!

"Please summon the police!" she cried, entering the office as if it were her own dining room.

"We've done that already," said Mother Zaleska in a sepulchral tone.

"Have you? Splendid!" said Zofia, in overdrive, though she wasn't sure what was going on. Could someone else have seen through Fikalski's machinations? Could the police have come up to the mark at last, or had Alojza managed to put two and two together? She reined in her triumphant mood as well as her physical speed, came to a stop in the middle of the office, and looked around attentively.

Mother Zaleska was not sitting at her desk but a little further off; the place of honor was occupied by another nun, whom Zofia hadn't seen here before . . . But of course! A couple of years ago, on the memorable day when Helcel House was opened, she had been standing beside Count Tarnowski himself. Zofia summoned up her rather rusty French.

"Allow me to introduce myself," she said. "Zofia Turbotyńska, wife of Professor Turbotyński."

"What a lovely name," replied the nun, looking at her from under half-closed eyelids; of course she was incapable of repeating it.

"Excuse me for not introducing you," said Mother Zaleska, waking up. "This is Mother Juhel, our order's mother superior, who oversaw the construction of this house."

Compared with Mother Zaleska, who must have lost at

least ten pounds, if not an entire stone from worry in recent weeks, Caroline Juhel was in the pink: small and plump, with a head as round as a radish under her wimple.

"What brings you here, madam?"

"The sisters and I are planning a small act of charity. Under the patronage of Countess Żeleńska."

"Another lovely name," she said with dignity, "yet I fear that in the present circumstances . . ."

"Mrs. Turbotyńska is fully acquainted with these matters," added Alojza, knowing that Mother Zaleska was unlikely to come to Zofia's defense; she couldn't actually speak French, but she understood the odd word, so with some clumsy hand gestures she made it known to Zofia that she was to translate. "She has already helped us greatly."

Zofia viewed this act of courage with gratitude, and was reminded of Mr. Kieszkowski's French pug, which was often just as valiant as Alojza. Reassured by these words, Mother Juhel adopted a benign expression, which meant nothing, of course, then leapt to her feet abruptly—as did Mother Zaleska—and announced that she was going to settle into her room. Evidently even she believed the trouble at Helcel House had gone too far, so she'd decided to move from the order's headquarters on Warszawska Street for a few days and see to matters on the spot.

Only now could Zofia find out why the nuns had summoned the police of their own accord, but she didn't know where to start; luckily Alojza asked first. "But how did you know that Mrs. Czystogórska has gone missing?"

Zofia blinked nervously, but tried not to let it show.

"Oh, this is a small town," she said, laughing, or rather blowing air through her nose a few times. "But gossip is not the same as fact. Would you please tell me what you know?"

"We only know what you know, and that's nothing at all. Last night she went to bed, but this morning she'd vanished. None of her belongings are missing," said Mother Zaleska reluctantly. Then, with a mixture of fury and despair, she listed the losses: "First Mrs. Mohr disappeared and we found her dead, apparently poisoned by the cook. The kitchen maid has had to replace her. Then another corpse, Mrs. Krzywda's, and we lost the watchman. His duties have been assumed by one of the gardeners—there's not much more to do in the garden and the orchard at this time of year—and now a third old lady has vanished into thin air, Mrs. Czystogórska. And I don't know who else I'm going to lose—the chaplain, Father Mazurkiewicz? One of the sisters? As soon as I look around I'll find that Dr. Wiszniewski himself has murdered Mrs. Czystogórska . . . *Kyrie eleison!*"

"The watchman didn't do it," said Zofia, interrupting her with a dismissive wave. "As for the cook, I cannot be sure, but even if she is guilty, in the words of the poet, we should punish the hand, and not the blind sword. She was just a blind sword, persuaded to do evil by another."

"By whom?" said Alojza, livening up.

"I have my suspicions," Zofia began cautiously, but decided to retreat. Alongside another death the whole intricate web of connections that she had discovered would not make sense, unless Mrs. Czystogórska . . . "But it's too soon to cast aspersions. Please can you tell me something about this woman?"

"An ordinary resident, she kept herself to herself. Still entirely fit."

"Did she have anything to do with the previous victims? Or did she work in the kitchen?"

"No, in the laundry. As far as I know she was not acquainted either with Mrs. Mohr or Mrs. Krzywda."

"And did . . ." said Zofia hesitantly, "did Mr. Fikalski ever make advances to her?"

Alojza laughed, but seeing Mother Zaleska's reproachful glare, she shielded her mouth with her hand.

"Out of the question—she was too old and too poor for him. He does with Mrs. Wala . . ." At this point Mother Zaleska shot her another murderous look. "There's no need to gossip. But no."

"What about the police? When will they arrive?"

"They're already here," said Mother Zaleska. "They're searching every corner thoroughly. We preferred to ask them rather than our employees, as we did the first time. I can't help wondering if the shock of discovering Mrs. Mohr's body caused the poor watchman to lash out at innocent Mrs. Krzywda, may the Lord shine on her soul . . . The human heart has some dark recesses . . ."

"The watchman didn't do it," Zofia repeated automatically. "I'm sure of that. And so far, they haven't found anything?"

"They said they would let us know if something comes to light," said Alojza, eagerly doing her best to answer all the questions. "There are four of them searching the entire house, the garden, and the orchard. We have no idea where they'll find her. Maybe in a basket of dirty laundry? Or in a storage space? Maybe shut in one of the coffins in the basement?"

"I fear you have been reading too many secular books," hissed Mother Zaleska. "Shut in a coffin, what an idea! Well," she added after a pause, "we must wait. And pray. We must be sure to pray."

Zofia sat and waited for as long as she could — she spent two hours in the office, just once leaving her post for a brief visit to Countess Żeleńska, with whom she discreetly shared some gossip about the Cracow and Bochnia communities, and also learned that Mrs. Mohr's sister had finally arrived in town, so her funeral, as well as Mrs. Krzywda's — now that the police had returned her body — would be taking place soon, both on the same day. But Zofia was on tenterhooks, and quickly excused herself, saying she had to talk to Mother Zaleska.

In fact, she rushed straight to Sister Alojza to ask why she hadn't been told about the return of the woman with whom she had been wanting to meet and talk for ages, but the nun raised her hands in a helpless gesture. "I didn't tell you because although she was here, she only came once, and immediately said she had no time for any conversations."

Now and then one of the policemen appeared and reported on events; despite a careful search, they hadn't found Mrs. Czystogórska anywhere, either dead or alive. Naturally, officers had been sent to the homes of all her known relatives, but none of them had any news of her or had seen her for a long time. Several policemen went to search the squares and streets in the neighborhood, scoured the gateways and courtyards, and questioned the concierges, but with no success. The gardener who had assumed the role of watchman was questioned too, reducing him to nervous convulsions and tears, but he hadn't seen anyone creeping into the building, nor Mrs. Czystogórska sneaking out of it. She had simply evaporated.

Roughly once every fifteen minutes, Zofia thought of summoning one of the junior officers, or magistrate Klossowitz himself, and screaming into his face: "Arrest Fikalski, the murderer of two victims! Put him in chains! Throw him into jail! Shut him behind iron doors!" But in fact she knew that everything had changed—if he really was the criminal, the case was far more serious. Could another resident of the house have got wind of his schemes, forcing him to eliminate her? But if so, why had the previous murder been so brutal, and this one perfectly discreet?

The grandfather clock kept striking the quarters, the half-hours, and the hours, but finally Zofia's life could not wait; apart from decking the grave, she had a multitude of plans for today, on top of which she could sense that with

every minute she spent in the office Mother Zaleska's irritation was intensifying. Finally a ratchet, a cogwheel jumped
in Zofia's mind and she leapt to her feet, curtly took her
leave, and headed home in a very different mood from the
one in which she had arrived.

❧

"Zofia, what a misfortune!" Ignacy was plainly agitated as
he greeted his wife on the threshold.

In the first instance she thought he was talking about
the disappearance of Mrs. Czystogórska, but then she realized that he couldn't possibly be aware of it.

"Calm yourself, Ignacy, what on earth has happened?"
she asked as she took off her cherry-red hat. "Not another
murder?"

"What are you saying? No, it's worse than murder! It's
Mr. Matejko!"

"Yes, I know he's unwell . . ."

"Aha, but not more than half an hour ago the curate prepared him for the road to eternity, and then the great man's
noble existence came to an end!"

She didn't know what to say. For a while she couldn't decide between the following remarks: "He whom the gods
love dies young!," "It's that wife of his who's driven him into
an early grave, may the Lord shine light on his soul," or
"Well I never, only last month he had the energy to shout,

stamp, and write letters of protest!" None of them seemed appropriate.

Many years ago, when she was young and silly, she had fantasized about making Ignacy vice chancellor of the university, and then Matejko would paint him in his ermine cloak and chain, holding the golden scepter of office. And then, for good measure, they'd commission a joint portrait, where this time Ignacy would be more modest, in a black frock coat, while she would shine in a satin dress, every fold of which the master would paint precisely, as if it were the robe of Queen Jadwiga. But for years she had known she'd never make her husband the vice chancellor, and that this dream, like many others, would remain simply and only a dream forever.

"It's the end of an era," she said at last, sensing that she'd hit the right note.

❧

Her plans for the day included washing her hair; she wanted to look dazzling at the graveyard tomorrow. She stood in the middle of her boudoir beside a tub of warm water. She undid and loosened her plaits, and with her hair reaching to mid-thigh, she looked to see if there was any more gray in it than last time. Then, with Franciszka's help, she washed it in suitable preparations, towel dried it, and spread it wide to dry fully before nightfall. The final ritual in this lengthy ceremony was to brush it—she usually did it herself, but after washing, just like her mother, her mother's mother, and her other forebears, she placed herself in the hands of her servant, who brushed her tresses very gently and carefully.

"If you please, madam," said Franciszka, suddenly leaning forward; she must have been summoning up the courage for a while. "Today the master asked me . . ."

"Yes?"

"A strange question . . . Today the master asked me if . . . if madam might be going to Helcel House so often to test the ground for disposing of him there?"

At first Zofia was lost for words, but then she started to giggle.

"Franciszka, next time tell him he's not a pair of shoes or a basket to be disposed of anywhere. Secondly, he may be a professor now, and professors are usually fairly advanced in age, but he received that honor extremely early in life, for he is an outstanding individual. Out-stand-ing. He is not just at the top of his intellectual capacities, but his physical strength too—he is in his prime."

For a while neither of them spoke, and the only sound to be heard was the soft swish of the brush gliding through the hair.

"Dispose of him!" said Zofia. "What an idea."

But then she thought about his prematurely gray sideburns and the habits he might only have adopted ten or twenty years from now, but had acquired already, and a surge of affection flooded her heart.

"That will do, Franciszka, that will do," she said, as if in a hurry to go somewhere. "It is splendidly brushed."

In fact, she was in a hurry; she wanted to reach the bedroom before Ignacy fell asleep, and for the first time in many months fulfill her marital duty. And be absolutely sure to praise his youthful vigor.

᭢

As every year on All Souls' Day, countless crowds of people were heading for the public cemetery. All Cracow seemed to be flowing toward the Rakowicki toll gate and further north. All along the road to the cemetery, right up to the gate, swarms of beggars had been gathering from first light, counting on the exceptional generosity of those visiting the graves: they made a public display of their twisted limbs, their ulcers, and the stumps of their legs and arms ripped off by grapeshot in one of the wars waged by the empire, just as if they were first-rate goods set out for sale. Apparently in the afternoon, when the crowd grew thinner, there was usually a brawl among the beggars fighting over the handouts, after which they'd make up and drink the lot away at a vagabonds' Mardi Gras in the Rakowicki tavern. A very different company had assembled by the cemetery gate, but it too was lying in wait for donations with equal rapacity—the ladies from the Charitable Society, wrapped in capes, were collecting money in tins, which they were shaking maybe excessively, but tenaciously. *Between the Scylla and Charybdis of philanthropy*, thought Zofia, and was pleased by the comparison, which cast her in the role of Odysseus, sharpest of all the heroes, placing cunning before brute force. Rather than the many-headed Scylla of the beggars, she decided to opt for Charybdis—the whirlpool that sucked everything into a bottomless abyss—and having raised her dress like a sail, she cruised toward the ladies of the society, towing Ignacy behind her. At this time of day, the ladies on duty were Mrs. Cypcer and the vice president, Mrs. Gwiazdomorska, so Zofia dropped five one-crown coins into the tin—"To wipe away the tears of indigence and misfortune," as she put it. She took care to drop each coin in turn, unhurriedly, so that it could briefly be seen in the chink of the collecting box.

Once they had laid a wreath and relit the candles on the Turbotyński grave, Ignacy and Zofia made their usual annual tour, adding new sites to the old route, where over the past year closer or more distant acquaintances had gone to rest: Cousin Orkusz, Mrs. Hanewicz who had lived next door, and Mr. Gralewski the pharmacist. They advanced slowly amid the human throng. In the distance they could hear singing coming from deep inside the cemetery, where some patriotically inclined young people had gathered at the tomb of the Society for the Care of Veterans and were singing suitable songs in memory of the victims of the 1830,

1846, and 1863 uprisings. Former comrades-in-arms of those fallen in battle kept watch by the actual tombs, hoping to stand straight as ramrods, but mostly stooping and grizzled, both literally and metaphorically with one foot in the grave.

"Look, Ignacy, what a fine monument the architect Talowski has erected for his future demise — Egyptian."

On a stepped plinth sat a sphinx with one forepaw resting on a skull and with a snake coiled around the other.

"Just like the rubbish they're putting up at the corner of Retoryka and Smoleńska Streets. Obelisks, sphinxes, and other modern nonsense," said Ignacy indignantly.

"You mean ancient."

"Either way, it's idiotic. That Talowski fellow designs nothing but spiders, frogs, donkeys, dragons, sphinxes, and other oddities . . . Whoever saw such a thing? And who on earth needs it?"

Zofia let this comment pass in silence. She liked the almost-completed Egyptian House, though not as much as the houses designed by Talowski that lined the banks of the Rudawa. She would have no objection to moving into one of them, equipped with all the latest amenities, but Ignacy refused to hear of it. Every attempt to broach the subject ended the same way: "Move out to the suburbs? Into a new building? Over my dead body."

"And that — what on earth is it meant to be?" he said, pointing at a statue of a winged youth.

"I must say I like it very much. It's so . . . full of energy."

"The cemetery is the last place where one should expect to find figures full of energy, my dear," muttered Ignacy, adjusting his top hat. "But now they put up weeping women, angels with children, and scantily clad men all over the place, as if we were in a museum. I hope they don't erect something like that for Matejko."

"It's up to his widow, and one can expect anything at all from her," said Zofia sourly, irritated by the topic. Fortunately, Ignacy had forgotten that only a few weeks ago she had insisted Matejko would live to a hundred and would certainly make peace with the city authorities well before then. But Mrs. Dutkiewicz was quite another matter — she would certainly remind Zofia of yesterday's speech about Matejko's state of health. She looked around hesitantly, but luckily her cousin was nowhere to be seen.

"Now *that* I understand," exclaimed Ignacy, as they passed the bust of a man with whiskers and a large nose. "Classical, distinguished, tasteful."

"Kolberg," said Zofia, putting her lorgnette to her eyes and reading out the name. "'A credit to his motherland,' it says. I don't recall the name."

Here and there among the grand mausoleums adorned with columns and marble stood unfinished edifices, which some tradesman or butcher had started to put up for himself at a time of temporary success in business, but had later had to abandon.

"Do you know whose that is?" she said, leaning confidentially toward the rather apathetic Ignacy, who was finding this funerary vanity fair, this graveyard fashion show, extremely dull, and then she whispered a name.

"Really? But he's buried somewhere else entirely."

"That's just it! He spent so much money, he wanted so many cherubs of Carrara marble that he was reduced to penury and his family had to put him in a mass grave for paupers! They were left with his debts and this great lump of stone that they cannot possibly sell."

"They'll find another button-making millionaire who'll buy it. Then he'll go bust and his heirs will sell it on to a corset-making millionairess."

Once they had completed their tour of the family graves, holding a number of casual conversations with the cousins and acquaintances they met along the way, in which they exchanged comments on the statues and the costumes, as well as the decorations — almost all of which Zofia regarded as "banal," "tasteless," "shabby," or even "proof of parsimony" — they went back to the Turbotyńskis' neo-Gothic monument, where they took another look to see if the garlands, wreaths, and lamps duly sang the family's praises. And finally they said goodbye to Franciszka, who, muffled in thick woolens, remained by the grave. Like many other servants, she was to guard the flowers and candles until midnight, as they were stolen by the dozen here. Meanwhile the flames would burn down to the last right here, on the grave of the late lamented Turbotyńskis, and nowhere else, while the everlasting flowers would be useful next year too.

"Don't you think she could come home a little earlier?"

said Ignacy, walking away. "Who'd be tempted by those dry flowers?"

"You appear to have forgotten . . . ah, good afternoon, good afternoon," she said, returning someone's greeting, "that only a couple of years ago they even stole the gutters from the . . ."

"Conveniences."

"Exactly. They were tempted by the gutters, but they'll leave the flowers? Ignacy, sometimes your faith in human honesty is exaggerated . . . Besides, it's far from being the coldest All Souls' Day I can remember!"

On leaving the cemetery, they stopped at the stalls. Ignacy chose a few roast chestnuts, while Zofia preferred something sweeter. Generally she kept an eye on her figure and denied herself treats, but it was a holiday, and on holidays our decisions are run on different rules. The salesman chipped a few smaller pieces off a large lump of honeycomb toffee and wrapped it in a paper cone. They ate in the cab in silence, ignoring the fact that luncheon was waiting for them at home.

CHAPTER XI

❧

*In which Cracow impatiently prepares for its favorite kind of
ceremony, Zofia Turbotyńska burns with shame in a fourth-
class funeral procession, the mysterious young man appears
in the foliage, and Mrs. Mohr's sister in torrents of mourning
tulle; it's also Sunday, and as such there is a prison visit, and
a threat to wreck the prison governor's family home.*

Next day no news came from Helcel House; feeling impatient, Zofia sent Franciszka, who had caught a chill
while keeping watch on the candles at night, to inquire
about some details, but Mrs. Czystogórska hadn't been
found; no one knew anything about her, not at the house,
nor the police, nor in town.

Meanwhile, still digesting the treats sold outside the cem-
eteries and the equally delectable gossip exchanged on All

Souls' Day, all Cracow was preparing itself for the imminent event of the season, which is to say Matejko's funeral; for in Cracow no celebration, no ball, military parade, or theater premiere, not even the visit of a member of the ruling house, was conducted with such pomp as the funeral of a great Pole, whether recently deceased or exhumed somewhere in exile and transported to the Wawel Cathedral or the pantheon at St. Michael's. Posters featuring a large cross and the great artist's name were put up everywhere, the postmen delivered telegrams with black edges to his home on Floriańska Street by the ton, the seamstresses cut crepe to drape the streetlamps, the florists' nimble fingers wove exquisite wreaths and wrote out words of mourning on silk ribbons, while at many a desk condolence notices were composed for the national press and—as someone scrupulously counted—thirty-two foreign publications, and also funeral speeches, over which the high foreheads of the luminaries of Polish culture sweated in search of phrases that would duly *escort Matejko to his eternal resting place.* Ignacy played a small part in these preparations, too, as one of the doctors who were asked for advice on embalming the painter's corpse.

To mark the occasion, Zofia spent the entire afternoon wondering whether to write an epic poem, in which she would compare the embalming of a body by an ancient art, using scented oils, with the embalming of Polish antiquity using oil paints, as Matejko had done, but got no further than a single quatrain:

In King Krak's city, where the Vistula rolls its gray-
    green waves,
Racing time toward the sea without stop,
The graying master shuts his weary eyes
And from his hand his gilded brush lets drop . . .

But she wasn't sure if from these words it wouldn't
emerge that time races not ahead of itself but toward the
sea, so she tried to put it another way:

And like time it races yonder to the sea,

"Yonder" didn't sound right, though, and "without stop"
grated too, so she set the poem aside until lunchtime.

In any case, Zofia had some more serious funerals in
mind: both — or maybe just two out of three — murder victims were to be buried, one after the other, three days before Matejko. And Zofia had to be present at these events
without fail. She had already seen the death notices posted
in town — low down or to one side, pushed out by the huge
signs featuring the artist's name — with a small image of a
distraught mourner sitting on a grave, one hand shielding
her face, the other pointing to a name. The name Mohr, of
course, because the wealthy family had taken care to com-
memorate her as grandly as possible, especially as she had
left them a generous legacy; there was no mention anywhere of Mrs. Krzywda's funeral.

And so the procession that set off from Helcel House on Saturday, November the fourth, was extremely modest; it was the first time Zofia had ever attended a fourth-class funeral, the cheapest kind, with a two-horse hearse and two cabs for the mourners, which was quite sufficient; there was no drapery, no flowers, just a simple coffin made of soft wood, with no particular adornment. Of course, one sometimes saw processions of this kind on the way to the market, or if one accidentally set foot in a poorer district, but to be part of such a cortège . . . oh well, it wasn't the first discomfort Zofia had experienced as a result of the inquiry.

The final upshot was that she forgot to ask if Mrs. Krzywda herself had bought the site where she was laid to rest in her fourth-class coffin, or if Helcel House had paid for it. Was it among the graves of other almswomen, or had she been given special treatment in view of her tragic death? If she had, then the site was hardly prominent, in a dull corner of the cemetery. There was a Mass, of course, but a quiet, rapid one, muttered rather than celebrated by a young and distinctly bored priest.

Two nuns walked behind the coffin, neither of whom was Alojza, who was probably busy with preparations for Mrs. Mohr's immeasurably more important funeral; then came three old women, including Mrs. Andrusik, who had found the body in the bedroom, and whom Zofia recognized by the characteristic birthmark thickly sprouting hairs on her cheek, and finally Zofia herself. There was also an altar boy with a cross, and the young priest. The cof-

fin was carried out of the chapel — without much rever-
ence — by the gravediggers. Just at the last moment, as they
were lowering the ropes into the pit, Countess Żeleńska appeared. She had come in her own carriage, for Mrs. Mohr's
Mass, in fact, but had decided to arrive in advance to attend
the earlier funeral too. In the custom of olden days she was
dressed in full mourning, as if she had close ties of kinship
with the deceased: her face was obscured by a black veil,
and she had a black satin dress under a wool cape, a black
bonnet, an umbrella, and even a black lambskin muff.

Apparently focusing on the burial — as if at such a poor
funeral there were anything to hold one's gaze — Zofia actually kept looking around in case someone from Mrs.
Krzywda's former life turned up: a relative, an acquaintance,
anyone at all. But there was no one. She had lost hope of
learning anything new here, when suddenly, far off among
the graves, she saw the face of a young man, overshadowed
by the brim of a bowler hat; his forehead was bisected by
two vertical lines and two horizontal lines, and beneath
firmly drawn brows, his keen eyes were burning. She knew
him, or rather she recognized him, as one couldn't say they
were acquainted; it was the smartly dressed youth whom
she had once passed on her way into Helcel House, and of
whom Alojza could tell her nothing.

When the short ceremony came to its end, without another word, the priest bestirred himself and raced off, pre-
ceded by the altar boy, who had to speed up every few paces
to stop the priest from treading on his heels. Now Zofia

would have run between the graves, ready to buttonhole
the youth and hold on to him until he revealed his connection with Mrs. Krzywda, if not for the fact that even in such
a modest cortège she couldn't extract herself; surrounded
by extremely feeble old women, caught in a dull conversation with the countess (who had been regaling her with
comments on various topics ever since arriving), wherever
she turned there was either a resident or a nun, all apparently dressed in lead. Saying "excuse me, please" wouldn't
work — they couldn't leave the narrow path and were quite
incapable of gathering in their skirts a bit. When she looked
for the young man again, he was gone. She asked the nuns
about him, but neither of them had noticed anyone at all,
except for the group from Helcel House. "Probably just a
gawker," said one of them. "He came, stared, and went away."

Gradually they had to make their way from the far corner of the cemetery and return to the chapel in time to take
their seats for the next service; everyone who had escorted
Mrs. Krzywda to her grave — apart from the mystery man —
was planning to attend the second funeral. It had far more
to offer: more mourners, more carriages, more horses, candles, and plumes — in short, a spectacle to be discussed
with other residents of the house for many weeks to come.

By the time the coffin and the friends and relatives of the
deceased had arrived from town, the seven female mourn-

ers from the earlier funeral were sitting in the pews on either side of the cemetery chapel, under the watchful gaze
of their old acquaintances, the Helcels, who looked down
from their commemorative plaques. Zofia also recognized
two ladies who were well known in town for carefully study-
ing the list of funerals posted by the cemetery gate each
morning; they spent entire days at the cemetery, attending
all the more significant ceremonies.

The cemetery chaplain said Mass. At first glance one
could see that the priest was in a wretched state. When they
endowed the chapel, the Helcels had stipulated that a Mass
be said for them on each anniversary of their deaths, but
the family's bloated ambitions had gone way beyond reason. The funds contributed by another Mrs. Helcel, Ludwik's sister-in-law, obliged the chaplain to say Masses for
the founder and her husband once a week, for his parents
once a month, and for their siblings once a quarter. As a result, for the Helcels alone the poor chaplain had to say seventy Masses a year. No wonder he looked so haggard after
only a few months in his post.

It was the best and grandest of first-class funerals — no
one knew if the deceased had paid for it herself in advance
or had provided for it in her will, or if the family had decided to do her this honor; after all, following her husband's
death she had willingly moved into Helcel House, where
she lived a modest life, without depleting her capital, which
the relatives were already calling their "legacy" while she
was still alive, and must have imagined spending several

times over before it actually fell into their hands because of the murder. In any case, this was a lavish affair.

Naturally, Concordia, the best funeral firm, was in charge, providing as many as twenty carriages for the mourners—yet they were not entirely filled, because most of Mrs. Mohr's erstwhile friends had long since been lying in their graves, and though others were present, many had come in their own vehicles. The coffin was made of metal, in the latest style, decorated with a crucifix, the heads of cherubs, and other such wonders—but in view of the passage of time, it was closed, so there was no opportunity to admire the satin pillows and no doubt exquisite lace.

"A first-rate catafalque, as ever, from Concordia," whispered one of the ladies approvingly. Indeed, the firm had provided not just the catafalque, but also the black drapery covering it, a black rug, and strips of pitch-black velvet, which wreathed the chapel's double pilasters and arches. The decor was completed by some tall, beautifully burning candles set in massive candlesticks, and flowers, perhaps less impressive at this time of year than in spring or summer. A rather theatrically dressed master of ceremonies oversaw the correct course of events.

But the most striking feature was the hearse, Concordia's grandest, known as the "gala" hearse, harnessed to four black horses with equally grand plumes on their heads and cloths on their backs; it was a truly royal coach for the deceased, topped with a large black-and-silver crown with a cross; the four corners were guarded by four full-figure angels with their wings spread wide, who formed the main framework for the cut-glass jewelry box, carved like a real gem, that was just about to carry Mrs. Mohr away and finally lay her at her husband's side.

⚶

The longer one looked at the hearse, the more details caught the eye: the lamps with panes of glass that had crosses etched in them; the extinguished torches, cherubs' heads, columns, cartouches, and acanthus leaves—a real swarm of details. Yet Zofia was more eager to look to either side and listen in on the conversations; Mrs. Mohr's sister walked in front, right behind the coffin, in a huge, swirling veil, as if she were a brokenhearted widow, not a woman who, on learning of the death of her far older sister, had not interrupted her stay at a health spa. Fortunately she was not sobbing uncontrollably—the torrents of black tulle were quite enough for her.

In the procession, as ever, there was plenty of conversation—anecdotes were being told about the dead, and a lady was swearing that although she hadn't actually seen her "dearest friend for years," she'd been just about to pay her a visit when the death notices appeared in the newspapers. There was also gossip about Matejko's final moments.

"His last words were, 'Let us pray for the motherland! God be blessed!'"

"What are you saying? His last words were, 'O God! Save my motherland!'"

"Not at all, dear lady. I know from the curate that his precise words were: 'O God, save my motherland and bless my children.'"

But the greatest excitement was prompted by the murder, which had only now made its way into the papers. Everyone had plenty to say about it, but — as Zofia found — nothing relevant, unfortunately. So she didn't gain much from eavesdropping on their prattle.

She looked around the crowd, checking to see who was there; there were several of the wealthier ladies and a number of the almswomen who had no trouble walking; they hadn't known the deceased in person, but there was nothing they craved more than any kind of happening in their monotonous lives. And a first-class funeral was not just beautiful but also entirely free of charge. There was no sign of Mrs. Wężyk, who was generally kept within the grounds of Helcel House, or of Baroness Banffy, who as an outsider probably wasn't terribly concerned about people she didn't know; whereas Polcia, her maid, was there, but she was thrilled by anything to do with the upper spheres, if only the middle classes. For obvious reasons the watchman and the cook were absent, but the wimples of several nuns glided past in the procession, headed by Mother Zaleska. To Zofia's surprise she also noticed Lidia Walaszek née Campiani in the distance, who was walking slowly, leaning on the arm of Fikalski, a head smaller than she was. *What a nerve!* thought Zofia. *Even a murderer should have some sense of propriety!* Judge Mohr's former colleagues had made sure the younger, fitter court officials bore his widow's coffin, too, at least for a short while; there was divided opinion on this among the commentators, some of whom thought it an abuse of honors, others that it was a fine gesture toward a lady who in her time had made the finest possible impression on Cracow's judges. Naturally, for the time being the pallbearers did not share their opinions, but in fact the hearse bore the coffin most of the way, and the deceased was small and thin, so even though they were officials, the six fellows had no trouble carrying it. But there were plenty of people in the crowd who remembered Judge Mohr's huge coffin; he had been a renowned gourmand, and afterward people had said it should have had at least twelve rather than just six handles.

Countess Żeleńska had rather skillfully placed herself at the front of the queue to offer condolences — then with a slight nod to Zofia in farewell she toddled back to her carriage; she was driving straight from the cemetery to the nearby gala opening of a refuge for boys run by the Lubomirski Foundation. Zofia obediently took her place in the long line, keeping her eyes and ears wide open to hear and see what was going on around her.

"May I please have a moment of your time? Let's step aside," she suddenly heard; she turned and was surprised to come face-to-face with Baroness Banffy's maid. She looked just as unfriendly as ever, but Zofia's expert eye detected that something about her had changed. Not her hairstyle, not her clothing . . . yes, she was wearing very nice, expensive jewelry: beautiful earrings with rubies circled by tiny diamonds, and a large brooch shaped like a sprig of flowers, set with various gemstones — not many servants went about in such valuable things.

"It's incredibly awkward for me to talk about this," she began once they had moved away from the crowd, "but you are in such close contact with Mother Zaleska, and above all with the police . . ."

"Yes, what is it?"

"I am afraid my mistress and her nephew are in great danger."

"Her nephew? I had no idea she had any family . . ."

"Yes, he's actually her husband's nephew. He lives in Cracow, and sometimes he comes to see my mistress, but every time she's greatly affected by it." She paused, and then in a solemn tone said just one single word: "Italians."

"Italians?"

"Italians."

"Excuse me, but is the nephew an Italian, or is an Italian firm chasing him for a debt, or is he in trouble with the Italian police? Surely not the baroness herself?"

"No, no, these are very serious matters. Deadly serious! Vengeance from the past! They're on the prowl," said the servant, grabbing Zofia's arm and squeezing it tightly. "They'll stop at nothing! They're just waiting for an unguarded moment, and . . . bang! You're dead."

"Is that why lately the baroness has been so . . ."

"Agitated? That's exactly why! A ball of nerves. And she's such a good woman, a real lady. Her estates in Transylvania were really something! Why should she have so much suffering in her old age, so much fear?"

"Would she be willing to talk to me about it?"

"God forbid! I'd be in awful trouble if she found out I'd been blabbing her secrets. Out of the question."

"What about her nephew?"

Polcia made a strange face; she let her head drop, raised it, and lowered it again, then said, "No, I can't."

"But what if the baroness's life depends on it? Do you want to have her on your conscience?"

"I can't, I can't."

"You don't have to persuade him to talk to me," sighed Zofia, losing patience. "All you have to do is tell me where I can find him."

"If only I knew — he's young, rich, a gadabout. One of the gilded youth — nothing but cards, recreation, and beautiful clothes."

"But he has to live somewhere. Does he have a house? Does he rent an apartment?"

It was plain to see that under the maid's hat a fierce battle was being fought between her sense of loyalty and her need to be protective, which finally ended in victory for the latter.

"The Hotel Krakowski," she whispered at last. "I don't know the room number."

She looked as if she wanted to say something else, but dropped the idea; she merely grabbed her dress, bowed slightly, and headed for the gate without offering her condolences to Mrs. Mohr's sister or relatives. Meanwhile Zofia eagerly returned to the queue, which was rapidly getting shorter. She deliberately stood at the very end to be able to talk a little longer.

The dead woman's sister was hardly visible under her layers of thick gauze, but now and then among the folds an eye or a rouged cheek glimmered; judging by her voice — which Zofia heard uttering the same formulaic thank-you again and again: "God bless you for those kind words" — she must have been much younger than her late sibling.

"I'm sorry to say I never had the honor of meeting your sister," said Zofia, "but please accept my deepest sympathy. I know from the Sisters of Charity, as well as from the other residents and employees of Helcel House, that they all esteemed her highly for her kind heart . . ."

"God bless you for those kind words," came the voice from behind the veil.

"Today my thoughts are with you in your great loss. Especially as you parted on bad terms, and often in such cases . . ."

"On bad terms? What are you talking about?" Suddenly the mourner turned out to be more than just a machine for uttering the same set phrase.

"I'm talking about the quarrel you had on the day when

the late lamented Mrs. Mohr departed this world in such a tragic way . . ."

"But Antonina and I did not see each other on the day of her death," said the other woman indignantly. "That morning I left for the spa with my daughters at first light."

"I was told that you spoke to your sister that evening . . ."

"Stuff and nonsense! What sort of story is this?"

"Apparently you quarreled about food?"

"This is quite intolerable. Henryk!" she cried, raising her voice. "Henryk! Talk to the lady, please — I won't hear any more of this."

From a cluster of men emerged a thin, bald man with a long, drooping mustache that hung on either side of his mouth like linen thread, almost reaching his wide lapels.

"Marianna? You called?"

"It's no matter," said Zofia, forestalling an attack, "merely a misunderstanding. My deepest sympathy."

Then at high speed she turned on her heel and, as if someone were chasing her, raced down the cemetery path. She had a lot of things to think through and couldn't wait until she sat down to a game of Napoleon's Tomb to make sense of it all. Somewhere in the distance, behind her, yet another judge's widow had latched on to Mrs. Mohr's sister to offer her condolences and was just about to hear "God bless you for those kind words."

Meanwhile, from the direction of the city an abrupt wind broke loose, pushing some massive clouds across the sky; the rooks began to crow more noisily and the last few leaves showered down on the heads and hats of the assembled crowd. Autumn was deeply palpable, right inside one's bones.

＊

Exactly twenty-four hours later, straight after Sunday Mass, Zofia presented herself to the prison guard on Mikołajska Street again. Naturally, he recognized her from a week ago, and treated her extremely politely, but he insisted that despite the noble gravity of charitable deeds, he couldn't let her into the visiting room without another letter of recommendation.

"I see," said Zofia, smoothing the silk lapel of her overcoat. "In that case I shall have to go and see the prison governor's wife, disturb her peace and quiet on a Sunday, interrupt her observance of the Lord's day, distract her from her primary duties as a woman who . . . yes, the one o'clock trumpet call has only just sounded from the tower . . . a woman who is sure to be serving the governor his Sunday luncheon right now. And as I am sure you know, the governor likes nothing less than to have his meals disturbed. Is he bad at his job?"

The question hung in the air. It took a few seconds for the guard to realize that it wasn't rhetorical.

"What a suggestion! The governor is the most dutiful employee of all!"

"Has he for some strange reason been sentenced to lose his day off?"

"The governor has never been sentenced to anything! He is a man of spotless character!"

"Or perhaps those above a certain threshold of significance within the public services should forgo their family meals? Lose sight of their children, blithely toying with their junket? Forget about their wife's tender smile as she serves His Majesty's favorite dish, which is boiled veal . . ."

"In horseradish sauce."

"In horseradish sauce?"

The guard, a man in his prime, was almost brought to despair.

"Do you want me to go to the governor's lodgings this instant and reduce their domestic bliss to ashes in the name of some general rules?"

His left eye twitching nervously, he came up to the door, turned the key in the lock, and with the simple words "Sundays are sacred," he let Zofia inside.

❧

"I didn't kill ze lady, madam."

The cook, Mrs. Sedlaczek, looked as if she had spent several years in a dungeon, not just a few days in the custody cells. She was pale, maybe because of the chill prevailing here, and her hair, usually tied in a tight bun and carefully covered by a mobcap, fell untidily to her shoulders.

Her appearance reminded Zofia of a scandal widely reported by the press all over Europe in her youth, involving a mentally unstable nun called Barbara Ubryk, who after many years shut away in isolation was released from a cell at the Carmelite convent on Kopernik Street. Well, thought Zofia, exposing the killer of Mrs. Mohr and Mrs. Krzywda wouldn't bring her European fame, but she wasn't expecting it anyway. Besides, she wouldn't want Ignacy to feel oppressed by his wife's renown.

"You've killed someone before," she said in an icy tone. She was annoyed at having to pay another visit to the local jail. First the watchman, now the cook—someone might start to think Professor Turbotyński's wife kept company with criminals.

"I did," admitted the woman. She spoke softly, sounding very different from when she'd been bossing the kitchen maids about. "Sedlaczek was a violent, tyrannical man. He abused, bullied, and beat me; he injured me. Ten years I put up wiz it, but zen I couldn't stand it any longer. One day when he came home from ze workshop . . . he was a carpenter . . . I sprinkled it into his food . . . goulash wiz dumplings . . . May God forgive me . . ."

"God is merciful, but you are not. You never forgave Judge Mohr."

"But ze judge was right to condemn me," said the cook, shaking her head. "I had committed a cruel sin. Sedlaczek was a horrible person, but he was a person. And my huzband, sadly."

Zofia felt a strange ache in her heart. Ignacy could be difficult, it was true, but the idea of murdering one's husband seemed to her . . . in bad taste.

"Ze judge was fair," the cook went on. "He took ze . . . what was ze word? . . . circumstances into conzideration. 'Violent mental confusion.' Zey sentenced me for manslaughter, not murder. Ze counsel appealed to His Majesty for a pardon. I spent zree years in jail in Bilsk before zey issued ze amnesty. I wasn't angry."

"So you didn't poison his widow out of revenge?"

"I didn't poison her, I tell you!" said the cook, raising her voice a little for the first time. "Ze old lady did me no harm. I didn't even know she was ze judge's widow. Why would I have murdered her?" She paused for a while. "I was a good cook, madam, I worked at ze hospital in Bilsk. After ze amnesty I decided to come to Cracow, because it's a big city. Zey had just opened Helcel House, and ze mozer superior at ze hospital wrote a letter recommending me to Mozer Zaleska. I zought zat zrough Christian aid for ze poor I would somehow serve ze Lord God and repair ze harm I had done. For death is always death. *Úzkost* never ends . . ."

"What never ends? I don't understand."

"Anxiety. Guilt never ceases to poison ze soul. Fear zat ze crime will return from ze past like a ghost . . ."

Zofia was filled with sympathy for this woman, agonized by pangs of conscience because of the crime she had committed and atoned for, and now, it seems, accused of a crime she hadn't committed, but for which she might have to pay. As she said goodbye, Mrs. Sedlaczek was sitting with her face buried in her hands. In the doorway she turned and asked: "Just one more question. What did you use to poison your husband? Cyanide?"

"What did I use?" The woman raised her head and looked at Zofia blankly. "No, madam, it was rat poison . . . Strychnine or arsenic, whatever came to hand in the kitchen."

So that's how it is, thought Zofia as she walked along St. Thomas's Street. *Even crimes have their style. The devious murder deviously, the cruel do it cruelly, and the practical practically. With whatever comes to hand.*

CHAPTER XII

✤

A short but eventful chapter, in which the major funeral procession of the season doesn't go to St. Michael's or the Wawel Cathedral, while Zofia plays truant from the burial, or one could even say: makes a dubious rendezvous.

By the time the Turbotyńskis arrived outside Matejko's house, Floriańska Street was full of people, who had been gathering since early that morning. *Quite a crowd,* thought Zofia, *but not like three years ago. Ah. Mickiewicz's funeral! That was a real occasion.* The burial of the remains of the greatest Polish poet, exhumed abroad and returned to his native soil, had attracted the entire city, as well as a vast number of outsiders. The procession that went ahead of the coffin was so long that, by the time the hearse finally set off from Count Tarnowski's palace on Szlak Street, its front end was passing St. Mary's. The Harmonia Society band had played beautifully, and the chorus of the Lemberg opera had sung just as finely. The hearse carrying the bard's coffin, artistically draped in red plush and decorated with white lilies and purple poppies, had been drawn by six bay horses. The strings attached to the pall had been held by the greatest of the great: Prince Jerzy Czartoryski, Prince Sapieha, Count Tarnowski, the historical novelist Henryk Sienkiewicz, and Jan Matejko — today, three years on, to be laid to rest on his own ornate catafalque.

"I wonder if it'll come off without a hitch this time," said a man behind the Turbotyńskis.

"My dear sir, what on earth do you mean, 'this time'? Mickiewicz's funeral was superbly organized," another man answered him.

"Oh, I see you've forgotten that the canopy didn't fit beneath the new telephone wires that cross at the top of St. John's Street."

Zofia remembered that perfectly. In the time it took to remove the poles from their bases, she'd been able to go home, freshen up, have a cup of tea, and return to her place in the procession.

Now, as the clocks struck nine and the trumpet call resounded, the coffin bearing the great artist's body emerged from his house, carried by students of the Academy of Fine Arts. Zofia almost blinked in disbelief. Surely she was seeing things.

"Look, Zofia," said Ignacy, confirming her observation, "it's Józefa's son! What an honor!"

Jan Nepomucen, the youngest of the Dutkiewicz boys, had lost his hearing as a result of scarlet fever, but apparently at a special school for deaf mutes in Lemberg he had shown talent, and the drawing master had recommended him to the academy. He painted landscapes, quite decent ones, in fact, though Zofia was sure he would never be Rembrandt. Now, wearing a white sash edged in black, with a serious expression on his face, he was helping to place the coffin on the catafalque erected outside the house.

"Indeed," she muttered, "an honor. But your enthusiasm is inappropriate to a professor, Ignacy," she said reproachfully. "At a time like this your role is to be dignified, not excited by trifles." She had to admit that she'd been so absorbed by the inquiry that she'd neglected no less essential matters, and had failed to make proper arrangements for Ignacy to be given the task of carrying the wreath from the medical faculty. Three years ago, as an ordinary doctor, he'd had no chance of such an honor, and had marched almost at the back of the university deputation, but this time, if she had taken more trouble, he could have had the chance. Unfortunately, only the day before had she remembered to go and see Professor Cybulski's wife, whose husband was active within the Medical Society. She had spent a boring hour there over a cup of tea, merely to discover that although Mrs. Cybulska's husband held Professor Turbotyński in high regard, it was too late to do anything about it. She had taken her leave and gone home feeling chilled to the bone and irritated. Yet she could still have gone to see Mrs. Gwiazdomorska, the deputy chairman's wife, or Mrs. Teichmann, almost next door, whose husband, as a government adviser and Knight of the Imperial Order of Franz Joseph, might have been willing to help his able former student. But as things stood, today Ignacy was to march in the company of all the academics again, in the middle of the deputation. *Never mind,* she thought, *people are always dying—the great and the good are no different from the rest of us in this particular respect. This won't be the first or last funeral of its kind—there'll be other opportunities.*

Then came the speeches. Wearing a *kontusz*, the traditional robe of noblemen, Count Tarnowski declaimed: "Your godlike toil on earth is done, now rest in peace, great master, inspired and alone!" and then began to praise the late genius to the skies and to bemoan his "severe anguish." Zofia looked around for Mrs. Matejko, but she was nowhere to be seen. Plainly she wasn't the only person to have this thought, for she heard a low voice uttering a malicious comment aimed at the widow. The count spoke at great length, to Zofia's astonishment—Tarnowski, whom she had always regarded with admiration, seemed to her uninteresting, and his speech was very dull. Finally, she stopped listening, as her thoughts escaped to the deaths of Mrs. Mohr and Mrs. Krzywda.

The speech ended with a repetition of Matejko's last words—or at least one of the versions of them: "O God, bless my motherland" — and then the procession began to form, heading to St. Mary's for the funeral Mass. Guided by the masters of ceremonies, the marshals held up boards with numbers on them to show the various deputations where to stand in the procession.

"Oh, that's mine, Zofia! Thirty-six," cried Ignacy, and went off to take his place. Zofia was left alone in the huge crowd of onlookers. This was the moment she'd been waiting for — earlier she had planned that in these circumstances she could easily slip away and visit Baroness Banffy's nephew. The day before she had sent a boy to the Hotel Krakowski with a verbal message that his "aunt" was going to pay him a visit on Tuesday "before noon," but without specifying an exact time. Yet before she had determined to wander off unnoticed toward Planty Park, she ran into a neighbor, Mrs. Zajączek. Once again, the old truth was confirmed that slipping through Cracow without being noticed was simply not possible — one couldn't walk across the Market Square without encountering at least one familiar face. Sometimes a polite nod of the head sufficed, but usually the done thing was to stop — or, as in this instance, walk a short way together courteously exchanging remarks about the weather and one's health. And so, accompanied by the garrulous Mrs. Zajączek, gushing about "the moving solemnities," she advanced with the procession toward St. Mary's Basilica.

Outside the church she was about to say goodbye and walk — or even run — off to the hotel, when it turned out that the enterprising Mrs. Zajączek, as wife of a member of the funeral committee, had a two-person ticket for the Mass. In normal circumstances, Zofia would probably have gasped with excitement, but the situation was unique. She was afraid the Banffy nephew wouldn't wait, but would leave the hotel as soon as the midday trumpet call sounded. Yet if she refused Mrs. Zajączek, news of this highly unusual occurrence would spread about the city at the speed of light, quickly spawning all sorts of tall tales. *City of rumormongers!* thought Zofia angrily, but politely thanked Mrs. Zajączek for the invitation. She handed the ticket to the fireman keeping order and entered the church as if about to be tortured, to emerge an hour later after a particularly grand Mass that hadn't thrilled her at all.

She hadn't admired the cardinal's silver hair; she hadn't delighted in Tarnowski's noble appearance; she hadn't even tried to spot Ignacy in the distance. After the Mass, the procession formed again and set off on a round of the Market Square, moving clockwise. By the time she came out of the church, the head of it was out of sight behind the Cloth Hall. All the shops, restaurants, and cafés were closed for the day. Wrapped in black crepe, the street lamps had been lit, there were black-and-gold imperial flags and black mourning flags fluttering from the houses, and people were leaning out of the windows to scatter flowers on the procession. Twice Zofia almost broke free, once at the top of Bracka Street, and once at Szewska Street, but each time she felt as if someone who knew her were staring at her.

Outside Gralewski's pharmacy she finally plucked up the courage and turned into Szczepańska Street, at which point she heard a man say: "But in all honesty it has to be said, my dear, that the Lutnia choir doesn't sing as well as the Lemberg opera chorus . . ."

"And there was no canopy," added a woman's voice sadly.

✻

Of all the hotels in which Baroness Banffy's nephew might have been staying, the one so banally named "the Krakowski"—despite its fine location on Planty Park, at the corner of Podwale and Garbarska Street—was among the shabbiest. And the shabbier it was, the more Zofia feared the embarrassment of being recognized there; though on the other hand, she consoled herself, no one decent would spend their time in such a place, and anyway it was a very unusual day, when the entire beau monde was taking part in the procession.

The building itself—a sort of red-brick, neo-Gothic manor, bristling with pinnacles like turrets crossed with chimneys, did not resemble a real hotel in the slightest. And that was no accident; it had been built ten years ago by a banker named Marfiewicz as the New City Baths. Next to it he had built his own very attractive house. *How odd,* thought Zofia, *to have such a beautiful garden and a villa in Italian style, and then put up this brick box right under your nose, for all of Cracow's grimy populace, caked in a week's*

dirt, to converge on every Saturday. Either way, this particular business had clearly failed, for ten years later the baths
were only on the first floor; on the two upper floors, the
tubs and tiles had been removed and replaced with hotel
rooms: small, dark, and ugly, so they said in town, though in
fact no citizen had ever spent the night there. Yet the general view prevailed that one shouldn't stay at a place where
until recently every Tom, Dick, and Harry had washed the
filth off his body, so visitors were firmly advised against the
Krakowski.

After a good look around, in case some worthy lady just
happened to have broken free of Matejko's funeral and was
eager to observe her suspicious movements, Zofia went
through the front door, situated on the street corner under
a wooden veranda. She could smell an odor of damp, soap,
and sweat emanating from the depths of a corridor. *How
strange,* she thought, *for a person of his social standing and
undoubted wealth to be staying in a place like this.* But she
carried on, trusting that eventually she would find the reception desk. And indeed, under the stairs leading up to the
second floor there was a scratched mahogany counter with
a fellow behind it; bald as a coot, he had a pince-nez planted
on his large red nose, which bore witness to a great fond-
ness for drink. He was just in the middle of yawning.

"At your humble service, madam," he parroted, shielding his gaping maw.

"I am here to see Baron Banffy."

"I'll see if he's in his room," said the man, removed his

pince-nez, rubbed the lenses on his coattail, put it back on his nose, and began to search among the keys. "He should be . . . Whom shall I announce?"

"Banffy," said Zofia, and then, with an audible note of pleasure, she added: "Baroness."

Noticing the receptionist's scornful look, she also added: "I am his aunt. His uncle's widow." She pointed at her black dress, put on specially for the artist's funeral.

"Juuurek," yelled the bald man. "Juuurek!"

From inside, from the direction of the baths, a burly, fair-haired man emerged, rough-hewn and wide as a barn door, with a rather dim expression, evidently the bathhouse attendant, his face red and shiny from the hot steam.

"Go to room fourteen and tell the gentleman his *aunt* is here to see him," said the bald man emphatically. "The *baroness*."

"Fourteen," repeated the other fellow, nodding. "His aunt. The baroness."

And thumping his great big feet on the stairs he went up to the second floor, while the receptionist disappeared behind the scenes, no doubt to knock back a glass of plum vodka.

As well as being devoid of the luxuries typical of a genuine hotel, the Krakowski had no spacious vestibule where Zofia could duly pose while waiting for the Hungarian baron to come downstairs — no marble mantelpiece to rest an elbow on, no portrait to admire with her back toward the stairs, before suddenly turning around to surprise her so-called nephew. For want of choice she could stare up at a corner close to the ceiling—and that was what she did. She heard the bathhouse attendant's heavy footsteps, but he came back on his own. It seemed Banffy needed a little time to make himself presentable. The smell of soap was becoming intolerable.

At last she heard him running down—a light step, so he must be relatively young—calling from a distance, in Polish, which gave her great relief: "What an honor . . ." He broke off in mid-word when she turned around, and instead of the large funeral hat, he saw her face, which he had in fact seen before, in another place, on a different flight of stairs.

They stood motionless, eyeing each other—the irritating woman who'd been sniffing about at Helcel House and the mysterious youth whom only three days ago she'd seen among the gravestones at Mrs. Krzywda's funeral. She couldn't make head nor tail of it. Why would the baroness's nephew attend the burial of a common almswoman? For a while it was so quiet that from somewhere inside the building she could hear the remote echo of splashing and jolly banter.

"I don't think they have a hotel restaurant," she began coldly, "and besides, today it would certainly be closed . . . Are we going to stand here like this or will you invite me to your room?"

"Oh! That's very forward of you . . ." he said, scowling wickedly. "I don't know if it's appropriate . . ."

"The matters which we shall discuss are not to do with good or bad morals, but life and death," replied Zofia firmly, once again feeling like Sarah Bernhardt onstage.

He cocked his head to one side like a bird and cast her a mistrustful, inquiring look. Zofia didn't shudder at all. Her eyelids, her hands, even the feathers on her hat were perfectly still.

"All right, be my guest," he said, turned, pointed at the stairs, and moved up them. "*Sprechen Sie vielleicht Deutsch?* I understand everything in Polish but I prefer to speak in German."

"*Aber natürlich,*" she replied, stepping onto the first stair.

❧

Banffy's room confirmed all the hearsay about the rooms at the Krakowski. It was small and dark, with just one window, a small one at that—the window of a former bathing cabin —badly furnished and even more poorly maintained. There were clothes lying about everywhere, and on the chest of drawers beside a basin and a jug of water there were several books, some crumpled newspapers, a couple of plates with the remains of smeared sauce, and two empty beer mugs; it stank like *un ménage de garçon.*

"Please sit down," he said, scooping a heap of clothes from the only armchair and tossing them onto the floor beside it; he seated himself on the rumpled bed, which the counterpane only roughly covered. "And amuse me with talk of matters of life and death. *Auntie,*" he added after a pause. Zofia let it pass without comment.

"Let us begin with death. What connection with Julia Krzywda prompted you to make an appearance at her funeral?"

"What connection? Well I never, does one need special permission to go to funerals these days?" He picked up a deck of cards from the bedside table and toyed with it, shuffling them from one hand to the other. "Who gives that sort of permission? The local council? Or perhaps it's you?"

"Don't you regard it as odd? To go to the funeral of a total stranger?"

"Even if it is, it's hardly unusual. I am drawn to the majesty of death," he declared in an exaggerated tone, and then smiled wryly; he was handsome, and conscious of the fact; not like young Żeleński, who had only just begun to sprout a mustache, but like a man who is aware of his own charm and knows how to use it. "You may just as well accept, Mrs. . . . ?"

"Glodt."

"Mrs. Glodt, that I am attracted by causes célèbres. And as two murders have been committed in the place where my dear aunt resides, it is quite normal for a young person enjoying life to be interested in such incidents."

"Gapers come closer; they push to the front. You kept your distance."

"Evidently I have good eyesight."

"In that case, perhaps you have noticed the dangers threatening your beloved aunt?"

"Dangers?" he said, laughing. "Well, yes, one could die of boredom in this dying place."

"Are you talking about Helcel House?"

"I'm talking about Cracow," he quipped. "Vienna is a day's train ride away, and Paris is not much further, but here she sits in this stuffy little town. If I had her fortune, I'd be on the other side of the toll gates in no time, far away from here."

"Are you in such a hurry to get hold of your aunt's fortune? Are you her heir? Maybe there aren't any Italian conspirators lying in wait for her at all?"

Banffy frowned and stared hard into Zofia's face.

"Italian conspirators? What Italian conspirators?"

"I know from the baroness's maid that both you and her employer are in mortal danger because of some Italians who are planning revenge for deeds done in the past."

"Revenge? Against me? But I've never set foot in Italy in all my life!"

"Maybe it's to do with your uncle. The person who connects you with your aunt."

"My uncle is dead, and for his entire life he was as taciturn as a Transylvanian bear. He shut himself away on his estates, where his only occupation was crossbreeding cattle. Anyway, where is Transylvania, and where Italy? What does the one have to do with the other? It's pure nonsense."

"What about Mrs. Campiani? Might she have something to do with it?"

"I've never heard of her before."

"Her married name is Walaszek, she lives at Helcel House, and she's involved with a man named Fikalski . . ."

"My dear Mrs. Glodt," said Banffy, standing up, "surely you can't expect me to be acquainted with every lady who resides in the house where my aunt is living? Actresses— absolutely. Dancing girls—yes, please. But old ladies?"

"You're claiming to be a bon vivant, but you're plainly living in conditions that wouldn't satisfy the simplest little actress . . ."

"I'm surprised you're such an expert on that particular milieu," he joked. "Indeed, you may well make fun of me for not flinging forints left and right, but I can't see a reason to sneer at anyone's privation. As I read in a French novel, money is round in order to roll. Now you have it, now you don't."

"I would never have imagined a member of the Banffy family to be suffering from privation . . ."

He leaned nonchalantly against the chest of drawers with his thumbs thrust into the pockets of his pinstriped waistcoat.

"Where do you get that idea from? All right, would you like to hear a story? Jolly good. I'm sure you won't have heard of the fair Angela, chanteuse and circus rider . . ."

"I do not generally hear about young ladies of that kind."

"But believe me, in all Vienna, probably in the entire

empire, there was never a more beautiful woman. Suffice it to say that Krayevsky, a Russian count, offered her his hand, a comital coronet, and estates in Crimea. Indeed, she accepted his support, but she refused to marry him. Why was that? Because she loved another. But whom? You can easily guess. We were both mad about her. We showered her in diamonds, Krayevsky bought her an entire circus, and set off with it to Raab, then to Brünn, anything to get her away from the Viennese environment, or rather from me. I hadn't a penny left, but as that was the case, I persuaded a lady friend to lend me several thousand crowns, promising to pay her back out of the fortune I would inherit, and then I went after the circus and got myself a job there as the lowliest minion. I carried water for the elephants and swept excrement out of the tiger cages" — at this Zofia rolled her eyes — "but I had Angela all to myself. Nothing could thwart our love!"

"And what did the Russian count do about it?" she asked with feigned interest, though she was sure this was some sort of poppycock; now she would have to put pressure on Polcia, the baroness's maid, to extract more information from her.

"He shot himself. Out of love. He didn't want to stand in our way. But just then, when our beautiful dream was about to come true, the lady who lent me the money accused me of cheating her out of vast sums . . . I said farewell to Angela as lovingly as I could, then gave the Viennese police the slip, and that was how I ended up in this miserable hotel in

Cracow, without a penny to my name, and here I am, planning how to . . ."

Suddenly, a volley of gunfire rang out. Matejko's funeral procession must have reached the Riflemen's Garden, where the marksmen's fraternity were paying homage to the great man.

"My God!" exclaimed Zofia in Polish, after glancing at the niello-inlay mourning watch pinned to her dress, and then stood up abruptly. "Do forgive me, it's time for me to go. I hope we shall have the opportunity to talk again."

She ran out of the room, while he stood there in amazement, staring at the door that slammed shut behind her.

As she ran breathlessly under the arch of the Florian Gate, the tail end of the procession was already disappearing down Lubicz Street. The crowds had grown thinner; most of the citizens had chosen not to escort Matejko all the way to the cemetery. Zofia was having a mental battle, but her sense of duty came out on top. Not without some difficulty she managed to hail a cab, and told the driver to take her as fast as possible along the Warsaw road to the cemetery. Once there, as she was paying the driver, she realized a dreadful thing: Matejko's tomb had been set up in the newest part of Rakowicki Cemetery, just where Cousin Dutkiewicz had bought herself a plot. *That* part of the cemetery suddenly became *that* part in a totally different sense. *Nothing is forever in this world,* she thought sententiously. She reached the vicinity of the tomb, where yet another of the day's speeches was just beginning (*Whose turn is it now?*), then she stopped at the edge of the crowd and waited for the ceremony to end, bravely enduring her hunger. By the time she found Ignacy among the dispersing crowd of mourners, dusk was starting to fall; at once she began to reproach him for neglecting her and failing to seek her out in the throng when he reached the cemetery with his deputation.

"My dearest, once people have parted in this sort of crush it's impossible to find each other again." He timidly tried to excuse himself. "I did ask you not to wander off . . . But never mind, what matters is that we both took part in this grand national event."

"Though it wasn't the same as for Mickiewicz."

"No," he said, nodding sadly. "Well, these days everything's gone to ruin . . . But why be surprised? People are confused by all these novelties. Have you any notion of what I read in the *Cracow Times*? Just imagine, an apprentice came to his master, a boilermaker or a leatherworker, I can't remember, with a social democrat journal in his hand and announced that present conditions were impossible, that the working day should last no more than four hours, and other such absurdities."

"And what did his master do?"

"He instantly realized he was dealing with a madman whose wits had been addled by reading social democrat journals, so he made every effort to have him put in hospital."

"As a doctor," she asked him, "do you think recovery is possible?"

"My dearest Zofia, forgive me, but I am an anatomist, not a psychiatrist. Did you see the wreath made of palettes?"

"Of course."

"What an exquisite idea!"

⊰●

That evening, she carefully studied the newspapers. Prime Minister von Taaffe had resigned, the composer Tchaikovsky had died . . . Unfortunately there was nothing about the condolences sent to Matejko's family by Professor Turbotyński and his wife. But there was news of a hypocritical woman called Mrs. Koźmian who had sent ten crowns to the poor instead of buying a wreath for Matejko, oh yes indeed . . .

Later, over a game of Napoleon's Tomb, she tried to make sense of all these stories again, but nothing added up. Where did Fikalski come in, where did the mysterious young Banffy fit, and what connected them? Could Fikalski have used Banffy to murder Mrs. Krzywda? Indeed, the young fellow had something bestial about him, a beast that had been through various misfortunes, knows how to bite, and when necessary will do anything to survive. But even if for whatever reason he was struggling with penury and would be willing to strangle an old woman, he wouldn't do it for the sort of trifling sum Fikalski could offer him. *What if Mrs. Krzywda killed Mrs. Mohr, Mrs. Czystogórska killed Krzywda, and young Banffy killed Czystogórska . . . No, what*

an idiotic chain of events! And why hasn't Mrs. Czystogór-
ska been found? The watchman didn't see anything, neither
her, nor the murderer, but a body is not a velvet reticule or
a hatpin. It has to be dragged, carried, lugged ... The most
peculiar thoughts went racing through her mind, that poor
Mrs. Czystogórska had been chopped to bits and served in
a stew to the almsmen and almswomen, or that her body
had been burned in the boiler room, but all these ideas
were highly exaggerated. *There are too many court cards*
in this game of patience. Unless, of course ... she thought,
reaching for the bell pull. Soon after, a rather sleepy Franciszka appeared.

"Franciszka," she said, "tomorrow morning ... no. The
day after tomorrow. The day after tomorrow, I shall ask you
to go on some very special errands ..."

CHAPTER XIII

❧

In which Zofia Turbotyńska discusses cruel monsters, and later, when two important expeditions beyond Cracow are undertaken, she delves in the bushes and the armorials, and comes close to solving the puzzle.

As she ascended the stone steps of Helcel House again, Zofia felt almost at home. *Who knows,* she let her fancy fly, *maybe one day, many years from now, in the twentieth century, once Ignacy has lived a very long life, in the reign of another emperor, I shall come to reside here myself, in one of the apartments on the third floor? Franciszka will have her own little room nearer the entrance, and she will receive the guests who have arranged to visit by telephone. By then I imagine everyone will have a telephone. As long as it's not the room where poor Mrs. Mohr was killed . . .* she added hastily in her thoughts. Then she knocked at the office door and went inside without waiting to be invited.

Only Mother Zaleska was there, still looking haggard and indolent, the shadow of her former chubby self. There were rumors abroad that Mother Juhel had accused her of employing "criminal types," refused to listen to any justifications, and was considering possible penalties, including appointing a new mother superior for Helcel House and sending Mother Zaleska back to Smyrna, where she had already spent over twenty years in the oriental heat. Zofia decided not to harass her with any conversation — she merely asked if she knew where Alojza might be, and indeed, two minutes later she found her in the library.

"I think we should go outside," said Alojza, winking a bulging eye at her. "In this place . . . the walls have ears!"

Zofia nodded. As she knew, the triple murder had prompted understandable fascination among the residents; it was probably of less interest to the convalescents, most of whom were younger people with plans for the future, just waiting to be "set free"; but the old and infirm, especially the almsmen and almswomen, who couldn't afford to go out, didn't have much entertainment here. Zofia had heard for herself a scrap of conversation in which one old woman said to another: "I worked as a costermonger. I had a stall at Szczepański market" — these were artless people, for whom the mysterious events were a sign heralding the imminent end of the world, or at least the collapse of modern morals, and it bade them fear for their own safety; for most of them it was one of the last thrills in their life — so they spent hours discussing Sedlaczek the cook and Morawski the watchman, spinning incredible yarns. Those who had been lucky enough to exchange a few words with either murderer boasted of their alleged "close acquaintance" with them, or fired off rhetorical questions: "God alone knows if I were going to be next . . ." or "She'd never have poisoned me — I can't bear the taste of almonds!" And so as soon as Zofia entered the library, where several residents were gathered, the room fell silent, and the ears under the mobcaps and snow-white locks seemed even bigger than usual. They sought another place for their conversation.

At this time of day there were people hanging about everywhere, and it was too cold in the garden, so they went up to the attic to talk amid the smell of timber and drying sheets.

"Well, Sister, is there any news of Mrs. Czystogórska?" asked Zofia just in case, though she suspected she knew the answer already.

"Unfortunately not. The police have registered her as missing: she has vanished from the house, simply dissolved into thin air."

"I'd like to help the poor woman's family in a small way, by sending them a few crowns."

"I can have them delivered," said Alojza unenthusiastically.

"I would rather bring them solace in person, or at least through my Franciszka."

"She used to live on Grodzka Street, but since her husband died and she came to live here she has no family left in the city," said Alojza, shaking her head. "Only in the distant outskirts, beyond Krowodrza."

"That is a long way," agreed Zofia. "But for a noble purpose, such obstacles can be overcome. I shall send my Franciszka; you know, Sister, my cook who has a grandmother here, old Mrs. Gawęda . . ."

"Yes, yes, of course, Mrs. Gawęda, a most devout lady . . ." replied Alojza mechanically, who had a good word, usually the same phrase, to say about every one of those in her care. In a remote part of the attic a rafter creaked.

"Could you please explain to Franciszka where the Czystogórskis live?"

"Her relatives' name is Orawiec," Alojza corrected her. "But of course I'll tell her."

There was a tone audible in her voice that Zofia had never heard before. Irritation? She realized the nun must be sick to death of the whole business of murdered and missing old ladies, of Helcel House, and most likely of her, and was probably cursing the day she had introduced her to the institution's internal matters. Sensing impatience from the nun who thus far had been her associate, Zofia decided to take her leave, but as they were coming downstairs from the attic, stepping carefully to avoid treading on each other's dress and habit, she said in parting:

"I admire you, Sister Alojza, for the truly Christian support that you offer me. I am not just grateful, but full of admiration. So much time and care, so much expertise . . . God bless you."

She may not have done a cookery course, and had gained all her culinary knowledge at home, from her mother and grandmother's advice, but she certainly knew how to add sugar.

❧

As she was already on the top floor, she decided to postpone her conversation with Lidia Walaszek, with whom she planned to investigate the "Italian theme," and instead knocked at the door of Countess Żeleńska's apartment. This time she found her in, and it was almost like the first day—her maid, Ludwinia, opening the door, the countess calling *Entrez!* from the small sitting room, the same armchairs and the same bell jar clock as then, but the countess herself was far more cordial. Not so cordial as to rise from her chair to greet, plainly put, a commoner, but she told the maid to fetch tea and Pischinger cake. Naturally the conversation began with the event of the week — Matejko's funeral, which the countess had watched from the windows of the Pod Baranami Palace, home to her cousins, the Potockis. She had read the detailed report in the *Cracow Times*, of course, and talked to several people who had joined the procession, but she still longed to know more and was eager to hear every detail: how certain people were dressed, what comments were made about various bons mots from the speeches, and so on. So, partly making use of what she had managed to see, and partly fabricating, Zofia told her this and that, passed on one or two rumors, and then shifted the conversation to other tracks.

"Apparently Baroness Banffy did not honor the funeral with her presence. Though her nephew was there . . ."

"Her nephew? That's the first I've heard of him. And as for her, I don't think she's at all interested in Cracovian affairs. And I can understand that—after all, she spent half her life in the wilds of Transylvania. But this was a national event!"

"Indeed it was. Does she still look so worried?"

"Worried? Enraged, more like. I'll tell you," she said, leaning toward Zofia, "before Ludwinia comes back from the kitchen, that she and that maid are at terrible loggerheads over which is better. Polcia only serves a baroness, Ludwinia a countess, yet to the hoi polloi these things matter. They say spiteful things to each other, petty rebukes . . . but when Ludwinia saw the jewelry that Polcia's wearing these days . . ."

"I noticed that at the cemetery."

"Exactly. Not at work, perhaps, but whenever she's out on her own, she dresses up, as if she were at least a second-class resident with her own room and savings set aside . . . Not much more and Ludwinia will start to expect diamond necklaces from me. But I think the luxuries have come to an end, because lately the baroness is terribly at odds with her Polcia. I'm sure she won't take back the things she's given her, *mais c'est fini.*"

Just at that moment Ludwinia came in with a tray of clinking teacups, and the countess asked: "What about the prizes for our raffle? I hope you haven't forgotten them. Christmas is approaching!"

"Mother Zaleska doesn't seem willing to provide them free of charge . . . oh, that's enough, thank you, just half a cup for me and then I'll be on my way."

"I know, I even brought the matter up with her myself."

"That's extremely gracious of you, your ladyship . . ."

"A mere trifle," said Żeleńska, waving dismissively. "I like to do my bit on behalf of the general good. But she informed me that now it all depends on you — apparently you and she have an arrangement."

"I'm pleased to hear she hasn't forgotten," replied Zofia, not betraying what it was about, and began to contemplate the little china basket of sliced Pischinger cake, wondering whether it was appropriate to reach for a second piece.

❧

From the countess's apartment she went in search of the Italian, from whom she hoped to learn the answers to several important questions. She knew that Mrs. Walaszek had once tried to establish her own order in the kitchen, but her eccentric culinary ideas had not found favor either in the eyes of the nuns or the residents of the house, so she had been thanked politely and advised to occupy herself with embroidery, where her "southern ways" couldn't do any harm.

Zofia found her on the first floor, in a large room where, in the company of some other permanent residents and a couple of convalescents, she was busy embroidering napkins and tablecloths. Engrossed in her work, Mrs. Walaszek did not notice Zofia standing in the doorway, who in her turn was watching the Italian extremely closely — and suspiciously. *Should I tell her about Fikalski's wife, who is living out her days with relatives in Bochnia?* she wondered. *Or perhaps she's perfectly aware of that already, because she's that bigamist's accomplice, and they teamed up to murder Mrs. Mohr, who could have exposed them. A crime committed by lovers . . .* The world had seen that sort of thing before — she'd read about such cases.

"What beautiful embroidery, my dear!" she cried with delight as she went up to Mrs. Walaszek's chair, immediately feeling that her own tone was exaggerated and artificial.

"Good morning, Meesees Troobotyska!"

For a while they chatted about embroidery, the superiority of cross-stitch over chain stitch, and vice versa; only then did Zofia decide to get down to brass tacks and ask about "that amiable bachelor." Mrs. Walaszek became distinctly saddened and suggested they go into the corridor; it occurred to Zofia that in this building everyone had their secrets, but hardly anyone had a quiet corner in which to confide them to an intimate friend. They sat down on a bench beneath—as Zofia noticed from the corner of her eye—a crooked, little picture of Saint Joseph, sure to be the work of one of the residents with artistic pretensions.

"Lately 'e 'as been avoiding me," the woman whispered sadly.

"Ah, dear lady," said Zofia, trying to play the role of a woman with experience in affairs of the heart, "that's what men are like . . . We can never be sure of their feelings. If their only concern is a base physical urge . . ."

"Lurge?"

"Lust."

"Oh," she laughed, "maybe that ees 'is only concern!"

Zofia had plenty of sympathy for a carefree approach to life . . . or to put it another way, she told herself she had plenty of sympathy for a carefree approach, but she found this attitude scandalous. However, her reason for holding this conversation was not to see to the morality of a woman who was actually a stranger to her, and a foreigner to boot.

"Or whether their only concern is a dowry, the lure of easy money."

"'E theenks I 'ave money, that I am reech, because there's a Campiagni family from Veneto, great *borghesia.* But I am Campiani, from Udine. Deefferent family, leetle money. I do not tell 'im. Why should I? Let 'im theenk that."

Now Zofia saw her in a completely different light—now she didn't know which of the two was more cunning, which was better at playing romantic games . . . maybe their only aim was to beguile each other, and old people are just as likely to do things that Zofia thought only fitting for courting young couples. She decided not to say anything about Mrs. Fikalska — may the battle continue.

"Indeed," she said, laughing, "let him think that. Unfortunately . . . it's getting late, and my husband will be home from the university for luncheon soon, so I must return on the double. Goodbye."

"Goodbye," replied Lidia née Campiani, hunter of dowry hunters, rising from the bench to go back to her needlework.

"Oh, I almost forgot!" said Zofia, turning back a few paces. "One more thing. A mere trifle. I wanted to ask if you happen to know a certain resident of this house, Baroness Banffy . . ."

"*Sciacallo di Piacenza!*" hissed Mrs. Walaszek.

"Who?"

"The wild dog of Piacenza," she repeated, but seeing a lack of understanding on Zofia's face, she raised a finger, dashed down the corridor, and entered the library. A few minutes later she was back with one of the ten volumes of *Brehms Tierleben;* she was carrying the book carefully, using a finger to mark a particular page. She opened it to a color plate showing a rather timid-looking jackal, with the caption: *Schakal (Canis aureus) 1/6 natürl. Grosse.*

"Yes, yes, I know, I understood that. We call it a 'jackal.' But what is the reference?"

"Everyone in Eetaly 'as 'eard of the ye . . . the Hyena of Brescia," she began to explain.

Not just in Italy. Of course Zofia had heard of the Austrian general von Haynau, who was famous for his exploits during the 1848 revolution in Italy and Hungary, where he hanged anyone and everyone as if it were still the Middle Ages and not the nineteenth century. But what did it have to do with Baroness Banffy?

"But not of the Jackal of Piacenza," Mrs. Walaszek continued.

"Piacenza?" Zofia could not pinpoint this city on the map.

Mrs. Walaszek seemed to be wondering whether to go and fetch an atlas from the library, but finally replied: "Een Lombardy. You see, in Piacenza a *duchessa* ruled, from the 'ouse of *Absburgo*, but she was a good lady, weedow of the *imperatore* Napoleone. But the *signora* died, and a new ruler came, *duca di Lucca*, from the 'ouse that ruled before the *duchessa*, but then just in Parma . . ."

Zofia felt herself getting lost, not just in Italian geography but in the twists and turns of the local politics, too. Here, at the center of Europe, things were simpler — from the day she was born she had spent her entire life under the rule of one single emperor, and for the rest of her earthly existence she hoped to be subject to just one more at the very most. Stability and order, not some form of southern belligerence.

"When the *rivoluzione* and the war broke out, the *Austriacchi* captured Parma and Piacenza . . . *maresciallo* Radetzky, you know?"

"Yes, the man the march is named after," Zofia recalled at once. Ignacy loved marches; he often went to Planty Park on a Sunday to listen to the military band that played there.

"*Allora*, when Radetzky beat the keeng of Sardinia's army, a teerrible defeat, a catastrophe, so in Lombardy and *Toscania* was *rivolta*. In ten days the cruel Hyena, von Haynau, captured Brescia and keelled the men, weemen, and even the cheeldren. *Molto crudele!* The soldiers whipped the weemen in the *piazza, o Dio!*"

"And this jackal?"

"'E was *tenente* . . . lertenant?"

"Lieutenant," Zofia corrected her. "*Leutnant.*"

"Exactly. Right-'and man of the Hyena, who sent 'im to Piacenza. He 'anged twenty men in one seengle day on Piazza Cavalli, and beat the weemen 'imself with a *gatto a nove code* . . . wheepping them to the blood . . . My father told me everything, 'e saw eet with 'is own eyes."

"And that was Baron Banffy? Husband of the baroness who lives here in Helcel House?" exclaimed Zofia, on whom this grisly tale made quite an impression.

"*Si, Barone Banffy, bastardo!*" At that instant Mrs. Walaszek, or rather Lidia Campiani, became the Italian *Carbonaro* of Zofia's imagination. Like a Roman goddess of revenge, ready to attack Baroness Banffy with a dagger for the crimes committed by her husband who'd been lying in the family crypt for years, somewhere in darkest Transylvania. It was true that General von Haynau had come a cropper later on—she remembered that in France or England some working-class men had given him a sound thrashing, obliging him to stop traveling about Europe. Nor was it hard to imagine some Italian patriots wanting to be revenged on their nation's oppressors. After all, there were plenty of reports in the newspapers about Russian or Italian anarchists assassinating people, like that Orsini fellow, who had tried to blow up the emperor Napoleon III outside the opera, or that man called Hryniewiecki, who had succeeded in killing the tsar, and himself as well in the process.

Indeed, she found the vision of Cracow as a hotbed of Italian revolutionaries terrifying, but also alluring in its own way. She imagined the eyes of the entire world turned on her city, reports in the global press . . . Not that Cracow was without its fair share of political murders—fifty years ago an investigating magistrate called Wolff had been shot dead in Planty Park. He had so doggedly pursued a young people's conspiracy that there was no space left in Cracow's jails. Afterward they sang: "They killed a Wolff, one of a thousand more, you thousand wolves, be full of fear" . . . But that was long ago.

However, she wondered, *what sort of publicity would they get half a century later from the treacherous murder, using poison, of the aging widow of an Imperial-Royal lieu-*

tenant, even if he were a cruel brute? She took another close look at Mrs. Campiani-Walaszek, widow of an official for the Galician Railway of Archduke Carl Ludwig, convalescing at Helcel House after an attack of kidney stones. Temperament aside, she did not exactly look like the emissary of malevolent conspirators. Besides, why would she have employed Mrs. Krzywda when she herself had access to the kitchen?

"I understand that you're not fond of the baroness?" she asked cautiously.

Mrs. Walaszek spat out a few words in Italian; there was no need for Zofia to request a precise translation, as their meaning was perfectly clear to her.

"A drrreadful wooman," added Mrs. Walaszek, switching back to Polish, "but not because she's a Banffy—she was only Banffy by marriage . . . she must 'ave 'ad a different name before. But she ees a *signora antipatica.*"

After this next outburst, without batting an eyelid, she calmly picked up the volume of Brehm.

"I won't keep you from your fabulous embroidery any longer," said Zofia, smiling radiantly. "Thank you very much for our talk."

They said goodbye and headed in opposite directions: Walaszek to the library to return her study aid, and Zofia to the exit. As she was passing through the main gate she realized that for today her true detective life was at an end; she would have luncheon with Ignacy, and supper that evening, but she wouldn't send Franciszka to see the Czystogórski family until tomorrow morning, when she herself would set off on another expedition. Today all she had left to do was to inspect the work of the new maid, who had already started to annoy her by being slow, listen to Ignacy rustling the newspaper, and maybe read a novel. Far more terrifying than the horror of finding corpses among the rumpled bedsheets or in a corner of the attic.

〰

Yet even this depressing autumn evening was to bring a spark of interest, and from the least likely direction: from a column in Ignacy's copy of the *Cracow Times*.

"Ghastly business in Barcelona," he cast into midair, but Zofia didn't pick up the thread.

"Truly ghastly."

Silence.

"Listen to this, dear heart. An anarchist threw a bomb at the theater there, just like Orsini. Twenty-two people were killed and forty injured—a bloodbath."

"What were they performing?"

"*William Tell*. The explosions were during act two."

"I've never been fond of Rossini. There's nothing of interest after the overture anyway."

Another quarter of an hour passed in silence, while Ignacy cut something out of the newspaper, and Zofia thought about people who disturb public order. *That's it, all these anarchists,* Carbonari *and rebels act in a similar way, they're recognizable . . . yes, quite — by style. In fact, it takes no effort at all to recognize one, because they don't try to conceal their crimes. All these troublemakers are relying on publicity, their aim is to sow terror . . . Surely if they really did want to kill a resident of Helcel House, they'd have done it with a bang, not on the sly?*

❧

To travel to Krzeptów, a village near the city of Tarnów, and back in a single day, and also to have time to talk to Countess Wielhorska there, who had penned the letter of recommendation for Mrs. Krzywda, or some of the servants perhaps, or someone else who knew the murdered almswoman, Zofia had to set off early in the morning, at a time when she was usually still in bed. Maybe that was why she dozed through most of the journey — the train rocked gently and her fellow passengers did not impose themselves to excess by being talkative, or corpulent, or malodorous, so not much of the trip stayed in her mind. But there was another reason, too: despite being excited by each new lead and each new idea, she was weary now; gradually she was losing faith in her chances of identifying the killer. None of it fitted together, and whatever facts she established instantly slipped from her grasp; so far, her only success had been proving to the police that Mrs. Mohr was poisoned. But if the price of this success — which tickled her sense of self-regard nicely, more so perhaps than having a poem published in the *Illustrated Weekly* or running a charity collection in cooperation with a countess — were to be condemnation of the utterly blameless Czech cook, then it was a success she could do without. And the more this dispirited her, the sleepier she became; she very nearly missed her stop.

She emerged in front of the station — a wide building, formed of three smaller ones joined by ground-level passages, but squat and provincial; the turrets at either end were a joke, like sticking a tower on a peasant cottage. People had been muttering for ages that Galicia's railway stations should be bigger, more modern, and more attractive, but so far few of the buildings were as fortunate as the one in Cracow, which had been considerably rebuilt some twenty years ago, and was now being decorated and made higher. One could only hope that the empire's mission to civilize would reach Tarnów too . . .

"Is the honorable lady looking for a hotel? In need of a place to stay?" asked an obsequious little man, trailing his left leg.

"No, on the contrary — I need to travel on from here."

"How do you wish to travel? By train? By carriage? By droshky?"

"By carriage. To Krzeptów."

"At your service, honorable lady," he said, bowing, and hobbled off to a group of three bearded men who turned out to be carters; one of them came over with the intermediary, and then the arrangements, bargaining, and wrangling began. Heatedly, because Zofia was not prepared to overpay. Though even so, she told herself, in Cracow for the same money, including a tip for the lame man, she wouldn't travel as far as St. Benedict's, the little church on Krzemionki hill, where in any case she only went once a year, in spring, for Rękawka, the traditional egg-rolling festival. (Personally she abhorred it, but Ignacy was fond of eccentric Cracow customs and loved scrambling up the hill to toss gingerbread, cooked sausages, and small coins to greedy urchins; she regarded it as an apology for profligacy, but as a good wife, every year out she went to the mound and gloomily watched the wealth of the Turbotyński household being squandered.)

So in Krzeptów she left the carter outside the inn and went for a walk. She had no intention of driving up to Countess Wielhorska's palace in a shabby Tarnów cart, to be taken for a boor. Krzeptów was like hundreds of other villages throughout Galicia: a road that ran down a small valley, lined with cottages that were falling apart with age, from which poverty was driving people to the other side of the ocean, and on two opposite hills stood two strongholds: a solid stone church, its tower broadcasting the piety of the local people, and an ancient comital palace. Or rather what was left of it.

For the further Zofia went up the neglected, potholed road, the clearer it became that she wasn't going to a palace, but the ruins of one. Finally, a wide, charred facade, topped with a tympanum, loomed from behind the bare crowns of some large parkland trees. Below there was a porch propped on columns, overgrown with creepers, and higher up a wall cut open by three arches. Through the broken first-floor windows some dark inner rooms were apparent, though their decaying ceilings did not admit much light; whereas the roof must have caved in long ago, because the arches were open to the dull gray sky. Here and there the remains of former outbuildings were visible too —collapsed brick walls preserved the outline of erstwhile stables, a coach house or a workers' block. In the middle of the courtyard, which was thickly overgrown with maples, acacias, and lots of prickly thistles that kept hooking on the flounces of her dress, Zofia could make out the casing of a round pond. A fountain must once have played in it—there were some rusted pipes protruding from the bottom of it, but the stone figure must have been looted years ago.

There wasn't a living soul in sight. The birds that flew away for the winter had already gone; the occasional jaded rook called lazily in the distance. If one could imagine nothingness personified, the Wielhorski Palace was it: a wide, dismal facade with nothing but ruin and decay lurking behind it, topped as if ironically by a large heraldic crest. Beneath a crown with nine tines adorned with ostrich feathers there was a horseshoe with two crosses—one on top of it, slightly peeling, and the other ringed by it. Zofia was no great expert on heraldry; she could identify her husband's family crest and a few of the most common ones, but she was almost certain this one was the Lubicz coat of arms. Just in case, she took her notebook out of her bag and copied it. At first she was going to do a rough sketch, without any detail, but here in this desolate spot she suddenly felt sad and uneasy, so she decided to draw it precisely, just as Miss Buchbinder, the woman who had taught her drawing, deportment, and French, had instructed her long ago, with shading and contours. Carefully crosshatching its gloomy recesses brought her a sense of calm, though of course, it wasn't a matter of great importance. More to the point, Countess Wielhorska definitely could not have sent a letter from Krzeptów a year or two ago — she certainly hadn't been sitting at her splintered desk or forming shapely script with ink made of mud. Unless by some miracle she were living not in the palace but in one of the tumbledown cottages festering at the bottom of the hill.

❧

The inn, probably more than a century old, sat brooding by the main gate like a large mother hen. Wide and solid — plainly the drinking here was on the same grand scale as the building — it had a hip roof with broken shingle, which stuck out a little at the front, where it was supported on six massive columns forming an arcade. In summer, that was where the customers sheltered from the heat and the innkeeper's helper laid out those who had drunk too much, but at this time of year the roof kept off the rain instead.

Around midday there wasn't a living soul here, except for a grizzled old mongrel dozing by the wall. Zofia ran up three small steps and opened the wide, semicircular door into the inn.

As she was in the countryside, she remembered to offer the traditional greeting — "The Lord be praised" — but realizing a Catholic greeting was inappropriate here, she bit her tongue and said, "Good morning."

"Good for some," said the innkeeper, casting her a reluctant look from behind a long row of solid mugs made of poured glass lined up on the bar, which he was wiping with a rag of dubious cleanliness. "A day like any other."

"It's coming up to one o'clock," said Zofia, comparing the hands on her watch with a large round clock that hung behind the innkeeper, between a shelf full of glasses and a shelf full of bottles.

"Somewhere, but it's always a quarter to eleven here," he calmly replied.

"I am looking for the countess . . ."

"Yes? I thought you were a countess. We don't usually see such . . . fashionable ladies in here."

"Countess Wielhorska, from the palace."

The innkeeper stopped wiping the glasses, put the next one down on the tabletop, and raked his beard with his fingers.

"Well, you've some searching to do . . . There ain't been counts nor countesses here since . . . my grandpa Chaskiel's day."

"From what year would that be?"

The innkeeper sighed and put down his rag.

"The year . . . Not since the year when the sheriff in Tarnów said the masters were going to wipe out the peasants — so peasants came from elsewhere, with flails, pitchforks, and boat hooks, across deep snow because it was the winter . . ."

"So were they killed? Or did they leave?"

But plainly he loved telling this story, and it had to start at the beginning.

"The first night, the masters defended themselves: they summoned their domestics, they had shotguns and rifles, they barricaded the doors with armchairs and beds, and when those outsider peasants started to smash them, they shot through the doors, and laid two or three of them out dead." At this point he paused; he had his favorite pauses in this tale, not to give himself time to remember the facts, but just to increase the tension. "That lot went on their way. Only on the third day did our local peasants get agitated, deploy themselves around the whole village, and post sentries. Up in the palace they were debating whether to defend themselves or escape . . . the two young masters tried to gallop on horseback across the park and on, through the woods, but the peasants caught them in an ambush: 'Where are you going, you brutes?' Then another cries: 'Kill the brutes, take their horses, and flay them alive — the authorities have said anything's allowed.' The young masters whipped up their horses, but that lot was after them, with pitchforks, this lot was hammering at the doors, while that lot was close on their heels . . . And this time it ended up with them taking the whole palace without a single shot — they went inside the place and herded the whole family into the drawing room. First the peasant women cried, saying: 'We work for you, but you want to kill us.' But they already had blankets with them, so they forgot about their weeping and got down to looting. Throughout the palace they smashed the furniture, broke the locks off the doors searching for valuables everywhere, but they didn't find any, so they ended up tearing the material from the walls and hacking out the door frames. But there was nothing, not a single jewel, nothing but the earrings they ripped from the countess's ears" — this made Zofia shudder at the thought of her own earrings — "and the wedding rings, all of which came off easily except for the old count's, so they broke his finger. Mind you, it didn't matter to him anyway, for he was dead by then. They were going to torture them, gouge out their eyes, cut off their hands and feet, but a tumult arose, they suddenly went for them with those sticks, and ten minutes later they even began to fight among themselves, all trying to hit the masters, but there wasn't enough room, stirring such rage that their women screamed to separate them, while other women and children taunted the nobles, shouting: 'It's all because of you, it's your fault they're fighting like that!' Finally, the peasants were reconciled and started beating them with flails, and soon only those two young masters were left alive, clearly the strongest. They took them, now very weak, their arms broken, covered in blood, naked—their clothes were ripped off, I saw it with my own eyes as a little boy, and two men arguing so hard for a leather boot that they ripped it apart. Someone out of mercy gave the young masters a blanket, a sheet, a little straw so they wouldn't freeze to death, and they took them on a sledge across the snow to the sheriff, and only there did they butcher them, for the Austrians paid ten florins for a dead noble, eight for a wounded one, and five for one un-injured."

The Galician Slaughter—of course Zofia had heard of these horrors before, not least from the young Żeleński. It was less than fifty years since the Austrian powers that be had incited the peasants to attack the nobles as a way of suppressing their imminent uprising.

"And there have been no Wielhorskis since then? No Countess Wielhorska?"

"I've not heard of any, but I was a little boy then, so high." He leaned over the counter and stretched out his hand about three feet from the floor. "The last countess I ever saw was that one, with blood dripping from her ears. After that, as they tortured her to death, I couldn't look no more."

Zofia glanced through the low, grimy windowpanes—good, the carter was still in the same place where she had left him. Yet another trail had proved to be a dead end— for the sake of form she asked the innkeeper about Mrs. Krzywda; maybe she really had lived somewhere nearby, and this was her source for the fictional countess who'd supposedly penned her letter of recommendation. But no, he had never heard of her. Zofia was cold, angry, and tired. It occurred to her to ask for a shot of strong drink, but she warmed herself instead with the thought that she hadn't spent a single cent in Krzeptów. She thanked the man for the conversation, wrapped her collar more tightly around her neck, and went out into the November chill.

❧

"My dearest Zofia, where have you been?" said Ignacy, greeting her in the doorway with a question; in fact, she hadn't the time to make up a convincing story about her all-day whirl of activity—above all she had to have an urgent chat with Franciszka, who was sure to be back by now from her own outing to Krowodrza.

"All in good time, Ignacy," she said in a raised tone, as she took off her gloves and put them in their box. "If you're hoping for supper before midnight . . . no, if you're hoping for supper at all, then I'm sorry to say you must gird yourself with patience and let me go to the kitchen first."

"What are we having this evening?"

"Carp in gray sauce?"

"With a cucumber salad, please."

"All right, there'll be cucumber salad too," she said, trying to adopt as calm a tone as possible, though she was quivering all over with curiosity about how Franciszka had got on with her mission. From the hall she could see the girl's back as she cleaned the kitchen, carefully polishing the stove lids.

"We must make supper. It's high time," she boomed from the threshold, so that Ignacy could hear her in the drawing room, and then she came down to her usual tone, or lowered it slightly to ask Franciszka: "How did it go?"

"Oh, she's alive, madam, she's alive! You were right!"

Since the day Franciszka first set foot in her house Zofia had never seen her so overjoyed; she was sure it wasn't because the woman in question was alive — her welfare and existence were certainly not important to Franciszka — it was simply that Zofia and her cook had both developed a taste for exactly the same thing: poking about in people's fortunes, and proving that reality was actually quite different from how it appeared to others.

"I knew it! Tell me, tell me everything," she said, and then loudly added, "carp in gray sauce it is!"

"And cucumber salad!" came a faint reminder from the drawing room.

"And cucumber salad!" she shouted back.

"First I went to see Sister Alojza. I showed her your letter, she looked at something in it and made a face, but she told me what those people are called and where their cottage is. So off I go, a long way, on and on. It's not Krowodrza, where the rich farmers are; no, it's even further, the very last houses, and they're not decent ones, but squatting on top of each other, almost collapsed. So on I go, asking where the Orawiec family live, and finally this skinny little urchin tells me it's over there. So I rap on the door, and I rap again . . ."

"And cauliflower too!" cried Zofia for the sake of form.

"This woman opens the door. She's not old yet, so I can tell it's not her. I ask if she's Mrs. Orawiec. Yes, she is. Aha, I say, I've come all the way from Cracow to see you — my lady has sent me to your aunt, Mrs. Czystogórska. And she stands up straight, she does, and gives me such a nasty look. Auntie's not here, she says. I nod my head and say, all right, but I have business with her, so I'll wait. Then she says: Auntie's not anywhere, probably killed, the police have been looking for her. They ain't found a corpse, but we all think of her as dead. Mother of God! I exclaim in reply. Mother of God! I've come all this way from Cracow and she's as good as dead. My mistress will be upset with me. And I can see she's eager to shut the door in my face. I've a pot of soup on the fire, she says, it's about to burn. So take it off the fire, I say, I'm only here a while, on important business. And she says her bit again: Auntie's not here, she's as good as dead. I shrugged and said ah, maybe you'll be glad instead of angry, for my lady had a big sum of money to give back, everything your aunt had put away for her coffin and funeral, albeit a fourth-class funeral, but even so it's fifty crowns . . . Well, I see the pot on the fire doesn't matter now. Fifty crowns, she cries, fifty crowns! Hand it over! We're her only heirs. Aaah, I say to that, it won't be that easy, there's no bill of exchange, it was just a verbal agreement. My lady said to give the money back, but only into the right hands. If she's dead, she's dead, peace on her soul. But she might turn up, then I'll give it her back . . ."

Zofia was all but flushed with satisfaction; in this story she could recognize the essentials of the plan she had made Franciszka etch on her memory, but she could also tell how much the girl had added of her own accord, and how craftily she had cranked up Mrs. Orawiec's greed.

"God be with you, I say, turn on my heel, and go. And she stands in the open doorway. Come back, she cries, once I've gone twenty paces, come back! I turned around but I stayed put. What am I to come back for? If your aunt is found alive, send to the Helcels and ask . . . Come back, she calls. So back I go. Auntie's here, she says, but they're murdering everyone at those Helcels. They've killed ten of those old women already. So auntie escaped. They sent the policemen after her, but she's so cleverly hidden they won't track her down—let them think she's not alive! And she leads me inside, and there she is, hidden in an alcove behind a wardrobe. I look, and there's a rug hanging on the wall, the wardrobe's in front of the rug, but the rug is moving, it moves aside and a little old lady with white hair comes out from behind it. She says to the first one: may lightning strike you down, you've brought a stranger, you're showing me to a stranger, she says, and that woman says I'm to give back the borrowed money. I never lent money to no one, she says, she insists, what an honest woman, I think to myself, to which I say: Are you Czystomorska? Czystogórska, she bawls at me. Czystogórska! Aaah, that's all, I say, my lady's mixed it up, for I'm to go to Czysto*mor*ska with the money. And quick as a flash I was out of the door."

"So she's hiding because she thinks . . ."

"She thinks they're going to kill her next. As if there weren't anyone else to kill," said Franciszka huffily.

"Splendid, splendid!" said Zofia, almost raising her arms to hug Franciszka, but she restrained herself and just went a little closer to the girl. "You've done very well indeed . . . What's that on your face?" she suddenly asked, inspecting her closely. "You're all red."

"It's nothing, madam," replied the servant, blushing in addition.

"Franciszka!"

The girl bowed her head and shrugged.

"Franciszka!"

"It's for the pimples on my forehead."

"What pimples?"

"I get them, I do. Here. And here," she said, pointing at two spots on her hairline.

"But what have you done to yourself?"

"Well . . . well, I went to Krowodrza, a long way away, to a place I've never been," she began, but then broke off.

"Yeees?"

"So I thought maybe I'd never go back there again either. And there was this old stone wall . . ."

"Franciszka, for pity's sake, what are you talking about?"

"It's all in *The Angel's Aid for Defense and Protection in Dire Need*," she finally plucked up the courage to say. "If you've got pimples on your forehead, then Marianna Werner, she was a famous clairvoyant . . ." — Zofia felt like asking what exactly this Marianna Werner saw so clearly, but she bit her tongue — "advises you to go to a place where there's an old stone wall and to rub your hand against it till it's moist, and then wipe your face, chest, and arms with that hand. You're to do it three times, then leave without looking back and never return. So as I was in Krowodrza and I saw an old stone wall crumbling away, I'll never be here again, I thought . . ."

"I don't wish to hear another word. I refuse," said Zofia in a dry tone. "Not a word. I won't be surprised if after rubbing that wall the skin comes off your hands, and even worse pimples appear on your forehead. *The Angel's Aid* — I ask you! A clairvoyant. Witchcraft in Krowodrza."

She couldn't understand how this bright — why not admit it? — *intelligent* girl, who had dealt with Mrs. Czystogórska so cunningly, could at the same time faithfully believe in those cheap fairground pamphlets that propagated old wives' tales and other nonsense. She could feel the anger making her chest ripple above the edge of her corset, so to calm herself she took several deep breaths and merely said: "Cauliflower à la hollandaise. Cucumber salad. Carp in gray sauce. For dessert, cranberry jelly. With cream, if there's enough left. And if there isn't," she added with resignation, "then let it be without cream."

❦

By seven, Franciszka had managed to make the entire supper. *She really is a treasure,* thought Zofia for the umpteenth time. Dish after dish appeared from the kitchen, brought in by the new girl, whose name Zofia still couldn't remember. She did her best to address her impersonally, or simply passed her by in silence, focusing instead on some mundane task, such as picking bones out of the fish, coated in sweet gray sauce with raisins and almonds.

"Why so quiet, my dear?" said Ignacy, battling with his own set of fish bones. "There seems to be something bothering you lately."

"Me? Not in the least."

"But something's wrong. Overworking, perhaps? Today you slipped out while I was still in the Land of Nod, and you vanished like a golden dream — you were probably at Helcel House again . . ."

"If I were there as often as you imagine . . . would you pass the cucumber salad, please . . . I'd have no time to run the house at all. Indeed, sometimes I have to discuss the details of the charity collection — it's becoming increasingly urgent, and it would be far more convenient for me to do it by telephone instead of having to head out of town each time" — Ignacy skillfully turned a deaf ear to that — "but today I had quite other matters to attend to."

And, in an effort to distract her husband, who was showing too much interest in her activities, she changed the topic to one of his hobbyhorses.

"But just imagine, I actually found a moment to get you a small gift."

"A gift?" He rested his knife and fork against his plate. "What can it be?"

"It's just a trifle, really," she said, waving dismissively, and then turned around. "Could somebody please hand me my reticule? My handbag, the velvet one," she added, seeing that the girl didn't know that word, and then held out her hand in a meaningful, expectant gesture. The maid looked around uncertainly to left and right, spotted the red velvet bag lying in the hollow of an armchair, ran to fetch it, and handed it to her.

"Thank you. Now where did I . . . ah, here it is," she said, taking out her notebook; to avoid revealing too much of its contents, with a single precise tug she tore out a page. "Here you are, it's a drawing of a coat of arms that I thought you might like. It's rather an old one."

Ignacy patted the front of his jacket and waistcoat with both hands until he found his pince-nez, set it on his nose, and examined the drawing.

"Indeed it is. Very nicely done — I've always said you have a talent for drawing. Of course, it's . . ."

"The Lubicz coat of arms?"

"No, look at this: one arm of the upper cross is missing. One of the Lubicz clan, while dividing up his patrimony, ran down his brother and did him harm, hence the cross has an arm missing, in eternal memory of the harm that was done, and hence the name of this coat of arms — Krzywda."

Of course, thought Zofia. Krzywda — she had only thought of it as a surname until now, without paying attention to the literal meaning of the word *krzywda:* harm. The arm of the cross hadn't peeled off — it had never been there at all.

"It's very fine," Ignacy went on. "I'm going to have it framed so I can hang it above my desk. A comital crown — now, whose might it be? The Rzewuski family, perhaps? I think they were the only counts who bore the Krzywda coat of arms . . ."

"And the Wielhorskis too," said Zofia mechanically; she had stopped listening to Ignacy at all, and when he said, "Oh yes, the Wielhorski family too," it didn't get through to her. In an instant she was experiencing something she'd only read about in novels featuring brilliant detectives to whom almost the entire picture of connections and dependencies suddenly becomes clear. The facts began to mesh together like the cogs in a machine; suddenly it all made sense, and she knew where to look for the facts that remained unclear. With her fork and knife suspended in midair, for the first time in her life Zofia Turbotyńska was having a genuine revelation, as a curtain of appearances was ripped aside, exposing the truth in all its splendor.

"And if my memory is not deceiving me, the Znaniecki and Huściło families, too," said Ignacy, completing his recitation of the list of families that bore the Krzywda coat of arms — Ignacy the amateur heraldist and cucumber salad addict, as he helped himself to a fourth portion.

✼

"My dear Zofia, where on earth are you going?" cried Ignacy from the drawing room half an hour later, when he saw Zofia, wrapped in a fur stole, creeping out of the house. "Surely you're not off to organize your raffle at this time of night?"

She had already taken hold of the doorknob, but briefly she hesitated. She took a few steps back from the hall and said: "Ignacy, any woman who wants her husband to love her must preserve a touch of mystery. Otherwise she becomes as flat as a board and as dull as ditchwater. Do you really want me to lose all my allure?"

Ignacy folded his newspaper and stared at his wife in amazement. But seconds later a playful smile she had rarely seen appeared on his kindly face.

"Go on, off you go! If that's the price I'd have to pay, then upon my word I'd rather not know a thing!" he said. For a moment she thought he ever so slightly winked.

✼

"Just a moment, madam, just a moment, where are you . . ." said the receptionist, trying to stop her, but at this time of night he could hardly stand upright; he clutched desperately at the counter for the support of solid timber and to give his own presence substance. Before he'd had the time, Zofia was urgently rapping at the door of room number fourteen. She heard the creak of the wooden bed, then footsteps, and the grate of a key in the lock.

"Mr. Banffy, we must have a serious talk."

CHAPTER XIV

❦

The Last (Not Counting the Epilogue)—In which Zofia Turbotyńska, bourgeois citizen of Cracow, solves the mystery of the murders at Helcel House, brings punishment for the crime, and in the process obtains the prizes for her raffle for the benefit of scrofulous children.

On November the eleventh, at ten o'clock on the dot, a sizeable group of the dramatis personae gathered in the office at Helcel House under the watchful gaze of its founders, each having been persuaded to attend by slightly different means. Their host, Mother Zaleska, had agreed to this stratagem when told that she would find out who had killed the residents, and that the names of the falsely accused employees would be cleared, benefiting the reputation of the entire institution. And then she would no longer be threatened with a return to the hot sands of Smyrna.

This morning Sister Alojza — now standing by the door, leaning against one leaf of it — had gone about the rooms with the invitations. She had simply summoned Sister Bibianna on official business. In keeping with Zofia's instructions, she had told Countess Żeleńska there was an interesting piece of information that Mother Zaleska would like to share with her; she had uttered the word "information" in such an alluring way that it sounded like "gossip," and so the countess had duly presented herself ahead of time and was sitting in the most comfortable armchair. Next to enter, at an even pace, were Baroness Banffy and her maid, who had been asked to come supposedly in connection with a letter that had come from Hungary; she had invited Lidia Walaszek née Campiani and Alfons Fikalski jointly, as "closely associated," purportedly to discuss financial matters.

Each person or couple that entered the room was surprised to find the others there, but for the time being nobody spoke except to exchange greetings and to comment on the weather — which was foul. Even greater amazement was prompted by Zofia Turbotyńska, who came in at three minutes to ten with Baroness Banffy's nephew (who nodded to his aunt in the first place, and then made a single bow to everyone else), and also investigating magistrate Klossowitz, who was impeccably dressed as usual in a perfectly cut uniform. Now the whole room and the assembled company were reflected in the toes of his highly polished

boots: the three nuns, four residents, the maid, the relative, and the tireless busybody whose clever ploys had lured
them all here.

"I am pleased you've all found the time to come to this
meeting," she began, "and to sacrifice half an hour or more
to hearing a few words I'd like to say about the dramatic incidents that have recently occurred at this august institution . . ."

Klossowitz crossed his legs. Fikalski, who had been
standing until now, leaning on his cane, finally sat down
on a chair dragged in from another room by Alojza. The
baroness's nephew unceremoniously moved some papers
to the edge of a desk and sat down on it, which Mother Zaleska noted with a scowl of disapproval.

So now they were almost all sitting in silence—some
fidgeting nervously, others with indifferent looks on their
faces, yet others excited. Zofia, in a specially chosen, smart
green taffeta dress, circled the room like a satellite, now and
then diving into the middle before returning to the outer
ring around the chairs, her skirts shuffling across the floor.

As we know, she was a self-confident person and had a
special way with words. But she would never have dreamed
of being so bold as to enter the province of esteemed scholars and professors, nor did she see herself as speaking *ex ca-
thedra;* nevertheless, she had decided to deliver something
akin to a university lecture, combining elements of crimi-
nology, ethics, and even aesthetics. She kept telling herself
that as it was a serious matter, she should talk about it with

due respect. She brought out her notebook, now filled with tiny script, cocked her head a little, and began in a calm, but ever so slightly trembling voice:

"Just as an antiquarian expert on Renaissance painting can ascribe a work of art to the hand of a particular master, so too a felon commits a crime in an individual way, applying his own personal style, so to speak . . ." At this point Klossowitz rolled his eyes. "What exactly is it that surprises us about the mystery of Helcel House? Here we have three deaths: Mrs. Mohr, poisoned on the sly and removed to the attic, so that no one noticed it was murder. Then Mrs. Krzywda, brutally strangled in broad daylight, almost in sight of other residents. And finally, Mrs. Czystogórska, who has gone missing without a trace." She paused to glance at the notes she had made the day before, poring over an album in Ignacy's library. "First a discreet nocturne, then a battle scene full of blood and passion, and finally . . . finally a white square on a white background, as if anyone were to think of painting such a thing," she said, laughing. "The perfect vacuum. Where is the consistent, recognizable style, the murderer's signature?"

Klossowitz was clearly impatient to interrupt her; first he started tugging at his mustache, and then he opened his mouth, but Zofia shot him an angry look. And picked up her thread again.

"Nothing here makes sense. The murderer must have changed his method, by force of circumstances. As we know, Mrs. Mohr was poisoned . . ."

"By Mrs. Sedlaczek, the cook," said Klossowitz, unable to restrain himself.

"We shall come to that later, if you will allow me to continue. She was poisoned with cyanide, served in a goblet of almond mousse. Not by Mrs. Sedlaczek, but, as I am about to prove, by Mrs. Krzywda, who worked in the kitchen." Mother Zaleska almost leapt from her seat. "The presence of poison has been confirmed by a medical expert, as not all of you may be aware; the body was then dragged up to the attic after death had occurred, or at least after the loss of consciousness. Those were the thumping noises Mrs. Wężyk complained about. Evidently, even a deranged person sometimes talks sense. Could Mrs. Krzywda have managed to lug a corpse up those stairs? She wasn't a weak person, and Mrs. Mohr was small, sickly, light as a feather; but while it may be possible to creep along a corridor silently, nobody can drag a body wrapped in a blanket along one if there's a vigilant guard in the little room by the door." Sister Bibianna went a deep shade of crimson. "But that was not the case, because, as the guard on duty that night has admitted to me in person, she experienced a moment of spiritual alarm and ran down to the chapel to pray, lying prostrate." A look of immense relief appeared on the nun's face, though she knew Mother Zaleska would not pardon this neglect of duty, even if the cause was religious in nature. "Taking full advantage, Mrs. Krzywda dumped the body in the attic and went back to her room without being seen. But why on earth would she kill the innocent old lady?

Mrs. Sedlaczek did at least have a motive, because the victim was the widow of the judge who sent her to prison for poisoning her husband long ago. It all looks very neat — poison then and poison now — but the desperate woman who puts rat poison in her husband's food would do it the same way again — she'd use the first poison to hand in the kitchen, and not a sophisticated, undetectable substance like cyanide . . . please let me finish, Dr. Klossowitz," said Zofia, heading off an attack. "It will all become clear. But what about Mrs. Krzywda?"

At this point she paused and cast her gaze around the gathering.

"Let us suppose for the time being that a person exists whom we have invented. An artist, to return to our earlier metaphor, acting not in person, but by means of the brush of an apprentice whom he has instructed to produce a painting. Let us imagine this vile person who issues a contract for the death of Mrs. Mohr. Why? I'll come to that in a moment. Suffice it to say that he either bribes or terrorizes the impoverished Julia Krzywda into committing murder. He supplies a suitable poison and makes sure he won't be suspected of complicity."

"But can we just invent somebody out of the blue?" asked Mother Zaleska hesitantly.

"Only in theory, please have no fear. Let us also suppose that Mrs. Krzywda then has pangs of conscience. Or the contractor, who promised her some money, now skimps on it . . . she threatens to expose the crime, the contractor has to act quickly, there's no time for subtle methods like poison . . . knowing the design of Helcel House and its residents' occupations, he slips into the room and rapidly, brutally strangles Mrs. Krzywda; it's dangerous, but he's desperate — he too is at imminent risk of the scaffold. He takes a risk and carries it off. No one noticed him; he can calmly go on enjoying life."

"You have thought this out very cleverly," said Baroness Banffy, "but does this person invented by us actually exist?"

"The answer is yes, and no. Yet I can betray that he is here with us in this room."

A murmur ran through the office: whispers, offended sighs, the shuffling of chair legs, people fidgeting in their armchairs.

"So why does he kill Mrs. Czystogórska?" Zofia continued. "And how does he do it, seeing that the Cracow police have still not found her body? If the contractor were Mrs. Sedlaczek, we might suspect that Mrs. Czystogórska witnessed the second murder and was then craftily eliminated by the cook and made into veal stew."

"Mrs. Turbotyńska!" said the countess indignantly, but in a tone that was too excited to sound convincing.

"On the day when Mrs. Czystogórska's disappearance was discovered, veal stew was indeed served. But Mrs. Sedlaczek couldn't have had a hand in it because the police had already arrested her. The fact that Mrs. Czystogórska was not made into a stew has been proven by facts that I would venture to call key evidence. While Dr. Klossowitz's subordinates have failed to find the body, I — that is to say my maid has succeeded. The body is . . ."

Klossowitz frowned and tried to speak again, but this time she didn't have to restrain him because he wasn't entirely sure what to say.

"Alive and well. That is to say, Mrs. Czystogórska is living with her relatives, the Orawiec family, in a cottage beyond Krowodrza."

"Thanks be to the Lord," cried the nuns in unison, and their exclamation merged with Klossowitz's shout: "That's impossible! My men checked that cottage!"

"They're obviously not as bright as my Franciszka. Which frankly" — here she fixed her gaze on him — "I don't find particularly surprising. There's a wardrobe with a rug hanging behind it; the rug conceals an alcove, and Mrs. Czystogórska is in the alcove, alive and well, though somewhat alarmed by the murders; she got it into her head that she would be the next victim. Thus we have solved the riddle of one 'murder,' but we still have two left, far more serious because they're real. Could there be someone among us who'd be suitable as the contractor of the murder? Indeed there is. He's sitting right here," she said, pointing a finger at Fikalski, whose face expressed outrage.

"Enough of this tomfoolery," he shouted, "enough of these fairy tales! This isn't a game of charades — you're putting on some sort of theatrical performance here, all very well and good, I'm fond of the theater myself, but you're making serious allegations against people of spotless honesty! And in front of the ladies!"

"Spotless honesty? Indeed? So you won't deny that you were personally acquainted with Mrs. Mohr?"

"That's not a crime!"

"And that you quarreled with her . . ."

"I had every right to do so, just like the next person!"

"Because, out of concern for Mrs. Walaszek here present" — at this point the Italian, until now eagerly supporting Fikalski with a series of snorts and grunts, stiffened — "she had threatened to tell her a certain secret that would have frustrated your matrimonial plans?"

"Alfonso? What does thees mean?" Mrs. Walaszek stared in surprise, now at her beau, now at his accuser.

"I haven't a clue . . . These are vile insinuations!" insisted Fikalski.

"So you won't deny that you are already married? That your wife, whom you drove out of her mind, is living out her days in seclusion, with nothing for her keep but a small pension left her by Mrs. Mohr, who not only took pity on that poor soul, but also on another — your victim here, whom you wanted to wed, committing the crime of bigamy, and then grab her fortune?"

Countess Żeleńska, so very keen on gossip, all but blushed with contentment; the nuns were horrified, Baron Banffy watched with some amusement, while his aunt and her maid seemed bored. Fikalski, at the center of attention, of course, suddenly lost his composure; turning red, he pulled at the tight collar pinching his thick neck and gasped for air.

"I never . . . I . . . I never intended . . . it wasn't . . . it wasn't for a dowry . . . no bigamy . . . never . . . at a certain age a man . . . needs affection, love . . . he needs attention, flirtation . . . a pretty little foot in a slipper, peeping from under a skirt . . ." At this point Mrs. Walaszek couldn't stop herself; she leapt to her feet and whacked him on the head with her fan with such force that some slivers of ivory fell to the floor, and the comb-over covering his bald pate was completely ruined.

"You will move thees over there!" she said to the young Banffy, showing him her chair, which he immediately shifted as she demanded, to the opposite corner of the room, as far from Fikalski as possible.

"I may be flattering myself," Zofia continued, "but by mentioning the fact that some individuals try to trick unfortunate single women by luring them with the vision of a marital idyll, I think I am fulfilling Mrs. Mohr's last unwritten wish, which was to deprive Mr. Fikalski of a lucrative marriage to Mrs. Campiani . . ."

"Walaszek," came a muffled, teary voice.

"Walaszek. We have a motive . . ."

"I won't stand for it!" the failed bigamist quietly protested, but no one took any notice of his grumbles.

"But here too nothing fits, because Mr. Fikalski not only

suffers from gout and would have extreme trouble making a quick getaway, but on the night of Mrs. Krzywda's murder, like many of us he was at the gala opening of the Municipal Theater. Countess Żeleńska, Baroness Banffy, and I were there too, and we all . . ."

"So was I," said Klossowitz, raising a finger.

"We all saw each other and can provide alibis for one another. You too?"

"Yes," confirmed the magistrate.

"Well, we didn't all see everyone else, but even so, there were enough people at the theater to certify that we couldn't have murdered Mrs. Krzywda with our own hands."

"But he could easily have commissioned the watchman to do the killing," said Klossowitz, brightening. "And Morawski happens to be in jail, tracked down by the city police, and is waiting for a fair sentence. Of course, if it turns out he was urged to commit the crime by Mr. Fikalski . . ."

"And that Italian," exclaimed Polcia the maid, who had been following it all closely, but without understanding everything. "Case solved!"

"I won't stand for it!" spluttered the dejected beau. "I certainly didn't commission a murder!"

Mrs. Walaszek merely snorted.

"There may be mitigating circumstances," Klossowitz continued, "and yet the action taken by the police —"

"Has brought nothing good," said Zofia, finishing his sentence, "because the watchman did not have a hand in it."

"Is that a fact?" said Klossowitz, laughing. "If he didn't, he'd have made a statement. He was seen in the building, in rooms where he claimed never to have set foot . . ."

"Because he had other reasons for saying that. And I must say, as far as I know this city, which Countess Żeleńska describes as a hornet's nest, his decision to keep silent was entirely justified. Though of course for him it could have had tragic consequences. Fortunately I am in possession of his statement, which I hereby submit to the police for the purposes of the trial." She took two handwritten pages out of a document case and passed them to Klossowitz, who wasn't sure how to behave in this situation, so he took the sheets of paper in his fingertips, like a fragile object made of glass, and held them like that for a while; finally he came to his senses, scanned the text, folded the statement in four, and put it in his uniform pocket.

"So far we have assumed that the key to the riddle of the murders is the killing of Mrs. Mohr — who was determined to kill her, who caused her poisoning, and later murdered the poisoner too. However, dear ladies and gentlemen, absolutely nobody was out to kill Mrs. Mohr."

The silence that followed these words was only broken by a plaintive, "But how can that be?" from Sister Alojza, who was being very careful not to get in Zofia's way, but this time couldn't hold back.

"Because she was poisoned quite accidentally," Zofia went on. "A while ago a Brazilian tried to assassinate

Admiral" — she glanced at her notes — "Mello by sending him a gift, an album filled with dynamite."

"Mother of God!" cried Sister Bibianna.

"Imagine what would have happened if a careless postman had delivered the packet to someone else. So it was in our case. Countess, do you remember that on the evening before she vanished Mrs. Mohr had a quarrel with her sister, just after dinner?"

"Perhaps," replied the countess hesitantly. "That was a month ago . . . one can't possibly remember every quarrel one overhears in this institution. There's someone arguing about something every day here." Then she added: "I thought I was going to live out my days in, if not idyllic, at least comfortable surroundings — not in an old people's *un*rest home!"

Still mindful of the raffle, Zofia let the countess make this theatrical gesture, and then picked up her broken thread: "Either way, the first time we spoke, you told me you had heard the two sisters quarreling that evening. Indeed, the younger one often reproached the older for not looking after herself, for eating too little and starving herself to death. What an irony — she perished not because of fasting but eating. If she had refused the dessert that evening . . . But I'm jumping ahead. Two women really did have an argument in the room next to yours, but Mrs. Mohr's sister had long since left for the spa by then. The other person you heard was the almswoman, Mrs. Krzywda."

"Was she trying to feed her by force?" asked Sister Bibianna, an experienced nurse after all.

"Quite the opposite. She was trying to take the dessert away from her."

A murmur ran through the room.

"Are you saying she must have been the murderer, because she knew the pudding was poisoned, but she also knew it had ended up in Mrs. Mohr's room by accident?" asked the young Banffy.

"That's it. By an unfortunate coincidence, which I will explain shortly. She must have implored Mrs. Mohr by everything she held dear . . . we can only guess what arguments she used, though we know it didn't come to fisticuffs because the minor abrasions on the dead woman's body were caused when it fell behind the trunk, and not by a fight. Suffice it to say that Mrs. Mohr had simply turned Mrs. Krzywda out of her room. She may have threatened to kick up a fuss, but Krzywda couldn't let that happen because she was counting on keeping things quiet. So ultimately, in a panic, she decided to steal in there at night, once Mrs. Mohr had died of cyanide poisoning, and hide the body. Quite unnecessarily, in fact, because if she had simply left her corpse in the bed, the old lady's death would have been regarded as quite unsurprising and natural, her funeral would have been held, and she'd have been laid in her grave. But panic is not the best counsel for a murderer," she moralized.

"Why would somebody want to poison one of us?" asked

the countess. "We ladies who live on the top floor have our faults, each of us might give cause, maybe not for murder, but certainly for irritation . . . in spite of all . . ."

"There could have been various reasons. For example, on the day when we buried both victims, Baroness Banffy's maid came up to me and revealed that her mistress had been anxious for a long time . . ." At this the baroness started jabbering to Polcia in Hungarian, unfamiliar to anyone in the room except for the Banffy family members. "She said it was to do with vengeance from the past, to do with Italian avengers."

"*Sciacallo di Piacenza!*" cried the ideal person to produce the right effect at this point — Lidia Campiani-Walaszek.

"Quite so! Could it have been to do with hatred of her husband, infamous for commanding the brutal slaughter of the citizens of Piacenza?" The young Banffy looked amazed; clearly he had never heard about his own uncle's inglorious youth. "Did she receive letters containing threats? Here in Cracow she has a close relative by marriage," Zofia continued ironically, "her husband's nephew, who's living at a second-rate hotel . . ."

"Do we really have to —" Banffy tried to object.

"Which one?" said Fikalski, cheering up; he found everything to do with hotels, restaurants, theaters, and entertainment deeply fascinating.

"The Krakowski," said Zofia emphatically, to which the countess responded with a meaningful gesture, covering her eyes with a slender, ring-adorned hand. "Nevertheless, as you can see, he leads the life of a bon vivant and certainly wouldn't spurn the family fortune, his own part of which he has lost by some twist of fate, though not in the way he claims." She turned to face him before continuing: "He found the story about aristocrats fighting for the favors of a beautiful circus rider in a newspaper. I had a feeling my husband had read it to me some time ago, and indeed, I found the report in his book of cuttings. However, the central character was not Baron Banffy, but Count Tibor Sztaray."

"Sztaray?" said the countess. "I knew a Sztaray. I danced with him once at a ball at the Pálffy de Erdöd Palace!"

"That isn't really relevant to the case," said Klossowitz, who was now bursting with impatience.

"It is and it isn't," said Zofia. "Very few people are who they claim to be, Dr. Klossowitz. Each of us plays various roles. We present ourselves to others from the best side, but sometimes we take it too far. Mr. Banffy here had no idea about his own uncle's military past and thought he had spent his entire life on his estates . . . Whatever, if he were to inherit from the baroness, he could expect to patch up his financial affairs. So too does the maid, Polcia, who was counting on a large legacy in her employer's will . . ."

"But I would never harm the baroness, not for anything in the world," swore Polcia. "Of course we've sometimes had our differences — that's normal among members of the same household, but the idea that I would poison her . . ."

"Or maybe the killer's motive for poisoning the baroness

dates back to the days of her famous parties in Transylvania, attended by all, even a dancing bear? Or even further back in time, to her childhood spent in a convent? Maybe that was when someone first developed the taste for murder?"

"The taste for murder, in a convent? But that's impossible," protested Mother Zaleska, "amid such spiritual wealth and the care of the sisters . . ."

"It's perfectly possible."

"Where is all this heading?" said the baroness, who had behaved fairly indifferently until now, but had clearly lost patience when Zofia began to talk about her. "Please focus on the real perpetrator of the crime, whom somehow you still haven't addressed, rather than these made-up or irrelevant details of my life!"

"Made up! Indeed they are." Zofia interrupted her. "Not by me, however, but by you. You were never in a convent, you weren't left an orphan in childhood . . ."

"Madam! I refuse to listen to any more!" protested the loyal Polcia. "I've heard plenty already, but for a commoner to speak like that to those who are highly born . . ."

"You're not going anywhere," said Klossowitz, standing up and applying the argument of his general bulk, mustache, and dark eyes, which gave him the look of a tenacious warrior. "Sit down and listen, please. Do go on," he said, turning to Zofia.

"And so: you never lived in a convent . . . your life as we know it, as we can read in the *Almanach de Gotha* and the social columns of the Hungarian press, starts very late, and your earlier history is known only from stories that are hard to connect with any real people or places. And no wonder: you quite simply stole your biography from someone else!"

Baroness Banffy didn't say a word, but if looks could kill, not just Zofia but all the witnesses to these words would have been dead on the spot (except perhaps for the loyal Polcia, who still wouldn't have squeaked a word to anyone); Countess Żeleńska settled more comfortably in her chair, looking forward to a real treat. She was sure she'd have plenty to say at her tea parties for the next month. The young Banffy didn't even bat an eyelid.

"It's the life story of another woman, a real aristocrat, who also lived in this house." The countess adopted a look of doubt, but Zofia immediately explained: "The life story of Countess Julia Krzywda-Wielhorska, who swore vengeance many years ago and who served at Helcel House as an ordinary almswoman, Mrs. Krzywda . . ."

Briefly most of the assembled company began whispering to each other, talking and exclaiming, causing a terrible commotion; peace was only restored by Alojza, who jingled a bunch of keys, clanging them against the brass door handle.

"In the February of 1846, that memorable year of rebellions, in a village called Krzeptów, the entire Wielhorski family was murdered: the count, by then an old man of eighty; and his wife, for many years bedridden by paralysis; their son, the only one left since the other had gone into exile in France as a national insurgent and died there without issue; and their daughter-in-law and two grandsons. The only family member to survive was their ten-year-old granddaughter, Julia, who was hiding in a wardrobe, though when she heard them start to smash the furniture, she crept up a chimney above a hearth where no one had lit a fire that morning. At one point the looting peasants threw some documents onto the hearth, thinking they were property registers and wanting to set them alight, but luckily the thick covers wouldn't catch fire so they soon dropped the idea. The girl ... You're not going anywhere," she said to the baroness, who had risen from her seat. "There's one policeman under the window and another by the door. Please don't fret, just listen carefully ... The girl was spared just one thing — she didn't have to watch her family being murdered, because she was hiding in one of her parents' bedrooms. But she did happen to see something she'd never forget for the rest of her life: Marychna, who used to work in the palace as a chambermaid, and who now, at her fiancé's side, was the chief instigator of the massacre at Krzeptów. Even from inside the wardrobe the little girl could hear Marychna, barely ten years her senior, loudly inciting the rest to hit harder and harder until their victims' brains burst. But above all Marychna had a precise and cunning plan of her own, for she was a sly creature: when the crowd poured into the palace, she didn't head for the drawing room, into which the Wielhorskis were herded, but set about ransacking the rooms. She told some of the others to guard certain areas to make sure nobody else could grab the most valuable items — for she knew where they were hidden. She removed all the jewelry, the bank documents, and the cash and gold from every nook and cranny, leaving the rest of the looters with nothing but the earrings, wedding and signet rings they tore from the victims. Through a chink in the wardrobe door, little Julia saw Marychna opening the secret drawers in the escritoire, filling her apron with necklace cases, watches, and strings of pearls, and stuffing valuables down her fiancé's shirt front as he walked about the rooms hesitantly, awkwardly, gaping at everything in amazement. And that was when Julia swore that if she survived, she would not rest until she had taken revenge on Marychna, in memory of her parents."

Zofia paused to catch her breath.

"And then what happened to her?" asked Alojza, who was listening with flushed cheeks.

"The victim, or the aggressor? The victim slipped away after dark, before the palace was set on fire. She was cared for by relatives who sent her to a convent school, and who took over the property, though they soon mortgaged it and lost it. When she grew up, she couldn't rely on making a good match, so first she became a companion to an old lady near Lemberg, then later she worked as a governess, in Lemberg and its environs. She lived extremely modestly, which won her the gratitude and respect of her employers. She never married, and led an innocent, virtuous life. But that was just a front. She saved a small legacy from a distant aunt and all the money she earned, setting it aside for her life's main goal: to take revenge, in keeping with her oath. One could say that she stalked Marychna worldwide, hiring adventurers and spies, even bribing the police in various countries. What did she establish? That Marychna, who was supposed to share the booty with her fiancé, had apparently moved the treasure to a safe place behind his back, then, without stopping to wave him goodbye, had set off around Europe. In Prague she had set up a shop, then another. She gained refinement and took lessons in manners. She married an old, but very respectable citizen. Seeing her wealth, he knew that she wasn't marrying him for his money. And indeed, she did it for his name. The old man left this vale of tears . . ." — she glanced at her notes — "only six months after the ceremony . . ." — she looked at the notebook again — ". . . held at St. Nicholas's church . . ."

"I don't think we need such precise details," said Klossowitz impatiently.

"Dr. Klossowitz, on the contrary: I think we do need them. They say the devil is in the detail. If one explores them properly, one can pick the devil out of the detail. Of course, Countess Wielhorska did not learn all these facts at once — various scraps of information reached her from different sources — some were lies, some mistakes, some plain gossip. Suffice it to say that at least ten years ago she found out that her sworn enemy was now called Baroness Maria Banffy, was residing comfortably in Transylvania at her husband's side and was on splendid form. The jewelry and cash looted from the Krzeptów Palace had been the foundation for a substantial fortune, increased by both her marriages. This bloodthirsty *coun-try bump-kin*," she chanted into the face of the furious Banffy, "brazenly putting on airs and lording it over others, had managed to achieve her aim, and married a real baron with a real castle."

"It wasn't much of a castle," hissed Polcia venomously, "it was just a provincial manor. Just a shell."

"And she knew all this from a clever young man, a quarter Polish, a quarter Czech, and half Hungarian, whom she went to find in a low dive in Prague, because she had heard a lot about his stalking skills. He was thin and down-at-heel, and time and again he would lose everything he had at cards or on other pleasures . . ."

"And there's nothing wrong with that either!" said Fikalski brightly.

"There are varying opinions on that matter," snapped Mother Zaleska.

"But he had a legendary talent for locating missing sons who were losing their health in bordellos, finding dishonored daughters who were hiding from their parents' rage in highland cottages, and discovering the hideouts of counterfeiters and handlers of stolen goods. He not only tracked down Marychna, but also discovered her plan to live out her old age in Cracow. Right here" — she cast her eyes around the company — "in the charitable institution founded by

Mr. and Mrs. Helcel. At that point things began to pick up speed."

It was so quiet in the office that the only sounds to be heard were Fikalski's gasps of amazement and voices and shuffling from the corridor on the other side of the wall.

"While it would have been extremely difficult for Countess Wielhorska to kill Marychna at her own estate in distant Hungary among numerous servants, Helcel House seemed a far easier place to do it. But she knew that to carry out the murder she couldn't just come from Lemberg, go through the main entrance, pass this door" — she pointed at Alojza, standing in front of it — "and find the victim. She had to get to know the place, its routine and its floor plan. She wrote a letter to the administration in her own name, asking for the admission of a Mrs. Krzywda, a woman of impeccable character. I do not know and I shall never find out why she used her own letterhead. She was acting with intent, after all. Could it be that in her heart of hearts she wanted to be discovered and restrained? She knew that Helcel House only accepted residents of Cracow and the immediate area — maybe she had no one to recommend her, so she decided to put her own title on the line? Or perhaps, in fact rightly, she foresaw that the letter would be put away in this large cupboard, where no one — well, almost no one — would bother to look at it? Whatever the case, Julia Krzywda was assigned a place at Helcel House, so she moved here, and billeted her assistant at a cheap hotel. But he . . . but you" —

she turned to the young man calling himself Banffy — "had no intention of leaving well alone, did you?"

Still sitting on Mother Zaleska's desk in the same nonchalant pose, the young man merely shrugged. After a while, he unfolded his arms and said: "Life has taught me to grab each opportunity on the wing. If I didn't, I'd have been dead long ago, but like a good Christian, I'd be lying in a pauper's grave."

"But at least as an honest man," Polcia hissed through clenched teeth.

"You preferred to blackmail Baroness Banffy," Zofia went on. "Not for huge sums of money, because she wouldn't have paid them. And not about major issues. You never threatened to reveal her part in the massacre of the Wielhorski family, because after all these years nobody would take her to court anymore. No — you threatened to reveal her origin, to drag out the peasant Marychna from under all the velvet and jewelry, from under that title, from under the polish. All your life, my lady" — she turned to the frowning baroness, sunk deep into her armchair — "you took care to rise in the world and to look down on others, just as you had been regarded. You learned manners, refinement, and languages, you worked your way up through successive levels of wealth, from one marriage to another, and there you were, at the summit, from which a young whippersnapper was threatening to topple you into ridicule by spreading gossip about the simple peasant from near Tarnów who'd made herself rich, beguiled an old Czech and then a Hungarian baron, and was trying hard to shine as a great aristocrat . . . there are too many recently self-appointed aristocrats in Galicia for you to be forgiven that." Zofia was standing right over her, staring at the woman's hands as they gripped the folds of her dress, but then she turned on her heel and addressed the so-called nephew again: "So you sucked out your share, like a leech. Not too much, but just enough to get by and enjoy yourself. As long as she was alive, you had your bit of money coming in. And enough decency to appear at Countess Wielhorska's funeral, maybe out of gratitude for bringing you to this goose that laid golden . . . well, silver eggs. For you offered Baroness Banffy not just silence but also your help to track down the person who'd been sending her anonymous death threats, which were pushing her toward a nervous breakdown . . . and which until not so long ago you yourself had been sending on the orders of your employer, Countess Wielhorska."

"Yes! Yes!" cried the baroness at last, raising her head proudly. "I was getting anonymous letters! Lots! I'd been mistaken for someone else, I can show you those vile messages threatening to kill me, telling me to go to confession, to humiliate myself and apologize for crimes committed almost fifty years ago! But it is no dishonor to be the victim of blackmail when one is accused of crimes one didn't commit! As you said yourself, we all saw each other at the theater, the countess, Mr. Fikalski . . . I even drove you home in my carriage."

"Indeed," agreed Zofia, "you're quite right. We did all

see each other, oh yes, from one box to another and in the grand foyer at the Municipal Theater. We were all at the theater — apart from your maid, who'd do anything for her mistress. Maybe she would even kill?"

"I wasn't at Helcel House!" cried the terrified Polcia, seeing where this was heading; the baroness grabbed her arm with fingers gripping like a vulture's talons.

"Of course you weren't," laughed Zofia. "You were at the theater. Ladies and gentlemen," she said, approaching the desk and turning to face the entire company, "this is exactly what happened. Julia Wielhorska, known here as Mrs. Krzywda, an ordinary almswoman, applied for a job in the kitchen by pretending to be a cook, which, of course, she was not, and then waited for the right opportunity. On the day the almond mousse was served in glass cups, she poisoned one of the helpings with cyanide. Unfortunately, Baroness Banffy's maid argued with her and insisted on taking a different one for her mistress — she was convinced that portion was smaller or inferior in some way, and at the last moment swapped it for another. That was how the poisoned dessert ended up with the entirely blameless Mrs. Mohr. Mrs. Krzywda may have been a murderer, but guided by her own peculiar sense of justice, she did not want to cause the death of an accidental victim. So she hastened to try and remove the glass cup, which led to her quarrel with Mrs. Mohr, which Countess Żeleńska overheard. But when the old lady threatened to kick up a fuss, eventually she gave in. She came back after midnight to hide the body in the attic. It was only found by me."

"By the watchman," protested Klossowitz.

"By the watchman, sent to the attic by me. Meanwhile the baroness, whose maid had mentioned in passing her argument about the dessert, realized that the time had come for the threats in the letters to be fulfilled, and that sooner or later she would fall victim to poisoning. And knowing who had argued with her maid about the two apparently identical portions of almond mousse, she identified who was out to kill her. So she confided in her maid . . ."

"Oh yes, indeed she did! She told me everything!" cried Polcia. "She told me conspirators were after her, Italians, the *Carbonari*, she said they wanted to murder her, so I must pretend to be her at the theater, and meanwhile she would see to an important matter that would save her life. And she gave me lots of jewelry. These" — she showed her earrings — "and this" — a ring — "and plenty more, which I keep in a casket . . ."

"Far too much," hissed the baroness.

"I realized the truth when I remembered what my clever Franciszka had said: 'In hats all the ladies look alike.' Especially in a hat with a thick veil. Both are of similar build, they could easily swap dresses. The baroness used the time to strangle Mrs. Krzywda, which explains the brutality of the murder. Above all, she was in a hurry, and besides, unaccustomed to subtlety, she had always been a tough woman who had cleared a path for herself through life with her elbows. And that's the reason why the two killings were so very different in style. They were the work of two different artists. Or rather, botchers: both were interestingly planned, but the first misfired, while the second has now been detected. During the interval she entered the theater by claiming to be a messenger with an urgent telegram for her master, exchanged dresses with her maid in the washroom, and calmly returned to Helcel House after the show. That's why she couldn't comment on the first half of the program. Why have you and your mistress fallen out so often lately?" she turned to Polcia. "Could it be that you began to suspect her of something?"

"First she told me those assassins had come and strangled Mrs. Krzywda by mistake," said the maid, clearly upset. "I even prayed for the poor woman, grateful that thanks to her my mistress was still alive . . . I went on fearing that something would happen to her, and then I spoke to you, madam . . . at the cemetery. But yes, yes, after that I started to guess . . ."

"And what did she say?"

"'Go to the police on Mikołajska Street,' she said. 'Tell them your mistress killed Krzywda. Then I'll say all Cracow saw me at the gala opening. But it was you who had a quarrel with Krzywda, you were at odds with her'"—her chin was quivering with emotion—"'and who are the magistrates going to believe? A baroness, or a common drudge?' That's what she told me. So what could I do? Just go to the gallows?" She looked at each and every one. "Well, what was I to do?"

"It's enough that you're speaking now," Klossowitz reassured her.

"Of course, one other person could have given the baroness away," said Zofia. "Her 'nephew.' But he was too fond of a comfortable life to have to be quite so loyal to the woman who used to provide his bread and butter . . ."

"Oh, how wise you are," said the so-called nephew, switching into German, "how moral. Loyal to the woman who provided me with bread and butter! Indeed, for the money she paid me I'd only have had bread. Without the butter. I should have been loyal to a murderer, should I? A poisoner? The one was as bad as the other, except that one was a real aristocrat disguised as a pauper and the other was a pauper disguised as an aristocrat. And what advantage would it have given her, eh? I came to the funeral, I did, and I'm not ashamed of it. But I wouldn't have got her back out of the ground by informing on her killer. She'd have gone on rotting in there anyway . . ." On hearing these words, Countess Żeleńska and Mother Zaleska raised their hands to their mouths in unison, like two puppets operated by a single string. "Just as she is now."

"But you'd certainly have lost your source of income. Just as you're losing it now. I'd advise you to start looking for an honest job —" said Zofia.

"The job will find me of its own accord," he interrupted her. "I won't croak from hunger."

"But you were afraid of croaking, as you put it. Because, ladies and gentlemen" — she turned to them all, speaking in Polish again — "I wouldn't have known half of this story if I hadn't warned this man that Baroness Banffy had hired some men who were going to kill him and then drown his body in one of the bathtubs at the Hotel Krakowski."

"That's not true!" said the outraged baroness, who finally had a real reason to be outraged.

"Of course it's not," said Zofia, casting a triumphant glance at the young man. "He let himself be taken in like a child! I only had to scare him a little by making up the nicknames of a couple of rogues supposedly prowling the dark alleys of Cracow, and he started to spill the beans like anything."

While glaring at the alleged nephew she didn't notice Klossowitz leave his seat, pass Sister Alojza, and open the door; when Zofia turned around, she saw a policeman leading Baroness Banffy out by the arm.

"Well, I see things are advancing at a giddy pace, and you have found a reason to believe my words again, Dr. Klossowitz. It's a great honor for me," she said, and bowed with an ironical smile. "But, ladies and gentlemen, please allow me to finish with a moral. And I'd like the baroness to hear it too." She raised a finger which acted like a magic wand, stopping the policeman who was towing the baroness toward the door. "If you had gone to the police at once, told them that Mrs. Krzywda was trying to kill you but

had slain the innocent Mrs. Mohr by mistake, your per-
secutor would have gone to prison for murder, and you'd
have continued to live in peace. Though not with the same
respect as before. Your maid would no longer have treated
you like a goddess, the nuns would have stopped whispering in corners that here at Helcel House they had a genuine countess and a baroness, and every almswoman would
be able to say, 'Don't put on airs.' It wasn't the crime you
committed years ago that destroyed you, but your own
conceit."

The great scene was at an end. Exhausted, the new
Sarah Bernhardt sat down comfortably in the only free
seat: the armchair in which Baroness Banffy had been sitting until now.

"Well then, Mother Zaleska," said Zofia, tilting her
head to glance at the nun, "Mrs. Sedlaczek is coming out
of prison and so is Mr. Morawski. We'll have those raffle
prizes, I presume?"

"I cannot imagine any other decision," said Countess
Żeleńska firmly from her place; she hadn't seen such an ex-
citing show in a long time, and as she was used to paying for
her entertainment, she'd decided to do so with her support.

"Amen," said Mother Zaleska curtly and with no great
enthusiasm, though she was clearly happy with the outcome of the case. "I simply need to discuss it with Mother
Juhel."

"Splendid," said the countess, clapping her hands to say

that the matter was settled. "Now please forgive us, everyone, but Mrs. Turbotyńska and I are due at a celebration."

As their amazement began to subside, everyone gathered in the office, including the nuns, began to talk, shouting each other down as they voiced their thoughts and grievances. They needed time to let off steam. The so-called Banffy was now standing by the door, pulling on his fine leather gloves.

"Congratulations," he said, smiling sourly at Zofia as she passed him by, "I think I've met my match."

Zofia laughed radiantly. "Do tell me," she replied, "what will you do now? And what are you really called? What are you? Austrian, Polish, Hungarian, or Ruthenian?"

At this point Mrs. Walaszek pushed her way past them, determined not to leave with Fikalski at any cost.

"What does it matter? There's no such thing as a nation; there are only kingdoms and empires. Under one power, under one crown. We're no more different than the citizens of Lemberg are from the citizens of Cracow. You'll see that twenty, at most fifty years from now there won't be any nations. I am myself. Now here, now there. What will I do? Whatever's needed. I won't perish."

"There can be no doubt about that."

"Zofia, Zofia," called the countess, and Zofia's heart skipped a beat on hearing her use her first name, "come along now, we can't be late."

Zofia turned again, nodded to Mother Zaleska and Sister Alojza, then ran down the stone steps. The strangest month in her life to date was over, crowned with undeniable success. It occurred to her that now she could dismiss the latest maid, whose indolence had been getting on her nerves for a good few days.

Outside Helcel House the carriage was waiting, with young Tadeusz Żeleński inside, who jumped out to meet the ladies, bowing low; then, with quite an effort, he helped his venerable cousin to get in and placed her on the upholstered seat.

"No, thank you very much," said Zofia, smiling, when he offered to help her too, then she nimbly hopped inside. She was as happy as a bubble in champagne.

EPILOGUE

✦

On the afternoon of January the first, Ignacy and Zofia were both feeling rather sleepy, trying to digest the ample New Year's luncheon, which had been cooked by Franciszka and served by the new girl engaged on trial; she had already prompted some reservations, but never mind.

"My dear Zofia," asked Ignacy from his chair, "have you read that the baroness with whom we shared a carriage . . . you probably don't remember . . . after the gala at the theater . . ."

"Yeees?" said Zofia, politely keeping up the conversation in her usual way, with a brief word or two.

"She turned out to be a murderess! We simply have no idea what a sea of crime is swirling around us. She was the one who killed the almswoman at Helcel House. Who in turn had designs on her! You could think for a solid year and you'd never come up with such a notion," he said, rustling the newspaper triumphantly.

"Of course, Ignacy. It sent shivers down my spine."

"They arrested her on November the eleventh, and now they've tried her. She'll be in jail until she dies."

"Oh, November the eleventh! It should have been a historic date for all Poland . . ."

"Well, quite," said Ignacy, folding the newspaper. "What a sad affair."

For on the eleventh, Countess Żeleńska had taken the exultant lady detective to one of the most glorious events of the season, radiating splendor not just because it involved one of the entire nation's most eminent people, but also because admission was reserved solely for the social crème de la crème. Zofia Turbotyńska had attended the marriage of the great novelist, Henryk Sienkiewicz.

"And what an idea," said Ignacy, sitting up, "for a man of my age to marry a slip of a girl aged eighteen! They say her stepmother is to blame for it all. Apparently the father, that Romanowicz fellow from Odessa, has everything he could want anyway, so he didn't insist. But the stepmother made it her greatest ambition to push the young lady into matrimony with a famous person."

"Or to push her out of the house."

"Maybe that too, maybe that too."

They both pondered this shameful incident: the separate return of the bride and groom from their honeymoon to Venice, the public scandal, and finally the jokes they had both heard, in his case told by the other professors over cigars; in hers—in a slightly milder form—told by the professors' wives over liqueurs, though neither would have admitted to the other that they knew them.

"But one must admit that the actual wedding at the chapel was exquisite. I think the bishop looked even more distinguished than at the opening of Helcel House—it was wonderful. What a pity so few people"—as she liked to repeat every time she spoke of the event—"so very few people were given the chance to see it . . ."

Naturally, this no longer made much of an impression on Ignacy, but the ladies with whom in the company of Countess Żeleńska she had conferred during the raffle —that highly successful raffle, to which the *Cracow Times* had devoted a separate note—were greatly impressed. She knew it would keep earning interest for quite some time, in terms of cordiality from those who saw her as someone who mattered, and envy from those who couldn't forgive her social advance. She was sure she'd be able to put both of these responses to advantage for her own aims when the need arose.

She was surprised to catch herself thinking that Sienkiewicz's nuptials, including the lavish wedding breakfast held in the mirrored hall at the Hotel Grand, had probably afforded her less joy than the wedding of Morawski the watchman. The "son of a dog" he'd mentioned had finally breathed his last in the dark basement on Długa Street, so at last his widow could settle down in the majesty of the law with her sixty-four-year-old heart's desire. His demise had come at just the right time for them . . .

For a while Zofia and Ignacy sat in silence. There wasn't a sound; outside, snow was gently falling on the cobblestones of St. John's Street, as a new arrival settled in around them — the year 1894, bringing 365 new days full of incident. In the servant's room Franciszka was reading *The Angel's Aid* for the hundredth time, sitting under a framed print of Saint John Cantius. Ignacy had been sure this Christmas gift would delight her, while also offering edifying religious values; his wife had chosen not to argue with him, but for her own part she had gone to the little room and placed beneath the pillow a set of tickets for the best seats at four successive performances of Sidoli's circus, which was due to visit Cracow again at the end of January with an entirely new program, full of extraordinary tricks and equestrian scenes.

"I almost forgot," said Ignacy. "The day after tomorrow the man's coming to install your *te-le-phone.*"

Then he dozed off.

ACKNOWLEDGMENTS

Our sincere thanks to Tomasz Fiałkowski and Konrad Myślik for their valuable pointers and advice about historical Cracow, and to Stanisław Kobiela of the Bochnian Society for information about the history of that town. A special thank-you to Barbara Grotkowska-Galata, manager of the L. A. Helcel Public Care Home in Kraków; Ewa Mosór-Radwańska, head of the therapeutic care department; and all the employees and residents of Helcel House for giving us such a wonderful tour of the building, and for the patience and kindness they showed us during our visit.

We'd also like to confirm that while some of the characters in this book were real people, most of the acts ascribed to them are purely the products of our imagination, while, as far as we know, Helcel House has never been the scene of any crime.

— Jacek Dehnel and Piotr Tarczyński